BITTERSWEET REUNION . . .

Delaney sat silently, studying his face.

"How long have you been back from Vietnam?"

Anthony eased out of his chair and walked to the kitchen. She could hear the clink of ice as he answered.

"Three weeks."

"Why didn't you call?"

He emerged from the kitchen, his glass full.

"I didn't call anyone."

"Before you left, I didn't think I was just anyone."

"And you were right."

He stood before her, uncomfortable. She crushed the urge to run.

"I needed some time alone. Some time to adjust to the sneers." He turned to face her. "Do you have any idea what it's like to be insulted, cursed, spat on? Well, try walking through an airport in uniform."

"Anthony, I know it's hard."

"Hard?" His voice rose, then he laughed. "Not true, Delaney. Nothing's hard—if you don't think about it. That's why I didn't call you. I didn't think about it."

She began to head for the door, then stopped, her heart thudding.

"Delaney, I can hear your heart beating."

"Anthony, it's obvious you don't want me. . . ."

He was on his feet, crossing the room. For a blinding second she fought. Then his arms captured her in a fierce embrace that seemed to last forever. He drew away, and silently, gently, wiped the tears from her cheeks. His mouth came down on hers, possessing, invading, conquering. . . .

Currents of Love

Judith Jett

POCKET BOOKS

New York London Toronto Sydney Tokyo

This book is a work of fiction. Names, characters, places and incidents are either the product of the author's imagination or are used fictitiously. Any resemblance to actual events or locales or persons, living or dead, is entirely coincidental.

An *Original* Publication of POCKET BOOKS

 POCKET BOOKS, a division of Simon & Schuster Inc.
1230 Avenue of the Americas, New York, NY 10020

ISBN: 0-671-65736-4

First Pocket Books printing March 1989

10 9 8 7 6 5 4 3 2 1

POCKET and colophon are trademarks of
Simon & Schuster Inc.

Printed in the U.S.A.

PROLOGUE

1983

There are approximately three hundred and eleven synonyms for the word *pain,* but to Delaney Rollins there was only one. Anthony. Anthony and Pain . . . Pain and Anthony . . . definitely synonyms.

The buildings blurred as the taxi sped down Wilshire Boulevard. Delaney closed her eyes. She fought for control as fear breached the walls she had carefully constructed through the years. Her mind darted wildly, searching for anger, the only feeling strong enough to devour the fear. But anger, her sentinel and ally, had deserted, leaving her defenseless.

"Coward!"

Her eyes flew open as the one word slipped aloud from her lips. The cab driver glanced in the rearview mirror. His eyes lingered longer than necessary, and why not? The face was unusual. Dark hair was pulled to a knot at the crown of her head, leaving the features exposed. The oval face was delicately curved, the slender nose bracketed between high cheekbones, and the mouth, positioned symetrically between the nose and chin, spoke of sensuality.

When her dark, worried eyes momentarily caught his own, he looked away, trying to decide if she was the looker he thought her to be. Furtively, he looked again.

"Sorry." She smiled lamely. "I was talking to myself."

The smile tipped the scales. Yep, he thought. She was something special. Real class. Pleased with his assessment, the taxi driver turned his attention to the traffic.

Delaney pressed her lips together and resumed her search for anger. There was no longer any doubt. It was gone . . . or in hiding. And to make matters worse, nothing but a void remained in its place. That void left her vulnerable. It was a luxury she could not afford, for Anthony would exploit any frailty he sensed. For fifteen years she'd shunned any contact with him. But now, she had no choice. If she intended to get what she wanted, she *had* to see him.

"You in the business?" the cab driver asked abruptly.

His New York accent identified him as a displaced person. And it jolted her. She hesitated before answering.

"No, not really."

"Hey," he said, rubbing his neck with a thick hand, "I'm not being nosy. What you do is your own business."

Obviously, he didn't believe her. And she didn't care. She returned to her own thoughts. It wasn't as though she hadn't *seen* Anthony. Oh, she'd seen him, numerous times, but that was on a screen in a darkened theater, or on television. Short of being a hermit, there was no way to avoid seeing him. In fact, anyone who didn't recognize his face was out of touch with the mainstream of American life. For

Anthony was legendary in a country that thrived on legends. Superstar. Director. The golden boy with his golden awards . . . his golden women. The stuff of dreams.

She braced her body as the taxi swerved around a stretch limousine. How long had it been since she'd seen his first film? Twelve years, or was it thirteen? A tight smile crossed her lips as she remembered a time when she'd counted how many days, how many weeks, months, it had been. And now, she wasn't sure.

But nothing could erase the memory of walking into that theater alone, not knowing what to expect, but hoping for an exorcism. It was afternoon, and the theater was only half-full. She'd huddled in her seat, her arms clasped across her breast, grateful for the darkness. And when it was over, she'd fled through the lobby, half-blind with tears as the credits rolled across the screen and the music soared.

The experience had *not* been an exorcism. Instead, it had been a slow form of immunization. She'd forced herself to return to the theater again and again until the tears dried up and stopped. The image of his face became bearable. Finally, when she flipped the dials of her television and found herself staring at him, all that remained was an emotional wasteland.

She wished she could say that she'd ended their relationship, but that wasn't true. It had simply self-destructed. And that was hard enough without suffering the added injury of his meteoric fame, having to see his face, hear his voice until she'd been buried in pain that had taken years to resolve.

And today she was to see him in person. Another shiver of fear tripped across her skin, for she knew, perhaps better than anyone, how dangerous Anthony could be.

3

The taxi slid to a sudden stop, jarring her back to reality. She paid the fare, watched the taxi pull away, and stood for a moment staring at the building. She took a deep breath and squared her shoulders, then entered the sweeping lobby. Her footsteps clicked across the tiled floor as she approached the elevators and stepped inside, pressing seventeen. The Muzak serenaded its single passenger until the elevator opened, and she was confronted by a set of glass doors.

CALLAHAN PRODUCTIONS

Her hand tightened on the strap of her shoulder bag, and she entered. The receptionist glanced up, and Delaney cleared her throat.

"Delaney Rollins. I have an appointment with Anth— Mr. Callahan," she corrected herself.

"Miss Rollins," the receptionist bubbled, coming to her feet so fast she almost tripped. Her face beamed like a searchlight and, for a moment, Delaney thought she was going to salute.

"Mr. Callahan's expecting you. Please follow me," and she proceeded down a long, plushly carpeted corridor with Delaney only inches behind. During the walk, Delaney glanced at her watch. She had agreed to thirty minutes. She could bear anything for thirty minutes. At eleven-thirty, it would be done with, and if she had her way, she'd be very rich.

"He's right in here." The receptionist smiled, pink lips against capped white teeth. She knocked lightly, then reached for the doorknob while Delaney's mind centered on a single thought, one that had become a mantra: If she had survived the past fifteen years, she could survive any-

4

thing. The door opened, and Delaney stepped inside as Anthony loomed into view.

"Delaney."

His voice, familiar yet strange, drifted across the room as the door closed behind her. He stood behind a desk, his body silhouetted by the Los Angeles morning sunlight. He appeared for a split second as a blend of colors, the red of his sweater glaring loudly while the washed-out jeans faded into the background. As he moved from behind the desk the air seemed to thin. Time had only slightly altered his features, endowing his chin with added strength and etching faint lines on his forehead. An almost imperceptible smile sat on his lips as he spoke again.

"It was good of you to come."

"Hello, Anthony." As she spoke he crossed the room, stopping short in front of her. Her eyes quickly swept his face, and for a brief moment, she felt herself caught in a time warp, able to view him from both the past and the present. She waited for him to speak. He didn't. His face flashed a series of contradictory signals. And his eyes, eyes that were the symbol of ice-cooled virility for millions of women, were curtained against any emotion. She waited. After all, he had demanded this meeting. He could take the lead. That was something he was used to doing.

"I've suddenly forgotten my lines," he said nervously.

"I didn't realize we had a script," she replied coolly.

"We don't unless you agree to write one. But that's why you're here, isn't it? Please sit down." He motioned toward the sofa, and Delaney crossed the room and sank into the soft cushions. His iron composure was back in place as he became the congenial host, asking the right questions. Had she had a pleasant trip? Was the hotel comfortable? Did she need anything?

"No, Anthony, I don't need anything." As she replied he pulled a wing chair closer to the sofa. He sat, his long legs sprawled in front of him. His hands were on his chest, fingers intertwined, and for a moment, he tapped his thumbs together. Delaney looked at an errant paper clip half-buried in the pile of the Persian rug. When she looked up, Anthony was staring openly, indulging his curiosity. Smothering her irritation, she allowed it, sitting quietly through his inspection. His expression changed, signaling his pleasure, and when his gaze settled again on her face, she held his look.

"Would you like some coffee?" he offered.

"No."

"A Coke? A drink?"

"No. I don't want anything."

Anthony's smile disappeared. He shrugged. "Okay, Delaney. No small talk. No questions about how you are and what you've been doing for the past fifteen years?"

"That's right, Anthony. It would be a waste of time." She averted her eyes from his stare.

"No references to anything except business," he pressed on. "No pretending we're old friends, right?"

"Right." Her voice was flat, but inwardly, she winced at his choice of words. Old friends? Hardly.

"Well, may I say you look wonderful?" Anthony asked. He leaned forward, his face eager.

"I can't stop you from saying anything you wish," she replied too quickly. And she heard the tinge of anger in her voice. Thank God. It was there. She might need it.

"Then you look wonderful."

"Thank you."

"May I also say you're very talented?"

"I didn't come here to be flattered, Anthony." Slowly and deliberately, she looked at her watch.

Instantly, his face clouded. He rose from the chair and moved toward the window, his vision traveling over the scene below him.

"Before we get into the business of contracts, humor me for a moment, Delaney. Answer just one personal question. Did you ever marry?"

"Is that question rhetorical?"

"Ah, hell," he muttered.

"Exactly," she replied.

He spun to face her. Anger spilled into his eyes, then faded. He watched her steadily. She stared at the floor. His shoulders dropped. He'd known this would be difficult, if not impossible, but the end justified the means. He ran his fingers through his hair and changed the subject.

"The book is good. You know that, don't you?"

There was no response from Delaney.

He tried again. "I want to do it, and I can do it *right*."

"That's odd," she interjected, resenting, but not surprised by, his display of ego. "I felt the same way when I was writing it, and modesty never was your strongest suit."

She watched his body coil like a spring. Then, abruptly, he relaxed and flashed a broad smile.

"I'd forgotten what a mean tongue you had, Delaney. Still fighting windmills. I wonder how many living bodies you've left mangled along the way." He cut his eyes back to the window, somehow unsettled by his own question.

"Not nearly as many as you, but that's beside the point. Look, Anthony, if you want the film rights to the book, all you have to do is meet the terms. My attorney told you no negotiating," she managed before Anthony broke in with a short laugh.

"Well, that's nothing new. We never could negotiate, could we, Delaney?"

"I thought I'd made it clear that I would not discuss the past, Anthony. If you can't cooperate and keep this off the personal level . . ."

"All right, all right, Delaney." He drew a deep breath. There was no right place to begin, no ending acceptable. He hesitated a second longer, then launched into his carefully rehearsed speech.

"I know what this book means to you, Delaney. I understand and respect artistic integrity." He began to pace. "This town is filled with barracudas who'd eat you and your book alive. And before you could stop it from happening, you'd be watching some film titled *Memories* with characters who were caricatures. I'm the only one who would bring it to the screen intact, *and* meet your price. And *you* know that, too." He paused, reading her face, and then plunged ahead. "Besides, we've already met your terms. My attorneys were instructed to sign the papers at eleven o'clock, the minute you walked in. The book's ours . . . and you've got the option to write the screenplay. Everything you wanted, Delaney."

His words struck her like a physical blow. For a moment, she was unable to move. *He had intended to sign all along.* She knew with sudden clarity what he'd done. He'd thrown his weight around, insisted there were artistic questions only she could answer. The ploy had worked, for he'd fooled both her attorney and her agent. She lunged from the sofa and headed for the door.

"You're still a real—"

"Son of a bitch?" he broke in, vaulting ahead of her. Both arms shot to the frame of the door. "I've never denied that, Delaney."

"Move your arms!"

He ignored her.

Blood crashed through Delaney's body. It wasn't just the book he was after. She had something else he wanted, something he wanted so badly he was willing to spend an enormous sum to get it.

"I'm sorry I lied to you," he was saying over and over. The sound of his voice fell on her ears like hot wax.

"From you, Anthony, a lie is a respite," she whispered in a voice so low that he had to strain to hear. "A lie, at least, is a change of pace from your use of truth as a weapon."

The knuckles of his hands turned white as his grip tightened on the door frame. His voice was low and contained.

"Don't you realize it was the only way I could see you? I don't know where you live, and believe me, I've tried to find out."

"I have nothing more to say to you." *He had been looking for her.* "Please," she pleaded. "Move."

"Look at me, Delaney."

Slowly, she lifted her eyes.

"Do I have a son?"

Anthony slammed open the sliding glass doors, stepped onto the sun deck, and began to strip his body of his binding clothes. A sharp breeze whipped around his bare shoulders, and for a moment, he breathed deeply. The sound of the waves pounding the shore was an irritant. He stepped inside, moving toward the bedroom and wishing it would rain. He wanted dark skies and gloomy afternoons when electric lights were a welcoming beacon and the artificial heat greeted you at the door like an enveloping blanket. He missed New York. Needed to go back. He craved the exhilaration of the city—its depravity—its frantic tension.

He pulled a bathing suit over his legs and shoved his feet into a pair of sneakers. Then he returned to the balcony, taking the steps to the beach two at a time. He had to run. Run until his anger ran its own course, and then both he and the anger would be exhausted.

He hit the wet, hard sand along the shoreline and sprinted for half a mile, his heartbeat signaling to him when to slow down. His lungs ached as he ran six more miles. His face was stinging from the salty ocean breeze, and sweat poured down his head and streamed into his eyes. Finally, he stopped, panted for air, and dropped onto the cold, damp sand.

For the first time in a long time, he felt himself on the brink of being out of control. Delaney's accusation had hit to the core of his emotions. How had she phrased it? Used the truth as a weapon? Well, if so, that weapon had turned on him with a vengeance.

It had not gone the way he had planned it. Somehow he'd blown the hell out of everything, and there he stood, helpless, while she walked away again.

He rolled onto his back, shading his eyes with his forearm. God, she was still so beautiful! What had he expected from someone thirty-six years old? Gray hair? Premature aging? Yes! That was exactly what he'd hoped for. Well, he was wrong. Dead wrong. The dark hair was as lavish as he'd remembered. There were no lines of any consequence on her face, and as for the body . . . he moaned as he rolled over again.

He'd spent three months preparing for that meeting. Three whole months, once he knew who she was. Delaney Rollins and Daria Rogers were one and the same, the author of *Memories,* the finest novel written in ten years. When he began frantic negotiations for the film rights, he uncovered that little-known fact.

Anthony had read the novel six months before, and upon reaching the halfway mark, he was on the phone to his attorneys to buy it. He didn't care how or what it cost. Here were characters who were alive, who had substance. A laugh broke from his throat and blended with the cries of the seagulls. No wonder. It was he, his soul laid bare. He knew it the minute he found out that Delaney was the author.

His attorney had been the one to tell him. Dropped it on him as if he were talking about the weather.

"We're not having much luck, Anthony. Anonymity was one of the stipulations handed to Harper and Row when they bought the book. We're having to deal with an attorney and her agent. All we've been able to get is her real name—Delaney Rollins—but we haven't been able to locate her."

"Hold it, Ed." Anthony stopped him cold. "Repeat what you just said."

"All of it?"

"All of it."

"Well, I said that Harper and Row won't talk. It's in the contract. No information about the author. No publicity. No interviews." Ed Stein laughed lightly. "Man, I don't understand writers. Why would someone write a book and not want anyone to know they had written it?"

"Just get to the rest of it, Ed."

"Sorry. We're hamstrung because we have to deal with some Atlanta attorney who imagines himself to be Clarence Darrow. And her agent won't open her mouth. But there was one small leak. A secretary who accidentally dropped the name Delaney Rollins . . ."

"Find her, Ed. Get me something." His fingers bit into the telephone.

"Anthony, we've tried—"

"So try harder. Get a picture, an address, anything."

Ed Stein sighed deeply. "Okay, Anthony. I'll put a private investigator on it, but I can't promise anything."

"Just do it, Ed."

For a while, nothing happened. The publishing company remained a giant sphinx. Her attorney was as elusive as an eel. Finally, Anthony jumped into the search himself and called her agent.

"Mr. Callahan, I'd love to be able to help you, but I'm simply not at liberty to divulge any information." Her voice sounded apologetic.

Anthony laughed softly as he cradled the receiver in his hand. "I know, I know," he crooned sympathetically. "Writers are a strange breed. It must be difficult for you, having to deal with such egos. And I know what some of these people look like. It would probably be impossible to put her face on a book jacket and still sell—"

"Wait just a minute, Mr. Callahan," her agent interrupted hotly. "I'd be more than happy to put her face on the cover. She's a lovely brunette with huge brown eyes! And she's normal, something you people on the coast wouldn't understand. Furthermore, her ego's nothing compared to yours! Why don't you guys give it up? I'm not telling you or anyone else anything!"

She'd hung up on him. But she'd broken. Admittedly, it was a small fracture, but it was enough for Anthony. He smiled as he hung up the phone. Delaney had been betrayed by loyalty.

From that moment, he had no doubt. It was *his* Delaney . . . and, if the book was as autobiographical as he thought . . . *his* son.

Wearily, he climbed to his feet, brushing the sand from his body. He kicked off his shoes and plunged into the waves, the water slapping at his face. Upon surfacing, he returned slowly to the shore, the pull of the outgoing tide pressing against his legs.

He'd lived with the idea of having a son for three months now, and today, Delaney had confirmed it. No matter what she'd said, he had seen it in her eyes, read it on her face. And there was something else. Fear. She was terrified.

His mind fired a torrent of questions as he started to run again. If he did have a son, where was he? And did he know about his father?

Shaking his head hard to chase away the demons, he sprinted the last half mile, climbed the steps to the deck, and collapsed in a deck chair. His mind shot back to 1968. That year filled with the best and worst of his life. He shuddered. If it hadn't been for the goddamned war! He could feel his fists clenching, and he willed them to relax. No. He rubbed his temples. It hadn't really started then. It had begun long before the war, long before Delaney. She'd simply been his ultimate victim. He felt rage rising like bile in the back of his throat. Who the hell was he all those years ago? And who the hell was *she* now?

13

CHAPTER

❧ 1 ❧

1942

Take him back to the nursery," Margaret Callahan ordered the nurse. "I'm not feeling well."

With a wave of her hand, Anthony Sean Callahan, eight pounds, six ounces, was dismissed by his mother. She had not looked at him. She did not want this child. He had been a terrible punishment, conceived without her consent, planted in her unwilling body by a drunk and angry husband. It was the one and only time during their marriage that Seamus had demanded his conjugal rights, and now she was stuck with an infant, a constant reminder, a living symbol of that sordid evening.

Margaret stretched her legs as she watched the nurse disappear from her hospital room. Then her fingers fell to her swollen stomach and she frowned. She would be *months* getting back into shape. She sat up and reached for a brush to remove the tangles from her magnificent red hair, exhaling puffs of air through her finely shaped nose as the brush resisted her vigorous strokes. What a ludicrous way God had chosen to populate His earth, she reflected, the frown spoiling her smooth, high forehead. Wasn't it enough that she had to bear the grunts and groans of Seamus plowing away at her body without also having to endure nine months of looking like a grotesque elephant? And the worst part was labor. It was humiliating, thrashing around in unbelievable pain as her body took over, making her yield to the will of the unborn child.

She had felt the same feelings when Michael was born, vowing she would *never* go through it again. Her full lips parted in a tiny smile as she remembered how well her lie had worked.

"The doctor says my pelvis is too small; another child might kill me," she'd told Seamus a few weeks after the birth of Michael. Her eyes had brimmed with false sorrow, knowing that Seamus would believe anything. For wasn't she his prized possession? Hadn't her father handpicked Seamus from among the many candidates who wanted to wed Tom Feeney's beautiful daughter? Not that Seamus had any money, her father had said, but Seamus was hard-working and ambitious. He would have more staying power than those born to wealth. The combination of her social connections and Seamus's energy would make for a good marriage. Margaret had been eighteen, fresh from the stifling atmosphere of convent school, and bored with her suffocating home environment. Besides, she wanted things, things of her own. Seamus was handsome enough, powerfully built, with strong Irish features. He'd been kind and gentle with her, so she'd gone willingly down the aisle, not knowing what price she'd have to pay.

For his part, Seamus had been elated at winning the

hand of Margaret Feeney. Not only was she lovely, but she was well-versed in the social skills, circulating comfortably among the wealthy, completely at ease discussing art and literature with a finesse that he not only envied, but admired. His own background had been brutal; he had gone to work at age twelve, contributing to the support of his large family. By depriving himself of the most basic needs, he'd managed to save enough to attend college. He'd met Margaret's father at a construction site where he was working as a brick mason. Tom Feeney was impressed not only with his skill, but also with his ambition. Tom had invited Seamus to dinner, and it was there he'd met Margaret, a vision of such rare beauty that he felt unworthy to be in her presence. When Tom Feeney gave him covert approval, he had courted Margaret tentatively and cautiously, attributing her lack of physical response to shyness. He completely overlooked Margaret's need to be the constant center of attention, a feat she managed with such skill that he was blinded to its implication. After all, he was in love.

Margaret was horrified on their wedding night. Seamus blamed himself. But if he had given it any thought, he would have realized that other women had enjoyed his sexual company—had, in fact, sought him out. But he refused to view his failure with Margaret as his fault.

Margaret had a vague idea of what would occur on her wedding night, but it was nothing like the reality. She'd been completely unprepared for the things Seamus wanted to do and his persistence in doing them. It was disgusting. Not once did Margaret question her own reaction, for she believed fervently *all* her reactions were correct; it was Seamus who was perverted. Then she became pregnant with Michael. She was miserable, but at least Seamus left her alone during those nine months.

It came as a surprise that she loved Michael. He'd been an easy and gentle child, and with the nanny Seamus had employed, Michael hardly made a ripple in her life. But she was determined never to go through the experience of childbirth again. And so she'd lied to Seamus.

And she'd backed it up by refusing to use birth control. It violated the laws of the Church, she'd said, pleased with the fact she could finally use the Church for her own purpose.

Seamus was devastated but stoically accepted his fate as Irishmen were wont to do. Outwardly he remained the devoted husband and father while taking his pleasures of the flesh elsewhere. Although Margaret knew about his indiscretions and occasionally played the role of martyred wife, she was secretly relieved. Those filthy, rough hands all over her body felt repulsive! Seamus could keep his string of sluts—never mind that she was the reason he had them —and she could keep her imperious body clean while indulging her selfish nature with the material benefits Seamus provided so generously. Her father had been right. Seamus had amassed a small fortune in real estate and development, and she had everything she wanted. And that hadn't changed even after Seamus found out the truth.

Carefully replacing the brush on the bedside table, Margaret turned her luminous gray eyes to the window, watching the snow fly as the wind howled and gusted. It was the worst snowstorm of the winter for New York and the surrounding area, and she had wondered if they would make it from Fairfield County to the hospital on time. What if she'd had that baby in the back seat of a car like some animal?

She slid down under the covers, pulling the blanket

under her chin, resenting the feel of the stiff hospital sheets. Even now she accepted no blame for the situation she found herself in. She called it rape. Pure and simple.

As to the lie—well, it would have worked if it hadn't been for that damned new shopping center Seamus was hell-bent to build. He'd needed investors, and that was how he'd run into Tom Larchin again. Tom had delivered Michael, but she'd changed doctors immediately after his birth. How could she have guessed that eleven years later, Tom would want to invest in a shopping center? Why didn't doctors just practice medicine and leave business to businessmen? What a wretched quirk of fate.

Seamus had invited Tom for a drink after a particularly long financial meeting, and one thing led to another. Seamus had confronted her with the truth—nine months ago.

It was an April evening, and Michael was visiting his grandparents for the weekend. Margaret had given most of her household staff a rare night off. Dinner, of course, was tucked in the oven, drying to a most unappetizing state, for Seamus was later than usual. When he arrived, he was drunk.

He appeared at her bedroom door, his eyes glassy, his clothes in disarray.

"The whole damn thing fell through, Margaret. Nine months of work. And they wouldn't sign," he slurred thickly.

She threw him a disinterested look. "Change clothes before you come to dinner, Seamus. And for God's sake, take a shower. You reek. The least you could do is buy your sluts a more expensive perfume!"

Seamus steadied himself on the door frame and glared.

"You don't give a damn about me as long as I bring home the money, do you, Margaret? Well, I just lost about a half-million dollars. Does that mean anything at all to you?"

"Nothing," Margaret replied, snapping her diamond earrings in place and heading for her closet. "You'll find a way to replace it. You always do." She emerged from the closet, her dress draped over her arm.

"Do I, Margaret?"

Something in his voice made her hesitate. She dropped the dress on the chaise longue and faced him, tightening the belt of her silk dressing gown.

"Seamus, I said to change for dinner. It's getting late, and I'm—"

"I'll change, Margaret"—an ominous expression lurked in his eyes—"but I'll wear what I want. It's my house, too, and if I choose to eat naked, that's what I'll do." He stripped, dropping his clothes in the hallway, and stood nude in front of her.

Margaret stared in disbelief. This had gone far enough. "Seamus," she said, forcing a hollow laugh, "you look like a fool. I won't allow—"

"I'm bone weary of what you allow and disallow, Margaret." He stumbled into the bedroom. "I talked with Tom Larchin today. Remember him?"

Margaret kept her face perfectly composed. "Of course I remember him, Seamus."

"He remembers you, too, Margaret. In fact, he wondered why you had changed doctors. Wanted to know if he'd offended you. Is there anything you want to tell me, Margaret? Anything at all?"

"What could I possibly have to tell you that you don't

20

already know?" she replied, keeping her voice light. She was on very dangerous ground.

"Why have you turned me out of your bedroom, Margaret? What terrible mistake did I make that you despise me so? Why did you lie? I've done everything I know—"

"Do we have to discuss this now?"

"Hell, yes!" he roared. "We have to discuss this until I get an answer. It's a miracle that Michael was born! I can count the times, Margaret. Count them! I want to know!"

"You're revolting. If you were any kind of man at all, you wouldn't sulk over something as insignificant—"

"Insignificant?" Seamus's eyes widened as anger flashed across his face. He drew a deep breath and let it out slowly. "Margaret, it is not insignificant. Not to me. If you ever once showed me any love, I would find no need for cheap perfume. Even the Church has told you—"

"Don't you dare refer to the Church and your sluts in the same breath! It's only because of the Church that Michael exists! I did my duty! I've given you a son! If you want more, you can have bastards!"

"I ought to kill you for that, Margaret, but you're not worth spending the rest of my life in prison."

"I refuse to discuss this any further." She moved toward the black dress lying on the chair.

"But I'm *not* through," Seamus said, his voice like iron. "You're incapable of giving—you only know how to take. Your soul is sick. Somewhere down deep you're warped. You don't know how to love a man."

"You're no man," she shot back. "Look at yourself! You're a sniveling, whining—"

"Oh, but I am a man, Margaret. Just a man. That's what

21

you can't handle, because you don't know how to be a woman."

"You sicken me," she hissed. "You and your filthy habits. You're right, Seamus. I hated every time you put your hands on me. I would have done anything to stop it! As far as I'm concerned, you serve one purpose and one purpose alone. Money." Her voice faltered as she caught the look in his eyes. She knew instantly her moment of truth had backfired.

He lumbered toward her, his jaws set in steel. Fury crouched in his eyes as he threw her on the bed. "It's time to balance the ledger, Margaret. Pay your account." His powerful arms and legs were too much for her. "Look at me, Margaret." Whiskey-soaked breath pelted her face. "I want you to know that you're none better than those I pay. What's the old saying? It's a matter of price. And you've cost me about a million dollars *and* eleven years of misery. You better be worth it."

He had taken her, and when he finished, he had fallen into a drunken stupor.

The next morning he apologized. Margaret played it for all it was worth, sobbing into her pillow, sneaking glimpses of his bleary eyes.

"Don't worry, Margaret." Seamus sighed wearily. "I'll never touch you again. But there will be *no* divorce to taint this family. You'll be a good mother to Michael and act like a loving wife in public. That shouldn't be too difficult for you. You're a good actress. But I'll do what I damned well want to outside this house."

And he did. And while he did, the baby grew inside her.

Her eyes closed. She had hated Anthony from the time she felt the first movement in her body. She knew that her

22

mortal soul was in peril, for what she felt was a cardinal sin. No one must ever know. Sin or not, she wanted nothing to do with that baby. She'd hire more maids, another nanny. She'd see to Anthony's material needs, but that was all. Her long eyelashes brushed open as she came to a startling and satisfying conclusion.

Pleased with herself, she smiled softly. God had given her this baby against her will. God could take care of him.

CHAPTER

❧ 2 ❧

Anthony

Anthony was colicky as an infant, big and strong as a toddler, and almost uncontrollable as a young boy. He managed to upset the entire household, Margaret included, in spite of her determination to ignore him. Although he was never aggressively rude or disrespectful, he seemed compelled to explore life as if it were uncharted territory, destroying most of his toys with the same fervor with which he rebuilt them.

As much as she could, Margaret stuck to her resolve, responding to Anthony's needs with disinterested neglect. Mostly, he ran wild, his blond hair in constant need of cutting. He streaked through the house, his blue eyes soaking up the world with a frenzy as he tormented the maids in whose care he was generally left.

"That woman pays no more attention to that little boy than if he were a street urchin," Hattie the cook grumbled as she swept the trail of food crumbs Anthony had left all over the kitchen floor. "Why won't she make him sit down and eat?" she asked Mary Katherine, the latest in a string of maids.

"I don't think she really cares if he eats or not," Mary Katherine replied tersely, reaching for the Lysol.

"He's such a cute little thing. But so wild. He doesn't get a haircut until it's almost on his shoulders, and he wouldn't get a bath if it weren't for you."

Mary Katherine frowned. "Well, I hope the next maid sees to him. I don't think I can bear Mrs. Callahan ordering me around much longer. She acts like she's the queen of England. Always wanting me to stay late. Nothing ever clean enough or tidy enough to suit her. You know, Hattie, I feel sorry for that little boy. He's got a rough road ahead with that creature for a mother."

Two weeks later, Mary Katherine walked off the job when Margaret threw a temper tantrum over a spot on her bathroom tile. And the string of maids continued unbroken.

Once he was old enough, Margaret tried desperately to give him back to God, sending him to mass every day, hoping for spiritual intervention, watching him as he said his prayers to recant his numerous boyish sins. As the years passed she reluctantly accepted the fact that God was not keeping His part of her one-sided bargain. Even God did not want him, and her attitude toward Anthony worsened.

Seamus would shake his head when informed of Anthony's latest incident, for Margaret was loudly verbal about the constant trouble brewing around her younger son. Seamus would mutter, "Boys will be boys" and retreat to the peace and quiet of his office, feeling guiltier than ever about both Margaret *and* Anthony. It was that guilt that kept him from interfering for his heart went out to the boy.

Michael tolerated him, but Anthony felt no great loss as he watched his brother march off to Harvard, launch his career, and become the focal point of Margaret's blatant pride.

For this reason, he showed no reaction when Seamus arrived home, his face ashen, one hot August afternoon. He watched his father disappear upstairs. He heard his mother scream, and the sound momentarily paralyzed him. He waited. The piercing sound did not stop. Terrified, he took the stairs two at a time until he stood at Margaret's bedroom door. Seamus looked up at him, almost through him, and quietly announced that Michael was dead. Michael had been sailing with two friends, and neither could recall how it had happened. Michael was simply there one moment, and gone the next.

After the funeral, Margaret went into a deep depression, staying in her bed for days on end. When she finally emerged, the eyes that she turned on Anthony were empty. She didn't seem to see him at all. He felt invisible.

But the effects were lasting. In essence, she banned him from the house.

"Play in the yard," she instructed. "Use the bathroom in the cabana."

Anthony's sense of isolation increased; the damage toll around the house rose.

First it was the oriental rug in the study (he burned holes in it with a poker made red-hot by holding it in the fire). Then it was the leather recliner (he cut it with his pocket knife), and finally he shot out the windshield of his neighbor's Cadillac, watching it shatter from his bedroom window.

Margaret confined him to his bedroom. He took his meals alone in the kitchen. There was no television. She withheld his allowance, but nothing worked. If she'd been interested enough to read a child psychology book, she would have realized negative attention was better than no attention, but she'd managed to raise Michael without expert advice. Besides, that would have taken some time and energy and Anthony was hardly worth it.

In spite of Margaret's calculated neglect, Anthony flourished and grew like a tangled weed—he was hardy, perennial, and unwanted. On his twelfth birthday, he took her Mercedes for a spin, leaving parts of it permanently imbedded in a maple tree. That did it.

Margaret went into a rage.

"I won't have it, Seamus!" she shouted, her face red and contorted. "I can't control him. You can't control him. Nobody can control him!"

Seamus stood in front of the wrecked car shaking his head.

"Can't you do anything with your son?" Margaret shouted. The police officer called to investigate the accident shot Seamus a look of sympathy.

"Margaret, this is not the time or place—"

"There's never a time or place for Anthony," she interrupted hotly. "He's going to boarding school. And that's final!"

Seamus tried to fight Margaret on the issue, but she refused to back down. As usual, he gave in. Anthony watched the scene play over and over, hoping his father would hold out and feeling shame when his father crumpled under Margaret's relentless pressure. January arrived, and he found himself banished to the rolling hills of Pennsylvania.

Anthony adjusted rapidly to boarding school, finding it, even with its plain food and stark furnishings, infinitely more pleasant than his sumptuous home. In spite of his attempts to hide his teeming intellect, it was uncovered, and his instructors mounted a frustrating campaign to tone down his exuberant high jinks and channel his energy into more productive goals.

He was popular with his classmates, and not always for the right reasons.

"I cut algebra," Leon Wilbanks whispered to David Carter. "I'm gonna get kicked out of here on demerits."

"See Callahan," David whispered back.

"What can he do?"

"He's got a stash of medical passes."

"What?" Leon's eyes widened. "How did he do it?"

"That doesn't matter. It'll cost you, but he can take care of it."

David Carter and his new roommate, Anthony Callahan, were quite a team. David marketed what Anthony procured, and the amazing list of items Anthony procured boggled even David's devious twelve-year-old mind.

And Anthony was funny, a feat that did not go unnoticed by the rest of his classmates. Early on, Anthony learned to mimic, the end result of watching so much television alone. Now, he did it with diabolical accuracy. Several teachers were targets of his lethal imitations as their backs were turned toward the class. He was unaware that he was using humor to mock the hurt that filled his soul. He only knew it was his first real acting triumph.

David became Anthony's first friend. In fact, one trip to David's topsy-turvy Chicago home, and Anthony was spellbound. Dave's father was a financier, lately involved in backing films, and Anthony was awed by the assortment of people who wandered in and out of the house at will. It only served to point out how bleak his own home was, and he opted to spend all of his free weekends with Dave.

But he couldn't avoid going home for the summer. He was thirteen and facing three long months of loneliness as he wandered aimlessly through the large house. And it was by sheer accident that he overheard his mother's conversation. The house was being carpeted, Margaret complaining the hardwood floors were cold on her feet during the long winter, and Anthony's movements were undetected as he headed for the kitchen. She was at her usual station, seated on a stool, the telephone cradled in her hand.

"Just make up something," she was advising. "I did, and it worked for twelve years. Lie. He'll have to accept it." She paused to listen as Anthony remained in the hallway, his ears pricked, waiting for her to speak again. "Of course, he was furious when he found out. You know how men are about sex—that's when he raped me." She laughed. Anthony held his breath, his face the color of parchment. "Of course, he apologized, and he hasn't touched me since. But I got pregnant. You know I didn't want another baby. Anthony's been so difficult—not at all like Michael was—but you reap what you sow. How could I have expected anything else? And now he's maturing. I'll have another dirty man in the house."

His mother's voice faded as he slipped down the hallway and out the front door.

Her words sat like hot coals in the center of his chest. Something terrible had happened, and *he* was the product of that terrible thing. His body heaved with sobs as he collapsed behind a rosebush. His mother had never wanted

him. Never loved him. His mind shot to his father. Why
had he done it? Slowly, his crying abated, and as he dried
his swollen face on his shirttail his childhood evaporated
with each tear, banished like a dark memory that nothing
could evoke. He didn't need them. He didn't need anyone.
No one, he didn't care who, would ever control him again.
He would never let it happen. Never.

During the next few years his body grew with a velocity
that astonished and fascinated everyone, himself included.
His shoulders filled out, his legs grew long, hair appeared
on his upper lip, and his face took on the hard angles of
manhood.

He could feel his mother's eyes following him as he
roamed the house during summer vacations, and his father
began to talk about business with him upon the rare occasion when he came home for dinner. Anthony kept his distance, and no one seemed comfortable. The sprawling,
colonial house looked picture perfect from the outside. But
inside, there was an air of perpetual uneasiness. Anthony
felt like a visitor, one who had overstayed his welcome.

He was now sixteen, and Seamus, feeling his usual guilt
for neglecting his son, had promised a new Corvette would
sit in their driveway if Anthony brought his mediocre
grades up to snuff. The car was an irresistible bribe, and
Anthony complied, producing all As. To Seamus, it served
to underscore Anthony's abilities when he truly dedicated
himself to a task.

But it was Lucy Curran who provided the real reward.

"Delicious!" Lucy Curran murmured as she drove her
Jaguar past the Callahan house. She said the word at least

three times a day, on her way to the beauty salon, to shopping, or to enjoy a leisurely lunch at the country club.

Sometimes she said, "Absolutely delicious!" Either way, the object of her delight was the sight of Anthony's tall, muscular body, sometimes mowing the lawn, sometimes washing his shiny new Corvette, sometimes tossing a basketball through the hoop attached to the garage. Regardless of the task, it was a most pleasurable and stimulating sight.

Lucy Curran was a woman of impeccable taste and specific desires. Her husband, twenty years her senior, owner of a most profitable import business, satisfied her needs for the finer things in life, as her bedecked and bejeweled body clearly reflected. As for her other needs—well, he fell far short in that most crucial area. Lucy Curran, who was endowed by nature with more than her share of physical allure, developed the habit of satisfying those needs by entertaining a select group of more-than-willing men during her husband's frequent and extended trips to Europe. She would issue a subtle invitation to an unsuspecting mechanic, repairman, or carpenter, for it really didn't matter much to her, as long as they were magnificent specimens of manhood. When they arrived at her home under the guise of Lucy's household emergencies, she would literally "make their day."

She was discreet, or so she thought, not knowing that it was rather common knowledge among the male population residing in her neighborhood that Lucy Curran was available. By unspoken contract this bit of information was never to pass the ears of the resident females.

When Lucy telephoned, Margaret listened with a sympathetic ear.

"My gardener was drunk when he came to work yesterday," Lucy said. "You know how it is with hired help. Naturally, I fired him. I'm absolutely terrible when it comes to hiring anyone," she lamented. "I always leave that to my husband, but this is his buying season, so he won't be home for weeks! I'm really in a bind." Actually, she had laid the gardener off with a generous severance check, knowing full well that she would rehire him in September. He had five children and needed the money.

"My upper-story windows are a mess, haven't been cleaned in six months, and that dreadful lawn furniture needs painting again! Would Anthony be interested?"

Margaret Callahan jumped at the proposition. "Oh, Anthony needs something to do," she replied enthusiastically. "It keeps him out of trouble. Anyway, I've always believed that idle hands are the devil's workshop." She might have added that this belief applied solely to Anthony, but she didn't.

Thus, Anthony arrived at Lucy Curran's house one Monday morning in shorts and T-shirt, his developing muscles rippling, his suntanned skin glowing, to Mrs. Curran's barely suppressed and utter delight.

Up to this point, Anthony's sexual experiences had been less than satisfying. There was one girl who let him discover the full meaning of manhood, but that had occurred on a sofa while her parents were out for the evening. Fear of discovery, and her feverish whispers to "hurry, hurry," rendered the incident less than earth-shattering. Anthony never bothered to call her again.

Mrs. Curran quickly became a different story. She appeared at the door each morning clad in some filmy negligee, like nothing Anthony had ever seen. She would murmur apologetically, "Oh, Anthony, I overslept. I'm sorry. Give me a minute to get dressed." She would climb the stairs, the sun streaming through the fabric clinging to her lush body. The acute aching in his loins was paralyzing.

Lunch was miserable. She insisted on serving him on the patio.

"Sit there," she said, pointing one long red nail in the direction of a round wrought-iron table upon whose top rested a pink-and-white-striped placemat and napkin and one tumbler of iced tea that might have quenched the thirst of a two-year-old. In spite of his discomfort, he never complained.

"I can make more sandwiches," she said as she emerged from the kitchen with two tiny, crust-free slices of bread stuffed with cream cheese and something else unidentifiable and placed them in front of him. "Don't be shy if you need more."

"This will be fine," he mumbled, trying to keep his eyes off her shapely legs. Usually she had on some flimsy halter held in place by a force that Anthony found totally mysterious.

"Here. You need more tea." She leaned over his shoulder to refill his glass, and he reddened as he felt the fullness of a breast on his back. He was eternally grateful for the cloth napkin resting on his sweaty lap.

"Take your time, Anthony," she'd instruct as she perched on a chair opposite him, legs crossed. And she'd watch him eat, to his total humiliation. He could feel those green eyes with their hint of laughter, and each bite he took stuck in his throat.

The afternoons were equally perilous as Mrs. Curran

sunbathed by the pool, her body barely covered by a brief bikini. His heart would lurch as she rolled from her back to her stomach, reached behind, and unfastened the top of her bathing suit.

Anthony made it through each day, following her orders like a stricken pup, completing each chore, shoving the money she handed him regularly into his very full pocket. But the nights were torturous, as he was unable to sleep, pacing the floor of his bedroom, while vivid fantasies involving Mrs. Lucy Curran played endlessly through his mind.

After two weeks in Mrs. Curran's employ, she asked him to clean the second-story windows. Retrieving the extension ladder from the garage and filling a large bucket, Anthony began the task, working his way around the house and peeking only intermittently at Mrs. Curran as she wandered around the pool area. After all, he had to maintain his precarious perch.

Late in the afternoon, he rounded the corner to the rear of the house when the sky darkened, and he heard the first clap of thunder. He glanced at his watch, wondering if he would finish before the storm hit. As the clouds clustered like thick smoke he picked up his pace, dragging the ladder along the back of the house, his body sweating from the humidity, the heat, and his accelerated activity. Three more to go, he thought as he competed with the wind and impending rain, determined to complete the chore, outrace nature as only a boy of sixteen would do.

"Anthony, come in before the storm hits. Your mother would never forgive me if you were struck by lightning," Lucy called from the back door. That was exactly what she had in mind, although it was to be lightning of a different sort.

The cold rain pelted his body before he made it to the ground, and as rivulets of water washed down his head and shoulders he rushed for the shelter of the house.

The French doors opened.

"Anthony, you're soaked! Now you'll probably catch cold, and your mother will never forgive me. You come right in while I get a towel!" He stood, dripping on the burnished tile of the kitchen floor until she returned, then reached for the towel she was holding.

"No, no," she protested. "Let me. Take off that wet shirt." Like a willing schoolboy, he obeyed. He stood, his soggy shirt in his hand, not knowing where to put it as she rubbed his back with the thick terry cloth. And then she was in front of him, rubbing his chest. His eyes fell to the ample cleavage above the line of her cotton tank top. The outline of her nipples strained against the fabric. Nothing could have stopped his growing desire. That desire had taken on a life of its own.

She lifted her eyes, held his look, and licked her upper lip. "Would you like to touch, Anthony?"

Miserably, he stared at her, face burning, groin throbbing. She took his hand and placed it on one of her breasts. A hot tide flooded his body as he felt the fullness, the softness. She dropped the towel. Her hands moved to her shoulders and she lowered the straps of the cotton so that it fell lightly over the tops of his fingers. Then she ran a hand up his lean thigh.

It was there, on the wet kitchen floor, during a raging thunderstorm, two doors down from his mother's house, with another man's wife, that Anthony learned about the power of sex. It was *not* a boring summer, for Anthony was a willing student and Mrs. Curran an excellent teacher.

When September arrived, it never occurred to Anthony to thank Lucy Curran. If he had thought about it, he would have realized that he didn't have to express his gratitude, because the relationship was mutually satisfying. A great deal of sex and a total lack of feeling. It suited his purpose to a tee.

CHAPTER

❧ 3 ❧

It did *not* suit Seamus Callahan's purpose. Anthony had underestimated his father's interest in him, and he had committed a most grievous oversight. He forgot that his father was a man.

Seamus Callahan viewed his youngest son with something akin to awe. He didn't fit the family portrait. Both Seamus and Michael had broad, square features and were rather short. Anthony, in contrast, was tall and lean. His startling blue eyes were set deep in an angular face below a mop of defiant blond hair.

If Seamus hadn't known his wife's distaste for matters of the flesh, he would have suspected Anthony wasn't even his son. But the calendar's precise pinpointing of that fateful April night couldn't be denied.

Seamus had tried in vain to erase the memory of that evening. He had done everything possible to atone for his shameful behavior, yielding to Margaret's demands, no matter how outrageous. During the long seventeen years since Anthony's conception, he never once touched her. Still, Margaret knew how to slip in the knife, shoot him a look, make life, in general, quite miserable. As a result, he continued his quiet infidelities, opting to avoid his home and her eyes.

But now, Seamus sighed, unable to repress the smile that passed across his lips, there *was* the matter of his son and Mrs. Curran. Not that she wasn't a looker! The smile widened to a grin. She was indeed, and he wouldn't mind seeing that dark hair splayed on his own pillow, but Anthony was much too young to know the pitfalls of toying with a married woman.

Maybe as a father he'd fallen short. But for the first time, Lucy Curran created a situation that only he could handle. Margaret, he was convinced, was unaware of the affair . . . thank God for small blessings.

Seamus made a first and last-ditch effort to be a father. He talked to Anthony about women.

"Now, I don't know how much you do know," he began, watching Anthony slouch in the kitchen chair. "But I know there's a great deal you don't know."

Anthony stared at him like he'd just arrived on a space ship.

"But if Margaret suspected that your conduct in this neighborhood was anything but sterling"—he paused as Anthony dropped his eyes—"she'd be hell to live with."

"She's hell to live with anyway," Anthony blurted.

Seamus nearly agreed. But boys were supposed to respect their mothers.

"I think you're too rough on her, Anthony."

"Rough on her? Nobody's rough on her. She gets her way about everything."

"Not everything, Anthony. Not everything."

And the conversation closed.

Discreetly, he studied his younger son, and he noted Anthony's expression with growing concern. The blue eyes were either overflowing with a wild, kinetic energy or brooding and tinged with hostility. Either signaled trouble. Anthony was too intense, too consumed by a need to try the limits of his endurance. The traffic violations were witness to his recklessness. His grades were far from satisfactory. His diving medals were tangible evidence of his athletic prowess, but his nature was going to be a real problem. He needed to be directed, disciplined, forced to proceed in some orderly fashion.

The next day, Seamus made some inquiries, calling in favors for his political contributions. Before the year was out, Anthony had an appointment to interview at Annapolis. A military academy would be a safe place for his son.

To his father's delight, Anthony accepted the idea and spent his last year in prep school producing another stellar report card. During that time, Anthony read everything he could about the Academy and was well-versed in its history and traditions when he presented himself as a candidate for the class of 1963.

Once Anthony conquered—or at least appeared to conquer—his "problem with authority," as it was aptly labeled, he took to the Academy as though he had been seeking a home his entire young life and had finally found it. Here, at last, were people who cared about his well-being, about his intellect, about stretching his physical strength. All they asked in return was eight years of his life. It seemed like a small price at the time.

Anthony funneled all of his physical and intellectual energy into meeting the rigorous demands of the Academy, determined to fulfill if not exceed each challenge. The Academy, in turn, reciprocated, sharpening both his mind and his body to a keen edge. His athletic abilities were nurtured, and his diving skills were honed to perfection. A new assortment of medals collected in his dresser drawer.

All of this left little time to socialize. On the rare occasions when he did choose to loosen up, slip out of the confines of the Academy's rigid discipline, he boggled the minds of his classmates with his devastating success with women. The same grace that allowed him to master intricate dives transferred to the dance floor. His body telegraphed formidable sensuality. That, coupled with his good looks and cunning persuasive ability, created an awesome combination. He always scored.

After graduating, he headed straight for Pensacola and put in a grueling sixteen weeks to obtain his commission. He elected to fly, ranking high enough to get what he wanted, and spent three years achieving that goal. Ultimately, and by some military snafu, he was sent to McGuire Air Force Base outside of Trenton, New Jersey, where a small contingent of navy pilots were flying transport planes to Vietnam and other military installations around the world. He tagged along wherever they headed —Germany, Africa, the Philippines—for it was easy duty. He was seeing the world, just as the recruiting posters said. He ignored the furor growing around the involvement in Vietnam, knowing that combat duty would come soon enough. The protest rallies were merely a distraction; he needed to view the war with a single eye.

One free weekend, he phoned his old classmate, Dave Carter, now living in Manhattan.

"It's about time you got in touch with me, you bastard!" Dave yelled in his ear.

"I've tried, but you're never there," Anthony replied, a laugh spilling across the telephone wire. "I'm sick of your answering service, Dave. I've talked to that woman so many times, I almost asked her out."

"You could've added that to your long list of mistakes, Callahan. She weighs in at two-fifty. And anyway, don't talk to me about staying home. Whenever I returned your calls, you were in England, Greenland, or some other exotic place. I'm afraid to go to Europe knowing you've been there before me."

"Watch it, Carter. Listen, if that high-powered talent agency you claim to work for ever let you stay in New York, we could get together. Tip a few. Talk over old times and—"

"Look over the 1966 crop of women? I know you, Callahan. Get this. I spend six months in New York and six months in L.A., I've got all the budding actresses, singers, and models I can handle. Strange how some females are willing to do anything to be discovered. Can you beat it?"

Anthony chuckled. "No way."

They met for dinner, and Dave gave him a key to his apartment.

"I'm never there, you lucky bastard. Just clean up your mess and replenish the booze. And just to prove I'm your best friend—no, make that your *only* friend—you have access to the little black book beside the telephone. The blondes have stars by their names. Just say you know me" —he grinned lasciviously—"and if you get shot down, remember I'm a tough act to follow."

At first, Anthony had been impressed with Dave's collection of females. The women were fine. The variety ex-

41

CURRENTS OF LOVE

hilarating. But his interest soon waned, both in and out of
the bedroom, as he discovered a lot of packaging but not
much substance. Each and every one of them seemed obsessed with her looks, her career. When they did talk, it
was about "the business," as though they were unaware
of the rest of the world. Anthony was completely disinterested in the frivolity of show business, and finally a
restlessness resurfaced. He got hungry for some real
conversation and set out on his own.

Anthony was fascinated by her accent, that long, lazy
drawl that dropped consonants as if they were so much
excess baggage. He met her at a party, one of those in-
spired New York gatherings that threw people together like
potpourri. He spotted her when he arrived, a little thing
clad in a lace dress, legs encased in black stockings, their
length exaggerated by satin heels. It was the time of mini-
skirts, and she'd been what the designers had in mind when
they'd created them. Dark brown hair was piled on her
head in an unconstructed arrangement so that wisps and
strands escaped at random, brushing her face as she moved
her head in conversation. His eyes swept the room again,
looking, always looking, landing on a busty blonde who
held his interest for a moment, but eventually they returned
to the brunette. The dress screamed to be touched as it
seemed to float over her body. The hands drifted through
the air as she talked, then she suddenly burst into laughter.
Dark eyes glittered as she listened intently to someone's
reply, only to burst into laughter again. Yes, he decided, it
was definitely worth investigating. He got a Scotch from
the kitchen and deftly worked his way through the mass of
bodies, planting himself strategically behind her. That's

when he first heard the soft drawl. Leaning comfortably against a chair, he listened.

"He's the most persistent obscene caller in New York," she was saying. "Six o'clock in the morning, please. The phone rings. Well, he sounds like Joe College. 'Is Mary there?' And she's out on a flight, of course, and besides, no one calls her Mary—everyone who really knows her calls her Mary Sue. With that he proceeds to let out a barrage of obscenity that would cause a Baptist preacher to faint. Nothing, and I mean nothing, has any effect on him. We've blown whistles into the telephone. We've had guys answer and threaten him. *Nothing* works. Looks like we either change our phone number, or we're stuck with him for life."

This was his cue. He lowered his head to the side of her neck and whispered, "Don't change it till I have the number, and then grant me exclusive rights to the new one."

Startled, she stepped backward, caught her heel on the toe of his shoe, and almost fell into his arms. Her face was inches from his as he steadied her.

"You scared the hell out of me," she said, her voice low and breathy.

"If I did, you're pretty easy to scare." He'd grinned down at the faint hint of freckles on the bridge of her nose before his eyes lingered on the well-defined dip in her upper lip. "I was voted 'Least Likely to Scare Anyone' by my classmates. I've devoted my entire life to being worthy of that honor." He continued to examine her face as he prattled on, knowing that he'd gotten more girls in bed with talk than with any other method. It was all in the head. "And now that we know each other so well, I'd like to marry you, have two-and-a-half children, and become a statistic like the rest of the world."

"I can't possibly do that before Sunday." She smiled up at him.

"You married?" he asked.

"Are you kidding?" she responded, a touch of iron in her voice. "Not me. Not ever!"

"A girl after my own heart," he replied. "Soulmates."

"No mates. I'm antimarriage. To quote Gloria Steinhem, I can't breed in captivity."

He was impressed. And he was absolutely convinced that he was walking, unimpaired, into the front lines of the sexual revolution. Her eyelashes dropped. God, what a flirt! It was time to obey his first rule once he'd singled out a woman: Cut 'em from the pack.

"Can you leave?" he asked, barely able to control the impatience in his voice as his eyes raked over her body.

"Now, that's an original idea," she replied, one eyebrow rising critically.

"So it's not original," he agreed. "What can I say?"

"You can say you won't ask again."

"What else can I say?" he said.

Her laugh held a hint of surrender.

He plunged forward.

"Well, *can* you leave?"

"I came with someone," she explained, her eyes circling the room and landing on the figure of a lanky redhead.

"So what?"

"So, I always leave with the man who brought me—that's what."

He glanced in the direction of his competition, shrouded his face with concern, and said, "Listen, I probably shouldn't even be telling you this, but you look like a nice

44

girl, and—well, I think you ought to know. That guy you're with, he looks okay in that three-piece suit, but he has a record. Five years ago he served time"—he paused dramatically—"Attica. Burned down a thread factory. Got fifty thousand dollars for the job."

Her eyes widened, flashing disbelief. "Is that true?"

He unleashed his most dazzling smile. "No. But it makes a hell of a good story. Anyway, all's fair in love and war."

"Which is this?" she asked, her eyes straying across his face. He felt as though he'd just been kissed by a hummingbird.

"Certainly not the latter." Keep it coming, he told himself. She's interested. She's relenting. "Look, at least give me a name."

"Delaney Rollins." The eyelashes dropped again. She was his for the asking.

"Anthony Callahan. Now give me a number—then give me your heart."

"The number's in the book, and in spite of your obvious attractions, no one gets my heart."

He called her the next day. He kissed her that night. And he fought with her on Sunday. It set up a cycle that was seldom broken.

Neither could quite believe that the other was for real. To Anthony, Delaney was a collection of impossible contradictions. She was southern, through and through, but she was also liberal. She was lovely, and she was exceptionally bright. To anyone else, those two qualities might seem compatible, but not to Anthony. His relationships were limited in duration and confined to a certain type—good-looking, easy, and not too smart.

And if it was Delaney's physical assets, the magnitude

of which mushroomed each time he saw her, that first attracted him, it was her mind that kept him coming back. He found himself, for the first time in his life, in the unenviable position of having to defend nearly everything he said.

She was into the forefront of the women's liberation movement, from which he had been insulated by the navy. Still she batted her long eyelashes and flashed that seductive smile to taxi drivers, waiters, and any other man who happened to cross her path. It drove him out of his mind.

She was punishing in her questioning of his motives for believing anything and everything, forcing him to delve into areas that he didn't want probed. After all, it was 1966, and the entire nation was polarized over something or other. To be challenged by a female? He still expected women to provide him with a haven from the turmoil that invaded his life.

Her delicate looks and soft manner of speaking belied the ferocity with which she defended her convictions. Sometimes, when she was unloading on him with machine-gun rapidity, he had an overwhelming urge to run for shelter. It changed his opinion forever about women in general and southern women in particular. Magnolias? Ha! More like roses—loaded with thorns.

"Would you mind getting me another drink, baby?" he'd ask innocently, expecting her to trot to the kitchen and return, drink in hand.

"Oh?" she'd reply, her voice casual and sweet. "When did you break your leg? Get your own."

And he'd scowl and slink into the kitchen to get his own, wondering what was happening to his world.

And she insisted on paying her way, sending him into an unreasonable fury. He didn't make much in the navy, but he outearned her, and that was a fact! *McCall's* and all the other women's magazines were notorious for attracting bright talent for pennies. But if she couldn't pay, they didn't go.

And still, she was warm and delicious and, he found out early on, incredibly innocent. He was confused. She continued to flirt flagrantly, flattering his male ego, exciting him, making him feel like he was the only man on earth. Her clothes were sexy as hell—not necessarily revealing, just sexy. It was something about the way she put it all together, some extra little detail—a flower, a scarf fluttering around her head, a ruffle down her back that signaled availability—and he, Anthony Callahan, who was used to being the pursued and not the pursuer, was being held at bay by this mere wisp of a girl. He was going nowhere.

As his frustrations mounted with amazing speed, so did the arguments. She would kiss him with a passion that astonished him, leaving him weak with desire. He wanted that small body more than he'd ever wanted anyone in his life, but as his hands would begin to claim it, she'd break it off, clasping his large hands in hers and utter a stinging and definitive "No."

In desperation, he turned to other women, trying to relieve his bruised ego with an injection of willing sexual partners, only to be left unfulfilled, and he'd find himself back at her door.

"You're sending such damned mixed messages!" he yelled at her one night after a particularly passionate encounter. "What the hell do you want from me?"

"It's what you want from me that's the problem, Anthony," she replied quietly while straightening her clothing. Her face glowed in the soft light of the living room.

"Yes, that *is* the problem, isn't it?" he answered angrily, a corrosive smile curling his lips. "You come on like a neon light, but that light turns into a bright red stop sign. Do you know what you're doing to me?"

"No," she answered, her voice almost a whisper, "but I do know what you'd do to me."

"What? Leave you a fallen woman? Get you pregnant and walk off? For God's sake, Delaney, it's 1966! There *are* such things as birth control!"

"Birth control is not the issue, Anthony. My soul is the issue. You can't have it, and that's what you want."

"Are you telling me if the body comes, the soul will follow?"

"With us, yes." Her voice dropped even further as her hand drifted across his chest, leaving him trembling with desire. It was becoming impossible to touch her without wanting her, wanting to take her any way he could get her.

"I'm not ever going to get married, Anthony."

"Who said anything about marriage?" he asked brusquely. So what if the idea had been creeping into his thoughts? Viciously he shoved it aside, buried it. He was not going to wind up like his father. Who the hell did she think she was?

"Nobody. But I wanted you to know how I felt about it anyway. No marriage. I don't want another human being to feel obligated to stay with me, bound by some invisible legal ties."

He exploded. "No marriage. No sex. What are you going to be? A nun?"

"Protestants don't have nuns. You know that very well. And I didn't say no sex. I said no sex with you."

His head was reeling. She was rejecting him. His face strained in harnessed anger as what she said registered.

"Does that mean that you will sleep with someone—or

should I say anyone—other than me? That's what I hear you saying, Delaney." That image now hurtling through his head sent him into a blue-black fury. Never! She couldn't! She wouldn't! He knew she wanted him.

"You want to own me, Anthony. You want me to fall in line—let you control my life. You almost own me now, and if we ever made love, you would own me, whether I wanted you to or not. I will not be owned."

He stormed out, got drunk, called one of Dave's women, and got laid, swearing to himself and to anyone else who would listen never to see her again. He stayed at the base the next weekend, and he was miserable. He sulked, he argued, he even got into a fight. He was used to getting his way with women, and some part of him simply refused to believe what she said. Thursday night he gave in and called. He kept his voice calm, never referring to their argument, and then he'd gone back with every intention of winning, claiming what was his and his alone, only to endure another velvet rebuke.

She knew his time was limited, for there was one topic they never discussed. The war. He knew without asking where she would take her stand, and she knew where he was going. Something inside him refused to raise the topic of his inevitable departure. But as the time approached for him to ship out, he seemed to accept her terms—never understanding them, never completely understanding her —but the burning need for her very presence by his side overruled his desire.

It was a time of calm. They both seemed to be storing up energy for the storm he was about to face and the emptiness she would endure. During the quiet lull, he thought more and more of marriage, but she'd made her statement about that, and if she meant it only half as much as she meant everything else, the issue was closed. What the hell was he going to do with her?

Maybe she'd change in the thirteen months he'd be gone.

He barely touched her now as they talked about everything except when he was leaving and how long he'd be there. He became more and more convinced of one thing. In spite of what she said, no one else would have her either—not as long as he was alive, for every fiber in her body told him that she loved him, that she wanted him, and that she'd be there when he got back, though not one word passed between them. Somewhere, sometime, someplace, he'd have her . . . after she got over being full-blown crazy.

CHAPTER

❧ 4 ❧

Delaney

D elaney Anne Rollins! I said to put that book down and come wash these supper dishes. Now!"

"Yes, ma'am," Delaney said, reluctantly closing *Les Miserables,* her mind still centered on the trials of Jean Valjean.

Carrie Rollins watched her youngest daughter walk through the kitchen door and view the pile of dirty dishes.

"I noticed you didn't clean your plate again, Delaney. I've told you and told you to eat more. You're too skinny. You look all spindly."

Delaney glanced at her mother from dark doe eyes, eyes much too large for her thin face.

"But I wanted to finish my book before—"

"Eatin' comes before readin', Delaney. Readin's good, but you'll die of starvation before all that readin' serves

51

any purpose." She reached out a hand and stroked Delaney's silky hair, then sighed and left the room.

Delaney washed each dish slowly, lost in her thoughts. It was becoming more and more difficult to resolve the world in which she lived with the world that she read about.

Being extraordinarily bright and equally poor put her at at a disadvantage, for nothing made sense. Nevertheless, she devised a method for dealing with the problem. Fantasy. She was constantly drifting away, her head filled with the deeds and misdeeds of characters who lived in books as she ignored the real people with whom she lived.

From poring over her sisters' cast-off comic books, she taught herself to read when she was four. That was the year she found her way to Valhalla's small public library. The first time she entered those doors, one of her sisters had taken her. And although, to her knowledge, Teresa never went back, Delaney's visits became a daily occurrence.

Shyly, she made her way to the children's section and stood staring, awestruck by the rows of books.

"Can I help you?" Mrs. Trent, the librarian, finally asked when she realized the child had been standing there for a long time.

"Yes, ma'am," Delaney had replied, and then she proceeded to shake her head no as Mrs. Trent chose books mostly full of pictures. Delaney wanted words.

"Why don't you sit with me a moment and we'll read it together," Mrs. Trent suggested, and she was duly astonished when the small child flew through each book until Mrs. Trent selected one appropriate for a third grader. After that, whenever Delaney slipped through the doors, Mrs. Trent smiled and left her to fend for herself. It was the greatest gift anyone had ever given Delaney.

By the time she was six, Valhalla's small library was

Delaney's second home. She spent hours perched at one of the large oak tables, her small feet dangling from the straight-back chair, reading with no direction or particular goal in mind.

"Where's Delaney?" her father would ask, settling in front of the television set, his tired legs propped on a threadbare footstool.

"Where do you think?" her mother would answer. "She's got her nose stuck in another book."

Nothing Delaney read helped her understand the world. Rather, she simply stored the information, never knowing why fascinating thoughts danced in her head like fireflies.

If her mother was less than pleased by Delaney's neglect of her chores in favor of reading, her teachers were astounded. They skipped her in the second grade, thinking that would suffice, only to discover that another skip was in order in the fifth grade. None of this was of any consequence to Delaney. She continued to drift along, dreaming of the places she read about, wondering if she would ever find that one particular spot (she was absolutely convinced it existed) where dreams were reality. Of one thing she was sure: That spot was not Valhalla, South Carolina.

Her parents did the best they could, both working at the mill, trying to put enough food on the table and clothes on the backs of their four growing daughters. But no matter how carefully they planned or how frugal they were, there was never enough. Life was raw. Not a single object in her home existed for the sake of beauty. Every item served a purpose and was intended to be used, and then used up.

It was only through fantasy that she could escape the sameness of Valhalla's dreary landscape, the shabby interior of her home, and the inevitable prospect of one day assuming her proper place at the looms in the mill.

By the time she reached the seventh grade, reality began to creep into the private places of her heart. She felt the first pang of humiliation at always wearing her sisters' hand-me-downs, and she was so slight that none of them ever quite fit. Quietly, she would stare at her sisters' curves and renew her belief in magic, for she was convinced it would take a large dose of it to transform her pencil-straight body.

She began to feel isolated, left out.

"Are you going to the seventh-grade dance?" a classmate mumbled as they munched their sandwiches in the rowdy cafeteria. Delaney stared at the Tangee-colored lips, bit down hard on her own naked one, and mumbled, "No. We're going out of town." Such a blatant lie from such a little creature. They never went anywhere except to Cushing to visit Aunt Dicey at the farm.

All her friends began to take on different shapes. They talked incessantly of boys. She would sit in class, peek at the array of pimply-faced, gangly males, and for the life of her, she couldn't understand the big attraction.

Lagging far behind socially, she buried herself deeper in her books and began to write. She wrote stories—mostly about animals, rather than people, for people were too odd to comprehend.

And if she developed some unconventional ideas, she kept them to herself. She continued to fuel her insatiable intellect with even more books. She read of heroes and heroines, but in Valhalla, there were none. She read about glittering wealth, but no one in Valhalla was wealthy. She read about scientists and explorers, but she'd never met one. Everything seemed just beyond her knowing and just beyond her reach.

What she did meet—in fact, was unable to avoid—was

a collection of robust young men who parked their pick-up trucks and souped-up cars in front of her house, although she was not the feature attraction. Having three older sisters, all pretty in their own way, guaranteed that she would be witness to the southern courtship rituals that unfolded on her front porch. The boys planted their bodies on the banister, long legs stuffed into Levi's and T-shirts stretching across their chests. Delaney took to entering the house by the back door, thinking how much they resembled a flock of strutting, preening peacocks.

As a very disinterested party, she observed her sisters practice the art of flirtation. When Delaney was alone, which was seldom, she would settle in front of the chipped vanity mirror and mimic until she perfected each subtle move. The exact tilt of the shoulder, when to lower the lashes, how long to sustain a sultry look (just so long, not one second more), the ribbon, the necklace, the flower in her hair, until she reduced the procedure to a science. When the time came, and if she chose, she would be just as adept as her sisters—a southern girl worth her salt.

Within three months of each other, Ellen and Diane were married. The weddings, held in the Baptist church, were lovely, filled with flowing bridesmaid dresses, flowers, and the breathtaking lace of the wedding gowns. As they all worked together to sew the gowns at home, the fabrics stretched across chairs and tables, for once magically transforming her drab living room into a beautiful flower garden.

What occurred after the wedding ruined the magic. Her sisters went back to work in the mill, their beautiful wedding gowns stuffed in a closet, never to be seen again. Both Ellen and Diane reverted to their usual shoddy skirts and blouses and, soon after, an assortment of secondhand

maternity clothes. Instead of flowers and ribbons and perfume, their world was filled with bills and babies. Tom,
Ellen's husband, turned sullen, constantly complaining
about the crying baby or his lukewarm dinner or anything
else that interrupted his pursuit of a "good time." Ellen
grew silent, never laughing or joking the way she had before. One night, Tom vanished, leaving Ellen and the baby
broke and in debt. Too proud to accept welfare, Ellen took
on a second job as a waitress. When she moved to Charlotte, where opportunities were better, she looked like an
old woman.

Diane managed to keep her marriage intact, but she, too,
changed before Delaney's eyes. She acquired the slump of
one who had worked too long at the looms. Delaney never
failed to notice the occasional bruised arm or discolored
eye, in spite of Diane's attempts to hide the marks with
heavy makeup.

Teresa was another story. For years Delaney's memory
was haunted by the sight of her sister, sobbing at the
kitchen table. Her father's face was set in stone as her
mother paced in front of the sink.

"He doesn't want to get married, Daddy," Teresa
moaned, her hands clutching her stomach as she rocked
back and forth.

Her mother glanced up and caught Delaney's eye.

"Go to your room," she snapped.

It was a futile act, for the frame house was poorly constructed. Every word was audible as Delaney curled in her
bed like a shrimp.

"How could you let something like this happen, Teresa?"
John Rollins roared. "We taught you better, girl!"

"I know, I know," Teresa moaned.

"Then why did you do it?"

"I thought he loved me. He *said* he loved me, Daddy. I believed him. He said we'd get married. Oh, Mama, what am I gonna do?"

"Where's he gone, Teresa?" John Rollins asked, his voice ringing through the house like an angry wind.

"I don't know. His brother just grinned when I asked about him"—Teresa heaved with sobs—"and it was a horrible grin, nasty, like he knew all about it."

Delaney put her hands over her ears, trying to drown out the sounds, but the voices droned on.

Later, when silence finally fell, Carrie Rollins slipped into Delaney's room.

"Honey, I need to talk to you, explain a few things," she said softly. Delaney lifted her eyes from the book she was pretending to read.

"Lord, child. You're gonna ruin your eyes before you're twenty, readin' in that kind of light." She flipped the wall switch, and the bare bulb in the ceiling vanished. A blurred triangle of light from the open door bathed the room in pale yellow.

"I like to read here," Delaney said as she buried her head deeper in the pillow. "Besides, there's no decent lighting in this entire house."

"Well, the lighting in this house suits the rest of us just fine. Maybe you shouldn't read half the night. Maybe you should confine your readin' to the day." Carrie heard the sharpness in her own voice and tried to correct it. "I'm sorry, honey. I'm just weary." She sat on the edge of the bed, calling forth her last crumbs of patience.

"I know you don't understand what's going on with Teresa—"

"It's okay, Mama. You don't need to explain," Delaney interrupted.

"But we need to talk about it. There's more to it than you can understand right now. Teresa made a mistake—"

"I know, Mama, and I promise you I'll never do what Teresa did."

"That's not what I'm tryin' to say, Delaney. What Teresa did comes natural—"

"Well, if it's so natural, why is Daddy so angry? And why are you upset?"

"You don't understand, honey. People would talk. People don't take kindly to—"

"Bastards?"

"Delaney Rollins! I've never heard you use such a word."

"Well, that's what they call them in books."

"That may be, but I don't want you sayin' it." Carrie wiped her hands on her apron and dabbed at the perspiration on her upper lip. "Love don't always come easy, honey. Sometimes it gets real confusin', and Teresa got confused. When you're older, you'll see what I mean."

Delaney's eyes were unreadable. "Whatever you say, Mama."

She watched Carrie leave the room, then rolled to her side, pulling the covers under her chin. Mentally, she tossed away her mother's words like chaff in the wind. For she knew the naked truth. Teresa got herself pregnant, and now she had to pay for it. Women pay and men don't. How could Teresa be so stupid? She turned her head sideways and stared through the window at the blackness of the night. If that's what she had to face when she grew up, then she just wouldn't grow up. She was glad she was skinny. Boys don't like scrawny girls with no bumps. As her eyes closed one last thought filtered through her mind.

She would simply never bother with sex. Besides, it was disgusting.

The next day, Teresa was packed off to Aunt Dicey's. Not a word was ever spoken to Delaney, but when Teresa returned eight months later, she was alone.

The lesson cut deeply. But Mother Nature had other plans, and soon Delaney's body began to change. Curves developed. Her stark features softened. Boys now tried to talk to her, but they only tried once. Using her intellect as a laser-sharp weapon, she sent them scurrying from the line of fire. With a viciousness that was excessive, she rebuffed all advances, determined that her life would not be tangled by the devious tendrils of love, for it was a trap. She had other plans. When she was a senior, her attitude had been so effective, she was not even asked to the senior prom.

And then a miracle happened. Her remarkable academic performance landed her a full scholarship to the University of South Carolina. She was the first one in her family to venture into that alien world, and they were bursting with pride and hope—hope that at least one of them was going somewhere. Even her sisters pitched in, sewing madly to fashion some kind of wardrobe for a college girl. They treated her differently and boasted about her achievement to other people in her presence. She was relieved when September arrived and she took her meager belongings and settled into the dorm. She was determined success would be hers one way or another, and her degree would be the first rung. When she thought of Valhalla or her family, she felt a sense of shame, and she reaffirmed that her life would be different. She wanted to see something other than the mountains and the low country of South Carolina. She was consumed with the curiosity that comes only from deprivation. She set her eye on her goal: Get the degree and get out.

By this time, Delaney's opinion of boys had mellowed. Mother Nature continued to prod, and now she responded to the eager young men who populated the campus. She lost her shyness and single-mindedness, buried her previous animosity, but managed to keep any serious suitors at arm's length. Being blessed with near-perfect features and form, she attracted more than her fair share. And because she knew no other way to handle men, she practiced her finely honed feminine wiles with consummate skill, finding herself in several sticky situations. But she had ample motivation for fending off groping hands in the back seat of a car. Not that she didn't enjoy the attention, the flattery, or the impact her physical presence had on the opposite sex, but it ended there. She watched her friends drop out of school to marry, drift away, and muttered to herself, "What a waste," as she submerged herself in her latest literature or philosophy course. There was the *real* challenge.

She wanted to write. But first, she had to have something to write about. With a youthful lack of wisdom, she dismissed her own experiences as unexciting and not worthy of closer examination. She concentrated on school, finishing in three years by taking advantage of summer sessions, and she racked up a grade-point average that was most impressive.

A short three days after graduation, at the tender age of nineteen, her suitcase packed loosely with her scanty wardrobe, she stood in the Port of Authority Bus Terminal in Manhattan.

"Delaney! Delaney Rollins!"

Delaney's head swiveled, her eyes searching through the crowd of people spilling everywhere. Finally, she saw a hand waving high above a mane of red hair bobbing through the sea of human bodies.

"Lord, I thought you'd never get here," Mary Sue Lipton gushed as she bussed Delaney's cheek. "Have you collected your suitcase?" Her eyes fell on Delaney's single bag, which answered her question. "I'm sorry I was late, but traffic was a nightmare, as usual. I hope you weren't nervous or anything."

Mary Sue was guiding Delaney through the endless terminal. Delaney's feet flew to keep up.

"I was afraid I'd get called on a flight. You know, I'm supposed to have three days off, but when crew scheduling runs short on stewardesses, sometimes they call you to come in. So I haven't been answering the telephone," she giggled. "And that has cut into my social life considerably." She laughed. "How was the bus ride?" she asked, then continued before Delaney could answer. Suddenly, they were through the doors, and Mary Sue was standing on the curb waving wildly for a taxi.

The noise was deafening. She listened to Mary Sue's chatter as the taxi hurtled through the streets of Manhattan. She felt nothing but euphoria. She was here! She was actually here!

"The apartment's really small, Delaney, but I can't afford it by myself. When Patty got fired and moved back to St. Louis, I didn't know what I was going to do."

"Why did she get fired?" Delaney asked absently, staring out the window. All of her senses felt bombarded at once. The noise, the traffic, the people.

"She couldn't wake up. Slept right through the alarm clocks, all three of them. And that's something United Airlines doesn't take kindly to—they expect you to be there when your flight takes off. Anyway, I was actually writing a notice for a roommate when I got your letter. Oh, Delaney, I'm so glad you came. You're gonna love it! Now, about the apartment, like I said, it's small—only one bedroom—but it has twin beds, and the sofa pulls out, too. Anyway, I'm so junior on the seniority list that I pull the worst schedules in the world, and I'm hardly ever there. And tomorrow's Sunday! We'll get up early and fetch a newspaper, and by the end of the week you'll have a job. Your being here makes it perfect. What if we hadn't met in college? What would we have done?"

Mary Sue was right about the apartment being small. It was minute, but Delaney loved it. But she was wrong about landing a job. That was a bit more difficult than Delaney had imagined.

She scoured the want ads, seeking a job in publishing. It was a month, a very lean month, before she landed a job with *McCall's* magazine in the typing pool. After weeks of tediously transcribing manuscripts, Delaney was promoted to a semisecretarial position in the food department—not exactly what she had in mind, but a step in the right direction. She was where she wanted to be and on her way.

She soaked up her experience in New York like a sponge, relishing the pulse of the city, the noise, the traffic, the pace. Everything was perfect, until she met Anthony. In one split second, the callow belief that she had control of her life trembled at its foundation.

Anthony was the most beautiful human being she'd ever seen. His blue eyes were fringed with jet-black lashes, sooty and thick, totally inappropriate for fair-haired people. His hair was both full and fine, and the texture was silken, like a child's. She was constantly running her fingers through it, never satisfying her need to touch, and never deciding on a word to describe its color. He was the right height—just under six feet—the right build—lean, yet strong—and his body exuded nuances of male scents, each one more fascinating and magnetic than the other. His long, artistic fingers were perfectly shaped, and she could have predicted that he would play the piano before she ever knew it. His legs were lanky and hard, and when she placed her hand on his knee, she immediately wanted to lean over and kiss it.

And that thought would bring her logically to his mouth . . . for which she simply had no words. When she tried to describe his mouth, her terms were all negatives: not too broad, not too full, not too soft.

"You're a mess of contradictions when it comes to men," Mary Sue said, after listening to Delaney extol Anthony's abundant charms. She opened the refrigerator door and screwed up her mouth. "Yogurt. That's all I ever find in this refrigerator. I think the stuff reproduces itself."

"What do you mean, contradictions?" Delaney asked, pulling the peanut butter from the cabinet and reaching for the bread.

"Yuk! Peanut butter again? Can't we order some deli sandwiches?"

"No. I'm broke till Friday. And you didn't answer my question."

"It's a cultural difference, Delaney. Coming from the south, we've been conditioned to act a certain way with men. You know, flirting and the whole routine that surrounds it. Men from the south don't take it seriously. In fact, most of them expect it. And it's a harmless pursuit. But"—and she hesitated, holding her peanut butter-laden knife in the air for emphasis—"here, you might be misunderstood."

"I still think being female is a blessing. And God's given

63

me all these wondrous assets." She crinkled up her nose and struck a pose, one hand on her hip. "I only wish he'd blessed me a little more in the chest department. Oh, well, what you see is what you get."

"Well, I don't think Anthony's gotten anything. Or have you relented and decided to bed the poor boy?" She picked up her sandwich and headed for the living room.

"No."

"Why not, Delaney? No wonder the man's half-crazed."

"I don't know, Mary Sue. It just doesn't feel right. It feels too"—she hesitated, searching for the right word—"too dangerous."

"Dangerous?"

"Dangerous. I think I'm in love with him, but I'm not sure who it is I'm in love with. He rarely talks of his family or his childhood. . . ."

"Well, do you?"

"Do I what?"

"Talk about Valhalla and your family?"

"No. Not much."

"Why not?"

"I don't really know. I guess because I'd just as soon forget most of it. Oh, I love my parents, but they're so"—she groped for the right word—"unexposed."

"Well, I don't think Anthony's parents are unexposed."

"Neither do I." Slowly she chewed on her sandwich. Anthony's parents were a total mystery. And that was an avenue she did not want to explore with Mary Sue, so she shifted the subject.

"Did you see the demonstrators in front of the army recruitment center?"

"Yeah. It's getting worse every day. That dirty little war is turning into a dirty big war." Suddenly, Mary Sue tossed the remnants of her sandwich onto the coffee table. "I'm going to the grocer's. I can't stand any more peanut butter, Delaney."

When she'd gone, Delaney deliberately put Mary Sue's comment about the war out of her mind. Just this once, she'd be like Scarlett. She'd think of the war and all its implications at another time. For Anthony and the war were so closely entwined that sometimes it was difficult to separate them.

But for right now, she would think only of Anthony, something she did on a regular and continuing basis. Why was she withholding? Everyone else seemed to be sleeping around.

She sat quietly on the sofa, rationalizing. She needed to be more objective about sex. She listened when her friends talked endlessly about the subject, and she got the impression that in spite of the fact that two people were involved, it was more of a solitary act, an accounting of who did what to whom. And she always heard a sadness, a loneliness in their voices. Intuitively, she knew that it would be more with Anthony. There was something about him that ripped straight to the core of her being.

She began to categorize what she did know about him. The first thing that popped in her mind was that he was her polar opposite. He was from the north, his family had money, he'd attended prep schools, and he was Irish. She'd never known anyone in Valhalla who was a full-blooded anything. Once, when someone asked her what nationality she was, she had replied "mongrel," for it seemed that every major nation in Europe had been a little responsible for her heritage. And Anthony was Catholic. She had known two Catholics before coming to New York, but they were nothing like the ones she now met. And he was conservative. Delaney, after mulling this over, decided that was because he'd simply never given it any thought. He was too spontaneous to be conservative.

But that was all superficial. She'd always said that she'd know a man, know everything about him, before giving up her body. The edges around Anthony were indistinct, like a fog. She might get lost in that fog and never find her way out.

And deep in Delaney's subconscious was a message she'd received in childhood, powerful and primal. She did not hear the words of that message. She only felt its impact. It came straight from her sister, Teresa. "Give in, and he'll abandon you."

All of this left her riddled with confusion. And it created fertile ground for misunderstandings. They fought. And she never saw it coming.

"You're just in a bad mood, Anthony," she'd accuse him, after he had fired off about one of her real or imagined defects.

He'd taken her to his favorite bar, where an impressive jazz pianist performed. She smiled warmly at the musicians, meaning to show her appreciation for their talent. That's all. Just a smile.

"The cello player is going to move on you the minute I'm out of here," Anthony muttered under his breath.

"What?" Delaney asked, unable to make out his words over the music.

"The cello player. He's after you."

"Don't be ridiculous," she replied, but the minute Anthony excused himself for the men's room, the cellist had been at her side. Anthony had caught him. Delaney braced herself for a confrontation, but Anthony had only laughed and said, "Your dress is too short." And then she'd been in a mood. Her dress wasn't any shorter than anyone else's. And the argument would start.

"I can't believe you're that naïve!" he'd shout on the way home. "Men take those little smiles as a come-on!"

"Well, that's too damn bad, 'cause where I come from, it's just being friendly!"

"Don't be friendly!" he bellowed.

"Don't tell me what to do!" she yelled back, and jumped from the taxi, racing for her apartment, leaving him growling and snarling. The week would pass. She was on pins and needles, wondering if he would come for the weekend, wondering if she should go to the base. But on Thursday, he'd call, act as if nothing had happened. The whole thing would repeat itself.

She knew women found him attractive. She could tell by the way they stared and went out of the way to touch him, always allowing their fingers to linger a bit too long. If she unconsciously exuded sensuality, he exuded sexuality—or was it unconscious? His body language issued invitations, and her intuition told her that those invitations had seldom been refused.

But the biggest stumbling block was that he overpowered her. His very presence made her feel inadequate. His voice scared her. His poise scared her. His religion scared her. Sometimes, it would take all of her energy to subdue the shaking and trembling inside her body when he appeared. As bright as Delaney was, she never properly defined those feelings. She was in love.

He didn't understand her refusal to go to bed with him. Manufacturing excuses as though she were in business, she hid her real reason. She wanted him more than she could put into words, but she didn't trust his opinion of women. His references to them, in general, were less than flattering. In fact, he openly admitted that he found most women manipulative—he would even accuse her of being so.

"If you don't want me, why do you wear that perfume?" he'd nuzzle in her ear. "Why do you wear those high heels and sexy little slips?" His hand was creeping up her skirt. "Delaney, I can *hear* your heart beating when I touch you. Why are you doing this to us?" His lips covered hers, his kisses tender, passionate, and then demanding as his hands slipped further up her legs. She relished the heat of his body, marveled at the miracle of how the curves and hardness fit together, ran her fingers over his skin in disbelief, and then pulled away.

He would be furious. He called her a tease. He called her a hypocrite. He called her impossible. Then he'd called her back the next week.

She was crazy with jealousy at his absence, wondering whose arms she'd pushed him into in Paris, Africa, or wherever the hell he was. The relationship was too intense, and yet too wonderful to let go. She was in serious trouble.

In spite of Anthony's valiant and fruitless effort to hide it, she knew his heart was full of vulnerable places. She sensed the tenderness lying just below the surface, if only she could touch it. Whenever he slipped, let it show for a moment, he'd crack a joke to divert her attention, or tease her unmercifully until she gave it up as a useless pursuit.

Sometimes, at night, she would lie in bed and try futilely to untangle her feelings. Maybe it was because Anthony wanted to compel life, swim frantically through it, ignoring its limits. Maybe it was because he seemed to thrash and circle, never seeing the horizon beyond him. Maybe it was because he didn't fully trust anyone, not even her.

Maybe it was because she sensed that underneath all that

carefully guarded discipline imposed upon him by the navy, a fire was raging, a fire that might consume her, too.

On rare occasions, when she allowed herself to face the bare truth, she realized that none of it mattered. She didn't care what he did, where he went, or what he said. She wanted him. She was playing for keeps. She was absolutely convinced that once she gave herself up to Anthony, there would never be another man who could replace him. She wanted to spend her life with this impossible, beautiful man who made her crazy. She wanted to get married. And Anthony never mentioned it. Never.

CHAPTER

❧ 5 ❧

Delaney studied Anthony's profile as the headlights of oncoming traffic pricked the early December nightfall. She was memorizing his features, storing images in her mind. Anthony laughing, Anthony stretching, Anthony watching her. In three days, she would be at the mercy of her memory, dependent on it for sustenance for her soul.

"Are you nervous?" The windshield wipers slapped against the driving winter rain as he skillfully wove the Corvette through the Friday-night traffic.

"Just don't tease me anymore. At this point, one wrong word and I bite."

The corner of his mouth curved upward as he pressed the accelerator, peering into the wet night.

"That bad, huh?"

"That bad," she confessed. "My whole body feels like it's made from spare parts, none of which fits."

"I like the way your body fits."

"Stop it, Anthony." She stared at the rain, and for the first time since arriving in New York, she longed for Valhalla. She missed those solid, familiar faces that had given her such a sense of belonging. There, few had ever judged her and found her wanting; no one ticked off her assets and liabilities; and never had anyone tallied up her social blunders. All of which she knew, with fanatic certainty, was about to happen. The edge of her discomfort sharpened.

"What if they don't like me?"

Anthony chuckled. A careless cynicism filled his eyes.

"So what? They don't like me either."

Delaney exhaled a sigh. "Anthony, that is so hard for me to accept." Maybe her family didn't have much, but it had always been shared equally—and that included love. Anthony's references to his family were always perplexing . . . even disturbing. He rarely spoke of them, and when he did, his voice bordered on contempt.

"The 'queen' will probably give you a hard time, but I think you're tough." He laughed again. "At least you are with me."

"That's different."

He flung her a look of skepticism. "Oh? That's different? And just how is that different, Delaney?" His voice was provocative as he made a flagrant attempt to change the focus of attention to himself.

"You know what I mean," she answered. "And anyway, you're fishing for compliments to feed your overinflated ego."

"Isn't that a woman's purpose in life? Her very reason for living? Because if it isn't, I can't seem to justify—"

"Stop it, Anthony! I know what you're doing, and nothing will work tonight. Not even that uninspired chauvinistic bait you're tossing at me."

"Okay." He dragged on the word, filling it with feined resignation.

"What have you told her about me?" Her hand was now fiddling with a strand of errant hair, twisting it around her finger.

"Nothing much . . . just that I picked up this hooker, and I really liked—"

"Anthony! You didn't!" Her eyes bored at him through the darkness.

"Of course I didn't." He laughed. "Lighten up, Delaney."

Lighten up? He would never know what an impossible task that would prove to be, for her nerves were racing through her body like an army in dubious battle.

He reached across the leather interior and grasped her hand. "Delaney, I hate to even admit this, and if you *ever* repeat it, I will, with both malice and forethought, break that pretty little neck of yours . . . but, if you can handle me—and you seem to be more than equipped for that job—you can handle the 'queen.'"

When she made no reply, he released her hand and renewed his grip on the steering wheel. "I haven't seen them in weeks. We wouldn't be doing this at all if I weren't shipping out Monday, and I really don't believe she would have asked if it weren't my birthday."

A leaden silence filled the car, and then he faced her again, winked, and added, "Happy Birthday to me."

Much too soon the large white house appeared in the beams of the headlights as they wound up the swerving arc of the driveway. Anthony killed the engine, leapt out, and was opening her door, a luxurious grin on his lips.

"Good-lookin' legs for a hooker," he whispered as she emerged from the low-slung depths of the car.

"Damn, Anthony. Don't you every quit?" she sputtered as she straightened herself, ritualistically touching her hair, her face, brushing an imaginary speck from her coat.

"Quit what?" He swung her into his arms, the slackened rain now misting his face as he lightly touched her lips. "Have I told what I *really* want for my birthday?" he crooned, his hand dropping to the curve of her hips.

"Only about a thousand times," she moaned in exasperation as she landed a playful slap on the top of his hands. "You are impossible."

"So I've been told." He smiled, steering her to the imposing entrance. He knocked lightly before pushing it open and then, his eyes dancing, hissed one last directive.

"Take no prisoners."

"Dad, this is Delaney Rollins."

Seamus Callahan was standing in the doorway to the study dressed in a dinner jacket. Delaney's first impression was of a stocky, solid man full of compressed energy. His still-full hair, only slightly gray at the temples, was neatly parted over a square, pleasant face, and his mouth was a carbon copy of Anthony's, the one and only resemblance she could find. An expression of surprise skimmed fleetingly through his brown eyes before it was replaced by a candid look of cordiality. He closed the distance between them, warmly shaking her outstretched hand.

"Well, well. What have we here, Anthony? Your mother didn't tell me you were bringing a guest. Miss Rollins, I am more than delighted." His eyebrows curved upward as his attention turned to Anthony. He placed a proprietary hand on his son's shoulder and continued. "This one"—his tongue clicked in mock disapproval—"seldom allows us the pleasure of his company. Leads me to wonder what goes on in his enigmatic world."

So Seamus was the source of Anthony's devastating charm, Delaney mused as Anthony's father ushered her into the drawing room. That was an intimidating experience unto itself. Her mind conjured up a picture of her own home in Valhalla for comparison. No perfectly appointed eighteenth-century English motif there. No original paintings adorned the walls, no antique porcelains, no sparkling silver. The contrast was stark and revealing.

"Tell me what he's been up to," Seamus continued as he took her coat. "Has he been behaving himself?"

Delaney's eyes were fixed on Anthony. His face was shrouded as though an impenetrable cloak had descended over him. A fresh whisper of unease consumed her as Margaret Callahan swooped into the room.

She was clad in a long green gown whose expensive lines flattered her slender figure. Her red hair was cut short and severe, exaggerating the high cheekbones of her face. Her nose was a trifle too narrow, her lips a shade too thin, but the total effect was one of aristocratic beauty, and about her was an air of superiority that telegraphed an immediate and unmistakable message: This was her home, and no one in it outranked her. Margaret aimed a darting but meaningful glance at Delaney. An acute sense of embarrassment flooded Delaney's mind as she deciphered the signal. Obviously, she was underdressed, her dark, tailored suit inappropriate for dining with the Callahans.

"Anthony, dear," she said as she gracefully planted herself in front of him, lifting her cheek to receive his awkward kiss. "But what is this?" She turned to Delaney.

"Anthony, shame on you! Why didn't you *tell* me you were bringing a guest?"

Anthony pulled a polite smile from midair as his face remained inexpressive.

"Oh, but Mother, I did tell you."

Margaret's eyebrows shot to sharp points as her mouth gaped ever so slightly. "You did? Well, I forgot, but that doesn't matter at all! Hello, my dear," she uttered, spinning back to Delaney. "I'm Anthony's mother, Mrs. Callahan, and you are . . ."

"Delaney Rollins, Mother."

Margaret's eyes, now the color of morning fog, were skillfully sliding down Delaney's body. "You'll both think I have a case of premature senility," she gushed as her vision flickered over Delaney's modest jewelry. Delaney felt like a reject in a bargain basement. "How could I have forgotten? But please, sit down. Talk to Seamus while I inform the cook there will be one more for dinner. Seamus *loves* to talk to pretty young things." She swept through the doorway, leaving in her wake an atmosphere of unwanted snowfall in April.

Delaney sat, her mind rapidly shifting gears. She had come with an open mind, in spite of Anthony's warnings. She wanted to love his family as she loved him, but in less than sixty seconds, she had reversed her position. Margaret Callahan was hateful. Furthermore, she was rude, dishonest, and a snob—everything Anthony said was true. Even the house itself, elegant as it was, seemed permeated by a sense of utter wrongness. She grappled with her disturbing assessment as Seamus spoke.

"We must have a drink." His voice was a little too loud. "Miss Rollins, what can I get you?"

A twenty-gauge shotgun would do quite nicely, she

thought as she answered his question. "Please, call me Delaney, and Scotch and water will be fine." Anthony tossed her a look of surprise. She rarely drank anything stronger than wine, and he knew it. Seamus excused himself, and Anthony, who had been leaning against the mantel, straightened his body as his face underwent a radical change. He now looked like an urban guerrilla.

"Delaney, forget it. I *told* her you were coming. It's her way of getting to me." His eyes dropped as his mouth set in two hard, parallel lines.

Delaney stared at him, and she felt the first wave of anger, deep-seated and beginning to grow. What kind of childhood had Anthony endured? Her anger was fueled as she considered the possibilities. She wanted to rush across the room, take him in her arms, and love him, an experience she now believed he'd never known.

Deliberately, she forced that thought to the back of her mind. How was she going to handle Margaret? If she didn't act, the evening was destined to be a disaster. She glanced at Anthony again. Clearly, he felt powerless in Margaret's presence, for she *was* his mother, but she was no relation to Delaney Rollins from Valhalla, South Carolina!

If Margaret intended to treat her like an intruder, Delaney would engage in sabotage. That thought, and that thought alone, propelled her through the evening.

"Whatever do you find to do in Valhalla? What a quaint name."

"But Mrs. Callahan," Delaney bubbled, "we stay so busy. You know how it is, shucking corn in the summer, tending the hogs in the winter. There's always something, but my favorite is animal husbandry."

"Animal husbandry?"

"Animal breeding," Delaney explained as she sipped her wine.

"You actually breed animals?" Margaret asked, the shock in her voice thinly disguised.

"Oh, yes. It's simply fascinating. I've been involved with cattle since I was just a scutter. It's a sight to behold, a bull and a cow. Why, when I was twelve, I raised a prize calf that I bred myself. Took the blue ribbon at the state fair."

Anthony was, for once, speechless. A hint of a smile appeared on Seamus's lips.

"So your family farmed?" Margaret coughed and wiped her mouth with her napkin.

"Among other things."

"What other things?" Seamus interjected, his eyes dancing with glee.

"Well, my daddy was a sort of distributor for a while."

"A distributor?" Margaret echoed, looking at Delaney from lowered eyelids. "What exactly did he distribute?"

Delaney rolled her eyes around the table. "Well, it's the tiniest bit illegal, but I guess I can tell you. After all, this is New York and not South Carolina, so I suppose it's safe. Uncle Henry makes the best corn liquor in the county, and Daddy sold it for him. You know. Distributor. But then Uncle Henry got caught. Those good-for-nothing hounds failed to sound the alarm soon enough. After Uncle Henry went to jail, Daddy quit the business."

There was a moment of unearthly quiet. Anthony

dropped his eyes to his plate, and Seamus chuckled into his wine glass.

"I'm sure that's all very interesting," Margaret managed, her eyes firing venom at Seamus.

"You were perfect!" Anthony whooped as the car sped back to the city. "I've never seen her so rattled."

Delaney's mind was wrestling with the image of Margaret as she walked them to the door. A strychnine smile was plastered on her mouth as her eyes flashed hatred, complete and unadulterated. Well, so be it, Delaney thought. The evening had been so wretched, it bordered on the absurd.

Delaney giggled. "I'm glad there was someone who enjoyed the evening. I've never been so uncomfortable in my whole life."

"Well, it didn't show," Anthony said, his face relaxing into another smile, savoring the moment. "That part about the calf? None of that was true, was it?"

"Every word of it was true, Anthony. As I recall, the cow's name was Cleopatra, and the bull was called—"

"Anthony," his voice exploded with disbelief.

Delaney burst into a new set of giggles as Anthony slowly nodded his head.

"I've got a long memory, Delaney. You'll pay for that one."

"How could you believe that? You know we don't farm. My family works in the mill." She paused, the thought of her family lingering in her mind. "Your mother's right about one thing, Anthony. It's probably the most lackluster existence known to mankind."

His hand reached across to caress t⟨...⟩
his body slouched in the driver's seat. ⟨...⟩

"Even Dad enjoyed it. But I bet he cat⟨...⟩

"Why? He was a perfect gentleman."

"Because he's *there*," Anthony answered f⟨...⟩

"That reference to the Civil War. I couldn't b⟨...⟩t!"

"She was desperate. That was her best shot. She sure clammed up in a hurry when you told her your grandmother belonged to the D.A.R."

"Why did that stop her?"

"She's sensitive about being third-generation Irish. The south hasn't had a monopoly on prejudice, Delaney."

"Thank God for Aunt Dicey," Delaney sighed. "Before she died, she bored us all to tears talking about who fought in which war. But if it helped tonight, I'm eternally in her debt."

Abruptly, she turned her head and kissed the inside of his wrist.

"That will get you in trouble, Miss Rollins."

"Maybe trouble would be nice," she murmured softly, surprising herself by her own admission. At that moment, she loved him beyond belief. Maybe she was ready. Maybe she could touch his heart, release him from the suffocating memories of childhood, teach him what love was. Her reasons for holding back no longer seemed valid. Time was short, and her heart was full of longing—longing to hold him, touch him, know him.

Anthony's mood changed. The air in the car thickened as silence hung like a trembling leaf in autumn.

"Why now, Delaney?" There was a reservation in his voice that somehow meant more to her than all the exuberance he had exhibited in the past.

...use maybe I'm a fool. Maybe you've been right all ...ng. Maybe . . ."

"I love you." His face was filled with something new, a staying power that she realized would be an everlasting reality in a world of uncertainty.

"I love you, too, Anthony. I don't know why I've put us through this. Maybe . . ."

"Why don't you quit saying maybe and engage that busy mind of yours in fantasy—which is, by the way, about to become a very real business."

He kissed her when he parked the car. He kissed her on the elevator. He kissed her as he struggled with the lock to the front door. His fingers trailed through her hair, touched her cheek, brushed across her shoulders. It was as though his hands were reaching for what his whole heart yearned for. He was undaunted by the sound of the telephone as the door swung open and he led her into the darkness of her room, slipping her coat from her shoulders, leaving it in a crumpled heap on the floor. He pulled her into the circle of his arms as if she were a promise that he never believed existed, somehow miraculously fulfilling itself before his astonished eyes.

As his hands floated lightly over her body, exploring, claiming, Delaney felt herself climbing, climbing to a new level of existence, aware that everything up to this point in time, even her most joyous moments, had been mediocre, if not less. She followed his lead on a very private tour to the center of her own being, and she gave herself up to the feast of hedonism he was offering while the phone continued ringing, the sound muffled and distant.

Reluctantly, Anthony pulled away from her mouth, an erotic sheen glowing under his skin.

"Answer the damn phone, tell whoever it is to go to hell, and leave it off the hook."

He followed her to the kitchen, as though unwilling to let her out of his sight.

"Hello," Delaney answered, her voice breathy and uneven as Anthony traced the neckline of her blouse, kissed her hair, nibbled on her fingertips. The pleasure of his touch was so intense that she hurt. A brand-new emotion surfaced in her body, a desire, violent in its vividness. She lifted her hand to touch his face when the voice on the other end spoke, and the desire keeled over, roared silently with disbelief, and exploded into agony.

CHAPTER

❧6❧

Margaret stood staring at her naked body. She hated what she saw. Her face had begun to sag as gravity pulled at her once-taut muscles. And now there was the sudden appearance of a sallow quality that seeped through her skin in spite of the host of cosmetic bottles lining her dressing table.

She was growing old. Sitting with that creature Anthony had brought to dinner the night before was more than she could stomach. The contrast was, to Margaret, devastating. A clutch of panic stole her breath, and then she blocked the image of the unflattering comparison. Delaney Rollins wasn't worthy of thought. But Anthony, even though he'd tried to hide it, seemed quite smitten. Well, with luck, a year's separation would take care of it. Granted, she was not considering Anthony's happiness; that would have been most unusual, even unique in Margaret's limited frame of reference, but she'd be damned if she'd let some little no-body marry into her family. What would people think? Never mind that she would only have to endure a daugh-ter-in-law's presence on special occasions such as holidays, but lack of breeding always surfaced. Trash. Well, what else could she expect from Anthony?

She peered into the mirror as she pulled the skin of her jawline upward. That was better. Much better. Maybe she should have a minilift. She skewed her mouth, thinking of recent compliments—how the meaning had changed. Granted, they were still doled out in generous portions, yet the words she heard seemed to imply that she looked good for her age—and, even more devastating, so did the ac-companying expression in the eyes of the bestower.

She turned sideways and patted her hips. The skin felt spongy. Five days a week, killing herself in that brutal aerobics class, and all she got for it was sponge. A very small smile stole across her mouth. For Simone had prom-ised that in three months that derriere would be as tight as a sixteen-year-old's.

Margaret felt her flesh tingle as she thought of Simone. Lovely, lovely Simone. Oh, to have such a body—firm, yet utterly feminine. A rush of heat consumed her as she reached for her dressing gown. Visions of Simone's silky blond hair spinning through the air fluttered in her mind. Strands of gold, resting on that graceful neck. Oh, what strength in that body, the perfection of the arms, the legs.

Margaret drifted back to the bathroom, powdered her body, and began to brush her hair. It was wrong. It was wicked. And it was *wonderful*.

Simone was so thoughtful, so interested in Margaret's progress. Sometimes, during class, she would single Mar-garet out, use her to demonstrate the proper positions, to point out which muscles were supposed to be working, and Margaret would feel positively weak from the touch of those long fingers. And Simone's eyes. Huge eyes under pale, arched brows. The purest green Margaret had ever seen.

"Oh, God," Margaret mumbled weakly, stumbling to the bedroom and collapsing on the chaise. "What am I going to do?"

Had she been intentionally loitering after class last Monday? Margaret wasn't sure now. Maybe she *had* dawdled unnecessarily, but then, she rationalized, she'd intended to go straight to her bridge club from exercise class. She'd actually had more than an hour to kill, a valid reason for taking her time. Margaret closed her eyes. A low moan escaped her lips. What did it matter? What had happened, happened, and nothing could alter it. Monday. Such a short while ago. And such Delphic meaning.

On that day, after class, Margaret found the dressing room deserted when she'd emerged from the shower. At that precise moment, Simone came gliding through the doorway, a lovely smile on her face.

"Well, Mrs. Callahan," Simone remarked pleasantly, "are we the only two left? What is the expression? 'Alone at last'?" She laughed, the tinkling sound falling on Margaret's ears like hand bells.

Margaret's eyes flickered nervously around the dressing room. "I think you're right, Simone." The air suddenly seemed charged with thousands of electrons. Sounds, including her own voice, amplified, then amplified again. Margaret snatched at words.

"I'm a little slow today, Simone." She forced a smile. It quivered on her mouth. "At my age it takes a little longer to get it all together," she added too quickly.

"Mrs. Callahan," Simone responded firmly, her voice lilted with the faint French accent that Margaret found irresistible, "I have no idea how old you are, but you look wonderful to me." Abruptly, she disappeared into the shower room. Margaret stood, hair dryer midair, virtually reeling. The phrase reverberated in her mind. *You look wonderful to me. You look wonderful to me.*

Margaret heard the shower running. The image of Simone's naked body flashed through her head. Funny, she'd never before thought of women's bodies. Other than her own, of course. Or had she? Frowning, she flicked the switch of the hair dryer. Her fingers flew through her damp hair as she shook away the unexpected thought. Leaning toward the mirror, she examined the roots of her hair. It was about time for more color. Maybe she'd try something a little more vivid—something with a touch of gold in it.

She dropped her head, blowing the hair up as Jason had instructed her to do.

"More body, Margaret," Jason had lisped, his weight on one foot, his hand propped delicately on his hip. "We all could use a little more body, couldn't we, Margaret?" He'd grinned lasciviously, even conspiratorially.

Margaret switched off the dryer and lifted her head. And there was Simone, standing behind her, watching her steadily in the mirror. Startled, Margaret wheeled to face her.

"I'm sorry, Mrs. Callahan," Simone began, "I didn't mean to give you a fright." The look in Simone's eyes was so intense that Margaret felt like one of the butterflies she used to have to pin to poster board for science class. Her heart thrummed loudly.

"I know it sounds silly, but I wondered if you would be so kind as to dry my back. I can never reach that little spot between my shoulder blades, and I hate dressing while I'm still damp."

Margaret's eyes floated over Simone's nakedness as she accepted the towel. Simone turned slowly, and cautiously Margaret dabbed at the satiny skin, so white, so smooth. Her eyes now fell to the gentle curve of Simone's waist, the firm buttocks, the long legs.

"Thank you," Simone murmured as she turned to face Margaret. The pupils of her eyes were huge, dark orbs as a tiny, satisfied smile curled the edges of her lips. The smile lingered as she watched Margaret's vision fall to her small, perfectly shaped breasts. For a split second, Simone hesitated. She could be wrong. But Margaret continued to stare at the pink nipples, standing at attention. She seemed mesmerized, and Simone's hesitation vanished completely.

"Let me show you," Simone intoned. She reached for Margaret's hand and cupped it under one breast. "Isn't that nice?" Simone was saying, her voice coming from a faraway place, a secret place, dark and full of pleasure.

With the other hand, Simone loosened the tie to Margaret's robe. A low whimper crept from Margaret's throat as the robe slid to the floor.

Anthony wakened and then wondered if he'd really been asleep. Sunlight filtered brightly through the window shades. It was still dark when he'd finally collapsed in bed, so yes, he must have slept. He rolled his head sideways and glanced at the digital clock. Ten fifteen. He closed his eyes again, computing the hours ahead. He'd planned on staying over another day before reporting to the *Chicamauga* in San Diego, but with Delaney gone, there was no reason to remain.

His lungs felt empty. He took a deep breath, and then

another. The empty place was still there. He lay perfectly still for a moment before the realization hit him. All the air he would breathe from now until he returned wouldn't make that emptiness vanish, for it wasn't his lungs, it was something much deeper, something that penetrated the very core of his being. It was the absence of Delaney.

He sat up and reached for the crumpled pack of Winstons on the bedside table. Lighting one, he inhaled nervously and stared straight ahead. Before last night, he'd thought he'd loved her. Now, there was no doubt. When that telephone call came, and she crumpled to the floor, he'd wanted to take on the world to protect her, and he'd been unable to do anything. Never before had he known such impotence. And never had he wanted so badly to fight something. He'd been filled with rage that he couldn't find an enemy, for the enemy was elusive, the enemy was life itself. He could not dissolve the pain. He could not change what had happened. And so he'd put her on that plane, knowing that something had shifted within himself, and that the shift was permanent. He was experiencing an almost forgotten emotion, familiar, yet distinctly foreign. For the first time since he'd been a child, he loved.

He glanced at the clock again, forcing his mind to shift back to the present. If he hurried, he could catch an afternoon hop from McGuire to San Diego. He'd called that morning when he'd returned from the airport, and yes, there was a plane heading west that afternoon. He stubbed his cigarette, threw back the covers, and headed for the shower. He had a great deal to do. Pack the rest of his gear, get to the cleaners, drop his car by the house, and return to the base in time for his flight. He'd think about Delaney later, when he had time. He hesitated, then laughed ironically. Resolving not to think about her was thinking about her.

He began to lather his face, wondering why he suddenly felt vulnerable, disturbingly vulnerable.

"Anthony," he addressed his mirror image, "you may be in a lot of trouble." The razor pulled at his beard, and he cut himself. "Oh, yes," he mumbled. "A whole lot of trouble."

The day promised to be beautiful and delivered its promise by way of a white, clear sun, all to Margaret's delight. The air, when she'd stepped outside to retrieve the mail, was crisp and scintillating, devoid of the usual winter chill.

She'd spent the morning snapping at the cook and rushing from room to room, fluffing a pillow here, flicking an imaginary speck of dust there, and once she'd even giggled when she heard herself fuming aloud at a flower that refused to fall at the proper angle. Simone was coming . . . she was actually coming, and everything must be flawless.

Margaret had spent hours prowling the health-food stores, buying just the right organic vegetables and fruits, for Simone was most particular about what she called "body fuel." A half-dozen new cookbooks were piled on the kitchen counter, and Margaret had pored over their contents, agonizing over which recipes to use, changing her mind again and again, sending the cook into more than the usual black funk.

But now, the salads were tucked into the refrigerator, the cheese casserole bubbled in the oven, and the silver tea service glittered, ready to receive any of the variety of herbal teas Margaret had meticulously selected. With a wave of her hand, she sent the cook out the door.

One last inspection of the table setting. Perfect. One last

glimpse in the mirror. The rust cashmere sweater she'd chosen highlighted her hair. One heavy gold chain around her neck. Perfect. The house was ready. The food was ready. And she was ready. Margaret felt like Cinderella waiting for the ball to begin.

She glanced at her wristwatch. A few more minutes. She wandered about the drawing room, glancing occasionally out the windows. Since that one occasion, Simone had virtually ignored her. Although Margaret had tried, she'd never succeeded again in being alone with Simone. And more than anything else in the world, Margaret craved Simone's exclusivity. Passionately, she yearned for Simone's undivided attention, Simone's emerald eyes trained only in her direction. All of Simone's spoken words must be uttered for Margaret's ears and Margaret's ears alone. Today, all of those yearnings would be realized. It was finally going to happen.

As she paced the length of the drawing room her mind stirred with thoughts of their one encounter. She could tangibly feel Simone's fingers tracing the tears as they slid down Margaret's face.

"Don't cry, sweet Margaret," Simone had soothed.

"But it's a terrible sin," Margaret sobbed, clinging to Simone's lean body as they lay on a mat in the deserted studio.

"No, no, my innocent," Simone had crooned, stroking her back with movements as sensuous as a cat's. "It's no sin to love! Isn't God the source of all love?"

Margaret had sniffled and nodded, blowing her nose on a tissue Simone fetched.

"Well," Simone continued, kneeling beside Margaret, her voice low and deliberate, "if that's true, then God is the source of our love, too. What difference does it make what form love takes, as long as it's love?"

Margaret pounced on the rationale. She needed it. She emblazoned the words in her mind. She carried it with her, nursed it, coddled it until it had grown into one of the commandments. Nothing that beautiful could be evil—so she conveniently decided to omit any reference to Simone from confession. For if there was no sin, what was there to confess?

The doorbell rang, and Margaret walked rapidly toward the front of the house, then forced herself to slow down. After all, she wanted to appear confident, not like some overanxious schoolgirl.

Simone stood in the doorway, smiling, a nosegay of pink sweetheart roses and baby's breath tucked in her hand. Margaret's world shrank. All it included was Simone's presence—no more.

"What a lovely sweater, Margaret," Simone said evenly as Margaret took her coat. "Earth tones are so good to you. They accentuate your lovely complexion."

Margaret blazed in the glory of such praise. She continued to blaze through lunch, although she was barely able to swallow. Simone kept up a patter of small talk, gossip about her students, remnants of her girlhood in Paris, vague references to education at some art academy Margaret did not know.

"Am I allowed to view the rest of this magnificent house?" Simone asked casually, dabbing at her lips with her napkin. Margaret's face had stained to crimson, but she willingly complied.

And now, with Simone's head nestled in Margaret's down pillow, Simone's glorious naked body lolling elegantly on the bed, blond hair fanning loosely in a parabola of wheat, Margaret experienced the first unselfish moment of her life. She would, if necessary, give this woman anything—even her soul.

Unwittingly, she expressed her thought, and it came out awkwardly and stupidly.

Simone laughed. "That's preposterous, Margaret. My needs are simple—and it is impossible for any one person to fulfill another person completely. I want you to understand, Margaret, that I am here and you are here temporarily. Nothing in this world is permanent, not even life."

But Margaret did not understand. And she did not want to understand. In her mind, she changed the subject, posing the next question carefully.

"How long have you known, Simone"—she hesitated—"well, that you were different?" she asked, her voice uncertain.

Simone's face clouded, then cleared. She watched Margaret closely for a moment before she replied.

"The word you are avoiding is lesbian, Margaret. You can say it. It is not a dirty word. And to answer your question, for as long as I can remember. Even when I was small, I was always attracted to women. I love the way they talk, smell, feel." She frowned as her mind surged forward. "I know I'm supposed to say I had this horrible father who beat me or raped me, but I didn't. He's a very nice man, so it must be genetic. When I began to mature, I thought for a while that I would change. But when my friends were in love with the latest male heartthrob, I was, very simply, in love with the starlet."

Simone rolled to her side and propped her head on one hand. Margaret's eyes grazed the small pink nipples. Simone smiled knowingly.

"We are not through, Margaret. We have all afternoon.

Love is better when it lingers." She peered at Margaret sideways. "My first lover looked very much like you. She was my teacher when I was fourteen, and she was lovely —red hair and gray eyes. Every day she would ask for someone to stay to help tidy the classroom, and every day I volunteered. I began to walk home with her, carry her papers and books. Then she invited me in for tea. From that point forward, I detested the touch of a man's hands on my body. I tried it—several times—but I found it similar to eating unripe fruit—not to my taste at all." She giggled at her double entendre and began to move toward Margaret.

"This," she whispered, one hand lighting on Margaret's midriff, "is much nicer."

Later, when Margaret would try to recreate the sequence of events, it would be a jumble, a series of disconnected images. Anthony, a look of unutterable hatred on his face, his words vile. Simone trying to dress as Margaret hugged the sheet to her neck, whimpering all the time. Simone's contemptuous replies to Anthony's insults, his delivered in shouts and hers in half shouts. Simone leaving. Her own voice pleading, pleading with Anthony not to tell Seamus, not to tell anyone. The names Anthony called her, his face distorted, the tendons in his neck corded tightly. And then the quiet, the terrible quiet when he'd gone.

An awesome fear filled her very soul. What if Anthony did tell? Would Seamus believe him? She thought of their disastrous sexual interludes. Yes, came the answer. Seamus would believe him. What could she do?

She stood by the window, shifting from one foot to the other. Thank God Anthony was leaving today. There would hardly be time to talk with Seamus. She tried to pray. The prayer went no higher than her ceiling. And why should

God listen to her? She tried again, her lips mouthing the unspoken words. The prayer lengthened and then took a violent turn.

"Let him die. Let him be killed. Let him explode until there's nothing left of him. Nothing, nothing, nothing!" She lifted her head, trying to force the words through the roof, through the sky. Somehow, she would get God's attention. She mumbled, over and over, "Please, let him die!"

CHAPTER

❧ 7 ❧

M ama, we need to talk," Teresa whined. Her eyes darted nervously around the room.

Delaney flinched at the sound of Teresa's voice. It was strung high, too loud. She sat on the edge of the bed, staring through a set of sliding glass doors, wondering if such doors were mandatory. With each new Holiday Inn constructed, was there a written rule requiring sliding glass doors? Her shoulders tightened. Why was she thinking about that? Who cared?

"Mama?" Teresa spoke again. The pitch of her voice climbed insistently.

"I know, I know, Teresa," Carrie Rollins answered. Weariness threaded through her words. "We can't live in a motel forever. Don't even want to." Her eyes roamed over the predictable furnishings. "I hate how they do these motel rooms. So cold and disposable."

"You can come to Charlotte, Mama. Live with us," Diane said cautiously.

"And where the hell is she going to sleep, Diane? Use your head. From what you've said, there's hardly room for you and little Carrie, let alone Mother!"

"You have no right to talk, Delaney. I haven't heard you invite her to New York City yet," Diane flared back.

"Hush!" Carrie broke in. "Settle down. Both of you! The last thing I need is the two of you bickering. And we all know I'd be miserable in New York."

Diane's mouth clamped in two thin lines. She doused Delaney with angry, dark eyes, then rose from her chair. "Things don't come so easy for some of us," she muttered. Immediately she sat down again, her back rigid.

Carrie closed her eyes, momentarily blotting out her three daughters. She was glad Ellen had already gone. Four of them would have been too much. She was tired, bone-sore tired. And there was more to come. She grappled for something to say, something that would shed some light, diffuse the anger.

"We don't come into this life with guarantees. I think there's some mention of a vale of tears." She opened her eyes and confronted all three of them. "I want you to remember something your pa used to say. It's been playin' around in my head all day, so it must need to come out. He always said life was like a circle. How birth and death are part of that circle. He talked about the seasons, and how nothing really died, and he thought about death that way, too. As long as you carry the memory of him, then he's part of you. And then you pass yourselves on to your children, and the memory of him goes with it." She paused, gazing at a spot on the carpet, and then went on, her voice soft and low. "Like the trees in winter. Just sleeping. But we can all remember what they looked like, full-leafed and green. And that gets us through the winter."

She stopped talking, letting her words sink in. She lifted her head and stared at each of her children for a brief moment.

"You don't have to take care of me. I'm not an invalid, and I'm not senile. I can take care of myself." She caught the doubt in Delaney's eyes. "I know it didn't seem like it when your daddy was alive, but believe me, I'm not helpless. I'm stronger than any of you know." She stood, crossed to the glass doors, and gazed at the brown, grizzled grass. Then she turned and pinned each of them with her clear blue eyes.

"But it ain't gonna be in a mill. Not this mill or any other mill. I'm almost fifty. I don't know how to do much other than cook and clean. Lord knows, I've put in my years doin' that."

"Well, you don't have to no more, Mama," Teresa shrilled. "I'll do it for you. I'll do it all!"

Carrie sighed. She folded her arms across her chest, the white bandages on her hands protruding like flags.

"I'm not talkin' about that, Teresa. Women cook and clean till the day they die. Fight dirt all their lives and then get buried in it. But"—she hesitated—"it's what keeps us alive, keeps us strong. We always got somethin' to do. I ain't ever seen a woman retire. No such thing." She faced the glass again, staring at the weak winter soil. "Still, I like the earth. Always have. I never wanted to leave the farm. It was your daddy's doin's to live in Valhalla. He never could stand farmin'. Now, things are different. I'm goin' back to Aunt Dicey's place. It's been sittin' fallow since she died. A farm needs to be worked and worked right."

"Aunt Dicey's?" Teresa echoed with disbelief.

"That's right, honey. Lord, Lord, we used to hope that farm would sell. I prayed for a buyer, we needed the money so bad. But it didn't, and I guess the Lord always knows best."

Delaney's eyes surveyed the bandages on her mother's hands. If this was God's best . . .

"I'm not sayin' what you can and can't do, Mama, but what you gonna live on?" Diane asked stiffly. "Workin' a farm is tough, and it takes money to get started. Most of that equipment is rusted and no good."

"There's a little insurance money, Diane. I'll make it. If anyone knows how to stretch a dollar, I do. I can make most anything grow. Your daddy knew that, too. Used to remark on how God had blessed me with the green thumb. Used to say it all the time."

Delaney suppressed the scream forming in her throat. How could her mother still talk of God's blessings?

"So I'm movin' to Cushing. I'm gonna do what I do best. Grow things." She stopped talking again. Fatigue etched lines around her eyes. "The Lord works in mysterious ways," she said abruptly. "It ain't up to us to question His will."

Delaney bit down on her tongue. She bit down hard. Mystery? What was the mystery? You were alive one minute and dead the next. It seemed to her that God was spinning a wheel or pointing a finger, deciding who would die and how they'd die. That wasn't mystery. That was cruelty.

Her hands clenched into fists as she called forth the look on her mother's face when the casket was lowered into the ground. She knew what was in that casket. That was no mystery. It contained a charred, blackened log, barely recognizable as human—that was God's work.

She dropped her head and caught a glimpse of the photograph sitting on the bedside table. She stared. It was a picture of Carrie and John Rollins on their wedding day. Young and full of hope, they leaned against the hood of an ancient Studebaker, laughing at the camera, laughing at life. Teresa didn't remember grabbing it as she'd raced through the house, shoving Carrie through the thick, black smoke. The photograph remained in her clenched fingers for eight hours before anyone could pry it loose. She felt a wave of sickness. What kind of life had God given them? Scrimping, working, year after year, with nothing to show for it.

"You moving to Cushing with Mama?" Diane asked curtly.

Teresa's face splotched. She looked like a rabbit caught in the headlights of a car.

"I hadn't planned on moving to Charlotte with you," she retorted, knowing full well that Diane was about to unload on her.

"You could try going to work. You might even like it." The words crackled with anger. Each one like the lash of a whip.

Teresa's head lifted. Her chin jutted stubbornly into the air.

"Jesus will take care of me. And He'll take care of you, too, Diane, if you'll let Him."

Diane snorted.

Carrie glanced at Delaney. Her eyes said: See? That's what I meant. Delaney knew that Carrie was worried about Teresa. She'd voiced that concern the night before as they were leaving the funeral home.

"She's always scrubbin' that face," Carrie had whispered. "She's got it plumb raw, and she won't let me put no cream on it. Says it's a sin to perfume your body. It's not

98

that I mind her religion, Delaney. It's her choice. Now, it bothered your daddy a heap—her leavin' the Baptist church when she'd been raised there and all. But now she won't let me as much as trim that hair—says cuttin' your hair's a sin, too." Carrie's face, illuminated by the pale December moon, was drawn and tense. "I heard they'd been handlin' some snakes in that church, too. I'm scared for her, Delaney. I'm afraid there's something more workin' here than religion. She can't get over givin' up that baby. Thinks God's punishin' her. And she's tryin' to atone for the sin she done."

Delaney had listened, smothering the reply that jumped into her mouth. The truth was, Teresa looked terrible. Snake-handling? Next she'd be drinking strychnine.

"Listen, Teresa," she began. "I don't have any problem with your living with Mama. But I don't want her waiting on you, taking care of you. You have to help. Remember what Daddy always told us. You can pray like it's all up to God, but you better work like it's all up to you. You have to face reality. You're too old to be leaning on Mama."

Teresa smiled vaguely. She rocked back and forth in her chair. Diane breathed a sigh of disgust, and Carrie shook her head.

"We've got to settle this," Diane interjected impatiently. "Delaney and I are leavin' tomorrow. Neither of us want everything hangin' in the air."

"Diane's right," Delaney agreed. "I think moving to Cushing is a good idea, Mama. It's a good farm. You've got Daddy's truck, and it's paid for. . . . " Her voice faded as she paused. "That means," she finished slowly, "there'll be no more Rollins family in Valhalla."

Fresh pain rolled across Carrie's face, then subsided. "I

don't care," she said with resignation. "Maybe we should never have been here in the first place."

"Mama!" It was Diane this time who was shocked.

"Well, it's the truth, Diane. We had some good times here, and I don't want to forget that, but now we've got a real bad time." She smoothed her skirt with her bandaged hands. "Grief is a place where nothing grows. Sometimes it's best to leave. Sometimes it's the only thing to do. It ain't runnin' away. It's just startin' fresh. This town speaks of heartache."

Delaney lunged for her coat. "Then it's decided," she said as she crossed the room. The door closed behind her with a muffled thud.

The December air hit her face as the white sun glared overhead. She walked. She had to see it, make the unreal real. Her mind swirled. Anthony on a carrier this very day, going somewhere she could never go, somewhere dangerous. Her father dead, dead, dead. Her mother moving. Her eyes burned with unshed tears.

When she'd received Diane's call, Anthony had taken the blows she'd landed on his chest, his face stiff with helplessness. He'd caught her as she'd crumpled in his arms, cradling her like a baby, listening to the moans until they'd stopped. It was he who had packed her suitcase. He made the reservations, paid for the ticket, watched as she boarded. She had not turned to face him as she passed through the doors of the plane. For none of it was real. None of it, until now.

Her footsteps slowed as she approached where the house once stood. She stopped. The chimney, scorched and scarred, reached toward the sky, an ugly monolith. Belief began to fill her mind. She surveyed the ashes, the blackened brick of the foundation. Why? The word reverberated in her head, violating the leaden stillness of the afternoon.

A faulty furnace. No money to repair it. Her parents pushed it, hoping it would hold up one more winter.

That night, Teresa had gone to bed. Carrie and John were watching television. Carrie had fallen asleep on the sofa, and John had left her there when he went to bed. Johnny Carson had just begun his monologue when Teresa screamed. The house was full of dense smoke. Flames licked at the back bedroom door, the door that locked John Rollins in a tomb of fire. Carrie had burned her hands, trying to force it open. Teresa had dragged her mother from the house and rounded the corner to the bedroom window, but it was too late. When the fire department arrived, the roof had caved in. There was nothing left.

Delaney stood motionless. Her throat scalded as she swallowed. She felt responsible. If she'd stayed in Valhalla, worked at the mill, she could have helped. But she hadn't. She'd walked out, turned her back, given her family little thought. And this was the price.

Roughly, she wiped at her face with the back of her sleeve. Well, it wouldn't happen again. Her eyes, bright with unshed tears, hardened. She spun, turning her back on the ashes. She knew what she was going to do.

CHAPTER

❧ 8 ❧

S AM! SAM! SAM!"

"Where? Where is it?" Anthony shouted.

Terry's head swiveled.

"I'm lookin'! I'm lookin'!"

The missile warning tone was constant, screaming in Anthony's ears. The lead plane broke high and right. Anthony followed.

"Shit, I can't see it!" Terry's voice was frantic.

"Must be in the sun!"

"Got it, Freeze! Four o'clock! Four o'clock! Dive! Dive!"

The plane ripped through clouds. The green earth loomed ahead.

"Shit, I lost it again! No, there it is! Right on our tail, Freeze!"

Anthony's body fought gravity and the plane's steep

angle of descent. He shot a glance at the altimeter needle. Dropping, dropping. His skin iced with sweat.

"Is it still there?"

"You bet your ass! Do something!"

Anthony hit the brakes. The heavy plane hung suspended for a split second. From the corner of his eye, he saw the missile, trailing fire the length of a telephone pole, glide over them. He tipped the nose and began to climb just as an F-8 sliced under him.

The whole formation had fallen apart. He'd lost Jeremy Blalock, his leader, and the last thing Jeremy had told him was to stick like glue.

Planes and flak choked the sky. The possibility of midair collision suddenly seemed a probability.

"Let's drop this load and get the hell out of here!"

"I'm tryin' to get a lock on the target!"

Higher, higher, the plane tore through the air.

"Almost, almost," Terry murmured, his eyes fixed on the computer controls.

"I've got it, Freeze! Two degrees left! Hold it!"

The plane strained as it seemed to hover. He scanned the earth below him, then plunged down. Gravity sucked at his body. The earth, sky, smoke, and planes merged into one insane kaleidoscope.

"Now!"

Anthony pressed the pickle and felt the bombs kick loose. The plane jolted forward.

"Jesus, Freeze, get us outta here!"

Flak exploded in puffs of smoke outside the windows. The radio crackled with the tense words of thirty pilots, dodging missiles, flak, and one another.

"Jesus, Jesus," Terry kept muttering, his eyes glued to the radar.

"When did you get religious, Fireball?" Anthony shouted as he pointed the nose up again.

"Just now, Freeze! Just now! I've had a complete religious experience!" Terry touched his body, as though reassuring himself he was alive. "Shit, Freeze, do we have to do this again?"

"Come on, Fireball. It was a piece of cake. Nothing but a walk in the park." He winked broadly as a grin flared across his mouth.

"'Walk in the park'? 'Piece of cake'? Man, you're full of clichés today." Terry's voice was loud and shaky. "Just get us back over the water! I'm feelin' real fetal!"

"Talk to me, Fireball," Anthony urged as he brought the plane back hard right. "Tell me about your first car. Tell me about the first time you got laid."

"Shut up, you asshole," Terry snapped, but his mouth formed a nervous grin. It was routine. After any close call, Anthony made him talk. Somehow, it worked as a tranquilizer, the sound of his own voice droning on and on about something familiar.

"How or when I first got laid is none of your business. You wanna talk cars? Let's talk Mustangs. Now there's a piece of work," Terry began.

The monologue continued, broken only by instructions as they landed on the carrier's deck. Terry was still talking when the canopy opened, still talking on the escalator, still talking when Anthony finally left him in the head—knowing that Terry would throw up. He would heave until his body was shaking and weak. Anthony had seen him do it once. Now he made sure he was nowhere around when it happened.

* * *

Anthony entered his stateroom. It was empty. Good. He needed time alone. He dropped to his bunk and then shot back to a sitting position. His breath was ragged. He fought to regulate it, sucking in air, holding it, then letting it out slowly. After several minutes, the hyperventilation stopped.

He stared at the bulkhead. No wonder nobody talked much about Alpha Strikes. Who could understand unless they'd been there? He'd tried to question Jeremy about it. Jeremy had mostly grinned and shook his head.

"It's kinda like sex, Freeze. You gotta be there." Anthony sensed there was more to what Jeremy didn't say than what he said. Now, he knew why.

Adrenaline still poured through his veins. He forced his mind to focus on something. February. It was February. Valentine's Day. George Washington's birthday. He groaned. That was at home.

Here, it meant the winter monsoon. He felt the *Chicamauga* roll into the wind, and he knew that above, rain would be pummeling the South China Sea.

He'd been flying combat missions for two months. Two months of being shot at. Each time he and Terry were launched from the flight deck, he knew what was coming. There was no safe space. If he took the A-6 high, the SAMs came in, tracking, always tracking, locking in, forcing Anthony to dive, flying at altitudes so low a farmer in a field could have taken him out—that is, if the flak didn't get him first. It was open season all the time.

"The enemy has the most sophisticated antiaircraft weaponry available," he'd been briefed, and it was true. And every time he went up, all hell broke loose both above and below him.

But today had been even worse. Up until now, he'd been

laying air-dropped mines into the Ca and Giang rivers. Today had been his first Alpha Strike. Thirty-five planes, each trying to do a specific job with the assumption that everything would go according to schedule. As far as Anthony could tell, nothing had gone right. Nobody knocked out the antiaircraft. SAMs were all over. Who in their right mind thought thirty-five planes could maneuver in a five-mile area of sky?

He was lucky to get in, drop his load, and get out. He thought that he'd hit his target, but he wasn't sure. He hadn't taken a second run. Not in that pandemonium. At least today's target made sense. A power plant near Haiphong was better than a truck. Sometimes he thought there were more trucks in the hands of the enemy than in the combined states of Alabama, Mississippi and Texas.

Terry stuck his head in the door. His face was the color of chalk, but his grin was back in place.

"See you at the movies?" he asked. "I hear it's *Who's Afraid of Virginia Woolf*. Burton and Taylor tearing each other apart in a whimsical tale of marital bliss." Terry widened his grin and his chipped front tooth flickered.

Anthony cleared his throat. "I wouldn't miss it," he replied in a voice that uncannily resembled Richard Burton's.

"How do you do that?" Terry asked incredulously. "One day you sound like Burton and the next day McQueen. Will the real Anthony Callahan please stand up?" He paused, waiting. "Jesus, who the hell are you, anyway?" He shot Anthony a puzzled look and closed the door.

Anthony felt his muscles begin to relax as he smiled to himself. The truth was, he didn't know how he did it. He just opened his mouth, mugged a little, and there was the voice of a stranger coming from his own lips.

Maybe tonight at dinner he'd do Terry. He knew he

could capture that antsy, hyperkinetic energy Terry generated, and there was that little tic in his right eye when Terry was nervous. He thought about Terry's rapid speech patterns, the excitability that accompanied his words. He and his navigator were so different. Contrasting bookends. Anthony showing no nerves and Terry all nerves. *But not in the air.* Terry knew his job and did it better than anyone else—at least in Anthony's opinion.

A deep and sudden loneliness gripped him. He wanted to talk to Delaney. Tell her what it was like—what he was thinking. He could never get that down on paper. No matter how he tried, nothing would come out except garbage. Garbage like how everything in his world was fine. And lately, in the hours of flying and the hours of waiting to fly, the world in which he'd known her seemed to be slipping away. And when that world was gone, all that remained was the death that was hiding in the lush greenery of Vietnam. How could he tell Delaney about that? She'd tell him to turn in his wings and come home to her. And as much as he wanted to have her say it, he'd never do that. Never. Best not to think of her.

He stood and headed for the doorway. How long were his insides going to shake this time?

January lingered too long. The news was not good. Two records were set in South Vietnam and duly reported by the press. The casualty toll for American servicemen was the highest to date—144 killed and 1,044 wounded—and the second record was rife with gnawing alarm for Delaney as American pilots flew 549 missions in one week.

Three astronauts were killed in a fire that engulfed an Apollo 1 spacecraft. And the draft board turned down Cassius Clay's request for exemption from military service because of religious convictions. Changing his name to Muhammad Ali had made no difference.

Delaney watched events unfold on her television with growing apprehension. Each night, consumed by a feeling of helplessness, she would resolve that she must do something, something to make sense of the insanity that seemed to feed upon itself. And then guilt would filter through her conscience. Guilt that she completely loved a man who willingly participated in the madness growing like a virus in Southeast Asia.

January stayed much too long. Snow stained the streets of New York. Sooty snow that blanketed the city in a film of grime. The lights that glittered at night no longer spun their magic. She was caught in the throes of a grief where time had little meaning, and yet its passage meant everything.

On Sundays, she combed the classifieds, determined to find another job, one that paid well. She interviewed on her lunch hour and after work. She lost the chance at several because of lack of experience. Disappointed, disillusioned, and depressed, she watched as January slipped into February. She wondered where the days had gone while at the same time wondering why they seemed so endless.

Letters from Anthony came occasionally, and from these she drew life. The job search continued to be fruitless. And the long dark nights seemed even longer.

But in February, her diligence paid off. Answering an ad for a marketing services trainee, she found herself on Park Avenue at the corporate headquarters of Universal Business Equipment. Résumé in hand, she was led into a posh office and came face to face with Leo Edelstein. Tall, polished, articulate, he conducted a perfect interview, and Delaney knew, even as he told her he'd let her know something in a week, that she had the job. The chemistry was good. The job description was diversified enough to whet her interest, and the salary was irresistible.

"Your position will be unique in the company," Leo began. "Introducing new products to a sales force requires not only knowledge, but an ability to sell that product better than our top salesmen. In fact, you will ultimately be training our sales force on new products. If you can sell it to them, then they can sell it to the customers. In other words, you have to be better than the best—and don't think they won't challenge you every step of the way."

Leo watched Delaney appraisingly as she soaked up his words. He knew she had the right look—appealing, yet demure. There was a confidence in her demeanor, softened by a sense of ultrafemininity, qualities she would need upon occasion. Leo prided himself on his ability to judge character, and he knew instinctively this girl had it. Even the accent would be an asset, just as his New York accent was sometimes a liability.

"This position is multifaceted. Because you will be our expert, you'll be required to work the convention circuit. And I'll be honest with you—this is no easy task. You'll be responsible for every detail, and when working conventions, the details can be innumerable. You'll ship equipment, work with electricians, carpenters, and telephone installers. You'll hire temporary help, train them, even dress them on occasion. You'll stay when the convention is over to pack equipment and ship it back to storage or to the next city. Not to mention the long hours and aching feet."

He gazed searchingly into the brown eyes for reaction. He'd been interviewing for two weeks, and his monologue either sent candidates scurrying for cover or appealed to their sense of glamour, neither of which he wanted. It was a difficult job. And it was his idea to hire a woman. He was convinced that, in this case, a woman would command attention better than a man. When you needed an electrician in a hurry, he was betting that a pretty face concealing an excellent mind was the answer.

"I'm interested, Mr. Edelstein. It sounds challenging and eclectic. I'd certainly like to try."

It was no surprise when Leo called in person.

"Miss Rollins, I'm offering you the position. I know you're currently employed and need to give notice, but we'd like you to be in Hartford at our training facility no later than February twentieth. That is, if you're interested."

She was. So was Leo.

Not familiar with the intricacies of corporate politics or corporate intrigue, she was unaware that Leo's frequent appearances at the training center were unusual. She only knew that when he arrived unexpectedly, every three-piece suit seemed to come to attention. And being naïve, she did not find it unusual that Leo would take her to dinner, ostensibly to discuss her progress.

It became known, at least among the sales training staff, that Delaney "belonged" to Leo. She was his special project. No stone was to be left unturned in her education. She was on the grill.

Most trainees stayed in sales school for three weeks, but Delaney stayed for three months. On Sunday nights she'd take the train to Hartford, returning to New York on Friday. She learned each piece of equipment Universal made from the inside out, and from each instructor she gleaned some subtlety of sales technique until eventually she was running circles around them when they role-played difficult customers.

110

Leo received a call from the manager of sales training in May.

"There's nothing left to teach her, Mr. Edelstein. I'm sending her back to New York. She's on her own."

Not quite. Leo went with her to her first three conventions, heady business for Delaney: Chicago, where he watched her with customers; then San Francisco, a breeze for her, with the exception of her aching feet; Leo had been right. After fourteen hours on a concrete floor, they complained relentlessly.

Leo kept his distance, until Las Vegas. But the more time he spent with her, the greater the temptation. He'd taken her to a show at the Dunes and wound up watching Delaney more than the voluptuous assembly of bare-breasted showgirls parading on stage. That's when he realized he was in a dilemma. His policy of "hands off" when it came to female personnel was proving a Herculean task. And in Las Vegas, he finally failed.

"Leo, don't." The voice was velvet, but the underlying tone was steel.

"Sorry, sorry. I shouldn't have done that, Delaney. I vowed I wouldn't, but you've been on my mind so much lately, you're damned near an obsession." His arms still encircled her as his eyes grazed her mouth. He almost kissed her again, but she pulled away, and his arms dropped to his sides.

"You know that I'm involved with someone else. In fact, I'm totally committed to Anthony. And this is not only bad for you and me, but it's also bad for business."

"Right. So now who's the teacher and who's the pupil?" he asked pensively. "I want you to know that this is a first for me. It's a breach of business ethics, as far as I'm concerned, and I recognize the potential danger, Delaney. I'll make you a promise. And I'll try my best to keep it. As long as you're involved with what's-his-name, I won't try anything again." He gave her a small grin as she rolled her eyes at his refusal to say Anthony's name. "But if it ever falls apart, you promise that I'll be the first in line. Deal?"

"Deal," Delaney agreed, then she added, "but don't count on it, Leo."

As Delaney disappeared into her hotel room Leo sagged against the wall and stared at the carpet on the floor. "Oh, but I am, Delaney," he said. "I'm counting on it a lot."

CHAPTER

❧ 9 ❧

The air intelligence officer's eyes sent a direct message.

"How many did you get?"

"I don't know," Anthony replied. His head pounded and his eyes burned. Sweat trickled down his underarms as exhaustion hit him in the pit of his gut.

"How many did you see?" There was a stronger signal in Hal Sweeney's voice.

Anthony met his stare in silence.

"Come on, Callahan," Hal said uneasily. "You know and I know we've got to do this. Give me a number."

"Ten."

"You saw ten initially?"

"Ten seems like a nice round number."

"Okay. Ten. How many did you take out?"

"I don't know. I can't see through smoke."

"Look," Hal said wearily, "I'm just trying to do my job.

Just like you do yours. The admiral won't stand for anything as vague as what you've given me. Shit, man, he knows nobody can see through smoke. What do you think this is all about?"

"Numbers," Anthony replied curtly. "It's about numbers."

"Right, Callahan, it's about numbers. Now give me some."

What the hell, Anthony thought. Give the admiral what he wants. "I got seven."

"Seven. Now we're getting somewhere." Hal's eyes dropped to the paper in front of him and he began to write.

Anthony slumped in his chair. He knew the debriefing was necessary, knew that what he said would eventually work its way up the chain of command, but he hated it. Keeping score, he thought. He then reminded himself not to think.

The interrogation droned on as Anthony mumbled replies. On some level he had a feeling that Hal probably felt no better about it than he did. Who really gives a damn about a suspected truck park?

Finally, it was over. Anthony strode toward his stateroom, caught between exhaustion and anger. Precision bombing. That term might apply if conditions were perfect, a situation he had yet to confront. Sometimes, moving at five hundred knots with flak exploding all over the sky and SAMs on his tail, who the hell could know what he'd hit?

He needed a shower. Outside, the heat and humidity combined to drench his body with sweat. Then the air conditioning would cause the sweat to evaporate, making his skin itch. Sometimes, the heat made him nauseous, and that's how he'd begin his flight, nauseous.

Mechanically, he stripped and headed for the shower stall. The water streaming over his body helped, but as he dried he began to itch again. He wondered if he had caught some fungus—some jungle rot. He snorted at himself. He hadn't been near the jungle.

He stumbled back to his stateroom, scratching. He couldn't remember being relaxed, comfortable. In fact, he couldn't—wouldn't—remember much of anything except the last sortie or the next sortie. Remembering was dangerous.

He threw himself on his bunk and closed his eyes. He'd now been on the *Chicamauga* for five months. Five endless months of pretending there were no nerves in his body. He rubbed his forehead and thought of winter, of snow, of sleet, of icy winds blowing through the streets of New York. An image of Delaney materialized. She stood on a corner, stamping her feet to warm them, laughing, dark hair tumbling around her head.

He sat up. Rarely did he allow her in his thoughts, for it was an intrusion. Any thoughts other than flying were expendable.

He collapsed again, closed his eyes, and there she was. Tonight he gave in to it. He saw her with unbearable clarity.

"Oh, God," he murmured. He braced for the loneliness, for the emptiness that always followed when he thought of her. He'd never been good at expressing his feelings, particularly not in writing. Besides, even trying to write had caused his loneliness to grow to gigantic proportions. So he'd stopped.

But she had not. Her letters to him appeared with regularity. At first, he'd devoured them, savored them, worn the paper thin unfolding and refolding them. Gradually, he'd realized they were distracting him, making him think. And they gave him something that was better ignored. They gave him a future. A future beyond the South China Sea, the Intruder, and the *Chicamauga*. Thoughts of a future might cause him to make a mistake, lose his edge. He'd seen it happen. Seen guys turn in their wings.

He was convinced that most of the pilots assigned to the *Chicamauga* were the very best. And lately, some of the best were gone.

Two days before, Jeremy had bought it while Anthony was his wingman. The target had been the Ham Rung Bridge, which spanned the Song Ma River. The bridge had been hit time and time again, and the gomers rebuilt it time and time again.

"You're with me, aren't you?" Jeremy had grinned in the ready room.

"Try to lose me," Anthony had replied, but once they'd reached the target, the missiles had come in. He and Jeremy had split, proceeding to evasive tactics. He'd almost blacked out from diving and climbing, dodging the metal in the fiery sky. He'd forgotten everything except staying alive. Then he'd heard it, one voice over the radio.

"Hey, Jeremy! You got flames all over you! Eject! Eject!"

"Negative," Jeremy's cool voice responded. "I'm headin' for the water."

"Eject! Eject!" another voice shouted wildly.

"Aw, shit!" Anthony heard Jeremy utter. Then nothing. There was something perversely wrong about Jeremy's last word. Something wrong and something valid.

Anthony rolled to his side. He wanted to sleep. Needed to sleep.

"You awake, Callahan?" Tom Halston's voice drifted across the stateroom.

"Yeah," Anthony answered, watching Tom's form rise from his rumpled bunk.

"Got a cigarette?"

Anthony tossed a package of Winstons in Tom's direction. The lighter flickered in the semidarkness.

"How was it out there?" Tom asked, inhaling deeply. Anthony regarded Tom's hawkish profile.

"A fucking mess," he mumbled.

"A day like any other day, huh?"

"Yep."

"About Jeremy," Tom said, his voice low. "Better him than you."

"And better you than me," Anthony replied. The attitude was imperative. He had to believe it would never happen to him. Anthony watched Tom inhale again, his mind fixed on Jeremy. Jeremy had given him his call name, Freeze. He'd christened him during a poker game during flight training. Told him he was a subspecies of life. Told him he had no nervous system. No blood. Only ice in his body. Normal temperature was zero, he'd said. Freezing. He was a freezer. Then he'd been fortunate enough to fly with Jeremy. Jeremy, lover of women, cards, and speed, not necessarily in that order.

And he was gone, like the others. Memorial services were being held tomorrow. He still had to write to Jeremy's wife. Was he supposed to say that Jeremy died a hero? He did, but heroes usually have reasons for dying—and Anthony was beginning to doubt that one existed. Don't let it get personal, he told himself again. He almost said the words aloud. That's all he needed, to let Tom hear him talking to himself.

He leaned forward and opened a drawer. He fished through a packet of unopened letters, peering at the postmarks. He ripped open the most recent.

Dear Anthony,

I love you. I love you.

Why don't you answer my letters? I swore I wouldn't ask that, and I did. You're on my mind every minute of each day. Sometimes, I talk to you. I can hear you answer. I don't know what to say. I spoke with your father. He keeps a stiff upper lip. Wonder who inherited that quality? So, there are a million reasons you don't write. It's okay. No, it's not okay.

I love you,
Delaney

A tourniquet tightened in his chest. He couldn't read those letters anymore. It did things to him he couldn't handle. He shoved the packet back into the drawer and slammed it. With one swift incision, he cut the remembrance of them from his mind. He had to be a machine— like the A-6 he flew. Every cog oiled to perfection. Every part in prime order.

He rolled to his side, closed his eyes, and crashed into hard sleep.

CHAPTER

❧ 10 ❧

Grief is an animal that devours itself. Time is the leavening.

Healing began slowly. Waking was no longer synonymous with a piercing stab in the chest. Sleep, which had been elusive, reappeared, granting Delaney its healing properties. Eventually, something that had been broken between her mind and her body, something absolutely essential, connected, and with that slight shift, that welding, came sensation.

The August heat rose from the sidewalk, coiling around her until it seemed to scorch the ends of her hair. The same tall buildings that kept the wind swirling in the winter trapped the humid air in sultry, still pockets. Her head complained, her feet complained, and for the first time in months, Delaney was aware of her body.

She stopped at the produce store. Her mouth watered as

she watched the Korean proprietor drop six fat lemons into a sack. She could see them in her mind's eyes, sliced, squeezed, the semitransparent pulp floating over ice. The thought sent ripples through her nervous system, and in spite of the heat, she picked up her pace.

She entered the apartment and stumbled over Mary Sue's flight bag. Cursing softly, she headed for the kitchen. The antiquated plumbing sang a whale song as the shower droned. She extracted one lemon, sliced it in half, and licked the juice from her fingers.

By the time Mary Sue strolled into the living room, Delaney had downed half a pitcher.

"God, it's hot," Mary Sue groaned. A towel, wrapped turban-style, covered her thick red hair.

"Did you pick up the mail?"

Mary Sue nodded and dropped into a chair, one tanned leg sprawled across the upholstered arm.

"You know, Delaney, some people begin conversations with ice-breakers, such as 'Nice to see you. How was your day?' Not you. You always begin with: 'Did you get the mail?'"

"Well, did you?"

"Yes. Nothing, Delaney. How long has it been?" Reaching behind her, she flicked on the stereo. The sound of the Beatles blended with the monotonous hum of the air conditioner. "'Eleanor Rigby,'" Mary Sue grumbled. "Too damned sad." She changed stations and after several tries settled on Sinatra. "So, how long?" she repeated, watching Delaney anxiously.

"Two months, three days," Delaney replied. "But who's counting?"

Mary Sue nodded. Delaney's head was bent. A wan smile covered her lips.

"You know, Delaney"—she paused and laughed uneasily—"this is not an easy subject. I mean, it's not like he's on vacation or something." Delaney's head flew up. A cold stare filled her eyes.

"Well, it's not!" Mary Sue rushed on. "This war's escalating so fast it makes my head spin. It makes *your* head spin. There's no telling what it does to Anthony. Those jet jockeys are flying more and more each month. And to top it off, I heard on television the other night that we've got a pilot shortage. That's probably the reason he doesn't write. There's no time. I met a guy on my flight the other day, Delaney. He just got back, and he said nobody would believe the flight time the pilots are clocking over there." Her voice came to a halt.

"Don't, Mary Sue. Don't try to make me feel better by making excuses."

"But I don't think they are excuses, Delaney. The fact is, we don't know."

"There's always time to write something, Mary Sue," Delaney countered irritably. She curled her feet onto the sofa, nervously tapping a cushion.

"I suppose you're right, Delaney, but why don't you at least try—"

"Just shut up, Mary Sue! I'm not interested in your in-depth analysis of what's going down in Vietnam!"

Mary Sue's face registered shock. Her green eyes narrowed to thin slits. "That's very good, Delaney," she began. "That's the first genuine emotion I've heard in your voice for months. I don't mind being the target of your anger, 'cause anger's better than nothing. And that's what you've been. Nothing. I'd begun to think I was living with a zombie. Go ahead." She leaned forward. Her voice was taunting. "Tell me to shut up again, because I'm—"

"Shut up!"

"Good!" Mary Sue prodded. "Because I'm not going to! I've got something to say, and I'm going to say it. Listen to me, Delaney!"

"No! I'm sick of your stupid comments, your uninformed comments about the war! You go out and protest, but I don't think you have the slightest idea what it's all about. I think you enjoy it! The marches, the rallies, it's all one big party to you!" She jumped to her feet, glaring, then sat back down. "And while I'm on the subject of partying, I'm worn out with the string of hippies you parade in and out of here! Alley cats! They look like alley cats! Where in God's name do you find them? In the subway station? I don't get any sleep because the damned stereo thumps all night long! You never consider that I work regular hours, unlike your crazy schedule!"

Mary Sue's mouth dropped open. She leaned forward, her elbows on her knees. "That's it, Delaney," she breathed loudly. "Let me have it. What else bothers you?" She waved her arms wildly in the air. "Don't tell me. I know. I don't wash out the coffee pot. I leave panty hose strung in the bathroom. I don't hear the alarm clock. Anything else?"

"Yes!" Delaney shouted. Her eyes jumped to the middle of the room. "Will you stop leaving your flight bag where I stumble over it every time I come home?" She sprang from the sofa again, took two quick steps, and aimed one vicious kick at the overstuffed bag. Pain slammed through her foot. She collapsed beside the toppled suitcase, moaning.

Mary Sue sat silently. Delaney shot her a fleeting glance. Mary Sue looked like the proverbial cat, and Delaney felt like the canary.

"You finished?" Mary Sue asked calmly.

"Yes," Delaney groaned, cradling her foot in both hands. "Oh, God, Mary Sue. I'm sorry. I don't know what's wrong with me."

"I do. It's called life, Delaney. Welcome back."

"Come on, Mary Sue. I haven't been that bad. Have I?"

"No. You've been worse. I've been living with a total crazy woman. First you raced all over New York hunting a new job. Then, when you finally landed one, all I heard was Universal Business Machines. You pored over manuals, memorized sales spiels, detailed company policy, almost boring me into a coma. First I considered suicide. Then, when you didn't stop, homicide.

"I swear, Delaney. You were possessed. And about the time I adjusted, if anyone could, you switched gears. You never uttered an unnecessary word. Chatty Cathy turned into a mime. I was alone even when I could see you. No, no," she insisted as Delaney tried to interrupt, "I'm not finished. There's the mail. I know how important it is to you, but my God, you have full-blown anxiety attacks every time we pass a mailbox!

"And the war. You devour everything written about Vietnam."

"That's unfair, Mary Sue," Delaney protested loudly. "I'm only trying to understand what's going on."

"You and the rest of the world, Delaney! Yet you jump on anyone who doesn't know as much as you. Hawk or dove, it doesn't matter. You crucify them! What does matter is what they know, and it had better be as much as you, or else. With the conflicting reports from the government, the military, and the newspapers, who could know? Yet I've been out with guys active in the antiwar movement who are afraid to set foot in this apartment if you're here!"

"Who?" Delaney demanded. "Name one."

"Kevin. And Larry."

"Okay, okay. You've made your point." She returned to the sofa and sank into the soft pillows. Her hand shook as she reached for the lemonade. The accuracy of what Mary Sue said stung. It was true. Every syllable.

"Why didn't you shoot me and put me out of my misery?"

"I considered it." Mary Sue grinned. "You've had some big losses, Delaney. You've had shock, grief, anger, all those terrible emotions that none of us really understands unless we've been there. But you're coming out of it now. And that's good." She leaned back and shut her eyes. "Alley cats, huh?" A burst of laughter broke from her throat. "Damned if you're not right. Most of them are alley cats!"

Delaney shrugged sheepishly. "Well, maybe not all of them. Kevin's really nice, Mary Sue. I like him. I'm sorry I made him so uncomfortable."

"You can forget Kevin. He's in Canada."

For a moment, neither spoke.

"Have you talked to Anthony's father again?"

"Last week. He doesn't know any more than I do. But I'm not surprised. Anthony really doesn't get on with his parents."

Mary Sue sighed. "Let's forget it for a while. Let's go out tomorrow night. Just the two of us. Have some fun. Get theater tickets."

"Can't. Too expensive."

"Too expensive? If you'd quit sending all your money home to your mother, you could afford some creature comforts, Delaney. Like food."

"I eat!"

"At McDonald's. How long has it been since you've had a good steak?"

"As a matter of fact, I'm going to have one tonight. I'm having dinner with Leo."

"Is he still trying to get you in his bed?"

"No. He's given up. I think. Anyway, I don't want to talk about it."

"No, I guess you don't. It's not easy when your boss develops a case of lust. Testy situation."

Delaney nodded. Leo's attentions had been overwhelming at the beginning, but he soon realized he was wasting his time. Now he kept the relationship platonic, but Delaney knew at what expense. She was fond of him, even admired him, but she was incapable. That was the right word. Anthony had rendered her incapable.

"I've got to dry my hair," Mary Sue said, heading for the bedroom. "I've got a hot one tonight. I want you to meet him. First-class tomcat. You're gonna love him!"

Delaney watched as she left the room. She stared through the grimy window, her thoughts drifting like the heat waves wafting toward the sky. Eight months. What had she been doing for eight months? Where had spring gone? And now summer was in its last burst of strength. Over half a year spent and another half to go. She smiled cynically. Maybe Mary Sue didn't like Eleanor Rigby, but she was living with her. Delaney Rollins and Eleanor Rigby seemed one and the same.

Leo felt his shoulders knot. Conversation was impossible.

"Look, Delaney, this is supposed to be a relaxing, pleasant, social dinner—not the firing squad. Let's discuss something else."

"What? Business? The weather? The taxi strike?" Her mood was belligerent. Leo could see it in her face, hear it in her voice. He leaned back in his chair and sighed heavily. His gray eyes darkened as he shot Delaney a look that was, quite simply, disapproving.

"You are obsessed, aren't you?"

"What I fail to understand is why you're not," Delaney stated caustically.

"Because it doesn't do any good, Delaney. All the sound and fury that you antiwar people are making won't add up to a hill of beans in the scheme of things."

"I don't believe that, Leo. If I believed that, I'd just roll over and play dead—or be dead. Someone has to do something."

"Okay, Delaney." It was futile. No matter how he tried, he couldn't get Delaney to focus on anything except the war.

"Okay? What does that mean? I'm not a child that needs to be placated, Leo. I have a right to my opinion, and in case you haven't noticed, I'm not the only one who feels we shouldn't be there."

"I'm well aware of the growing numbers opposing our involvement in Vietnam, Delaney. I saw what happened during the Tet offensive. The whole world saw what happened during the Tet offensive. I just feel like you've lost all objectivity. I know it looked bad, but looks can be deceiving. The truth of the matter is we won militarily."

"The truth of the matter?" Delaney echoed. "The truth of the matter? Who knows the truth of the matter? Did you watch as the police chief executed a prisoner in Saigon? Blew a hole in his head. And we see it on television. There's no truth in that. Just murder. How can we support this kind of government?"

"I hear you, Delaney. And I know you mean everything you're saying. But what are you going to tell Anthony when he comes home? Even more, what do you say in your letters?"

Delaney picked at the salad in front of her. "I don't mention it."

"Oh? You simply avoid the subject? Maybe that's possible in a letter, but it won't be possible when he comes home. You going to square off with him?"

"I don't know. I truly don't know, Leo." Her voice trailed, all the anger spent. "I just know that this whole war seems reduced to a body count. Every night it's the same thing. We killed ten thousand and they killed ten. It just doesn't make sense, Leo. None of it makes sense."

"War never does make sense, Delaney."

"Maybe I won't have the opportunity to discuss anything with Anthony—even if he comes back alive."

Leo knew it was pointless to continue, but now, at least, the conversation was personal instead of political.

"How long are you going to hang on, Delaney? How long are you going to torture yourself with this? He's chosen a career in the military, Delaney, and feeling the way you do, you'd make a lousy navy wife. And you would never, never be able to keep your mouth shut." He grinned, momentarily breaking the tension.

"I don't know, to all of the above, Leo. I can't answer until I see his eyes, hear what he has to say. I don't know what he's been through or how he feels about it."

"Fair enough, but he's coming back to a different world, Delaney. Feelings are running high, too high."

Delaney sat silently, fingering the napkin in her lap.

"All I'm saying is that it could be much rougher than

you think. And if you can't handle it, I've got a good shoulder."

"I don't need a shoulder, thank you very much." She smiled tautly. "Let's change the subject. You still think Eugene McCarthy doesn't have a chance at the Democratic nomination?"

Leo groaned. "Try again, Delaney, and this time find something neutral, like the food, which, by the way, is delicious. Eat."

"I'm eating, I'm eating," she relented, breaking off a piece of bread and poking it into her mouth.

"Good! You know, I have to admit, eating is not my original idea. It's a custom that's been around for centuries. I've known about it for a long time." He picked up his fork. "Now, this is an interesting instrument. It's used for spearing food. Try it."

She skewed her face in a menacing expression. Holding her fork as though it were a spear, she aimed it in his direction.

"Now, that's an act of aggression, Delaney. Not appropriate at dinner." He reached across the table and scooped up her knife. "We'll learn how to use this at another time."

Delaney laughed. "I can handle it," she said, reaching for the knife. The comment seemed to hit both of them on two levels. I hope so, Leo thought.

As for Delaney, she wasn't sure. She wasn't sure of anything. She might believe her own arguments about the war, but she no longer really believed her arguments about Anthony.

"You writing anything?" Leo asked abruptly.

"Nothing to speak of," she replied vaguely.

"That's not good, Delaney. You need to do it."

"I still keep my journal, Leo."

"For someone who intends to be a writer, you're doing very little about it."

Delaney nodded patiently and waved her hand in the air. "I know, I know. But you keep me so busy that all I'm able to manage is my journal. And would you get off my case? I don't seem to be doing anything right."

"Okay, okay. But when you write something you're satisfied with, let me know. Nancy Tyler is a personal friend of mine. And she happens to be one of the best literary agents in New York." Tilting his head, Leo observed her down the bridge of his nose. "Now I'm off your case. Don't mistake my concern for criticism, Delaney. You're operating on a short fuse."

"Do I detect a note of condescension?"

Leo rolled his eyes. "Well, if you detect it, it must be there. And I won't apologize for it. Sometimes you can be maddening, Delaney. Can't you accept . . ." He halted in midstream, narrowed his eyes, and then continued. "I think I answered my own question. I have the right to disagree with you, Delaney, but every time I do, you lay siege to my position. I've been taking it personally. But I don't think it's personal at all. I think you'd attack any man who disagreed with you."

"That's absurd, Leo," Delaney huffed, but the thought refused to leave her.

CHAPTER

❧ 11 ❧

"Get your ass in gear, Callahan. We're crossing into the promised land," Terry announced loudly.

"The promised land? Give me a break, Fireball. If we go to the promised land, the navy promises a shot of penicillin, 'cause we're sure as hell gonna need it."

"You got a real problem, Callahan." Terry leaned precariously on the table, his liquor-soaked eyes aimed in Anthony's general direction. "You know what your problem is?"

"No, Terry. What's my problem?"

"You're a pessimist. That's your problem." He dropped, grinning, into a vacant chair. "In my book, a dose might be preferable to an endless hard-on. Have you considered that?"

"I consider everything, Fireball. I have three-hundred-and-sixty-degree peripheral vision. Nothing escapes me, including the fact that when it comes to women, you're all mouth. Oh, yeah. If you have a wet dream, you think Ginny knows about it. God, Terry, you feel guilty when you do nothing but look! Man, I'd rather troll with the Pope."

Terry grinned wider and stuck his tongue in the chipped front tooth. His eyes sidled around the Cubi Point Officers Club.

"That's what I like about you, Anthony. Your inability to call it the way you see it."

"Inability? Not in my vocabulary."

"Well, it ought to be," Terry slurred. "You goin' or not?"

"I'm giving it some serious thought. But I can't think with an empty glass. Why don't you get a refill while I consider my options?"

"You do that, Freeze. You consider the options. That's what you do best." Terry wove an uneven path through the crowded room. The atmosphere was heady, charged with energy. Sated with Scotch, Anthony viewed the scene through myopic eyes, everything a little fuzzy, a little distant.

The *Chicamauga* had arrived in the Philippines the day before. Five full days of liberty stretched before him. It would take four of them to quiet his nerves. He wished to God he could stop dreaming. He propped his elbows on the table and drained the last of his Scotch just as Terry slammed a full glass in front of him. Tom Halston was at his heels. Terry flicked his head in Tom's direction.

"This is our host for the evening, Freeze. I handpicked him. Actually, he was the only applicant. Besides, he's still relatively sober."

Anthony's vision shifted from Tom to Terry. "Do I have a choice?"

"No!" they whooped in unison. Anthony wasn't sure who dragged whom or who was propping whom up, but in five minutes they were in a cab headed for the bridge separating Olongapo City from the naval base. The stench from the river, a total misnomer to Anthony's thinking, soiled the air. There was no doubt that the sewage for miles around was floating in that water, not a pretty sight.

"Where are we going, and how fast we gonna get there? I can't stand this smell!" Terry complained loudly, holding his nose.

It was the last thing Anthony remembered clearly.

"You're fucking crazy, Freeze!" Tom was saying.

The words exploded in his ears. Anthony rubbed his pounding head as Tom persisted.

"What the hell gives with you?"

"Please, Tom. Do you have to shout? Besides, I've got no idea what you're babbling about, and I need a Bloody Mary or I'm gonna die."

"You should be so lucky."

"What do you mean?"

"I mean if the Shore Patrol gets you, you might as well be dead."

"What are you talking about?"

"You don't remember?" Tom's eyes were level, serious.

"Remember what?"

"Jesus, Freeze. What's the last thing you do remember?"

Anthony racked his aching brain. An image of a taxi materialized.

"A taxi?" he said.

"You need a shrink, Callahan. You don't remember Kitten? Or Mick Jagger?"

"I don't know what the hell you're talking about, Tom."

He sat up and immediately wished he hadn't. Blood rushed through his temples, and his tongue felt like a truckload of alum had been dumped on it.

"Anyway," Anthony said, gripping the edge of the bed, "I've got a feeling that I don't want to hear any more. Kitten? Mick Jagger?"

"Well, you're gonna hear it, 'cause you're gonna have to explain it—that is, if anyone recognized you other than the entire population of Po City and half the United States Navy."

"Is this a joke?" Anthony asked, forcing his brain to attention.

"No joke, partner. We've got us some big trouble. You tried to kill a marine last night—and you were buck-naked when you did it."

Commander Johnson looked at Anthony with a set of cold piercing eyes. Anthony stood at attention. His blood seemed to freeze.

"Your conduct was abysmal. And your judgment worse," the commander began quietly. "How do you think it reflects on your squadron when one of its officers causes a riot in a civilian bar—notice I didn't say participates in a riot—I said *causes* a riot—and how do you explain that your naked butt was on view for the world to see?—not that it's worth seeing." His voice was rising at a steady rate. "And I'm not sure it's worth saving." The commander's face was red and getting redder.

"Sir, I—"

"Not yet, Lieutenant! I'm not through! There's a fucking marine in sick bay with your fingerprints all over his neck! I'm not overly fond of the marines, but nevertheless, they are not the enemy! I suggest you reserve your energies in case you ever confront him face to face, and right now, I'd relish that sight! If we didn't need pilots so damned bad, I'd ship you to the Canal Zone or somewhere equally stimulating so you could vegetate until you rotted! Do you understand me?"

"Yes, sir!"

"I will not have my officers making public spectacles of themselves! Now you go see that marine, and you kiss his ass or any other part of his anatomy necessary to see if you can keep him from pressing charges! And I don't want to see your face until this blows over, Mister Callahan! Dismissed!"

"What'd he say?" Terry hissed. He'd been lurking in the hallway, trying to look inconspicuous.

"He told me to kiss a marine's ass," Anthony replied, smiling weakly.

Terry shot to his side. "What'd he say about you being naked? I mean," Terry's eyes fired brightly, "it was great! When you grabbed that mike and cut loose with 'Satisfaction,' I swear, if I hadn't been watching, I'd bet my life it was Jagger himself!"

"I wish it had been," Anthony mumbled.

"If you just hadn't stripped. I mean, nobody cared, and we were goading you, but . . ."

"Seemed like the thing to do at the time." Anthony forced an uneasy laugh.

"And that marine—well, if you hadn't called him a motherfucker—"

"And if a frog had a tail he wouldn't bump his ass every time he jumped," Anthony snapped irritably.

Terry followed Anthony into his stateroom.

"Damn, Terry, can't you lay it to rest? I mean, it's bad

enough that I have to depend on your less-than-reliable account of what happened."

"We shouldn't have drunk that moonshine, Anthony."

"I thought in your part of the country it was the American way."

"Well, it is, but I was saving it for something special. Somehow I thought last night was going to be special, so I tucked it in my jacket. Only seemed proper to share it."

"Next time, don't."

"Can't. We drank it all, and I don't think they make corn liquor in the Philippines."

"I probably need to thank Kitten," Anthony said, sinking to his bunk.

"Ahh, forget it, Anthony. She's just a hooker who let us use her apartment to get you dressed. Anyway, we gave her twenty bucks for her trouble. Man, I've never tried to dress a belligerent drunk before. It's hard as hell! The only way we could keep you still was by singing 'Dixie.' Weird!"

"Whose idea was that?"

"Yours."

Anthony's head dropped to his hands. " 'Dixie'?" he repeated. "You're right, Terry. I do need a shrink."

The marine turned out to be a nice guy. Fortunately, he remembered less than Anthony about what happened. But the sight of the bruises on his throat triggered an unwelcome and frightening feeling in Anthony.

Later, when he thought about it, he tried to fill in the blanks, piece what happened together in his head. But he could only recall vague images. The loud bar, the Filipino girl on his lap, the local band crucifying "Satisfaction." He could feel more than remember being on stage. He'd been told his rendition was sterling. The song reverberated in his mind. "And I've tried/and I've tried/and I've tried." He shook his head—a drunken stunt. Not to be repeated. The part that bothered him was the feel of the marine's neck beneath his hands. He hadn't admitted it to anyone, but he remembered trying to choke someone. He just hadn't known who. And when he looked hard at that memory, he knew he was in trouble. He *had* meant to kill. And for the life of him, he didn't know why.

CHAPTER

❧ 12 ❧

Summer yielded to autumn; then autumn bowed to the first sharp winds of winter. Thanksgiving came and went, and Delaney was alone. The weeks piled on top of one another, and not a word from Anthony.

Still, she watched the nightly news, trying to make sense out of the senseless. Body count. Progress in Vietnam was measured by body count. Last night's figures were typical. Fifty-eight Americans dead. Two-thousand-four-hundred enemies dead. Out of kilter. Too many questions. How did we know?

A priest was arrested for pouring blood on Selective Service files in Baltimore. The protest movement was growing. The nation was angry, confused. Delaney was angry, confused. She searched for logic in what she read and found none. She felt splintered, unable to understand, desperately seeking answers when she was beginning to forget the questions.

"Waiting for Scotty to beam you up?" Leo stood in the doorway to her office.

"No," she smiled wanly. "Just waiting."

"For you, that's become an art form, Delaney." He took visual inventory as he entered and sat in a side chair. Delaney looked tired, her face pinched. It was getting harder each day, harder as the time came for Anthony's tour of duty to end.

"Well, how'd you like to hear about your raise?"

"You know I want to hear." She leaned forward, linking her fingers as she managed a laugh.

Leo felt his breath catch as he gazed at her expectant eyes. For that one second, he hated Anthony for what he was doing to Delaney. Immediately, guilt moved in like an avalanche. Leo gritted his teeth. He was jealous, jealous of someone he'd never laid eyes on—and furious because Delaney was hurt.

"Well," Delaney prodded, "are you going to tell me or not?"

"You got what you asked for," Leo grinned, delighted at the brief spark of life he saw in her eyes.

"You mean, *you* got me what I asked for."

"You deserve every dime, Delaney."

"I know I've worked hard, Leo, but if you hadn't gone to bat for me, I'm not sure it would have mattered." She smiled again. "Now I can go home for Christmas."

Leo straightened his body and grimaced. "You sound like the little match girl, Delaney. You weren't earning peanuts before the raise. What do you do with your money?"

"Isn't that a little personal, Leo? What if I asked you the same question?"

"I'd tell you to mind your own business. But that's the chauvinist in me. I have a hard time believing women have much sense when it comes to handling money."

"Well, think again, Mr. Edelstein. My mother was a financial whiz. She stretched a dollar till it yelled for mercy. And I'm my mother's daughter."

"Okay, okay. I stand corrected. But you still sound like the little match girl. 'Thank you, sir. Now I can go home for Christmas,'" he teased lightly.

He watched her for a moment. A new pang of envy rushed through his mind. Why did she have such a hold on him? Why not any of the beautiful women he filled his evenings with? Inwardly, he sighed. Trying to analyze it did him no good. It was Delaney he wanted, and he couldn't have her—at least not yet. Not until Anthony came home and they resolved it, one way or the other.

He broke the silence softly. "I'm caught in this waiting game, too, you know."

Delaney dropped her eyes. "Don't, Leo. Please don't. You know how I feel, and nothing's going to change that."

"Never say never, Delaney. The two of you may be worlds apart, figuratively as well as literally. How's he going to feel when he finds out how polarized the two of you have become? And how are you going to feel when you find out—I mean really find out—what he's been doing for the past year?"

Delaney stiffened. "You're getting too personal, Leo."

"I've always been too personal with you. Look, Delaney—"

"Leo, I'll cross that bridge when I come to it. *If* I come to it," she said firmly.

Leo knew the subject was closed. At least for now. He threw his hands into the air, a gesture of capitulation.

"Okay, okay, Delaney." He rose. "Congratulations on the raise."

"Thanks, Leo." She watched his back as he left her office, feeling as though she'd hurt someone who hadn't deserved it. A shadow of doubt passed through her head. Why hadn't she met Leo instead?

She turned to the stack of papers sitting in front of her and stared numbly. She felt split in two pieces. She didn't make sense, not even to herself. Her eyes drifted to the telephone. Abruptly, she picked up the receiver and dialed.

"Mr. Callahan? This is Delaney Rollins," she began.

"Delaney! I'm delighted to hear from you."

"I'm sorry to bother you at work. I know how busy you are, but I needed"—her voice stumbled—"no, wanted to know if you'd heard anything from Anthony."

A small silence filled the telephone line. "No, Delaney. I haven't. In fact, I intended to call you this week—find out if you'd had a letter."

"Not a word in months."

Seamus caught the anxiety in Delaney's voice. He wished he could reassure her, but most of the time he himself needed reassurance. And it was in short supply. He fumbled for words.

"Now, you know we'd hear something if the news was bad. I hate to sound trite, but in this case, perhaps no news truly is good news."

"I know, Mr. Callahan. It's just been so long, and I have a tendency to—"

"Worry," Seamus completed her sentence. "I worry, too, Delaney. I tell myself it does no good, but I can't seem to stop. Margaret says that I've turned into a foolish man, trying to be a parent at this late stage." He stopped. "But that's not your problem, is it?" He rushed on. "If I hear

140

anything, I'll call. And if you hear anything, you do the same."

"Thank you, Mr. Callahan," Delaney mumbled. She cradled the receiver in her hand as she pressed the disconnect with her finger. Oh, Anthony, she breathed inwardly. Where the hell are you, and what the hell are you doing?

"He got what was coming to him," Anthony said dismissively. His voice was chilling.

"What?" Tom asked, although he'd heard correctly.

"I said," Anthony repeated, "he got what was coming to him."

Tom toweled his body furiously. Sam Wilcox might not have been the best pilot in the navy, but still, Anthony's comment was out of line. Sam had disappeared during last night's sortie. Blown into the dark sky as though he'd never existed. True to the code, any pilot that went down became fair game. To go down meant you'd made a mistake. Not that they didn't all make them, but there were errors and then there were errors. The point was not to make a fatal one. Anyway, it was okay to talk about your own stupidities in the air, but it was not okay to die. If you admitted that something couldn't have been prevented, you admitted your own fallibility.

As Tom lathered his face he glanced at Anthony in the mirror. There was something in Anthony's eyes lately, something that bothered him.

"I think you're being a little rough on Sam," Tom stated flatly.

Anthony gave a short laugh. "As opposed to what? Sam's problems are over. He's dead. He made a stupid mistake. There's no room for stupidity up there, and no room for stupid pilots."

Tom started to say something, then changed his mind. There was something new in Anthony's voice—and Tom didn't like it at all.

"What the hell is wrong with Freeze?" Tom asked, sliding into the chair next to Terry Watson.

Terry stared at the mountain of scrambled eggs on his plate. He didn't answer. In fact, he had no answer. All he felt was anger that the question had been raised. It validated his own suspicion.

"The same thing that's wrong with all of us," Terry shot back.

"I think he's nuts!" Tom rolled on, dragging on a cigarette. "Lately he's been taking crazy chances. You have to have noticed."

"Jesus Christ, Tom! You're really a dumb shit, saying something like that to *me* of all people! I fly with him, remember?"

"I know, I know, Terry. And he's about the best we've got," Tom said with uncharacteristic generosity. "It's just there's something in his eyes lately, something in his voice. I think he actually looks forward to these sorties—that he *likes* it up there."

"Now who's crazy?" Terry's voice rose as he glared at Tom. "We shouldn't even be having this conversation."

"I know, I know. But it seems that since we came back on line, ever since the Philippines, Anthony's been different. I mean, even that incident in Po City. Up there wailin', dancin' around like some Motown pro—not that there's anything wrong with that," Tom added hastily, noting the blatant hostility in Terry's eyes. "I mean, we all get drunk and get nuts, and he was good! Really good! But I turned my head once, and Anthony's down to his skin trying to kill some poor bastard for just being there. It's a bad scene, Terry."

"You're a total asshole, Halston!" Terry exploded. "We're *all* dangerous. Or haven't you figured that out yet?"

"What are you so hot about?" Tom asked. "You saw him, too. What he did wasn't normal—and you know it! But I can pass on it because what he does on the ground doesn't matter. But in the air, it does. And I'm not sure I want to fly with him any longer. He takes too many chances. He goes in too low. He thinks he's infallible."

"Don't we all?" Terry spewed sarcastically. "And ain't nothin' normal over here, including you." He waited for his voice to settle. "Look, Tom. Colson has nightmares. I hear him screaming. Palmarie pukes, just like I do, after every flight. And you got a bad case of insomnia, and your hands shake every now and then."

Tom's body tensed. "You noticed?"

"I look!" Terry broke off. He felt a little guilty. Tom did a good job hiding his tremors, shoving his hands in his pockets when necessary, but it was true. "All I'm saying is we're all affected. The symptoms just differ." He shoved his plate away and rose. "Don't worry about it, okay?"

Rapidly, he left, his stocky legs crossing the deck in record time. He didn't want to discuss it. For if he did, he'd have to admit his own concern. Something was wrong with Freeze. He was becoming more and more remote. Not even Terry's down-home humor made a dent in Callahan's thick iron hide. His brow creased deeply as he entered his stateroom. Aside from the obvious reasons, he was glad this tour was almost over. Callahan was like a man with one foot in the stirrup of two horses.

CHAPTER
❧ 13 ❧

G forces tore at his body. His eyes flickered over the gauges. Normal. Everything looked normal. Yet the plane hurtled down. He turned toward Terry. He was shouting something, something crucial, but Anthony could not hear. Terry's mouth formed an O, a dark hole in the middle of his face. The earth rose to meet them. His lips parted, and he gagged, gagged on the taste of terror filling his mouth. The plane hit, exploded.

He bolted up. His heart crashed against his rib cage as his eyes took in the familiarity of the stateroom. Breathing hard, he glanced at Tom's bunk. Empty. He wondered if he'd screamed . . . again.

He rose and lit a cigarette. He smoked nervously, pacing the length of the stateroom.

"Okay, okay," he muttered aloud. The sound of his voice helped to reestablish reality. "It was a dream, and it's over." Sweat drenched his forehead. He felt sick. Out of control.

He collapsed on his bunk, staring sightlessly at the ceiling. Every night. Now the dreams were coming every night . . . some so real they haunted him, and for hours he'd touch things, reasserting his sensibilities, validating sanity. The worst were the face dreams, children's faces, still, lifeless, staring. He tried not to dwell on it, not to consider the possibility that he was responsible for the death of children, women, old men. But like an obsession, it lurked in his subconscious, ready to pounce, except when he flew. Then he was too busy reacting, dropping his bombs on the designated target, hoping that he'd been accurate. But afterward, if he let down his guard, that obsession surfaced and damned near brought him to his knees.

He wiped his forehead on his T-shirt. He felt trapped. He loved flying. He lived for it. He couldn't imagine life without it, but what he did with his flying rubbed a raw place in his soul.

And then yesterday, he'd almost unloaded on one of his own. The F-8 had zoomed beneath him just as he'd released his load. Climbing, he'd lost sight of what happened, wasn't sure everyone made it back. He'd been crazed, waiting for each pilot to signal "feet wet," indicating they were back to the safety of the South China Sea. This time he'd been lucky.

With each sortie, each close call, something inside him shut down. He earned his call sign over and over—displaying no sign of nerves, no sign of fear. He was the best, and he was paying the price.

He withdrew. First from Delaney. Then from the guys he flew with. And now, Terry. Pain avoidance. Why connect

145

when it might mean loss? Five more days. Five more days on line and then home. Home to what? He laughed bitterly.

Delaney? Out of the question. Still her letters came. Still unopened. But she'd be there. One telephone call away. He reeled back from the thought. No, he wouldn't contact her. He had nothing to say.

He pressed his fingers to his temples as though the physical act could quiet his brain. He might not have anything to say, but he had plenty to think. How do you shut down a brain? He stared at his hands. He was shaking uncontrollably. Then, another hoarse laugh escaped his lips as he answered his own question.

"With a bullet, you dumb ass."

The *Chicamauga* steamed toward the coast of California. Anthony and Terry stood on deck watching the horizon. Terry's voice droned on and on and then suddenly silenced. No matter what he said, he got no response. He glanced at Anthony's body locked in rigidity, his face a complete blank.

"So," Terry finally spoke again, "you gonna call Delaney?"

Anthony's eyes came at him like Zuni rockets.

"You bet." His voice made a mockery of the words.

"Look, man," Terry soothed, "it's gonna be okay. Once you get home—I mean, it's only natural that we're all tense."

"Do you have a job outside flying, Terry? A secret life as a social worker or something? Quit treating me like some mental case."

"Fuck you, Callahan!"

"Now there's an original idea."

"I just think—"

"Yeah? Well, that's your problem, Terry."

"Shit. Here it comes."

"Here what comes?"

"Ahh, forget it, Callahan."

"No. Go on, Terry. What do you think?"

For a moment, Terry felt uncertain. If he could get a fix on Anthony . . . ah, what the hell, he thought, and plunged ahead. "You need to talk about it, whatever it is. You need to let go of it. You're never going to—"

"So much for what you think," Anthony said, his jaw clenched.

"You know," Terry flared, "you got one thing wrong with you."

"And what's that?"

"You're stubborn, narrow-minded, and crazy!"

"Those are three things, Terry. Count them. Stubborn, narrow-minded, crazy . . . three things."

"Then you're just crazy."

Anthony's eyes dulled. "I wish you didn't think I was crazy, Terry."

"Well, are you?"

"Yes, but I wish you didn't think it."

A porpoise broke the water, a streak of gray against green water. The carrier rolled forward as the coastline sharpened. Terry was nervous, wondering what was coming, but unlike Anthony, he had a wife who loved him, someone to buffer the growing tide of criticism chronicled daily in the press.

Terry turned to Anthony and smiled uneasily. "Keep the faith, man. Whatever comes, I'm on your side." Christ, he thought. He doesn't hear me. No matter what I say, he doesn't really hear me.

CHAPTER

❧ 14 ❧

Margaret thumbed through Seamus's personal Rolodex, pausing here and there. There were no first names. Just initials. She smiled to herself. Seamus was so obvious. Omitting first names to camouflage his inventory of sluts!

There it was! D. Rollins. Quickly, she glanced at the grandfather clock. Six-twenty-four. Nervously, she bit the inside of her cheek. Should she call? She sat for a moment, staring through the tall study window. Night was closing in, merging with the lingering dreariness of day. The March wind gusted and whistled around the corners of the house. Meticulously, she began to weigh the consequences of what she was about to do. It could make Anthony angry, and that was something she needed to avoid. But he had promised . . .

Yes. She'd do it. Picking up the receiver, she leaned

back in Seamus's worn leather chair and dialed. It rang
. . . once . . . twice . . .

"Hello."

"May I speak to Delaney Rollins?"

"This is she."

"Miss Rollins, this is Margaret Callahan. Anthony's
mother." The statement sounded like a question as her
voice inflected upward.

"Mrs. Callahan?" Delaney repeated, and Margaret could
hear the fear leap through the telephone line. She smiled
again, this time smugly.

"Yes, dear. I really hate to intrude, but—"

"Has something happened to Anthony?"

Margaret paused dramatically, allowing the smile on her
lips to swell. She'd guessed correctly.

"Mrs. Callahan? Is Anthony all right?"

"Oh, yes. Anthony's just fine. But I thought you'd know
that. Haven't you seen him?"

Utter silence deadened the connection. Margaret's eyes
glinted as she stroked the gold chain dangling from her
neck.

"No, Mrs. Callahan. I haven't seen him. I didn't know
he was back."

"Oh, my dear. I'm so sorry. I assumed he would contact
you. I mean, I thought—well, I've been trying to reach
him at Dave's number, and there's no answer. I hope I
haven't upset you."

"How long has he—"

"Been back in the States? About three weeks. He's some
sort of flight instructor. I can never remember the names of
those military bases—there are so many of them—but it's
near San Diego. Of course, that hasn't stopped him from

149

popping in and out of New York." She sighed audibly. "I suppose that's one advantage of being a pilot—all those free rides." She hesitated again. "But I'm boring you to death. And I've interrupted your evening. Seamus and I wanted to have Anthony and you to dinner, since he'll be here for the weekend, but . . . again, I'm so sorry."

Delaney was mumbling something incomprehensible as Margaret extended one manicured nail and pressed the button. The dial tone hummed in her ear. She stood, crossed the length of the study, and snapped out the light.

Feeling quite pleased, she climbed the stairs and entered her bedroom. Seated at the vanity, she gazed at the reflection in the mirror. The utter satisfaction that filled her soul spilled over her face. And she smiled. *Nobody* made Margaret Callahan look foolish—not without paying for it. She would have her pound of flesh. It was simply a matter of being patient, waiting for the right moment. And she was capable of waiting months, even years. Anthony had cleared the way, albeit unknowingly. He hated her. She could see it in his eyes. Whatever power she'd held over him had vanished, with one exception. And that was Anthony's desire to protect Seamus. What did they call it? Male bonding? She snorted derisively. It was an absurd concept, but it worked to her benefit. There had been no need for the fear she'd suffered. Anthony had no intention of revealing what he knew, what he'd seen. All those months of worrying for nothing. When the confrontation had finally occurred, it had been anticlimactic.

After Anthony returned, he'd flatly refused to come to Connecticut. So Seamus had insisted on going into the city. He wanted to see with his own eyes that Anthony was still in one piece. Margaret had been weak with fear.

During an agonizing dinner she tried to talk to Anthony,

but he'd cut her short, more with his eyes than with his words. She'd been subdued in his presence, threatened, eaten by terror. She had difficulty swallowing her food. Then, when Seamus had gone to the men's room and she and Anthony were alone, he'd broached the subject.

"You seem uncomfortable, Mother," he said. His eyes filled with amusement, a cruel amusement. She squirmed under the microscopic look in those eyes. He laughed at her, sensing her fear. When he spoke again, his voice was full of hate.

"Don't worry, Mother. I'm not going to tell a living soul. But it has nothing to do with protecting you. I don't give a damn what happens to you." He leaned back in his chair, his stare coming harder and harder. "For the first time in my life, we're on equal footing. You've never given a fuck about me, and now I don't give a fuck about you."

Margaret blanched. Her mouth opened to respond, but Anthony went on.

"I think it would kill Dad. Not that you haven't been doing that by degrees for years."

Again, she started to speak, but his look stopped her cold. Those blue eyes, frigid, frightening. Fleetingly, she wondered which Irish ancestor had such eyes and where the British had hanged him. Then, oddly, he smiled at her. And there was something about the smile that wasn't a smile at all, but something new, which she found formidable and dangerous. Inwardly, she shivered. In spite of his reassurance, and her belief in that reassurance—for he was correct in his assumption that it would kill Seamus—she did not feel safe.

When Seamus returned, and for the sake of appearances,

she'd tried to converse with Anthony, but he had cut her short. Dinner was awkward. And Seamus noticed.

"Something's not right," he said worriedly as he steered the Mercedes toward Connecticut.

"I don't know why it's taken you so long to see the obvious," Margaret retorted furiously. "I've always said Anthony was strange, but you never listened to me. And this war seems to have exacerbated whatever is wrong with that boy."

"He's not a boy, Margaret!" Seamus glowered.

"You don't have to bark at me, Seamus. I have a right to my opinion. Besides, nobody knows a child better than a mother. Do you believe I like thinking he's not normal? Anthony's my son, too."

"Well, well," Seamus murmured wryly. "That's the first time I've heard you acknowledge it. It's a little late for parental concern, isn't it, Margaret? Where the hell were you when he was young? When he needed you?"

"Don't you dare make accusations at me," Margaret spat. "You weren't exactly father of the year. You never had time for him. You only had time for whores."

Seamus slammed his hand onto the steering wheel. "You don't ever quit, do you, Margaret?"

"All I meant was—"

"Let's drop it! We both botched it." For a moment, he lapsed into silence.

But his comments triggered a plan in Margaret's mind.

"Seamus?" she began tentatively. He turned weary eyes in her direction. "I think there's something terribly wrong with Anthony."

"What do you mean?"

"I mean something mental."

"Goddamn, Margaret," Seamus exploded. "He just left a combat zone. That has to have an impact! Give him time!"

"Just mark my words," she warned, her eyes glittering in the dark. Yes, she breathed inwardly, it would work. If Seamus thought Anthony was unstable, sick, it would totally discredit anything he might say. No one believed the rantings of a lunatic. All she had to do was plant the seed, nourish it a little, and watch it grow.

Delaney stood in the doorway of a deli, her arms wrapped across her chest. The wind, sharp and cutting, whipped through her raincoat. She hadn't realized it was so cold. She stamped her numb feet, her eyes glued to the entrance of the building across the street.

Briefly, she thought of the telephone booth. She could call again. It was possible that he'd been in the shower, or that Dave had been in the shower. Or maybe one of them —please, please let it be Dave—was asleep and hadn't heard the phone ringing.

Time, and the wind, whittled away at her resolve. She shouldn't have come here. She didn't even know if he was truly in New York. So calling again was futile.

She should go in the building. Ring the buzzer. See if anyone answered. Besides, if she waited in the foyer, at least it would be warm. But what if Anthony were in New York? What if he walked in with someone else? The pain that burned in her chest needed no fuel.

She glanced at her watch. Twelve-thirty. Early, by New York standards. It could be hours before he appeared, *if* he appeared. Was Mrs. Callahan lying? It was possible, but doubt kept her huddled in the shadows of the door. She could not wait for morning. She had to know tonight.

A taxi rounded the corner, throwing twin beams of light onto the wet pavement. One passenger. Delaney's eyes pierced the darkness as a lone figure emerged. Tall and lean, the wind blew through blond hair, and Delaney stood in frozen helplessness as Anthony entered the foyer and disappeared from view.

She swayed on her feet. So Mrs. Callahan hadn't lied. He was home, and he hadn't called. Why? She choked back the question, and then asked it again. It would be unbearably hard, but she would understand if he'd found someone else. What she couldn't stand was the obvious stench of indifference.

Anger, relief, elation swarmed in her mind, warring with one another. Then the grief that had collected in her mind like dust in the corners replaced them all. The feelings grouped, then regrouped, momentarily blinding her to the obvious. He was home. She'd waited too long for this moment. She would not wait another minute for an answer.

She crossed the street, entered the building, and pressed the buzzer. No answer. She pressed it again.

"Yeah! Who is it?" His voice reverberated in her ears, and for a split second, she was speechless.

"Okay, okay. You want to play games. Well, Dave's not here."

"Anthony?"

"Yeah. Now you know who I am. Who the hell are you?"

She forced sound from her constricted vocal cords. "Anthony, it's Delaney." There was hesitation, short and interminable, before he replied.

"Delaney?"

"Yes." Another silence. "Can I come up?"

The buzzer sounded, and she pushed open the door. Gravity dragged at her feet as she climbed the stairs. Her pulse accelerated wildly as she approached the door to the apartment. She hesitated. She could leave right now. Save her pride. The thought dangled, then faded. Her mind set, she raised her hand and tapped lightly. The door flew open.

Anthony stood in the frame of the doorway. Her eyes swept his face, landed on his eyes, and she reeled from the vast, hollow blue reflected back. The stillness of the room behind him deepened.

He stepped back, waved one arm in the air.

"Come in. Come in."

She crossed the threshold, passing in front of him, close to him, close enough to touch, close enough to feel his body warmth.

She stopped in the middle of the room and turned to face him. Suddenly, she felt foolish. She racked her brain for something to say.

"You've lost weight" was all she could manage.

"A little." He moved in front of her, then lowered his body on the arm of a chair and reached for the glass on the end table. He swallowed, then stared at her, then laughed.

"Well, this is awkward enough."

"Awkward?" She considered the word. "Yes, it is. I shouldn't have come." She headed for the door.

"Well, at least have a drink before you go."

A drink? After fourteen months that was all he could offer? A drink? She spun to face him, a rush of anger flooding her body. Whatever was going on here, she could handle it.

"Why not? I could use one."

"Why not, indeed," Anthony repeated, and Delaney was vaguely aware that they were echoing each other.

She waited until Anthony emerged from the kitchen. His fingers brushed hers as he handed her the cold glass. She turned it up and downed the entire drink. The Scotch, undiluted, burned its way to her stomach.

"Easy," he said, then halted, as though he'd embarrassed himself. "I mean, there's more where that came from. Do you want another?"

"No."

Anthony coiled his body into a chair across from her.

"Delaney Rollins," he said.

"I think that fact's been well-established." The Scotch rushed through her veins.

"You're looking good," he said. His eyes slid over her body.

"I'm glad I pass muster."

He ignored her sarcasm. "How did you know where to find me?"

"Your mother. She called to see if you were at my place. She wanted to ask us to dinner."

A brittle laugh broke from his throat.

"My mother has never tried to reach me in her life."

Red dots stained Delaney's cheeks. "You think I made that up?"

"No. I'm just surprised."

"I think she wanted to find out if we were seeing each other."

"She's being a bitch. That's what she does best."

"Well, are we?"

"Are we what?"

"Seeing each other."

"We are right now."

It was a flinching response. "I need some answers, Anthony." Her voice was quivering. The bluff she'd been running was wearing thin.

"In order to answer, I have to know the questions."

She sat silently, studying his face. It was the same. A little more angular, perhaps. The mouth, forehead, chin, all of it, all the same—except for the eyes. They were different. Something was there, then gone. In a flash, it came to her. Duplicity. That's what she saw. A fading in and out, blurring the man he had been, and blurring the man he was. Abruptly, she rose and closed the small space between them.

"How long have you been back?"

He eased out of his chair and walked back to the kitchen. She could hear the clink of ice as he answered.

"Three weeks."

"Why didn't you call?"

He emerged from the kitchen, his glass full.

"I didn't call anyone."

"Before you left, I didn't think I was just anyone."

"And you were right."

"But things have changed?"

He stood before her, uncomfortable. "Do we have to have this conversation standing up? I feel as though it's an inquisition."

She crushed the urge to run. But she had to have answers before she left the room.

She sat at one end of the sofa. He sat at the other, his body slouched low. Neither spoke for a moment.

"I needed some time alone. Some time to adjust to the

sneers." He turned to face her. His eyes, in spite of the liquor, were filled with raw energy.

"Do you have any idea what it's like to be insulted, cursed, spat on? Well, try walking through an airport in uniform. Or are you unaware of the reception committee convened especially for the military?"

"Anthony, I know it's hard."

"Hard?" His voice rose, then he laughed. "Not true, Delaney. Nothing's hard if you don't think about it. That's why I didn't call you. I didn't think about it."

She heard the words. And she heard the lack of feeling behind them. She said nothing.

He drained his glass and slammed it on the table. Leaning back, he propped his long legs on the coffee table, locked his fingers behind his head, and viewed her through slits of blue. Delaney returned his look. She didn't know this man. This was a stranger occupying a body she once loved. Slowly, she rose.

"I think I'd better go."

"What's the rush?"

"What's the rush?" Once more, she examined his eyes, distant, cold. She shouldn't have come. It would have been better.

"There's no rush, Anthony. Not anymore." Her mind would not still. She began to turn for the door.

"Delaney?"

"What?"

"I can hear your heart beating."

"Well, how much pleasure can one woman stand?" The strength of her voice grew with each word. Her head was clearing. She'd come for a reason. She would hear the words from him before she left.

"It's obvious that you don't want me here, Anthony. In

fact, it's obvious that you don't want me anywhere. But I'd like to hear you say it. I've waited a long time, and I like things complete, tied up in packages. Open your mouth and say: 'I don't want—' "

He was on his feet and across the room in two strides. For a blinding second she fought. A crippling anger, as fierce as her love, swerved through her mind, and then his mouth crashed down and her legs dissolved.

CHAPTER

❧ 15 ❧

Anthony had not meant for it to happen. It was as though his mind had taken a leap from one subject to another with no logical connection. And his body had followed.

He'd meant to simply shut her up. She had stood there, demanding explanations, wanting answers, answers he had no way of supplying. Not want to see her? Suddenly, he'd known that was *all* he'd wanted. It was the only thing left in his world that was worth wanting. Her dark eyes had blazed with the fiber of honesty, as though she were able to see some distinction he couldn't quite make out, as though life still revolved around right and wrong, reason and meaning. He did not want to hear it. He did not want to answer. Her face was suddenly living proof that he'd lost something. And he wanted it back. Even if it was at her expense.

So he'd kissed her. Crushed her to his body. For a brief

moment, she'd struggled, and he'd tightened his grip, reeling from desire. And then she'd stilled, and he was acutely aware of her mouth beneath his, the curve of her body leaning into him. She'd made a sound, a small whimper as his hands moved over her hips, pulling her to him. He had swooped her in his arms, carried her to bed, and nothing, nothing in the world could have prevented him from finishing what he'd started.

He was not gentle. Not the first time. He undressed her, his hands fumbling, trembling, and ultimately he'd ripped her blouse, dropping it to the floor. Her eyes were large and dark, listening intently to his half-finished phrases, words of desire mingled with pain, frustration, impatience. She'd listened as though she'd understood it all.

He'd been cruel only once, for her active participation had surprised him. Convinced there had been someone else, blinded by jealousy that other hands had been where his now lingered, he'd paused before entering and watched her head roll slowly from one side to the other. He'd reached for her, twisting her chin so she faced him.

"Let's see if you've cut your wisdom teeth on someone else while I've been gone."

He'd heard the sharp intake of breath before he'd taken her. And he heard it again, trickling into the distance, as he lost himself in the warmth and wetness of her body. Once, and only once, he'd hesitated, a stunned expression filling his eyes as he realized he was the first. Then he rolled off her small body, his breathing labored, his passion spent.

He waited for her to speak. When she said nothing, guilt began filtering through his mind. He had been too rough. He'd taken Delaney like some whore—talked to her like a whore. He had, in a moment of insanity, taken something beautiful and soiled it. He swung his legs to the edge of the bed and sat up. Slowly, he turned to face her.

"Delaney," he began, his voice hoarse and low. "I'm sorry. I didn't know."

"No, Anthony." She stopped him from going any further. She pushed to a sitting position, pulling the sheet to drape her breasts. "Don't say anything you don't mean. I'm not sorry, and neither are you. It was inevitable. I know that and you know that."

He reached for her, cradling her in his arms, and he held her until his hands began to drift and desire welled again. And this time, he was slow, relishing her pleasure. The skills he'd used in the past now seemed natural and necessary. And when she cried out, the world as he knew it vanished. For the first time in his young life, he knew no separateness.

Later, he watched her as she slept. One arm was thrown over her head, and her legs were bent. Her hair fanned the pillow, framing her face, still except for a slight fluttering of her dark lashes. He watched in silence. The light from the bathroom door outlined her features, throwing slight shadows beneath her eyes.

He straightened the crumbled bed covers, tucking the sheet under her shoulders. Unable to resist, he lifted a hand and smoothed her hair. Exhausted, he closed his eyes and finally slept. When he awoke, she was gone.

Leo raised his eyes from the sales contract when Delaney entered his office. Her face was pale and her eyes were ringed with fatigue.

"The governor has granted you a stay of execution," he started with a tease, but the expression on her face stopped him.

"Leo, do you think I could have Las Vegas?"

"Las Vegas? But I thought you hated Vegas. That's the reason I told Larry Hellman to handle it."

"I know, Leo. I did say that, but now I want to go."

"Oh?"

She dropped her eyes, one finger tracing the edge of his desk. "Anthony's back," she announced quietly.

A sharp stab shot through Leo's stomach. It caught him off guard. He thought he'd accepted Delaney's feelings, adapted to them. He'd had months to come to terms with the reality that Anthony actually existed, but obviously, he'd failed. He cleared his throat, buying time to smooth the edge in his voice.

"How long, Delaney?"

"How long? What do you mean?"

"How much time do you need to straighten this out?"

"I don't know, Leo."

"So, how is he?"

"Very different. It'll take a while to sort it all out."

"If it can be sorted out."

"That's a possibility, Leo, but one I'm not ready to face."

"And, for your sake, I hope it works out. But watch yourself, Delaney. From what I hear, these homecomings can be ominous. Just be careful."

"I will, Leo. I'll be just fine."

I hope so, Leo thought as he watched Delaney exit his office. I really hope so.

Anthony didn't call. He simply showed up, not quite as drunk as he'd been the night before, but well on his way. It had not been his intention to see her. So he'd drifted the day away, spending the morning in the Metropolitan Museum, staring at Monet's water lilies. There was a beauty and peace in the painting that spoke of another world, a world filled with harmony, a world he did not know.

He wandered down Fifth Avenue, jostled by people going somewhere in a hurry. Someone pressed a leaflet into his hands. He scanned it quickly. It was a stinging indictment against the involvement of American troops in Vietnam's "civil war." He crumpled it in his fist. He wanted to fight, to brawl, to use that fist to flatten someone's face. He kept walking.

As afternoon faded into early evening his mood shifted. He wanted a drink. And a woman. Any woman. Run 'em in, run 'em out. At P. J. Clark's he met a willowy blonde who smelled like vanilla, but when she went to the powder room, he split.

Fifteen minutes later, he was at Delaney's door. And this time, she'd come to him first. Come willingly, and he'd loved her twice, lost in the sanctuary of her arms.

If only she didn't ask questions.

"Stop it, Delaney," he'd ordered. "Don't ask me what I've been doing, and I won't ask you what you've been doing. Neither of us needs to know."

"Since when did personal relationships operate on a need-to-know basis?" she flared. "And don't speak to me like I'm a junior officer."

"Oh, God," he moaned, rolling his eyes. Then he grinned. "You still have quite a mouth on you. That, at least, hasn't changed."

"I'm serious, Anthony."

"I know, I know. You're always serious, Delaney."

"And you're never serious."

"I was serious a minute ago."

He watched in amusement as a blush crept across her face.

"So there are exceptions to every rule." Then she giggled. "At least I know how to keep you on track."

He grabbed her arm and pulled her against him. "So do it. Let's get serious together."

Mary Sue was out on flight, so Anthony stayed the night. It was one of those rare, heady times of loving through hours stolen from a world staggering from change. They made love to each other. There was laughter and omelets and insignificant talk of insignificant discoveries, important only to each other. Anthony relaxed, loving and teasing Delaney with equal fervor, and he momentarily escaped the beast asleep in his mind. She was his world.

And Delaney, the new fire of sex glowing delicately under her skin, gave herself to him completely, releasing her body to soar beside his spirit with absolute trust. It was a time of equilibrium, for regaining lost ground and renewing her belief in life.

The next weekend she met him in Las Vegas. At first, he was aloof, as though the five days apart had erased all tenderness toward her. Gently, she cajoled, caressed, and in a matter of hours the Anthony she adored was back. He gambled—roulette, blackjack, slot machines—while he kept her at his side, one arm encircling her shoulders or waist, as though her presence anchored him, filled him with a different reality, solid and secure while at the same time wild and contagious.

Her plane left first, and he took her to the airport in a rental convertible, driving much too fast, his eyes hidden by dark glasses. She could sense the tension mounting in his body as they sped along the highway. Abruptly, he pulled off the road, cut the engine, and turned to face her.

He removed the glasses, and the blue of the desert sky was reflected in his eyes. He draped an arm across the back of the car seat.

"Delaney, we have to talk." A small wind rumpled his hair, and she reached out to smooth it.

"I thought that's what we'd been doing," she countered lightly.

He grabbed her hand and held it tightly as he turned sideways in the seat and stared at her.

"No, we haven't been talking. We've been evading. Or at least I've been evading." His eyes left her and circled the snow-capped mountains rising against the desert. "You're a woman who won't tolerate exclusion—at least not for long—and if you stay with me, I'll exclude you."

"Anthony," she began, her face stilled by the gravity of his voice, "we all have places that are exclusive. It's part of life."

"Don't, Delaney."

"Don't what?"

"Don't make excuses for me or talk to me like I'm a child."

Delaney stiffened.

"You make it easy for me, easy for me to forget who I am, what I do. But you won't be able to ignore it forever. And there are areas of my life that I will never share with you, and there are subjects we'll never be able to discuss."

"Anthony."

He leaned over and kissed her. "For once, don't say anything, Delaney. Just listen. That mind of yours swirls in perpetual motion, and you verbalize it all." He frowned. "But if that were the only problem, I think I could manage."

"What are you saying, Anthony?"

His gaze shifted to the road in front of them. "I'm saying that I love you, and I don't know what to do with that. I'm saying that I'm obsessed with wanting you—and I can't afford obsessions." He sighed deeply. "I'm saying I don't know how to love. I'll probably screw it up. Right now, I do one thing well—and that's fly. And I know, even though we haven't discussed it, how you feel about it. And I'm smart enough to know I can't change you, Delaney. I may not fully believe in what I'm doing. I probably don't understand it all, but I'm committed. Maybe you're my alter ego—what gives me balance—if I have any left. Or maybe you could undermine everything I thought I believed in. I can't take that chance."

Delaney sat still as fallen snow, listening and not wanting to hear.

"Are you telling me you don't want to see me?" she finally asked.

Anthony groaned. "No. At least I don't think I am. Maybe I am. I want you to be aware that I can't make any promises. I don't believe in promises. Until you, I didn't believe in love."

"Well, believe it, Anthony. I'm real, and I won't leave unless you send me away."

He pulled her to his chest, burying his face in her hair. "I don't want to, Delaney. But I might. And I wanted you to know that. Protect yourself, baby. Sometimes, I don't feel sane, or even safe. And sometimes I think nobody around me is safe from me. When that happens, if it happens, I want you to run, run for your life."

She nuzzled deeper into the hollow of his shoulder. "That will never happen, Anthony. Never."

CHAPTER

❧ 16 ❧

"Why did it take you so long to call me?" Dave asked as the waiter served the prime rib.

"Been busy."

"Too busy to let an old friend know that the hunter is home from the hill and the sailor from the sea, or however that goes?"

"I thought you'd be in New York. I still had a key, and I used it. I left you a note, but I guess you haven't been back in a while."

"Nope. I'm actually thinking about letting the apartment go. You interested?"

"Might be. I'd like to have a place to store some of my gear. Something more permanent."

"Now that's a new word for you, Callahan. Permanence. Did you learn that in the navy?"

"Well, I sure as hell didn't learn it from you." Anthony laughed.

"You look a little worn, Anthony. Was it rough over there?"

"Rough enough." Anthony sliced into the large cut of meat and was silent.

"What you need is a little recreation. Nothing like a good workout to jump-start the juices. I know a couple of ladies who are experts at rehabilitation. Actress by day, nurse by night. Let Doctor Dave write the prescription, and we'll watch the women fill it." Dave halted, his smile fading when Anthony made no response.

"Look, Callahan, I know where there's one hell of a bash going on tonight. We'll drop by, see what develops, and if we don't like it, there's always the frustrated nurses." He laughed uneasily.

"Sounds fine, Dave." Anthony's eyes were distant as he refilled his wine glass.

Dave studied Anthony's taut face. He was worried. Anthony was a volcano. And his eyes seemed to fade out, as if he saw something nobody else could see.

"So," Dave said, fishing for a neutral topic, "you still going to make the navy your career?"

"Where did you get that idea?"

"Why, from you. You always said that."

"Who in his right mind would want to spend his life taking orders from a bunch of assholes? Give me a little credit, Dave."

"Okay, okay," Dave answered. "So I made a mistake. You're not going to make a career of the military." He reached for his wine glass, puzzled by Anthony's strong reaction. Anthony had loved the navy—loved flying.

Something had changed. Something was wrong. Dave tossed his knife on top of his half-eaten dinner and lit a cigarette, exhaling in short puffs.

Anthony lifted his eyes from his plate and grinned infectiously. Now, that was something familiar, and the stranger he'd been talking to seemed to vanish, as if driven by a sudden wind. Dave tried again.

"Well, what are you going to do when you get out?"

"I haven't given it much thought. I'm not into thinking, Dave. Particularly not about the future. I have a hard enough time dealing with today." He grinned again.

Dave's professional eyes viewed Anthony's features critically. Good bones.

"Ever think about modeling?" he asked casually.

"Modeling?" Anthony chortled. "Give me a fuckin' break, Dave. Can you see me among all those fags? What the hell do you think I am?"

"I think you're a smart man. I think you'll have to earn a living like the rest of us. I think you'll probably"—Dave hesitated, grasping for a subtle way to say it—"I think you'll probably need to take it easy for a while. Modeling is easy." He rushed on as Anthony shook his head from side to side. "I mean television, Callahan. I could get you some spots. You've got the bones and the body to go with them. You'd be good."

"You're outta your mind, Dave. Forget it. Finish what's left of that meat, and let's get out of here."

"Okay, okay," Dave replied. "But if you should change your mind . . ."

"That'll never happen, Dave. And where did you learn that shit about bones? I think you have a problem. You've been living in never-never land too long. Doesn't anybody ever say no to you? Do you ever deal with anyone normal, anyone whose ego doesn't revolve around his looks or voice or whatever the hell else it takes to make it in Tinsel Town?" Anthony laughed. "You need to touch base with earth people every once in a while."

"And you consider yourself an earth person? Why, Anthony, you're not even a member of the human race," Dave quipped, smiling at Anthony's assessment of his profession. There was more than a grain of truth in it. He had been buried in an avalanche of frail egos as his reputation for cutting shrewd deals grew—and his list of important clients had grown with it. He had some big names now—all demanding his undivided attention. And here sat Callahan, whose face was a camera's dream, laughing at him and saying no. But still, if that look which flickered in and out of Anthony's eyes could be captured on film, the look reflecting a hidden agenda, wide open for interpretation, it could be worth . . . ah, hell, forget it. Callahan would remain Callahan.

"Seen Delaney?"

Immediately, that elusive expression covered Anthony's face. God, it was great!

"Yeah. I've seen her."

"And?"

"And, nothing," Anthony lied.

"Don't tell me she dumped you!" Dave's eyes filled with malicious glee as he leaned across the table. "Now, that would be a first. The mighty Callahan dumped as though he were an ordinary mortal. She found someone else while you were saving the world. The great Callahan bit the dust."

The words were hardly out of his mouth when the wine glass in Anthony's hand shattered. Shards of glass fell to the table and mingled with bright drops of blood.

"Keep your fucking mouth closed, Dave. It keeps you out of serious trouble."

"It was a joke, Anthony. I was only joking." Anthony's face was white. His jaw was locked. "Look, man," Dave finished clumsily, "it's none of my business. Jesus, Anthony, I didn't know the subject was so touchy." He sighed. Anthony's hand was spewing blood. "Why don't you go wash, and I'll get the check," he said, motioning for the waiter.

Anthony nodded and rose. Dave watched his receding figure with alarm. From here on out, he'd watch what he said. Anthony was too unpredictable. Yes, he'd watch his step. And, he thought as he pulled out his American Express card, he sure as hell wouldn't mention Delaney again.

Anthony stood watching the cold water cascade over his bleeding hand. What the hell was he doing here anyway? What the hell was he doing anywhere? If only Delaney hadn't had to be in Miami this weekend. He hated it when she worked conventions.

He stared at his hand, watching the blood mingle with the water. Why had he broken the glass? Okay, okay, so he suffered from constant jet lag, speeding from one coast to the other. With a flick of his wrist he cut off the water. He caught his reflection in the mirror. He looked sick. He missed Delaney. Love was supposed to make you feel good. Or maybe it made you hurt. But, Jesus, were you supposed to be this miserable? Maybe Dave was right. Maybe he needed another woman. A change of pace. No. That wasn't true. He needed Delaney. And goddamnit, she wasn't here. And he was suddenly furious again, furious because he couldn't control his feelings. Need. He hated the sound of it, the feel of it. And suddenly, all he wanted to do was to be rid of it.

It was a night that Dave Carter would be a long time forgetting. And Heather Riley took great pleasure in reminding him of it.

He should have seen the danger signs when they entered the house. After the episode in the restaurant, he should have been more attuned to Anthony's state of mind. He should have known that the hippies, the grass, the cocaine, all the things he took in stride, were relatively new to Anthony. He should have stayed with him instead of circulating.

The evening was a disaster. Dave introduced Anthony to one lovely female after another and watched with amazement as all of them ran for cover. Anthony's tongue seemed coated with acid as he softly demolished each one with a continuous round of stinging insults. Only Heather held her own—but then, it was hard to best Heather. She was one of a kind among rock singers. Stable, well-educated, she took her career seriously, treating it as a business and blending her artistic instincts with the cold facts of the recording industry. Her success had been stunning. She was a normal human being, except when she was on stage. There, she was electric.

Heather had watched Anthony from a distance. At first it had been curiosity. Heather was bored by the same old faces, the same conversation—who was doing what to whom and when. This face was new, different. And hostile. The combination was most intriguing.

"Your friend has a problem," she said to Dave.

"Which friend?" Dave asked, smiling into Heather's dark eyes.

"The one with military written all over him."

Dave's eyes worriedly scanned the room until he spotted Anthony moving toward the bar.

"What's up?" he asked Heather.

"Just call it intuition, but I think he'd like to kill someone."

"Who?"

"I don't think he really cares, Dave."

And before Dave could wind his way through the crowd, he heard the crack of a fist against bone.

Anthony stood over the inert body of a stunt man who was vaguely familiar to Heather. Gently, she touched Anthony's arm, and he followed like a lamb. Dave remained for a moment, offering apologies to the host. He made no attempt to find out what had caused it. He really didn't care.

Outside, Anthony turned mean again. Heather had grabbed the car keys from the ignition, and Anthony was making it graphically clear that he intended to have them.

"Shut your filthy mouth," she snapped. Her eyes blazed fire as she stood her ground. "I've got four brothers, all of them bigger than you, and I'm not scared of them either! Who the hell do you think you are? Call me another name like that and you'll be singing soprano for the Vienna Boys' Choir!"

To Dave's astonishment, Anthony quieted, then grinned, then doubled over with laughter.

"My God," he mumbled to Dave as Heather helped get him in the car, "there are two of them." He turned to face

Heather again, and his arm, flailing in the air, crashed into her mouth.

"Get that son of a bitch out of here," Heather shouted over Anthony's slurred apologies. "And you owe me one, Carter!"

"You bet, baby," Dave muttered as he gunned the engine. He glanced at Anthony's torpid body. "I owe you one."

CHAPTER
❧ 17 ❧

Anthony tried to enjoy his duties as a flight instructor. But, as with most everything, he was impatient and demanding. His men respected his abilities while living in mortal fear of his wrath. Many a man slunk from his icy stare, feeling as though Anthony's latest tongue-lashing had flayed the very flesh from his body. Under Anthony's tutelage, there were no excuses.

But he came to New York as much as possible, hopping flights bound for McGuire. For weeks, he avoided discussing the war with Delaney. She stopped asking about his time in Nam, and he volunteered nothing.

On the heels of McCarthy's moral victory in the New Hampshire primary, running on a pacifist platform, Lyndon Johnson announced he would not seek a second term. Delaney was elated. Anthony glowered.

"I don't give a damn who they elect, as long as it's not

McCarthy. Goddamn traitor," he muttered to the television set.

Delaney bit her tongue to keep quiet.

Mary Sue, slouched on the floor, didn't.

"Traitor? You think McCarthy's a traitor?" Her voice was incredulous.

"You bet," Anthony asserted. "What do you think he is? The savior?"

"Well, traitor is a strong word, Anthony," Mary Sue said, sitting up and facing him.

"Strong?" Anthony forced a laugh. "I can think of stronger things to call him, but I wouldn't want to offend your delicate ears."

"Such as?" Mary Sue bridled.

Delaney caught Mary Sue's eyes. Not now, she urged silently. Please not now.

"I don't need to elaborate, Mary Sue. And I should have known you wouldn't have the vaguest notion of what's going on in the world—that is, outside of the Top Forty and who you're going to lay this weekend."

"Anthony!" Delaney exclaimed. "He didn't mean it, Mary Sue. He's been—"

"I meant every word," Anthony said, his face a storm warning.

"You know, Callahan, you were hard enough to take before you went to Nam, but now you're a total asshole."

Delaney's heart thumped wildly.

"Take a look around you. See what's going on here, right here in the good old U.S.A. There are a lot of people who don't think you're such a hero." She spun and left the room.

Anthony sprawled in his chair. The look in his eyes was chilling.

"Don't say it, Delaney."

"Don't say what?"

"Just don't say anything."

"So now I'm not supposed to talk at all."

"That's right."

"No, Anthony," she started slowly, "that's wrong. And you're wrong. You owe Mary Sue an apology. Who she lays or doesn't lay is none of your damned business." The words began to run together as she felt anger rising like a wind before a brush fire. "You are way out of line."

"Oh, so I'm out of line, huh? Well, then you tell me, Delaney, just what do you think of our little war?"

"I think I'd rather not discuss this. I don't like your frame of mind."

"You're dodging the issue. As usual. Or am I to believe that you've stopped thinking entirely?"

Delaney felt the heat of anger. "That's uncalled for, Anthony. Of course I haven't stopped thinking. My politics are my own—just as yours are your own. Can't we drop this?"

"No!" Anthony shouted, pushing to his feet. "I'd like to think that you cared, one way or the other, Delaney."

"Care? You want to know if I care?" She heard her voice rising, unable to stop it. She rushed on, knowing they were on a collision course. "I've been active in the antiwar movement for months! I think we're intefering in what is mainly a civil war. I think that every man lost in Vietnam died for nothing. I think the government lies on a daily basis about what's actually going on, and it sickens me! Every time you dropped a bomb, it was an act of futility. And to know that someone I love put his life on the line rips my heart. For what, Anthony? For what?"

Anthony leapt to his feet, poised like an animal ready to

spring. Then instantly his body tension dissolved. His face sagged. Delaney's chest clenched as she looked into his eyes. He was looking through her.

"You're right. We shouldn't talk about this. There are things you'll never understand, Delaney. You haven't been there."

"And you haven't been *here*."

"Delaney, did you hear me?"

"I heard you."

"I want to stop before we say things we'll both be sorry for." He took her chin and turned her head toward him. "I'll apologize to Mary Sue, okay?"

For a second or two, Delaney stared at him, silent as the rising moon.

"Okay," she agreed.

And he did apologize to Mary Sue. But the damage, although not fatal, was permanent.

In April, Martin Luther King was assassinated. In June, Robert Kennedy died in a Los Angeles hotel. Violence seemed ubiquitous, and the country, quite literally, reeled. With each passing event, Delaney's stand against the war hardened, and Anthony's trenches deepened.

Each month seemed to present a new precipice, a new juncture. Delaney fought to hold on to who she was as she gave herself to Anthony. And Anthony found in Delaney's body a sanctuary where, briefly, he did not have to defend himself. Loving her was the only respite from the rage he had unwittingly procured for himself.

But because of the pretense, each knew that a subtle scrimmage line had been drawn, and neither made the first move to cross it.

CHAPTER

❧ 18 ❧

Anthony stopped telling Delaney when he was coming. He never called, never made plans. He would suddenly appear, as though it were the most natural course of events, and sometimes he'd appear when Delaney was traveling, waking Mary Sue, who would send him away, watching as he disappeared down the steps like some figment of her imagination.

Delaney, contrary to her nature, tolerated Anthony's sudden arrivals and departures, hoping that eventually he'd realize how abnormally he was behaving. There were moments when she wasn't sure she knew him at all. Anthony's moods would swing wildly, and she had to believe that somewhere in the jumble of erratic emotions, the Anthony she knew was hiding.

It was not easy. She tried several times to talk about it.

But he stared at her vacantly and insisted it was her imagination.

The weeks spun into months, and the lack of routine became routine. Swallowing her pride, she left it alone, for on some level, she knew he couldn't help it, and she couldn't help him.

But the incident in the Village raised more questions.

He'd wanted to go out. He'd paced the length of the small living room like a caged cat. She recognized the signs and knew what was in store. It would be a marathon of bar-hopping, Anthony tolerating no more than twenty minutes in one place. He'd order drinks and never touch them, his eyes flickering everywhere until he'd mutter, "Let's go," and they'd be off to the next place.

The June night air was sweet, for New York, and the city celebrated itself, twinkling in the falling twilight. Anthony walked rapidly, and she had to rush to keep up with him.

In less than an hour they had been in four clubs. Delaney was barely seated before Anthony wanted to leave. Once, when an up-and-coming comedian blasted the establishment with acid wit, she had been afraid to look at Anthony. And when she did, he was laughing. Still, he wanted to leave.

They wound up in a small neighborhood bar that was deserted. The lighting was dim, and when they entered, it took a moment for her eyes to adjust. The bartender was watching a television set mounted on the wall at the far end of the room. He was wearing a leather jacket, the kind that pilots wore.

"Let's go somewhere else, Anthony."

"Why?"

"I don't like the atmosphere."

"Seems okay to me," he said, his eyes fixed on the bartender's back. He sat on a stool and tapped the counter.

When the leather jacket turned, Delaney was momentarily caught off guard. It was a woman.

"What'll it be?" she called, her eyes back on the TV set.

"Two drafts," Anthony answered.

"I'll have to see the lady's ID." She moved in their direction and stopped in front of Delaney, one leather-clad arm resting on the bar.

Delaney reached into her purse as Anthony watched.

"South Carolina, huh?"

"Yes. I've never bothered to get a New York license. I don't own a car, and I never drive except when I'm out of town."

"Makes sense to me, honey," the bartender said, pulling two chilled mugs from the refrigerator.

Delaney turned to Anthony, who was staring at a stain on the bar.

"Been in New York long?" The bartender smiled as she placed the glasses in front of them.

"A little over two years," Delaney answered, her eyes flitting to Anthony. The bartender was staring at her. Anthony's face was stony.

"Don't have much business, do you?" Anthony stated, his voice low and steady—too steady. "Don't you get a little nervous being here alone?"

"I'm not alone." A soft, piercing whistle came from her lips. A large black dog reared from behind the bar and placed its paws directly in front of Anthony. A growl came from low in his throat.

"Down, boy!" Immediately, the dog disappeared. "I'm Mitzi," she grinned—"and that was Plague."

182

"Plague?" Delaney repeated.

"Yep, 'cause when he goes for you, he's all over you like the plague." She laughed coarsely.

Delaney turned nervously to Anthony. His face was immutable. Delaney felt the stirrings of low-level anxiety.

"Is that a piano?" Anthony asked, nodding toward the back of the room.

"Yes. But nobody plays it."

"Is it tuned?"

"Yes, but as I said, nobody plays." Anthony stood and moved toward the back corner. Mitzi's eyes tracked him like an animal stalking its prey. The air suddenly crackled.

Anthony sat and began to play "Moonlight Sonata." The haunting strains of the melody drifted lightly through the bar.

Mitzi's eyes never left his back.

Delaney was silent, listening, and watching Mitzi watch Anthony.

Abruptly, Mitzi reached for the remote control to the television. With her thumb, she increased the volume. The strains of "Moonlight Sonata" grew like an incoming tide. Mitzi flicked her thumb. Canned laughter blended with the chords of the piano. The piano crescendoed. Mitzi flicked again. Pepsi Cola competed with the piano.

Suddenly, Mitzi slammed the control on the bar and walked to the back of the room.

"Get outta here!" she screamed.

Anthony played on. So did the Pepsi generation.

"I said," she screamed again, "get outta here!"

Grabbing the control, Delaney fumbled with the volume. Half the noise stopped. She came to her feet as Anthony lifted his hands into the air. He turned and smiled at Mitzi. But it wasn't a smile. It was more like a baring of teeth.

"Plague!"

The dog rounded the corner, snarling. He stopped, the hair on his neck bristling. Anthony, still smiling, glanced at the dog. Neither moved. Then, slowly, Anthony moved to Delaney's side.

"She can stay!" Mitzi shouted. "But you go!"

Anthony's shoulders shrugged.

"You want to stay?" he asked.

Delaney's mouth dropped open. "No," she said, her voice shaking.

"Okay." He shrugged again. He took her hand, and Delaney let Anthony direct her out the door as Plague charged. The door closed behind them as the dog's body crashed into it. For a moment, Delaney thought it would break. And Anthony started to laugh. Delaney's heart pounded furiously.

"What's funny, Anthony?" she demanded. "I don't think it's funny."

"I was thinking of Mother. She needs a dog. Where do you want to go now?" he asked.

"Home," Delaney answered weakly. "I want to go home."

"You could have stayed, you know," he said.

"Are you crazy? What is wrong with you? Why did you do that?"

"She was a dyke, Delaney. And, she carded you to get your address. That South Carolina license threw her. Don't you know a dyke when you see one?"

"No, I don't. But you obviously do."

"? all the time, Delaney, no : l the time."

CHAPTER

❧ 19 ❧

Anthony found himself avoiding public places. Although there were people who supported the war effort, they were mostly among the political right wing, mainly George Wallace supporters. Anthony knew that Wallace's American Independent Party had little or no chance of winning the election, and Wallace's history of racial prejudice bothered him. He was uncomfortable with the kill-the-gooks attitude such conservatives seemed to spout. Wallace's campaign slogan, "Send 'em a message," was somehow offensive, too simplistic. And yet, knowing his friends had given their lives in Nam, he fervently wanted those lives to count for something.

He felt caught in the cross fire. Bombarded by political rhetoric, he tried to make the pieces fit. He failed.

When he did venture into the local night spots, he clashed with his long-haired peers, and checking his temper became impossible. Words were exchanged. He felt alienated.

One night, bristling with nervous energy, he cruised the bars, hoping to find some escape in the music, in the pulse of life throbbing around him. He drank a little too much, ignoring the patent disdain from the hippies. But interspersed between the acid rock that was beginning to dominate the music scene, he heard one song, one antiwar song that ended such excursions. He left before learning the title, but the essence of it stuck in his memory like a blemish.

From then on, he confined his drinking to the Officers Club. He found relief in flying, drinking, and Delaney, but Delaney was a double-edged sword. While he loved her, communication was limited; each was afraid to upset the delicate balance. What kind of future could he offer her? And if he did, at what point would their differences surface like Hydra, stretch their multiple heads, and eventually tear them apart?

He seemed to have no place in the country to which he'd returned. He watched as draft cards were burned and the flag was desecrated. He listened to the arguments of protesters who'd fled to Canada. And the war rolled on, the death count rising. The world had lost its direction, and he had lost life's meaning.

"You think too much," Terry told him one night as they finished their fourth or fifth Scotch. Who was counting?

"What are we supposed to be? Robots?" Anthony said, his words spiked with cynicism. He signaled the bartender for a refill.

"Yep," Terry replied emphatically. "That's exactly what we are. Just get in there and do your job. And quit thinking about it, Freeze. You ought to get married."

Anthony laughed. "Why? What good would that do?"

"It would give you something else to worry about."

"Can you see Delaney as a navy wife? She's such a dove she grows white feathers each night and sheds them before she goes to work."

"I'd say you've got big trouble in paradise, bub. Why don't you let old Terry give you a word of advice?"

"As if any power on earth would stop you." Anthony grinned.

"You aren't cut out to walk the fences, Freeze. You're either in or out. Now, that's what you're going to have to decide with this woman. I don't give a damn what the libbers say. A woman's either with you or she's not. So marry her or cut your losses. It ain't easy, but what the hell is?"

Anthony nodded. "You're absolutely right, Terry."

"Well, that's a first," Terry laughed. "Having solved that tactical problem, I'm going home to my woman." He stood, weaving a bit. "And"—he grinned—"she's going to chew my ass for coming in loaded. And you know what? I wouldn't have it any other way." He staggered toward the door.

Anthony finished his drink slowly. What Terry said was true. He wasn't meant to walk the fences. And what Delaney offered him was a head-banging ride on an emotional roller coaster. Who needed it? He'd end it next time he was in New York. That's what he'd do. He knew cutting her from his life would be hard. What he didn't know was that it might even be an act of self-destruction. But not one done in solitude. For if he had to destroy all of the beauty in his life in order to survive, he had to take Delaney out first.

* * *

187

"When are you going to tell him?"

"I don't know," Delaney moaned, wiping her face with a cold wash cloth. Her stomach heaved as she brushed past Mary Sue, heading for the kitchen.

"You can't wait much longer, you know. You've got to decide, Delaney. Either you tell him or you have an abortion. There's no halfway point here."

"I know. I know. He's been so damned maddening. He's always been so damned maddening. I've talked to other women who had husbands or lovers in Nam, and Anthony is not unique. I was trying to give him time to adjust."

"Well, you don't *have* time, Delaney."

"Please don't start, Mary Sue. I feel like hell, and I don't need—"

"Start? Start? Now that's an original idea. Seems like you should have done that several months ago."

"Go to hell, Mary Sue," Delaney muttered. She opened the refrigerator and reached for a Coke, hoping it would settle her stomach.

"You're being a fool! I don't give a hoot what Anthony's frame of mind is. I care about you! I'm transferring in two weeks, and I won't be here to help you, unless you decide to move to San Francisco with me."

"We've been over and over this, Mary Sue. My job is here in New York."

"And just how long do you think you can work pregnant? Even Leo can't manage that one."

"Can't we drop this for now? I've got to go to work."

"That's your pat answer, Delaney. You may be an expert at delaying tactics, but they won't work with this one. You've got to tell him the next time he's in town."

"I don't know if I *want* to tell him!" Delaney shouted.

Mary Sue heard the desperation in Delaney's voice.

"Then *don't* tell him. I'm not sure he'd do anything about it anyway. Delaney, Anthony is one of the most complex men I've ever known. He can be utterly charming, caring, and sensitive one minute, but he can turn on a dime. Since he's been back, he's full of bitterness. He clings to it, surrounds himself with it, wallows in it. And I have this feeling that he won't let go of it because if he does, he'll have something worse to deal with—pain beyond his endurance. Make an appointment at the clinic. Delaney, *please!*"

"I won't promise that, but I will do something, and I'll decide before the week is over. Okay?" She nibbled a saltine, her hands shaking.

"No. Not okay. I want to hear your decision tonight!"

"Oh, God, Mary Sue. Give me a break. One more week isn't going to hurt. I've got time."

"Time is exactly what you don't have!" Mary Sue followed Delaney to the bedroom. "Someone has got to talk some sense into you. Honestly, Delaney, I don't know who's crazier—Anthony or you."

"He's not crazy!" Delaney exploded.

"The hell he's not! That man is looney tunes, Delaney, and you know it!"

"That may be true, Mary Sue," Delaney replied hotly, "but I'm the only one who can say it. Not you! Not anyone else!"

An angry stillness slipped between them as Delaney's eyes burned feverishly.

Mary Sue exhaled a sigh of frustration. "You're right, Delaney. After all, it's your life." She snagged her flight bag, spun, and headed for the door.

"Mary Sue," Delaney called after her. "I'm sorry."

Mary Sue halted. "I seem to be hearing that phrase a lot

lately." She turned and gave Delaney a crooked smile. "I just hope people on the west coast aren't as sorry as people on the east coast."

"Well, it can't be any worse. Have a good trip."

"Okay." She stepped through the doorway.

"And Mary Sue," Delaney added, "I'll tell him."

"Whatever." Mary Sue grinned and shut the door behind her.

Delaney stood for a moment, staring at the door. Mary Sue was right, of course. She had to do something. She'd known she was pregnant for six weeks and had done nothing about it. It was the stupidest thing she'd ever done, playing Russian roulette with her body. But the pills would be in her medicine cabinet, and she'd be at Dave's with Anthony. She'd only missed a couple, but apparently they counted.

She thought of telling her mother. How could she put Carrie through that again? But abortion? Kill Anthony's baby? Her baby? In principle she approved, but now that the issue was personal, she didn't think she could do it.

But how to tell Anthony? Her mind careened with fear as she tried to imagine his reaction. He might do anything.

She had to tell him. He had a right to know. But beyond that fact, her mind refused to function.

CHAPTER

❧ 20 ❧

I'm going back to Nam."

"When?" The voice that spoke was not her own.

"In ten days."

"Why didn't you tell me?"

"I don't know. Maybe I didn't want to hear what you had to say."

"You didn't want to hear what I had to say?" she repeated, then she forced a laugh.

"Delaney, try to understand."

"Understand? No. I don't understand, Anthony. I thought you loved me."

"I do."

"Well, this is the kind of thing you share if you love someone, Anthony."

"It has nothing to do with love, Delaney. Nam has nothing to do with love."

A silence stretched between them. Sounds sifted through. Laughter from the restaurant. Voices and the clinking of crystal.

"I don't want you to go, Anthony."

"I have to."

"What's happened, Anthony? Why won't you tell me what's wrong?"

"Because nothing's wrong."

"Then why are you doing this?"

"Because that's where I belong."

"That's not where you belong, and you know it."

"Oh? And just where do I belong? Working for some corporation in a three-piece suit? Riding a commuter train? Is that where you see me, Delaney?"

His words struck at her, quick and hard. It was over. It had been a long siege, but it was over, and she had lost.

"Maybe I don't want you at all, Anthony."

He watched her, a remote expression on his face. "Maybe you don't," he replied slowly. "Peace at any cost? Isn't that what you profess?"

"Don't blur the issue, Anthony. Don't use the war to shut me out."

"Okay, then what is the issue?"

"The issue is who you are, Anthony. I don't know who you are anymore."

His eyes slammed into her. "I am a man you don't need to know."

"But I wanted you. I still want you. I want to understand."

"You'll never understand, Delaney," he cut in sharply. "You spout idealistic platitudes, and you can't know what it's like."

"That's not the problem, Anthony. You need some help, and you won't face it."

"Do I have to sit through this whole movie?"

"No, you don't." She came to her feet. The napkin in her lap fell to the floor. She left it, stumbling slightly as she moved past spotless white tablecloths, glittering silver, and faces frozen in a tableau of expressions. She collided with a waiter, sidestepped, and passed through the door. She stood at the curb, one arm raised to hail a cab. The drizzle from the hovering clouds misted her face.

Anthony appeared.

"Delaney, please. I love you."

A taxi screeched to a halt. She opened the door and slid in.

"Delaney, I have to pay the bill. Wait for me."

"No, Anthony." Her voice was heavy. "I won't wait for you. Not tonight. Not tomorrow. Not next year."

She heard the door slam, and the taxi pulled away.

Anthony stood watching. He stood for a long time as the clouds tore at the tops of the buildings and the mist turned to rain. He had killed something in her, and something in himself. His head dropped, and when it rose his face held a new expression. It was the face of a fanatic.

Delaney moved through a dream world, making decision after decision. She hoped it would become easier. It didn't.

Leo's eyes had filled with anger mixed with concern.

"You can't do this, Delaney. I won't let you do this!"

"Leo, please, you're making this difficult. Very difficult, and—"

"I'm making it difficult? I think that distinction belongs to Anthony, not to me." His face was rigid as he paced the length of his office. Suddenly, he stopped. His shoulders sagged as he looked at her. "What can I do to keep you here?"

"Nothing, Leo."

"If this were a movie, I'd say, 'Delaney, please marry me. Let me take care of you and the baby.' But it isn't a movie. And I know that wouldn't work. Nothing I could do would get him out of your mind. And I'd go crazy trying. I think too much of you and too much of myself to put either of us through anything so foolish. But I want you to know that is my first instinct, and I'm fighting it." He moved again and sank wearily into the chair behind his desk. "So," he said, smiling sadly, "if you need anything, anything at all, I'm here."

She was amazed at how quickly she packed, how quickly the apartment was rented. She sold the remnants of furniture she had collected to the new tenant and shipped her clothes to general delivery in Cushing. And she tried not to think. She pulled a curtain around her mind to block the pain. She could hear it rustle as it fell. The past was gone. She would think only of the infant she carried. She would make sure this baby was protected, loved, cherished. This child would be strong where she had been weak. This child would make wiser choices. And last but not least, she would make sure this child never knew of Anthony.

CHAPTER

❧ 21 ❧

Anthony scanned the instrument panel and shot a furtive glance at Fireball.

"Everything okay?"

Terry's eyes were glued to the computer readouts. "I'm making the corrections for wind velocity. Looks like the weather guys were a little off in their predictions."

"So what else is new?" Anthony mumbled to himself. He was now level at twenty thousand feet. The cockpit windows were opaque as the plane sliced through the night. Overhead, the stars gleamed down on a layer of thin clouds.

Ahead, Anthony saw flak ripping at the darkness. Charlie knew they were coming. Charlie always knew they were coming. If only someone could invent a silent engine, he thought, then he scoffed at his wishful thinking. Beneath his oxygen mask a sheen of perspiration was forming on his face.

"The natives are restless tonight," he grumbled.

"The natives are restless every night," Terry snorted. "Don't these people ever sleep?"

"I'll bet they wonder the same thing about us," Anthony answered. Both men watched as the flak increased. Terry broke the temporary silence, identifying the initial point for tonight's target, an antiaircraft base near Haiphong.

"Heading two one five," Terry instructed.

Following the lead of the formation, Anthony began a gradual descent. As they dropped the airspeed increased. Anthony could hear the deep beeping of enemy radar as it swept the sky.

"Ten more miles and we push over," Terry said. His fingers flicked some switches on the armament panel as the beep of the enemy radar came more frequently.

"I've got the target," Terry shouted above the noise.

"Good. Let's attack and get the hell out of here."

Terry pushed a button, and the attack light activated.

Anthony lowered the nose of his aircraft as a stream of flak drifted overhead. He could hear Terry calling altitude as the heavy plane plunged earthward. Hundreds of lights seemed to twinkle from the earth's dark surface as the guns unloaded in the sky.

"Nine thousand . . . eight thousand . . ." Terry's voice was calm, steady. *Now!*

Anthony dropped his load at seven thousand, and the plane, devoid of the weight of its load, surged forward. For the next few seconds the Intruder split the night, climbing, descending, evading the deadly fireworks splattered in the sky. Terry continued calling altitude, louder and louder as the chatter of pilots over the radio reached a fevered pitch. The engine screamed; the radar still beeped ominously.

"Another hard day at the office!"

Anthony grinned without looking at him. "Yeah. It's a jungle out there!"

"You might say—"

Whummp!

The half smile froze on Terry's face as the plane convulsed. Anthony fought for altitude as the stick joggled in his hand.

"Can you see anything?" he shouted as his eyes flew over the instruments.

Terry's head swiveled like a bar stool. The plane shuddered.

"The right wing, Freeze! I think we're losin' fuel!"

Anthony's eyes flicked to the right wing. He peered into the darkness. Then he saw it. Fuel was spewing into the air like a small geyser. Sweat poured into his eyes as he automatically began to dump the fuel. He tore off his mask and wiped his head.

Whump . . . Whump! Whump!

The plane hung suspended between the black sky and the blacker earth. Anthony's breath stopped as he fought for altitude.

"Do something, Freeze!" Terry screamed frantically.

"Come on, baby!" Anthony yelled as he pulled at the stick. The plane quivered and then responded.

"Three thousand . . . four thousand . . ."

They were climbing, climbing. Below, the ragged darkness of treetops grew smaller. And then, another shudder.

Terry keyed the radio to the emergency frequency.

"Radio's not receiving, Freeze! I think we're in some deep shit!"

"Keep sending, Fireball!" He looked around the sky for other planes. They were alone.

Anthony swallowed hard. Going down anywhere was bad, but going down in enemy territory? Captivity? If they were lucky and fell into the hands of the NVA regulars. But what if the Pathet Lao found them? They were known to execute on sight. Or, there were villagers who might possibly skin the enemy alive. Anthony blinked, then blinked again, pushing the thought from his overloaded brain.

"Five-One Two is off target! We're coming out!" Terry shouted into the mike.

For a split second Anthony removed his eyes from the panel and glanced in the mirror. There it was—a weak glow flickering in the dark.

"Fire!" he shouted, knowing he had run out of alternatives. The rules were clear—written in granite. At the first sign of fire—eject.

"We're outta here, Fireball! *Eject! Eject!*"

Anthony saw Terry pull down the primary ejection handle. In a microsecond, he was gone. The noise level from the open cockpit deafened him. Without thinking, he pulled the alternate firing handle and exploded into the night.

The parachute opened, jolting his entire body. An eerie silence hung in his ears as his hands sought the risers and clamped down like twin vises. He fell steadily, silently toward the jungle beneath him. His mind raced, trying to remember what to do. Disconnect the oxygen mask. If he were knocked unconscious, the mask might suffocate him. He concentrated on his right hand, ordering his fingers to relax. Holding the riser with his left hand, he disconnected the mask. His hands fumbled for the seat pan. He'd have no need for it, since he sure as hell wouldn't be landing in water.

Wind rushed by as blood smashed through his body. He waited. Eons passed. Something tore at his arm. A blow to his stomach forced the air from his lungs. Branches slashed at his face. And then nothing.

Somewhere, far in the distance, someone was moaning. The sound slowly penetrated his consciousness, and he realized he was listening to himself. His eyes jerked open, then closed again. It made no difference, for both were equally black. Was he dead? Was this death?

He moved and felt the pain. No, he wasn't dead—not yet. The ground under his body was damp and uneven. A rock punctured his thigh. Carefully, one limb at a time, he inspected himself. He felt disjointed, aware that his body was composed of singular parts. One leg, then another. Okay. He moved his left arm, and it screamed at him. Gingerly, he traced his shoulder with his fingers. Pain slammed his senses. It was broken or dislocated.

After fumbling with his good arm, he found the harness-release fittings and eased himself free of the chute. He fished in his vest pocket for a flashlight and flicked it on. Slowly he circled the blackness with the beam of light. The jungle foliage came alive, shiny and wet. With the aid of the light, he located his shroud cutter. He slashed the lines entangling his legs and killed the penlight. The thick darkness entombed him.

His mouth felt like cotton. He gulped deeply from a plastic water bottle, then vomited. He rested for a moment or two, then took one small swallow and spit it out.

Terry. He had to find Terry. Reaching for one of the two radios he carried in his survival vest, he activated the silent emergency beacon. Now, if anyone was searching, they could find him. He set the radio to transmit/receive and spoke, his voice sounding thunderous in the quiet of the night.

"Fireball?"

Nothing.

"Fireball? This is Freeze. Can you hear me?"

Nothing. He repeated the message, waited again, then gave up. Maybe Terry was unconscious and couldn't answer.

A voice blasted from the radio. Automatically, he rolled for cover.

"Diamond Five-One-Two. Diamond Five-One-Two. Do you read?"

It wasn't Terry. But it was a voice. Someone was searching. Anthony's heart pumped wildly as he replied.

"Diamond Five-One-Two copies loud and clear!"

"Roger that. This is Dacron One-Niner. Give me thirty seconds of beeper, over."

"Roger, beeper," Anthony complied. He waited thirty seconds and switched the radio back to voice. "Did you copy, over?"

"Roger. We got you. Identify yourself."

"Anthony Sean Callahan, Lieutenant, seven-two-six-eight-niner-three."

"Copy. Please wait."

The silence, punctuated by an occasional rustle of leaves, jarred Anthony's nerves. He waited, elation and fear mingling like two streams crashing toward a river.

"Diamond, Dacron. Have you joined up, and are you hurt?"

"Pilot has shoulder injury, and negative join-up."

"Okay, Diamond. We're with you. Will call again in a few minutes."

More silence. Anthony wondered if his parachute had been spotted. He was having trouble believing his luck. This was his first major mission since he'd returned to Yankee Station. And now it might be his last. He heard a sound, and his eyes pierced the darkness, straining to see. Maybe Charlie was easing through the undergrowth. The radio sounded again.

"Diamond, this is Dacron. I need thirty seconds of beeper."

His hands shaking, Anthony watched the luminous dials of his watch sweep away the seconds.

"Okay, Diamond. Find a deep hole and disappear. We'll be back at first light. Your watch still working?"

"Yeah," Anthony replied. "I read 2257."

"We'll be in touch. Got it?"

"Roger—and thanks."

He sat for a minute longer, feeling his body register the delayed stun of his fall. Pain began to localize in his shoulder and his head. He stood, his eyes struggling to see something, anything, in the thick vegetation that surrounded him. He had to move, find Terry. He fingered the radio again, made one more attempt, but no answer.

Mentally, he tried to compute how far Terry could be from where he himself had landed. His mind failed, and he knew that he couldn't, at this moment, in this place, add two and two, let alone estimate where Terry could be. He took a deep breath, willed his body to move, and, with his compass around his neck, started through the tangled trees.

Immediately, he fell. Panic welled as he reached for his revolver. The cool metal settled him for a moment. Slowly, he stood and inched forward, glancing at his compass in the tiny ray of his penlight.

Every hour on the hour, he tried Terry again. Still no response. His shoulder pulsed with pain as he rechecked his compass. He'd traveled in a circle, adjusting his direction so that he wouldn't stray too far from where he thought Terry might be, hoping that Terry would hear him. Desperation clawed at his mind. He couldn't give in. He had to keep focused, keep moving. He plunged ahead, his feet tripping over roots. Then, suddenly, he stopped cold. The trees were behind him. He was on level ground. Wet, but level. He could barely make out a rice paddy. He was standing at the edge of a rice paddy! And in the middle of that paddy, he saw something gleaming, something white . . . a parachute!

Anthony lunged backward and lost his footing. His injured shoulder slammed the trunk of a tree. His teeth clenched against the pain as he fell to his knees, crawling to the safety of the trees. Vines whipped his face. Rocks tore his hands. He stopped, leaned against a tree trunk, and reached for his radio.

"Fireball?"

Silence.

He slid to a sitting position, his head spinning from exertion, fear and indecision. His legs felt heavy and his eyes burned. He couldn't stay here. There was no way he could stay here. Slowly, he turned around and crept to the edge of the jungle. The air was as still as the chute. The quiet hurt his ears. He looked upward, probing the sky. The black night was fighting the first light rays as the horizon began to lighten.

My God! What was he supposed to do? He gripped his revolver tightly in his fist, his mind floundering. If there were rice paddies, there were villagers. It was a miracle Terry hadn't been discovered. Something bad had happened, or Terry would have answered his radio signal. Was the radio out? Or was Terry beyond answering . . . ?

The sky began to gray. He had to hide. For all he knew, he was sitting on the outskirts of a village. No! He had to get to Terry. Get him out.

His heart pounded louder as he inched his way forward. He started to push himself to his feet when he saw a figure outlined against the silvery sky. He retreated again. He moved one small branch for a peephole. More forms were running into the semilight of dawn. He could hear distant shouts, staccato chattering. He fingered the radio, transmitting once more. His lips were moving, but no sound followed. His ears strained for the sound of aircraft—any aircraft. The minutes were endless as the sun climbed relentlessly. He could now see the paddy clearly. Villagers were clotted close to the chute. He could see that some carried small arms while others held hoes and spades.

His body, wet and sore, was shaking uncontrollably. His mind fired messages in fragments. Run! Hide! Got to get out! Help! Oh, Jesus, Terry, Blessed Mother of God.

He heard it. The drone of piston engines. He pressed the button on his radio and held it down. Someone up there had to know he was still here—alive. He pulled at the wet vegetation and eyed the rice paddy. Some of the villagers were running, running toward the jungle and cover. One small group remained near the chute. What were they doing? Some kind of dance? He watched as they raised their arms high, swung them in an arc. He blinked, wiped the sweat from his eyes, and caught a flash of silver in the morning sun. He looked back at the chute. One villager held something high in the air. They weren't dancing. It was a game! They were playing a ball game! He watched as the ball waved in the air, then fell to the ground. The sound of the pistons grew louder, then deafening. The remaining villagers started to run as the Skyraider swooped overhead.

"Diamond Five-One-Two, this is Dacron One-Niner. We're on you. Authenticity time. Who's your favorite jazz player?"

"Don Shirley!"

"And who backs up Ray Charles?"

"The Rayettes!"

"Stay put. We're gonna secure this area."

The sound of the jets coming in blended with that of the retreating pistons. He dove for cover under the cross points of two fallen trees. His hands dug in the soil as the earth seemed to explode. White on white, white on red, orange. The ground shook. Napalm crackled somewhere, the acrid smell burning his nostrils. He squeezed his eyes shut, moaning, moaning.

"Diamond Five-One-Two, this is Dacron One-Niner."

Somehow, he moved. He keyed the mike to reply. His voice sounded strange, not his own.

"The chopper's on the way. We think we cleared the area, but we could've missed a couple of dudes. If the chopper doesn't make it on the first try, he'll keep coming. When he lowers the penetrator, you hook on. Got it?"

"Got it."

"Let me know when the bird's right over you."

"Roger."

Smoke drifted through the air as Anthony waited. The chopper was heading in, louder and louder. Where the hell was the rotor wash? The foliage above him began to stir, bend, then lash as though driven by a hurricane.

He watched as the penetrator floated through the air.

"I'm here . . . I'm here . . . I'm here . . ."

CHAPTER

❧ 22 ❧

Delaney sat quietly, watching her mother fuss around the kitchen, lifting the lid of an iron pot, wiping the spotless counter top, straightening the coffee cups so that each handle was pointed due east. The warmth of the room was soothing, familiar, and for the first time in days, she relaxed.

Her mother had been busy since moving into the large farm house, and it showed. The walls sparkled with fresh white paint. The tile on the floor glowed with numerous coats of polyurethane, and the harvest table and chairs were now a vivid periwinkle blue. Here and there were spots of cherry red, a bowl of apples, a crockery pitcher. Gingham curtains framed the tall windows as the morning sun speckled the floor with shadows.

Delaney's mouth watered from the array of scents floating in the air. Beef stew bubbled on the stove while bread baked in the oven. On the table sat an apple pie, basking in its golden-brown glory, and the coffeepot growled as it perked, exploding the dark brown liquid into the glass top like a soft drum roll.

Delaney had arrived the night before, and thus far, Carrie Rollins had asked no questions. There would be ample time for that today. In fact, there would be ample time for anything she wanted to do for a while.

"I like the border around the ceiling, Mama," Delaney said, her eyes circling the room, lingering here and there on familiar objects. The old washtub had been converted to a planter. Aunt Dicey's battered pie safe had been scrubbed, exposing it for the genuine antique it was. She wondered why she'd never noticed the beauty in this house before. As a child, she'd simply taken the high ceilings and oversized windows for granted. And it was so large, rambling on, room after room, as each generation had built according to their needs.

"Well, it suits me just fine, Delaney," Carrie said, pouring coffee into the squat white mugs. "A little paint and a lot of scrubbing go a long way," she added, placing a pitcher of cream in front of Delaney. "Lordy, this old place has seen a lot of livin'. It's chock full of memories. And built to last. It'll be standin' when you and I aren't, that's for sure."

"What's in the cupboard?" Delaney asked, thinking of her tiny kitchen in New York.

"More canned goods."

"More?" Delaney repeated.

Carrie walked over and opened the cupboard doors. Shelves were lined with Ball jars filled with peaches, pears, jellies, jams, green beans, chow-chow, tomatoes, and Aunt Dicey's incomparable apple butter.

"This is only the tip of the iceberg. You should see what's in the basement!"

She watched her daughter cross the room and peer down the cellar steps, then disappear. Carrie knew Delaney was in trouble, and she knew better than to ask questions. Privacy was a birthright. She believed in it, and she'd raised her daughters to believe in it. Life was hard enough without everybody knowing everything. Delaney would tell her when she was ready.

The stairs creaked, and Delaney reappeared. She sat at the table and sipped coffee, unaware that Carrie was absorbing every detail of her appearance with parental clarity.

No, Carrie thought, she's not well. Her pallid face was marked by translucent blue shadows, darkening her already dark eyes. And still thin, she was much too thin. Carrie sighed inwardly, wondering what kind of food they ate in New York City. Why Delaney wanted to live there was still a puzzle to her. But then, she was always strong-willed, usually getting what she wanted. Of all her children, Delaney had been blessed the most. But Carrie did worry, for Delaney had always insisted upon swimming in the deep water. She just hoped that life hadn't swirled those waters too much. Judging from the look on her daughter's face, she feared it had already happened.

"The basement looks like Aunt Dicey was preparing for seven years of famine." Delaney smiled as she refilled her coffee cup.

"Well, you know how she was. Not that it's a bad way to be, either, Delaney. She didn't believe in wastin' anything —and I suppose I have a touch of that in my soul, too. Maybe it has to do with livin' through the Depression. Or maybe it's the nature of farmin'. But I can't seem to make an apple pie without usin' the peelin's for jelly."

Delaney laughed. "Then it's genetic, Mother. I do it, too. I wrap all the leftovers in foil and freeze them. Mary Sue called them UFO's—unidentified frozen objects."

"Hmmph. From the looks of you, I'd say you didn't eat any of them."

"Now, Mama, you've always thought I was too thin. Thin is in."

"Not in this house, Delaney Rollins. I expect you to eat and eat well."

Delaney groaned and quickly changed the subject. "I'm really going to miss Mary Sue."

"I know you will. But you'll probably get to San Francisco on business. That job of yours does keep you travelin'. I don't see any dust under your feet."

Delaney's brows pinched together as she paused before answering. "I don't think that's going to happen, Mama."

"Oh? Why not?"

"I've quit my job. I'm not going back to New York."

An unsettling quiet filled the room.

"Well," Delaney said when her mother made no comment, "aren't you going to ask why?"

"I'm just waitin' for the other shoe to fall, Delaney. You'll tell me in good time."

"I'm pregnant."

Carrie felt the blood drain from her face. "Oh, Delaney." The dish towel she was holding fell to the floor.

"I know, Mama."

Carrie sank into a chair as both scarred hands dropped in her lap. She said nothing but looked at her daughter with clear eyes, eyes filled with questions.

"It's Anthony's, isn't it?"

"Yes."

"Does he know?"

209

"No."

"And do you plan on tellin' him?"

"No."

"Where is he, Delaney?"

"He's gone back to Vietnam."

Carrie sighed. "I know you have your reasons, Delaney," she started, "but I think he should—"

"*No!* I mean, no, Mama." Delaney lowered her voice. "He shouldn't know."

Carrie looked at her blankly.

"It's very complicated. I don't think it would matter. He's been different since his last tour of duty. I can't reach him. He doesn't seem to care about anything, not even himself, and if he can't do that, he sure won't care about a baby."

"If you knew that, why didn't you do something to prevent it?"

It was Delaney's turn to sigh. "I was careless. It was an accident. But that's only part of the truth. I guess, somewhere deep down, I wanted it to happen. Maybe I thought it would make a difference, give me something to break through to him. I love him so much, Mama." Her voice broke.

"And you thought love would be enough, didn't you?" Carrie reached across the table and took Delaney's hand.

Tears filled Delaney's eyes. "I know you've been through this once with Teresa. I hate that it's happened again, but I considered abortion, and I just can't do it."

"I don't want you worryin' about me. Not at a time like this, Delaney. Besides, I'm not as naïve as you might think. It's one of the risks when you raise four daughters. Love is a powerful force. It can drive you to do the impossible and, sometimes, the unspeakable. It's the most powerful force in life, and it can be the most painful. I tried to warn you girls." She halted, shaking her head. "Obviously, I didn't try hard enough."

"Oh, Mama!" Delaney's voice rose. "Don't blame yourself. There's nobody to blame but me. I did it."

"Not by yourself, you didn't!" Carrie snapped.

And Delaney laughed.

"Besides," Carrie huffed, ignoring Delaney's laughter, "only one can do the carrying."

"I know, Mama, and I'm not laughing at the situation. But what you said was funny." The smile faded from her face as she continued hesitantly, "I thought maybe you'd tell me who handled the adoption for Teresa."

"I don't know about that, Delaney. I mean, I'll tell you his name, but I want you to give it a lot of thought. You know what givin' up a baby did to Teresa. That was your daddy's decision, and I went along with it. He was worried about the shame. In fact, I think he was more concerned with shame than he was with Teresa." She lowered her eyes. "Deep down, I thought it was wrong. But the only doctor doin' abortions in these parts was no more than a butcher, and I wasn't willin' to go that way either. What I'm sayin' is I want you to be sure. If you don't want this baby, and you've definitely ruled out abortion"—she raised her eyes—"you have, haven't you?"

"I think so."

"Well, then you must search your heart, Delaney. But I think you should know my feelings. I don't want to lose another grand baby. I'll have to accept whatever you decide, but I want you to keep it."

"But, Mama, there will be talk. This is a small town."

Carrie nodded. "Talk is nothing but talk. Besides, I have a feeling you wouldn't be here unless you'd already considered that. You need to protect the baby, Delaney. That's what's important. I don't care much what people say or think, but I don't want that baby bein' called names." She halted, her eyes skimming Delaney's face. "You say that young man's gone back to war? Well, what if he never comes back?"

"Mama! Don't even say that!"

"You're not catchin' my drift, Delaney. I don't mean Anthony. I mean a *husband*. Suppose you're married and you've come home to have this baby while he goes back to do whatever he does, and suppose something happens to him. It seems to me bein' a widow is better than not bein' married at all. And in this part of the country, nobody checks records. Too many babies are born at home, and nobody bothers with birth certificates. I'm only thinkin' of the baby."

"How did you know I'd decided to keep it?"

"I'm your mother, Delaney. I guess I know you as well as anybody could." She eyed Delaney for a moment. "Besides, you're a bright girl, and I have a feelin' I'm not tellin' you somethin' you haven't already thought of."

"It's crossed my mind."

Carrie smiled knowingly. "You always was good at stories, Delaney. But this is more than a story. It's a deliberate lie, and you never were good at lies."

"Oh, but I am, Mama. If I have a good reason, I can lie well."

"Now, that's somethin' I didn't know," Carrie said, raising her eyebrows.

"That's because I never lied to you. And besides, it's probably the only thing you don't know about me."

"At this moment, there's a lot I don't know. Like, what's your husband's name, and where's he from? How long have you been married? Things like that. I want to make sure our stories are straight. We can't afford no mistakes, Delaney."

"Okay, Mama. His name is David Anderson. He's from Chicago. I met him in New York. I married him the week before he shipped out. He has no family except for an elderly aunt. He's tall and blond. And he's a marine."

"That'll do just fine, Mrs. Anderson. Now I'm going to fix you a big lunch, and you can tell me all about Anthony." She saw the pain register on Delaney's face. "You need to tell it, and I need to know, Delaney."

"Why, Mother? It's over, and—"

"Because you need to say it—once. And then you need to forget it. Never think of it again. You need to put it in a room somewhere in your mind, then shut the door and lock it. This David Anderson has to replace Anthony, Delaney, if you want people to believe you."

"But I've already done that, Mama. I don't understand the reason for—"

"Because you never know what's going to happen, Delaney. One other person needs to know the truth, and I'm gonna be that person. After you eat, I want you to tell me." She pulled a skillet from the cabinet and placed it on the stove. Suddenly, she stood quite still. "A baby. That'll be nice, Delaney. This house needs children again."

As Carrie glided back and forth across the kitchen floor a truth, warm and comforting, revealed itself. Delaney saw this place and her mother in a new and brilliant light. She had fled from these mountains, fled from Valhalla because she had confused education with wisdom. She had mistaken poverty for poverty of spirit. The mountain dialect had embarrassed her. It had signaled stupidity. Yet here was this woman, her mother, full of wisdom, gentleness,

213

and strength. How many others had she cut from her life for the same reasons? She would not make the same mistake again.

Delaney rose, crossed the tile floor, and put her arms around her mother.

"I love you, Mama."

"Why, I love you, too, honey. And don't you ever forget it."

"I won't, Mama. I won't." She knew she was exactly where she should be.

CHAPTER

❧ 23 ❧

As night closed in, the sky swept the mountains in a graduated haze—blue to violet to purple. The last leaves of autumn spun in the wind, clinging stubbornly to life. The air, cold and damp, numbed Delaney's face as she crossed the pasture and took the path that snaked down to the creek. A startled squirrel scurried past, its thick tail arched high in a question mark.

During the two months she'd been home, her shape had already changed. She touched her thickened waistline. It seemed the body of a stranger, or at least one to which she could not claim exclusivity. Her privacy had been invaded absolutely. One body, shared ownership.

It had been a hard eight weeks. Outside of the usual morning sickness, which in her case came at night, she was passing through an emotional maelstrom that could only be described as mourning. And in the depths of one sleepless night after another, she'd come to a decision. The only way she could deal with thoughts of Anthony was to pretend he was dead. She could do that—would do that until she believed it herself. For he was dead to her.

And she'd had to face Teresa. She reassured herself that Teresa had been through a pregnancy and maybe that experience would cushion the moral platitudes Delaney had been sure Teresa would spew. But Teresa's reaction had surprised her. In fact, it had amazed her.

"You have to keep it!" Teresa had said, her eyes bearing witness to her words. "I know what it's like to carry a baby all those months and then give it away. Somethin' had hold of me hard while that child grew in my body. And it was shakin' me from the inside out. And there wasn't no way it could let go or I could get away from it. Me and that somethin' was stuck! And I'm still stuck!

"I don't care who says what about what. What counts is what's right for you, Delaney! And I know it sounds foolish, but we're more alike than you'll ever know. We been raised by the same parents. Taught the same rules. Just look at what givin' up my baby done to my life. You think you're stronger than me, but you're wrong, Delaney." Teresa paused for breath as Delaney stared in astonishment.

Teresa's shoulders dropped as she shook her head violently. "I don't care if you lie till you're buried six feet under. Invent all the husbands you need. If you keep that baby, I'll lie for you. Jesus will have to understand."

And from that point on she'd hovered over Delaney like a mother hen. "You had your milk yet? . . . Did you take your vitamins? . . . You ought to go for a walk. . . . Exercise and fresh air are good for you!"

Delaney smiled to herself. It was almost as though Teresa had been given a second chance, and she intended to see that everything was perfect.

The path took a sudden turn, and Delaney heard the creek crying as water spilled over jutting rock. When she reached the creek bed, the sound increased, roaring in her ears as water fought to find its level. That's what she had to do. Find her level and stay there. Chilled, she stuffed her hands into her jacket pockets and felt the letter—Leo's letter. She seated herself on a flat rock and, in the failing light, reread it.

My Dear Delaney,

How you are missed! In case you had any doubt, I thought I would begin with that understatement, for you have left a void in both my personal and my business life that is equivalent to a black hole. Until now, I had always believed that nobody should be irreplaceable in a business (in fact, I still do), but I must confess that even though she tries, Ann Evans is not Delaney Rollins. Perhaps those are just deserts for trying to find someone similar. Dark hair and dark eyes do not a Delaney make. So I have decided that next time, if there is a next time, I will hire a tall, busty blond.

I also want to relieve your mind about any speculation concerning your resignation. Everyone accepts the fact that you are off to marry a young man in South Carolina.

I will be in Atlanta next month on business, and I would like to drive to that secluded valley of yours and take you to dinner—or even better, enjoy some of that hospitality you southerners are reputed to dispense. Is that hint broad enough?

Don't worry about how you look. I belong to that peculiar breed of men who find pregnant women absolutely alluring—particularly if the woman was alluring to begin with.

Don't say no. You have a month to think it over. I want to help, Delaney, even if it just means being a friend. I remain,

Faithfully,
Leo

Delaney refolded the letter, stood, and started up the steep incline, carefully picking her way. She would have to hurry in order to reach home before total darkness. Mr. Longmire's redbone hound began to bay at the new moon, now cresting the tops of the trees.

Why couldn't she love Leo? His heart was full of goodness, and his mind was clear. There was never any doubt about where he stood. Anthony flashed through her head. Immediately, she cordoned off his image and erased it. No. She wouldn't allow Leo to come. It would do him no good and might even hurt him in the long run. Besides, he'd try to offer her money again, in spite of the fact that she truly didn't need it. Carrie had banked every dime that she'd sent home. It was all in that savings-account book. Seven thousand dollars in black and white. She'd be able to pay both the doctor and hospital bills and still have enough for a layette and any other items the baby would need.

A light began to flicker down the path ahead of her. Slowly, it grew closer, and Delaney recognized the vague outline of Teresa.

"Delaney Rollins! Don't you dare go walkin' this late at night again! Don't you know you could trip, knock yourself on the head, and lie there without nobody findin' you? You know people have disappeared without a trace in these mountains—and that's a mortal fact!"

"There's no need for horror stories, Teresa. If it upsets you, I won't do it again."

"You just better not! You don't have enough sense to fill a flea's weskit pocket! Why, folks say there's wild boars roamin' these mountains. Now let's get home. Supper's waitin'."

Waiting. That's what everything was all about. Ripples on ripples, wave on wave. And now, it would never end.

CHAPTER

❧ 24 ❧

"Lord, Mama. She's doin' it every night!"

"I know, Teresa," Carrie replied in a whisper. "But keep your voice down. She'll hear you."

"Well, I don't see why I should keep my voice down when she's keepin' me up half the night." Teresa leaned wearily against the kitchen counter. "I didn't mean that, Mama. I know she's pregnant and needs her rest. It's just that I'm tired today." She hesitated, drying her wet hands. "Do you think all that moanin' and wailin' is ever goin' to stop?"

"Everything stops, Teresa. Even the Bible says, 'It came to pass.' I don't believe it ever says, 'It came to stay.'" She grinned wickedly at her daughter.

"Mama! Shame on you! Why, that's almost sacrilegious," Teresa chided, unable to restrain her own smile. "Seriously, Mama, sometimes when I listen to that hollering and screaming, I think she's losing her mind."

"Everybody loses his mind when dreaming, Teresa. The lucky ones find it again when they wake up."

"Maybe so. But it don't help a body get any sleep around here."

Which wasn't quite true. For the dreams were not a nightly occurrence. If they had been, Delaney would never have slept. She could control her conscious mind with implacable will. But her subconscious erupted like a wild animal too long chained. When freed, it turned on her.

The dreams were sporadic. And they were always about Anthony.

She would sit up in bed, her body trembling, still caught in the mind-set of the dream, trying to determine what was real and what wasn't, and ultimately deciding that it made no difference. At that moment, the reality was as intolerable as the nightmare. In the deepest part of the night, she would weep, the remembrance of the dream battering her sensibilities, for the images of Anthony were too real, too vivid.

And when Delaney moaned aloud, it was a sound that pierced Carrie's heart. It was a keening of the sort that she'd only heard once or twice in her lifetime and hoped fervently that she would never hear again. She would rush to Delaney's bedroom door, listening until her ears ached. And then Carrie would be unable to sleep herself.

On such nights, Carrie would rack her brain, trying to imagine what the future held for her daughters. They were both young. Their whole lives were ahead of them. How could they get on moled up in this old farmhouse like two wounded birds? They both deserved better. What had she done or left undone that had contributed to this unholy mess? Had she left off some necessary bit of knowledge, something so essential that her daughters were not equipped to cope with life? Poor Teresa, swallowing religion like an opiate, and Delaney, her joy child, wasting all that education, all that imagination for what? Barnyard chickens?

She wished for John. She needed his warmth, the feel of his body. Loneliness was a killing thing. How she had loved him! Loved him enough to allow him to have the lead, never making waves about any of his decisions. A chill ran over her body, and she pulled the covers tightly to her neck. Maybe that was the problem. Maybe she should have spoken up, spoken up about Teresa's baby. But she'd taken the easy way, the way she'd been taught all her life. The man is the head of the house. Always right. Well, as much as she loved John, he wasn't right about that baby —and he wasn't right about allowing Delaney to rush pell-mell through school as if education was all that mattered to a child.

She should have told her daughters of her feelings for John. How strong they were. And how he'd loved her back. She and John had been so busy struggling to survive that they'd failed to teach their daughters about love. Like what to do with a broken heart. Now it was clear. Her daughters had only witnessed the floundering. They were unaware of the rewards, such as the depth of love she and John had shared.

She sat up in bed. She must do something. She had to convince both Delaney and Teresa that love didn't always hurt. She had to break through that awful barrier Delaney had wrapped around herself. And Teresa had to learn to live *this* life while she was alive instead of hiding in promises of a life to come.

The task seemed enormous. Too enormous for her alone. In the darkness, Carrie's lips began to move.

CHAPTER

❧ 25 ❧

I have something to say to both of you."

There was an odd tone in Carrie's voice, and it caught Teresa and Delaney off guard.

"The dishes can wait." Carrie pushed her chair away from the table and eyed first Delaney, then Teresa.

"What is it, Mama? Have I done something wrong?"

"No, no, Teresa. You haven't done nothin' wrong. Least not that I know of. Why would you ask such a thing?"

"Because," Delaney answered, "when we were small, that tone of voice spelled trouble."

"Looks to me like the two of you have enough trouble without imagining more."

Teresa's head snapped in Carrie's direction. Delaney's lips parted, then closed as she and Teresa exchanged a look of surprise. Neither spoke. The clock ticked loudly.

"What do you mean we've got trouble?" Teresa demanded.

"Nothing in particular and most things in general, Teresa. I want the two of you to talk. And I'm gonna tell you what to talk about. Neither of you is leavin' this kitchen until I say so. Understood?"

Now Teresa's mouth opened, but Delaney shot her a look of warning, and she closed her mouth in a stubborn line.

"I said, understood?" Carrie repeated.

"We understand, Mama," Delaney nodded. "At least I do," she added tentatively.

"Well, maybe Delaney understands, but I don't." Teresa chafed. "You're talkin' to us like we're five years old. Now, let's see. You want me to talk to Delaney. So, Delaney, how are you?"

"There's no need to get your back up, Teresa. I said I'd tell you what to talk about, and as a matter of fact, it is about how both of you are."

Teresa scowled as Delaney sat quietly.

"Now," Carrie said when both her daughters were staring at her intently, "Teresa, I want you to tell Delaney about being pregnant." She shook her head sideways as Teresa opened her mouth again. "I mean it, Teresa. I want you to tell her how it happened, why it happened, and how you felt about it. Don't leave out nothin'."

Teresa came out of her chair. "Mama! Why? You know I never talk about it."

"That's exactly why, Teresa. I think you need to tell it, and I think it'll help Delaney. Sometimes all we've got to go on is what we learn from each other. Tell her."

Slowly, Teresa sat down. She glanced at Delaney as the red in her face deepened. With one hand she began to brush the crumbs on the table into a small pile. She knew, from Carrie's voice, that there would be no respite. She was seeking words as she began to speak. Her voice was slow, and her eyes were glued to the small mountain of crumbs she was collecting.

"I was only sixteen, Delaney. And you were a little kid. I never gave much thought to the future then. I just sorta let things happen. You know how it was." She paused and looked at her sister. "No, that's not true, for you weren't anything like me at sixteen." Her eyes glazed as she drifted back in time. "I was interested in two things. Looking pretty and boys. I'm not a brain like you, Delaney. I hated school. Couldn't wait to get out. I knew as soon as I graduated I'd get a job at the mill, and that was as far as I could see.

"Wally Galyon started hangin' around all the time, and I was plumb swept off my feet. I thought he was the handsomest thing that ever come down the pike. He was so big, so full of himself, all that dark hair and them big brown eyes. Well, he just took my breath away, which probably wasn't hard to do, considerin' how empty-headed I was. One thing led to another, and before I knew it, I was meetin' him on a regular basis, and we were . . ." She shifted uncomfortably in her chair. "We were real close. I was so dumb! I thought he was takin' care of everything. He told me he was. He told me there was no chance I'd get pregnant, and I believed him. I found out the hard way he wasn't doin' nothin' to stop it.

"There I was. Sixteen and scared to death. I told Wally about it, and he said he didn't believe he was the father. He said it had to be someone else, 'cause he was using precautions. I didn't know if he was or not, I was so stupid." Teresa's voice fell as she paused for breath. "Finally, after

I'd cried till I felt like I had no more tears, he said he'd sell one of his guns and pay for the abortion, but I had to tell Mama and Daddy. Abortion was serious then, and the only doctor doin' it had a bad reputation. Wally said if anything went wrong, he didn't want to be responsible. And he told me that if my daddy came lookin' for him, he'd have two or three of his friends swear they'd been with me, too. Mama, do I have to go on?"

Carrie held firm. "I have a reason, Teresa. Yes, you have to tell it all."

Delaney could stand it no longer. "I don't see why," she blurted angrily.

"Delaney, just listen. For once in your life, just listen."

Delaney bit her lower lip as she resigned herself to Carrie's will. But she still didn't see the point.

Teresa's eyes were now bright, glittering with unshed tears. She lifted her face to Carrie with one last look of supplication, then stumbled on.

"At first, Daddy considered the abortion, particularly since Wally'd agreed to pay for it. But it didn't take Daddy long to find out Doc Hunter was a real quack. So abortion was out. And then Daddy did something I've never understood. I'd expected him to go for Wally, and I was prepared to talk him out of it, but he didn't. Daddy told me I was just as guilty, even guiltier, for it was my responsibility as the woman to keep Wally in line." Her cheeks were now wet.

"I didn't know nothin', Delaney. If you don't know nothin', how you supposed to stop somethin'? Anyway, Mama and Daddy decided to send me to Aunt Dicey's. I was there for six months. Stayed in that upstairs bedroom the whole time. The very bedroom you're usin' now, Delaney. Nobody knew I was there, except Aunt Dicey. That was Daddy's rule, so she had no choice. She brought me all my meals, and I stayed real still when company came. Aunt Dicey found a lawyer in Greenville. And those people that got my baby paid for the hospital over there. Two days after my baby was born, that lawyer came to my room with a nurse, and they took him. I never saw him again. Then I went back to Valhalla." She paused again, bit on a fingernail, and when she spoke again, her voice hardened.

"Wally was gone. He'd joined the army. But he didn't leave before he'd told tales on me, tales that weren't true. Wally was the only one, Delaney, I swear, but he spread the word around that I was easy. That I'd begged him to do it. I took to hidin', wouldn't go anywhere. And then the preacher from my church visited. He talked to me about Mary Magdalene, and how Jesus had forgiven her, and how He'd forgive me if I'd just ask Him. Church was the only place I felt safe. And that's where I've been ever since."

A silence adjusted itself around the three women. Carrie's eyes drifted across Teresa's face, a visual caress. The window glass grew dark.

"I've made Teresa tell you all this, Delaney, because I wanted you to know you aren't the first to make a mistake of this kind, and you won't be the last. Now, both of you have a home here, for as long as you want it or need it. But you must understand there's no place safe from the world. You can hide, but the world will find you. At some point, and none of us knows when, something will happen that will force you to deal with the world again. You'll have more choices—and you'll make more mistakes. You can only hide so long before something finds you. Death found me." Now it was Carrie's time to grope for words.

"Because I loved your daddy so, I gave into most every-

227

thing he wanted. I lived where he wanted to live. Worked where he wanted to work. I thought he knew best when it came to you girls. But I was wrong. I should have spoken my mind. Told him what *I* thought. I think he would have listened. In fact, when I can't sleep at night for missin' him, I get this sense he's tryin' to tell me he could have used my help, my advice. It's lonely when you make all the decisions, particularly when those decisions affect other people." She looked directly at Delaney. "And that's what you're gettin' ready to take on when you have this baby. What I'm tryin' to say, and not doin' a good job of it, is that I did it wrong by keeping my mouth closed. Maybe if I'd helped, Teresa would still have her son. And you, Delaney, wouldn't have been so bent on leavin' so fast. You never had time to become a woman. You were too busy bein' a brain. I want both of you to know I'm sorry. There's lots of things we do in the name of love, but givin' up what you know is right and true—givin' up your free-dom, your very soul—ain't right." Carrie's words dangled in the air.

"Teresa, losin' that baby wasn't the end of your life, although you thought it was. And havin' this one ain't the beginnin' of yours, Delaney. It's what you do from now on that counts." She stopped, letting her words sink in. "And plannin' on doin' nothin' won't work." She stood and smiled. "Now, let's get this supper mess cleaned up."

If Delaney thought she was off the hook, she was wrong, for once the dishes were washed and put away, Carrie put on a fresh pot of coffee.

"We ain't quite through, girls."

Teresa evaded Delaney's eyes as they waited in silence.

"Tell Teresa what happened to you in New York. Tell her about Anthony."

"Mama, I think I get your point. I don't see how . . ." Her voice faltered as she caught the iron in Carrie's eyes. "Okay." She sat back and quietly gazed at Teresa. "I did the same thing you did, Teresa. I just did it in a different city with a different man at a different age."

"But you're so smart, Delaney," Teresa interjected. "All that education—"

"That's the point I'm tryin' to make," Carrie said. She looked at Delaney. "Teresa thinks that you're different. She thinks because you know so much that somehow you have a better handle on emotions than she does. Tell her, Delaney."

Delaney reached across the table and covered Teresa's hand with her own. "Don't believe it, Teresa. Not for one minute. I fell in love just like you. I believed in someone just like you. And, obviously, I gave no more thought to the future than you did. And here we both are. Tucked our tails and came running home. Is that what you want, Mama? The common denominator?"

Carrie sighed deeply. "The common denominator is that the mind don't have much control over the heart. You've both been hurt, and been hurt bad. Maybe you can help each other heal. I don't know if either of you will choose to have a man help you through this life. Maybe I was lucky that I did."

Two sets of eyes registered surprise.

"I know, I know. I can see how it looked to you kids, like John and I were just two old workhorses, gettin' through each day the best we could. And that's true. But, oh, my dears, the nights."

Delaney watched her mother's face in amazement. In her eyes, Delaney could see the reflection of a past about which she knew nothing, nothing of importance. Slowly, a realization began to crystallize. What she had seen as a struggle for survival had been accompanied by a celebration of life. Her parents had *loved* each other—and Carrie wanted her to know it.

"When it comes to choices of the heart, all of us are vulnerable. There's no guarantees. Sometimes you win. I did. I want you to remember that. Now, we won't speak of this again. It's forgotten. From here on out, it's up to you."

Delaney watched her mother's back as she passed through the doorway. Her mind was a backwash of memories. How many times had she looked at her parents and discounted everything they stood for? How many times had she looked at Carrie and never really seen her?

CHAPTER

❧ 26 ❧

He came to town on rare occasions. He would appear at the hardware store, the single grocery store, or the bank, tersely state his business, then vanish into the hills. Sometimes he wouldn't be seen for weeks at a time, for Joe Harmon was a loner, a solitary man.

Joe's arrival in Cushing went relatively unnoticed for a while, for the month was July, and he melted into the ranks of the Floridians who swelled the summer population. He became more conspicuous when summer faded, for, unlike the Floridians, Joe stayed.

Although that made him something of an oddity, it was an oddity the local inhabitants understood. Joe was not the first to seek solitude in these hills, nor would he be the last, but that fact did not preclude his being the object of a brief but curious speculation.

The pharmacist who filled Joe's one prescription, a mild

sleeping pill, finally asked the mayor, who also happened to be the town's premier real-estate salesman, why Joe Harmon had settled so far back in the hills.

"Where's that Harmon feller from?" The pharmacist adroitly posed the question so that it appeared to be a product of idle conversation or boredom rather than of a chronic case of nosiness, with which he was severely afflicted.

"Not sure," answered the mayor, adopting a similar tone. "But he's not one of them Florida Yankees. He hails from somewhere in the south, though. Sounds just like you or me, when he talks, that is." The mayor reached across the counter and plunked a pair of magnifying glasses on his nose. "Need me another pair," he stated woefully. "I just can't seem to keep up with eyeglasses." He studied himself in the mirror as he went on. "Joe showed up in my office last summer with a pocket full of cash." The mayor clicked his teeth. "It's unusual for a man to carry that much cash these days." The mayor gave a chuckle as he reached for a second pair of glasses. "Except maybe Simon."

The pharmacist laughed out loud. "Well, you're right about that. Old Simon's always got money to burn." For a second or two both men shook their heads, thinking of Simon and how he roamed around town, talking, mostly to himself, and buying strange items that he paid for with Monopoly money. Billie Orr said she saw Simon fish that Monopoly money out of her trash can, but since Simon fished through trash cans on a regular basis, she thought nothing of it. It had been a bit of a problem when Simon first tried to pay for his Bazooka bubble gum and Orange Crushes with that phony money, but arguments proved useless. Now, everyone just took the money and billed Simon's daughter.

"Well, at least Joe ain't as weird as Simon."

"That's true, but then hardly anyone's as weird as Simon."

The pharmacist nodded his agreement.

"Anyway, as I was sayin', that Harmon feller bought the Yearwood place. Made me an offer the minute he laid eyes on it." The mayor snorted his disbelief. "I'd been tryin' to unload that piece of land for three years, ever since old man Yearwood died, but it's so dad-blamed isolated nobody wanted it. Even those damn-fool summer people drew the line at fordin' two creeks after a good thunderstorm. You think these glasses suit me?"

"I think they do just fine," the pharmacist agreed affably. Later he would tell his wife how silly the mayor looked in a pair of rimless half-lenses, but a sale was a sale.

"Yep," the mayor rambled on. "Joe Harmon, he liked it just fine. Nice-lookin' young man, but not much for talkin'. Bet he didn't say twenty words to me. But his money sure talked." The mayor grinned, then clicked his false teeth back in place.

Irma Lee Watson, who ran the one and only restaurant open year-round, speculated about Joe Harmon in different terms and for different reasons. After all, any female in her right mind would wonder about a man that looked like Joe.

When Joe first came to town, he'd eaten at the Country Kitchen twice, and Irma had fluttered and preened like a Rhode Island Red—at least that's what Bubba Howe told Andy Davis the next day.

"You wouldn't have believed it if you'd seen it yourself," he said to Andy. When Irma heard, she was mad as hell and refused to refill his coffee for a whole week. She told her sister that Bubba Howe was a damned fool who ought to mind his own business.

She also told her sister about Joe Harmon.

"His hair looks kinda like a cross between brown and gold, all mixed up together. It's a mite too long for my taste, but a trip to the barber would straighten that right out. Take that hippie look away from him and you'd have yourself a real handful!" She giggled as she sipped her Dr Pepper. "He looks like an eagle would look if an eagle were a person. Oh, I know that don't sound so good, but it *is!* Believe me, if the sight of him don't set your blood to racin', you might as well be dead!"

What she didn't tell her sister was how Joe had ignored her. Looked straight through her as though she was a ghost or something. She'd flashed him her best smile, cut loose with her sultriest walk (the one that never failed to snag an occasional truck driver), but he'd turned a disinterested pair of eyes at her in a glance that damned near leveled Irma.

"Lord, that man is sexy," Irma Lee giggled anew. "And I do mean sexy!"

Once the curiosity regarding Cushing's newest resident subsided—and it was short-lived, for Joe was rarely seen—Joe settled into an undisturbed life. And he liked it that way. It was as though he'd intuitively known that the mountain tradition, which still tolerated eccentricity, would certainly respect privacy. Joe was right.

Joe's cabin was set high on one steep slope at the head of a valley. There was a one-lane dirt road that led directly to Joe's front door, but it was barely visible from the two-lane, particularly if a person happened to blink while cruising by. And someone, some other long dead and long forgotten recluse had planted a row of hemlocks that almost swallowed the front of the cabin if some adventurous tourist did happen by.

After moving in, Joe had made one trip to the furniture

store and one trip to the lumber yard. Alone, he'd unloaded his purchases: one La-Z-Boy recliner, one mattress, one table lamp, and some heart-pine lumber. He set to work and built his own table, and he was working on a chair— only one.

His solitude was complete, the exceptions being the roosters that crowed at dawn, the baying of the hounds at night, and the raucous cawing of the crows during the day. The only human contact he had was with his own reflection while shaving—which was once a week—and even then, the face that stared back was immutable. Joe wasn't friendly even to himself.

He let the silence of the mountains settle around him like a cocoon and found himself needing his sleeping pills less and less as he tried to forget such things as body bags.

In the mornings, Joe liked to sit at his kitchen table, which was placed strategically by the front window. There he would drink strong coffee and watch the fog lift from the valley below. He kept a strong pair of binoculars by his cup, using them to home in on a doe, a hawk, a rabbit, or whatever wild thing happened to roam into his line of vision. And sometimes he'd see a human figure, too, although he never intentionally meant for that to happen. It was always some female wandering in and out of the large, rambling farmhouse that sat at the foot of the valley. Although he wasn't sure how or when he absorbed the information, he knew the place was inhabited only by women. As best he could figure, there were three of them, but his lack of interest and curiosity carried his speculations no further. It was quite by accident that he actually met one.

He'd been to town, an experience that did nothing to heighten Joe's good spirits, and he'd come upon that battered blue truck smack in the middle of the narrow dirt road. There was no getting around her and no reason to back up. He cut the engine and sat behind the steering wheel, cursing low under his breath.

The woman was struggling with a flat tire, pumping the jack for all she was worth. She'd lifted her head, looked at him with clear blue eyes, then gone back to her task, as if he weren't there at all. Which happened to be Joe's wish, too. He sighed irritably, got out, leaned against the fender of his own truck, and waited.

"Sorry," Carrie murmured, twisting the wrench and her mouth simultaneously. "I'll be out of your way in a minute."

That was it. She hadn't smiled helplessly. She hadn't asked for anything. And she was doing a damned good job.

"You must be Joe Harmon," she said, not lifting her eyes.

"Yeah," Joe mumbled.

"Thought so. I'm Carrie Rollins. We have the adjoining farm." She pulled at the spare, lifting it into place.

"Here," he said. He made a move toward her, but she stopped him flat.

"That's not necessary." Her words came in puffs as she fought with the tire, which in Joe's estimation looked as bad as the flat.

Joe halted. Ah, hell, he thought to himself, and he strode to her side. With one hand he lifted the spare. In silence he knelt beside her and placed it on the rim. She handed him her wrench, then stood, never saying a word while he finished.

As he tossed the worthless tire into the back of her truck she climbed under the steering wheel. With a slight wave of her hand, she gunned the engine and was gone.

The basket was sitting on his doorstep the next evening.

She must have left it while he was hunting, for he'd heard nothing. Inside were two loaves of homemade bread, three jars of peach preserves, a quart of chicken and dumplings, still warm, and an apple pie. There was no note.

He grumbled. But he ate it all.

For several days he worried that she might come calling, and the last thing he wanted was some female buzzing in and out of his private domain. But she didn't. And in spite of his fear, and without any conscious thought, he began to observe the Rollins farm on a regular basis.

Through his binoculars, Joe had world and time enough to know them all. The women formed an abstract pattern as they moved in and out of the house and around the farm. The older one, the one he'd met, seemed to work from dawn till dusk, roaming in and out of the storage sheds or the weather-beaten barn. Another one came and went with a timing he could have set his watch by—if he hadn't thrown his watch away. Sunday morning, Sunday night, and, regular as a heartbeat, Wednesday evening. A Bible thumper, Joe thought. The kind of female he'd grown up with and wanted no part of. Then there was that little one, the one he'd seen splitting kindling. The axe seemed almost as big as she was, but grudgingly he'd admitted to himself that she was doing an adequate job. And Joe was okay with everything he was seeing, until the morning he realized the little one was pregnant. Something began to gnaw at Joe's conscience.

Maybe that was the reason he'd dropped off a load of firewood when he knew they were gone.

In return, he'd received another basket—this time country ham, sweet potatoes, and pecan pie. Again, he fumed that he'd opened himself for some kind of gratitude that would necessitate conversation. But he was wrong.

A pattern developed. One that managed not to offend Joe's privacy and that proved beneficial to all four parties. Joe found himself tending to chores around the farm that he considered too much for the women, but only when they weren't at home, and the food began to appear on a regular basis.

The days passed with uniformity, one piling on top of the other as the weather chilled, then froze. Joe stoked his fire more frequently and gazed through his binoculars at the frost on the meadow below him. The door to the farmhouse opened, and the small one emerged and headed for the woodpile.

"Crazy woman," Joe fumed aloud. "Goin' out in this weather with no coat on." Although Joe didn't know it, a major breakthrough had occurred. He was suddenly swept back into the world of humanity. He cared what happened to another human being.

CHAPTER

❧ 27 ❧

I t's mine!"

"No! It's not. Joe bought it for me!" Adam screamed. His small face reddened as he tugged at the Tonka truck.

"You kids stop right now!" Teresa ordered, dropping the knife she'd been using to cut beef cubes for the stew. "Ain't we got enough confusion in this kitchen without you two fighting over everything in this world?"

Abigail rolled her eyes in Aunt Teresa's direction, a tiny smile tilting her mouth as she abruptly released the truck. The smile grew as Adam, unprepared for the release, tumbled to the floor. He began to wail, and Abigail eyed him with diabolical satisfaction.

"Now see what you've done?" Teresa chided. Kneeling beside Adam, she cradled him against her breast. "Aren't you ashamed?"

Abigail thought about it. "No," she answered, her six-year-old face set in innocence.

"Abigail! I'm surprised at you!" Teresa rocked Adam gently as his muffled sobs continued. Only Abigail saw him open one eye to peek at the frown on Aunt Teresa's brow before he turned up the volume of his wails.

"There, there, honey," Teresa crooned.

"It isn't fair!" Abigail shouted, incensed from being ignored. Her blue eyes blazed, and her chin jutted in the air.

"It *is* fair!" Adam yelled back, breaking Teresa's hold. He took two steps and stood belly to belly with Abigail. "Joe gave that truck to *me!* Besides, you're a girl, and girls don't play with trucks!"

"Who said?" Abigail demanded as Delaney stepped through the swinging doors separating the kitchen from the dining room. Delaney stood stock still, glaring at the twins. Tendrils of blond hair stuck to Abigail's face. Her cheeks held twin red spots. Adam's eyes were glued to the floor. Delaney smoothed his dark hair as she gazed down at Abigail.

"What's going on here?"

"Adam won't let me play with his truck, Mama! He says girls don't play with trucks!"

"It's true, Mama! Joe gave it to me, and he told me girls don't like trucks! He gave *her* a doll! And she threw it out her bedroom window! Now she wants *my* truck, and she can't have it!"

Delaney's mouth twisted with frustration. No matter how many times she'd told Joe to make sure the gifts were identical, he didn't listen. He was still a dyed-in-the-wool chauvinist, and none of her arguments had dented his tough hide.

"Even Joe can be wrong," she said wearily. She placed a

hand in the center of both small backs and guided the twins to the kitchen table.

"Delaney," Teresa called from the back door, "Mr. Johnson's here with four bushels of okra. Can we use it?"

Mentally, Delaney computed. Okra, okra. Yes, they could use it. What was left over could be canned for next winter. "Yes, Teresa," she called over her shoulder. "We can use them all."

"Mrs. Anderson, how many hams you want us to cook tomorrow?" The question came from one of the cooks, Millie Morgan. Although she'd posted a schedule for each day based upon an estimate of diners, Millie couldn't read, and she couldn't remember the schedule either.

"Four, Millie. On Thursdays we cook four. Then we use what's left over for the casserole on Friday." She turned her attention back to the twins. Abigail faced her defiantly as Adam concentrated on a nicked spot in the table. His chubby brown legs protruded from his shorts, dangling loosely. As the twins grew, so did their squabbles. How had her mother tolerated four children when she could barely handle two?

Her head pounded. The noise level in the kitchen seemed deafening, and it was only nine in the morning. Dishes jangled and oven doors slammed. And there was the constant bickering among the cooks, most of it harmless, but nevertheless loud.

In spite of the air conditioning, the temperature was already eighty degrees. At least the dining rooms were cool enough. She rubbed her head, wishing for November. Sweet November, when they closed for the winter.

"Upstairs. Both of you," she ordered. "I can't hear myself think." She herded the twins up the steps and into the relative quiet and cool of her bedroom. Abigail and Adam scurried onto her bed and turned contrasting eyes in her direction.

Again, she was astounded that they were so different. It was almost as though she and Anthony had been replicated, only Nature had muddied the waters by changing the sexes. Anthony's eyes sat in Abigail's small face. Violently blue under dark lashes, they were mirrors to Abigail's stormy interior, reflecting each nuance of her mind. Adam's eyes, on the other hand, were deep brown, almost mahogany, sometimes opaque. They were like dark pools where all his emotions could hide.

"Abbie," she began, "how many times have I told you not to fight?"

"I don't know, Mommy." Her small, dirty hand traced the flowers crocheted in the coverlet.

"And you, Adam. How many times have I told you to share?"

"Two?"

"More than two, Adam."

"But Uncle Joe said . . ."

"I know what your Uncle Joe says. And Joe and I disagree on this subject. It is perfectly acceptable for girls to play with trucks. And it's acceptable for boys to have a doll. There will be, at least in this house, no toys for boys and toys for girls. Do you understand me?"

"Yes, ma'am."

"And you, Abigail?"

"Yes, ma'am."

"I don't want this to happen again. Now go downstairs, get the truck, and both of you go outside. Fetch one of Grandma's hand shovels from the tool shed and build a road. Build a bridge . . . together! And no more fighting, at least not until dinner hour is over." If it's ever over, she thought as the twins grinned at each other and scuttled down the stairs.

Five minutes. She'd take five minutes to rest her head on that inviting pillow before she returned to the kitchen. Who would have thought that turning the lower part of the house into a restaurant would have been such a success? They'd opened with one small dining room, and the business had grown like a mushroom. Now, during tourist season, she felt buried in food, or dishes, or squabbles. She spent all day long putting out fires and half the night putting up food.

She rolled to her side and closed her eyes for a minute. The cotton pillow slip cooled her cheek. Every year, in August, she doubted she'd make it to November. And she doubted with equal fervor that the rest of the family would make it either. There were moments when she was convinced she'd created a monster.

She'd been desperate for a way to support the children. Something that allowed her to be with them. There wasn't a good restaurant in the area, and Carrie's comment about women cooking and cleaning until the day they died had triggered the idea. Her mother was an exceptional country cook, and Delaney had the business acumen. Teresa turned out to be surprisingly good at organizing, and the small restaurant had thrived. Diane came to help. Walls were knocked out to enlarge the dining room, and soon the first floor was completely converted. The family moved upstairs, making room for more chairs and tables. And Joe— if it hadn't been for Joe's carpentry skills, well, they never would have made it.

The local people came first, and they were the toughest critics. Then, as the word spread, the tourists followed.

After the write-up in *Southern Living,* the crowds never stopped.

"Authentic southern cooking at its best," the article had said. "Unique atmosphere . . . each dining room with its own decor, from porch swings to rattan tables. Each dish prepared from fresh produce raised mainly on the Rollins farm. Ham comes from the hogs fattened on scraps from the dining room, and eggs from the Rollins henhouse. The superb jams and jellies are all derived from the numerous varieties of berries growing on the grounds. Don't miss the Vidalia onion relish, and save room for dessert—a down-home gourmet's delight!"

From then on, they'd been swamped. Delaney's body ached from the physical exertion, and her mind reeled when she tallied the cash-register results. They weren't getting rich, but they were doing quite well.

She heard the door at the front of the steps open.

"Delaney?" It was Carrie.

"Yes, I'll be right down."

"Good. Joe's here with those three tables he repaired. He wants to know if we need them for the noon service."

"Tell him yes." Her feet slid off the bed. She glanced in the mirror of the oak washstand and smoothed her dark hair into a bun. She'd try to talk to Joe again about the twins. She didn't want Adam to be a sexist. Yes, she'd talk to Joe, for all the good it would do.

"Uncle Joe! Come see the road we're building!" Adam raced toward Joe's truck as Joe hefted a table from the tailgate of his truck.

"Got no time for that," Joe answered gruffly as Adam wrapped his arms around Joe's legs.

"When you gonna have time?"

"When I have it, that's when."

"When you have it, will you come see?"

"Yep."

"Thanks, Uncle Joe." Adam released his grip and flew across the paved parking area, disappearing around the corner of the smokehouse.

Delaney stood holding the back door open.

"Sam's coming to help you set them up, Joe." She stepped outside, her eyes drifting over the tables. "They look good. I've told Sam which dining room. Now, don't try to carry them yourself," she admonished, fussing with the strands of hair drifting around her temple.

She crossed her arms over her chest and eyed Joe steadily. It was, to him, a familiar look, and he avoided her eyes. Probably about the truck. But goddammit, boys should be boys and girls, girls. He really liked and respected Delaney. But she was wrong about this sex thing. Someone had to take that boy in hand, show him men things, even if his mother didn't like it. Anyway, he'd lost any fear he'd had that Delaney would keep him from seeing the twins because he disagreed with her. He kept what he did with Adam to himself. And Adam never breathed a word. Besides, every boy should know how to skin a squirrel and fillet a fish. All that nonsense about hunting being bad was a bunch of crap. What Delaney didn't know wouldn't hurt her. He hoisted another table from the truck, trying harder to ignore her steady gaze. Maybe it would go away.

"I don't have to say it again, do I, Joe?"

"Nope."

"Then I won't. But please try to respect my right as a parent in this regard."

"Okay." From the corner of his eye he watched her as

she stood for a second longer, then disappeared into the kitchen. He hadn't meant what he said. He knew it and she knew it. But it was okay. He worshiped the twins, would do anything for them. Anything except raise a sissy, a mama's boy. That he wouldn't do. Not even for Delaney.

"Tell us, Uncle Joe," Abigail pleaded as she snuggled her small body in the crook of his arm.

Joe leaned back against the trunk of the ginkgo tree. He chewed a blade of grass as he watched Adam push the dump truck around the curves of an imaginary road.

"I've told you that story too many times, Abbie. You know it by heart."

"Not yet, Uncle Joe. But if you tell it thirteen more times, I might know it by heart," Adam said as he scooted to Joe's feet.

Joe smiled. Adam liked numbers lately. Always counting to a hundred, his dark eyes beaming when he made it with no prompting.

"Tell us about the ice and what it looked like. We like hearing about when we got born. Please, Uncle Joe?" Abbie burrowed the back of her head into his shoulder. She smelled like soap, dirt, and shampoo. She lifted her pleading eyes to him, and he relented.

"How come you kids only like stories about yourselves?"

" 'Cause that's the best kind!" Adam said, a small cloud of dust rising as he kicked his feet in the dirt. He sat cross-legged, elbows resting on grubby knees, waiting for Joe to begin.

"Okay, okay. But this is the last time. I get tired of telling it." Adam seemed to freeze, sitting like a statue. His eyes, full of anticipation, were fixed on Joe's face.

"On the day you two were born, it was cold . . . mighty cold. But your mama was hell bent for leather to take a walk. . . ."

"Are you sure you feel like walking today?" Carrie asked anxiously. She watched Delaney don one of her father's worn jackets. It barely covered her stomach and brushed the backside of her knees. At that moment, Delaney looked like a child again—frail and vulnerable. But those qualities were deceptive. The past months had negated them. Underneath that delicate exterior was a core of tempered steel. She was coming through this pregnancy with her colors flying.

It was not only the pregnancy she was handling, for she had pulled off the deception of a husband, speaking of David with such tenderness that Carrie almost believed in his existence herself. And his "death" had lent an occasion for further privacy. Delaney simply kept to her room for a few weeks as her mother announced Delaney's widowhood, and when Delaney reappeared, she was left alone in her "grief." Seemed a shame to make use of war in such a manner, but it made Delaney's story plausible.

"Honey," Carrie repeated when Delaney didn't respond, "it's mighty cold. Are you sure you're up to it?"

"It hardly matters whether I'm up to it or not," Delaney answered. "The doctor told me to walk, and since my body seems to belong to everyone else but me right now, I might as well mind the doctor, too. Besides, I'm as uncomfortable sitting as I am walking. Might as well walk."

"You be back before evening. I wouldn't want you tripping over something. A fall could be dangerous at this stage. Don't go too far."

Delaney smiled. "You'd like it if I walked a circle in back of the house, Mama."

"Walkin's walkin'. What difference does it make where it's done?"

"It makes a difference to me. I like the scenery. Why walk in a circle when I can go to the creek?"

"Because I feel safer when I can see you. You're over eight months now, Delaney. It's time to be cautious."

"You worry too much," Delaney chided, slipping mittens over her hands.

"Hmmph! Wait till that baby's born, and we'll see about worryin'," Carrie muttered as Delaney opened the door. "I want you back here before twilight! Remember!" she called as the door thudded shut.

Delaney descended the front steps, holding tightly to the handrail. She could no longer see her feet, not even when she was in bed. But she knew they were there, for they hurt all the time. As her body inflated so had her feet, growing half a size, as though compensating for her added weight.

She felt exactly like a stuffed mushroom. A living stuffed mushroom. One more month and it would be over.

As she walked her breath formed puffs of white in the cold air. Pulling back one mitten, she glanced at her watch. Four o'clock. Plenty of time before the mountain darkness set in, shrouding the world in blackness. February nights were so long—the days so short.

Crossing the pasture, she carefully closed the gate behind her. The cows turned their heads in her direction, staring in unison, pair after pair of sad eyes. They began to low as the bell rang, calling them to the warmth of the barn. As if choreographed, they moved as one, shambling toward the east, one large shadow in the pasture. In her mind, the mushroom image vanished, replaced by a cow, shambling to the west.

As she walked she rummaged through her mind for something pleasant to remember. She tripped over Anthony's face and willed it to disappear. Leo. She would think of Leo. He'd been so kind during his visit. And his letters arrived faithfully, full of funny anecdotes about the company. Lately, he'd been hinting she should return to New York, but that was out of the question. She would not raise children in the city.

A sudden shiver shook her body. She pulled the jacket tightly around her shoulders. It was freezing, colder than she'd thought. She stepped over rocks, keenly aware of her center of gravity. Time seemed to loom ahead and behind. Back to Leo. His last letter was filled with a woman he'd met, and if instinct proved right, Leo was finally in love with someone else. Although she knew it would happen, she was surprised at her feeling of loss, for it had been comfortable knowing Leo was there. But it was time for him to marry, have children.

"Stop it, Delaney," she spoke aloud. "Feeling sorry for yourself never worked, and it won't work now."

The baby kicked her side as if for emphasis, and Delaney smiled.

"I get the message, Tiger," she whispered. "So what if your daddy wasn't normal? The one I've created for you is everything a father should be. Listen to me now, for I want you to grow up to be like your father. He's caring, loving, gentle, sensitive—all the things your real father wasn't.

No, that's not true. Your real father was sensitive, and he could be tender sometimes, but it never lasted."

A drawn smile crossed her lips. When the baby actually came, she'd say nothing about Anthony. She'd talk about David. David who was everything Anthony wasn't—except real.

She stopped short of the creek bank. No use going down the hill, for that would mean she'd have to climb back up. The water gurgled, plowing over smooth stones, smoothing them further. This was a good place to raise a child. Why hadn't she seen that when she was young? How had she missed the honesty in the people? When had she forgotten the comfort in watching the ebb and flow of nature?

She shivered again. The weak sun had vanished. Toward the west, darkness was falling. She glanced at her watch. Five fifteen. She'd stayed too long, and now she'd have to hurry. Carrie would be frantic.

The wind picked up force, now blowing wildly through the skeletal trees. Was the temperature dropping? No. It couldn't be. She quickened her pace as much as she dared, picking her way through the tangled roots of mountain laurel and sidestepping a large branch that fell in her path.

She reached the spot where the paths forked when she felt the first pelt. She glanced at the sky, roiling with thick gray, darkening by the second. Another pelt. She held out her hand and stared at the tiny ball of ice. The first wave of fear washed over her. Ice! Snow would be bad enough, but ice? She tried to remember the weather forecast. There'd been no mention of an ice storm. But the television had been off all day. She and Carrie had been busy making curtains for the nursery.

As she walked the first sheen appeared on the ground. Tree branches, bare and twisted, began to glisten.

Keep moving, she told herself. Don't think about it. Put one foot in front of the other and keep moving. She slipped and almost fell. A pain shot through her spine, stopping her in her tracks. She stood still, placing her hands on her stomach until it subsided. My God! Not now!

She moved again—faster than before, willing her frozen feet not to trip. The ice fell faster, tearing at her face. The thick leaves on the ground shimmered with new life, treacherous life. Breathing hard, she swallowed the panic that welled in her throat. Even if she couldn't make it, Carrie would send someone for her. But what if Carrie didn't know which direction she'd taken? Had she mentioned the creek? She was no longer sure.

"I'll crawl if I have to," she said, the sound of her voice wavering and faint. Tentatively, she lifted one foot and set it on the ground. She slipped, then regained her balance. If she went on, she'd fall. Sliding her back down the trunk of a tree, she placed her mittened hands in front of her and began to creep. The ground bit into her knees. Another pain shot up her back. She struggled to breathe as the pain engulfed her body, creeping up her spine, intensifying, then waning.

"Don't panic, Delaney," she heard herself saying over and over. She crept forward, inch by inch, the ice falling layer upon layer. Her hands were now numb. Another pain hit. She wasn't going to make it. She pulled her body under the limb of a hemlock, its wide branches sheltering her from the heavy fall of ice.

She was going to die. Her baby was going to die. Right here under this tree, they would both die. Someone would find them, maybe tomorrow, and they'd both be dead. No! No! her mind screamed. She was going to make it. Somehow she would make it.

Thirty minutes passed. More pains. Carrie would come. Would find her. She bit down hard on the inside of her cheek and tasted blood. She moaned. Then screamed. Then moaned again. Through the branches of the hemlock, the darkness was complete.

CHAPTER

❧ 28 ❧

When Joe first heard it, he thought it was an animal—a wounded animal. It was vaguely familiar, that sound of terrible pain. He heard it again and lengthened his stride, moving over the ice as quickly as he could. Even in his thick-treaded boots it was tricky, and he stopped now and then, following that sound with his hunting instincts.

Nam! That was it! That's where he'd heard that sound. The memory carried a pain as though a festering sore had been touched. No. No. He wouldn't think of that . . . not of that time or that place.

He paused, listening again, and there it was. Down toward the creek. He fell, the frozen earth slamming against his large frame, and he cursed under his breath. The moaning came again, ahead, around the bend.

"I'm comin'!" He righted himself. He tried to run over

the slippery ice, holding his balance by hanging to the ice-laden branches of the trees.

"Thank God. Thank God." It was a woman's voice.

"Where are you?"

"Here. I'm over here."

He headed for the hemlock, lifted the lower limb, and there she was, wadded in a ball, rocking back and forth, moaning that awful moan. Oh, my God! It was the pregnant lady.

"Can you walk?" he said gruffly, checking his fury at her stupidity. That would come later.

"I can try," she said, reaching for his outstretched arm. A pain hit, and she convulsed in a knot. He waited until she quieted.

"Hell, you can't walk, lady. Look, I'm gonna carry you." His mind raced as he tried to decide where to carry her. Not to the farm. That was straight downhill, and treacherous as hell. Besides, his place was closer.

He reached one arm beneath her knees and the other behind her shoulders, but she let out another cry, and Joe suddenly knew, knew beyond all doubt what that cry meant. He'd heard it before.

He pulled off a leather glove. "Here," he said, shoving it into her hand. "When the pain comes, bite down on this. Bite hard! Try not to fight the pain—or me. It ain't gonna be easy to carry you and keep my balance, and I sure can't do it with you thrashing around. We stay here and we both freeze."

He watched as she put the glove in her mouth, her head nodding up and down.

"Now put your arms around my neck." With one swift movement he scooped her up and began to inch toward his cabin. She was limp in his arms, surprisingly light for a pregnant woman. How the hell did she get way out here? And in her condition?

Although the moon was hidden, Joe knew every stick and stone on this path. By himself, he could have made it blindfolded, but carrying her was different.

All at once, she stiffened in his arms. He stumbled, cursed loudly, and yelled, "Bite down! Bite down!" He waited the seconds it took for her to relax and then moved forward.

Twenty minutes passed, stopping, starting, before his cabin came into view. Another hundred yards and he'd have her inside. God only knew what he'd do then.

"I'm sorry, I'm sorry," she mumbled over and over.

"It's all right. We're gonna be inside soon."

There. He was at the front door. He raised his right leg and kicked it open. Gingerly he laid her on his bed and watched her writhing. He had to warm her up. Blankets. Get blankets—and sheets. He was going to need them. He needed to boil water, but why? Why did they boil water? Sterile! Of course! Something needed to be sterile, but for the life of him, he couldn't think what.

Grabbing blankets from the closet, he crossed the room and covered her body. Quickly, he stoked the fire. And it wasn't until then that he reached for the light switch.

"Damn!" he muttered as he flicked the switch. "Power's out." He reached for a match to light the oil lamps.

Another wail from the bed. He rubbed his head, trying to think. For the first time he wished he had a phone, though it probably wouldn't help. If the lines weren't down, they soon would be. What had he heard on the radio? Temperatures dropping to twenty below? Or was it ten below? What the hell difference did it make? Cold was cold.

Another scream. This time he went to the bed.

"It's gonna be okay, missy. I ain't never done this before, but I've seen it with animals."

She looked up at him. In spite of the blankets, her body shook, but Joe didn't know if it was from cold or pain.

"Listen," he said, "I know you ain't supposed to do this, but as I see it, there ain't much choice. I got some whiskey. I'm gonna fix a big shot. Maybe it'll warm you and ease the pain some."

She nodded weakly and murmured a thank-you.

When he returned with the glass of bourbon, he lifted her head and held the glass to her lips. She coughed as the whiskey went down, but she drank it all.

"We're gonna time your pains," he said, glancing at his watch. "I know they're close, but we need to know how close." She gripped his hand as the seconds ticked away, the pains in a pattern, reaching a crescendo and then descending as her body arched and then relaxed.

"Two minutes apart," he said. "We don't have much time. I'm gonna boil some water over the fire, and I'll be right back."

"Don't leave me, Mr. Harmon." She clutched his hand with surprising strength.

"I'm not leavin'. Have to be a damn fool to go anywhere on a night like tonight." Gently, he pried her fingers loose. In a matter of seconds, he was back.

Her hands were icy cold, but her hair clung to her face and neck, beaded with perspiration.

He reached for the blanket. "We're gonna have to get some clothes off you," he began.

"And that's how the two of you got born," Joe finished, staring at two pairs of enthralled eyes.

"And who's the oldest?" Adam demanded, pride filling his voice.

"You are. By about five minutes, I reckon." Joe snorted. "You could have knocked me over with a feather when Abbie here came poppin' out."

"And what did you use for a blanket, Uncle Joe?" Abigail piped in, already knowing the answer, yet loving to hear it again and again.

"I wrapped both of you in a sheepskin rug. You looked like wet puppies. Not much bigger, either."

"And what did Grandmother Carrie say when she finally got to your place?"

"Well, Miz Carrie shows up with a rescue team. But not till the next mornin'. And I ain't never seen a woman so torn between bein' hoppin' mad and thankful. She scooped the two of you up and bawled all over that sheepskin rug. Damned near flooded my place." Joe grinned.

"Aww, Joe. Everybody knows Grandmother Carrie *never* cries."

"Well, she did that mornin'! Now you two get on back to the house. Eat your lunch. You know your mama likes you to finish before the restaurant fills up."

He watched as they raced across the pasture, headed for the house. He closed his eyes. There was another part to the story that he hadn't told the twins. It happened in a different country and at a different time, but it was still part of the same story. Maybe he'd never tell them.

He stood, brushed the grass from the seat of his Levi's, and headed for his truck. One visit a day was about all he'd allow himself. What a handful! And those women, working so hard at the restaurant. It was time to take Adam off their hands for a couple of days. Go camping. Take the canoe down the river. Yeah. He frowned slightly. He'd bring Abbie another doll to make up the difference. Too bad the one he had given her broke. Maybe he'd buy her one with golden hair this time.

Somehow Joe knew he was acting as a father figure to the twins. Taking up the slack, he called it, but only to himself. Occasionally, he wondered about Anthony. "Damned fool," he'd mutter, then add, "All of us— damned fools!" He knew that Nam changed people, could bring out the worst and best in a man. Mostly, he reserved judgment. Who the hell knew what had gone on? That flyboy had probably done what he had to do. And so had Delaney. And that was all there was to it.

CHAPTER

❧ 29 ❧

November finally came. The sweetest month of all. The twins were in school, the restaurant closed, and in the daytime the house took on a soothing quietness. Delaney had come to love winter, frosty days, long, deep nights, for that was when time slowed, and that was when she wrote.

She poured another cup of coffee and headed upstairs. She sat at her scarred desk and, for a moment, stared blankly at the sheet of paper already positioned in the typewriter. Although the typewriter was four years old, Delaney still thought of it as new. Carrie had given it to her for Christmas the year the twins were two. The restaurant had been open only one season, but it had turned a profit, and part of that profit had paid for her new typewriter.

"You need it," Carrie had said. "You worked your fingers sore in the restaurant," she explained, "and I know you don't really like it. Most folks keep workin' at something they don't like 'cause they have no choice, but you've got a chance, girl. Do it. Do it for yourself."

Carrie laid down an ironclad rule. Nobody was to disturb Delaney between nine in the morning and three in the afternoon. And each day, as sure as the sun rose, Carrie brought Delaney lunch at exactly twelve-thirty. For five months she was free to indulge her fancy, fly with her imagination—and thus she wasted the first year.

Even on this November morning, with frost still sparkling on the grass, Delaney blushed at the remembrance of her first attempts. They were terrible. And she'd kept the rejection slips to prove it.

Slowly, meticulously, diligently, she improved. But it was Teresa who put her on track—a track from which she derailed with alarming frequency. If Carrie had an ironclad rule, so did Delaney. No one, but no one was to read anything she wrote. And both Carrie and Teresa had ignored it.

Delaney had been furious.

"Well, you can just scratch your mad place," Teresa had said when Delaney confronted her. "What's the use of being a writer when nobody reads nothin' you write? Besides, it's stupid. All those rich people runnin' around the world fallin' in bed with each other and seein' who can buy the most. Stupid. Why don't you write about somethin' I can understand?"

Delaney had raged. She'd locked herself in the room like a child. She wouldn't come down for dinner. But she thought about it. And Teresa was right.

She started over, and the one sheet of paper had slowly, laboriously, grown into an impressive pile. And what's more, she almost liked what she had written.

For a moment, she stared anew at the blank sheet of paper. The book was near completion, and she was having difficulty with the ending. She couldn't get anything to work. And again, her mind was balking.

Slowly, she dropped her head against the cool metal of the typewriter. She'd never finish. She didn't know how. She'd be eighty years old, still unfinished, still staring at the same piece of paper, only by then it would be yellowed and dry.

She stood up and walked to the window. Maybe she wouldn't write at all today. Maybe she'd sit in front of the fire, think, and listen to the quiet. Oh, God, why was this so hard?

"Are the twins asleep?" Teresa asked as Delaney entered the den.

"Finally," Delaney replied, sinking into a chair. She propped her feet on the ottoman and pulled an afghan over her legs.

"Maybe they go to bed too early, Delaney. After all, they're six years old. Another half hour of television wouldn't hurt them."

"No, it probably wouldn't, Teresa, but it might kill me. You know, when I was a little girl, I used to believe that God didn't give you two things. He only gave you one. I mean, I thought He didn't have enough to go around, so if you wanted two things, you had to settle for one. I think I still believed that until the twins were born." She laughed. "I guess God showed me."

Teresa frowned slightly. "Sometimes I don't understand when you talk about God, Delaney. How could you believe something like that?"

"Let me see if I can make it clear." She thought for a moment. "It's like the restaurant's a booming success, and I can't write anything. So I either have the restaurant or I have writing." She caught the puzzled look on Teresa's face. "Or something like that."

"You need to get back to church, Delaney. The preacher could straighten you out in a hurry."

"Oh, Teresa," Delaney said wearily, "that's your answer for everything."

"And I'm right."

"Please," Carrie interrupted. "I've heard enough squabbling from the twins tonight without the two of you goin' at it."

"I know, I know," Delaney said. "Sometimes I think if they don't stop bickering, I'll lose my mind."

Carrie smiled knowingly, spurring Delaney on.

"Abigail has a three-minute attention span. And Adam is so dreamy that I have to tell him things over and over. He's like a balloon. He floats, and if I don't pull the string, I think he'd float away."

"He'll grow out of it, Delaney."

"How do you know?"

"Because you did."

"Was I like that?"

"Worse."

"Then I suppose there's hope for Adam."

"There's always hope, Delaney."

Delaney closed her eyes for a moment as contentment settled itself in the room. It was that small portion of the day when life winds down. The television droned in the corner, Teresa was stretched out on the sofa, and Carrie's knitting needles clicked rhythmically, almost hypnotically. She was half listening, her mind lingering on Adam, when a faintly familiar voice nudged her consciousness. Who was that? She played with the voice in her mind, trying to guess the owner, but the answer would not come. She listened a second longer. A car. An Audi. The voice extolled its beauty, its maneuverability. Irritation, like a bee sting, prickled in her mind. Who was it? Slowly, she opened her eyes. The image on the screen was that of a man. He reeked of success. The message he was sending was clear. Own this car and own these qualities. The camera zoomed for a close-up. Startling blue eyes shone from a chiseled face, the face of wealth, of the American aristocracy, of undiluted power. It was Anthony.

Carrie glanced up. Delaney's face was white, white as fallen snow.

"Delaney? Are you sick?"

Delaney said nothing. She sat in her stillness, the fixity of her gaze so intent that, for a brief second, she seemed like a bird, trapped and exhausted from beating its wings. Carrie rose and moved to Delaney's side.

"Delaney? What's wrong?"

"That was Anthony."

Carrie wheeled toward the television. The image faded.

"Anthony?" she repeated. The name implied, Anthony who? A quick anger leapt in her mind. She knew full well Anthony who. She stepped back, still watching the set as though he would materialize again. "Are you sure, Delaney? I mean, it could be someone who looks like—"

"I'm sure. I'd know him anywhere."

Carrie's eyes returned to her daughter. She reached a hand and rested it lightly on Delaney's shoulder. Teresa stared first at Delaney and then at Carrie. She was about to speak when Carrie shook her head silently. On the screen, Hawkeye quipped with Margaret. Canned laughter filled the room. Carrie returned to her chair, picked up her needles, and counted stitches.

The image remained in Delaney's mind. It remained like a specter. The possibility that she might see his face, a face she'd worked so hard to forget, everywhere, made the promise of life unbearable. A sob racked her body. And then she was weeping, weeping as she'd never wept before, her body convulsing with the effort. The wall that defended her emotions had cracked.

CHAPTER

⊱ 30 ⊰

My silver teapot, you fool! And you know what woman! That woman! That new maid! She stole it, and it's mine. I want it back!"

"A silver teapot." Seamus nodded, watching Margaret tear through the dining room, opening the china cabinet, closing it before she had time to see its contents. "When did you notice it was missing, Margaret?" he asked, trying to keep his voice level. He was tired, tired of the scenes, the imagined slights, the inexplicable bursts of temper. And this was to be another night of exhausting activity.

"Today! I've searched this house and I can't find it! She took it! She hates me! She's always hiding my things! But this time she didn't hide it. She stole it." Her voice began to break as she paced the floor. "I fired her. Ordered her out of this house. And now I don't have anyone to help me." She began to cry loudly, like a child. Her eyes smudged to black sockets as mascara ran down her cheeks. She balled a fist and rubbed her face, smearing red into black.

"Now, now, Margaret," Seamus soothed. "Let's go into the kitchen. We'll talk about it after we eat something."

"There's nothing to eat!" she wailed harder, but she stood and followed him meekly, sitting in a chair and staring into space.

He spoke gently as he made two peanut-butter sandwiches and opened a can of soup. He made a mental note to shop for groceries. The refrigerator was almost bare, and the cupboard was worse. While the soup warmed, he wiped her face with paper towels, then watched as she wolfed down the food he placed in front of her. It was obvious she hadn't eaten all day. She sat silently, smiling at him once, and he thought perhaps it was over. But then she started on the teapot again.

"I think she stole it," she babbled to herself. "But maybe she hid it. She doesn't like me, Seamus." She said his name, but he knew she was unaware that he was in the room. The last of his energy evaporated. He watched helplessly as she piled the contents of the kitchen cabinets onto the counter tops. Quietly, he slipped into the dining room.

He needed to think. And watching Margaret made that impossible. For months he'd been trying to ignore her strange behavior, for she'd always been difficult; but her outbursts were no longer simply strange, they were bizarre, and worsening, and now, he knew, he had to deal with it. She'd hired and fired maids and cooks so rapidly that Seamus thought of his house as a revolving door, never knowing who would serve him, who would clean, or who would be working in his yard. She no longer kept social engagements. No longer went to the club. Once she'd had the telephone disconnected and then denied she'd done it. That in itself should have set off alarms, but he and Margaret had lived separate lives for so many years, it had taken time for the reality of the situation to sink in. Well, she had his full attention now.

He had to do something. See a doctor. Maybe it was simply a hormone imbalance, the change of life. He sighed unevenly. Whatever it was, it had to be dealt with, and immediately.

He stood, crossed the foyer, and entered his study. Might as well let Anthony know they wouldn't be coming to the theater. No sense in upsetting Anthony's balance if he should happen to see two empty seats in the second row. Wearily, he picked up the phone and dialed.

"Mr. Callahan, I'm afraid the prognosis isn't hopeful. We've run a series of tests, and it's nothing physical. She's been seen by two psychiatrists, and they concur that we're dealing with schizophrenia. Your wife is a very sick woman. We suggest immediate hospitalization."

Seamus sat rigid in his chair. His voice was tight, controlled. "And what can I expect? I mean, how long? And what are her chances for a cure?"

"Your questions are difficult to answer, Mr. Callahan. There's still so much we don't know about schizophrenia. But you can be assured your wife will have the best care available."

"What caused it, Dr. Jaffee? I mean, was it always there and something triggered it? Or was it simply inevitable?"

"What you're asking is did you do something, or did anyone do something to cause it? Am I right?"

"I guess so."

"No. She seems to have led a fairly normal life up to this

point." He caught the look of pain that flickered in Seamus's eyes. "Or maybe she hasn't?"

"I wouldn't say that Margaret has ever been completely normal. When I look back on it, well, I always thought it was my fault that she wasn't happy. I blamed myself."

"That's not uncommon, Mr. Callahan, but if there's anything you can tell us, anything pertinent, it would be helpful. I'd like to set up some interviews with her psychiatrist, if you don't mind."

"No, no, I don't mind." His mind was churning with thoughts of Anthony. "Dr. Jaffee, I need to ask you one question. Is this genetic?"

"Why?"

"My son spent quite a while in the psychiatric hospital. He was in Vietnam and had a breakdown."

"Would he mind if we took a look at his medical records? I can't really answer your question until I've seen them. What did his doctors tell you?"

"It's not so much what they said, but more what they didn't say. A lot about stress from the war. And some about his childhood—particularly his relationship with his mother. That was never healthy, but I take responsibility for that, too."

"And how's your son now?"

"Completely recovered. In fact, you might have heard of him. Anthony Callahan?"

"The actor?"

"Yes. He's my son."

"Strange that Margaret didn't mention her son was Anthony Callahan." Dr. Jaffee was silent for a moment, lost in thought. "Let me venture a professional guess, Mr. Callahan. Probably the two are unrelated, considering many veterans had a difficult time after Nam. But I'd still like to view his records—that is, with his permission. Why don't you have him call me?"

"I'll do that, Dr. Jaffee. Thank you."

When Seamus left Anthony's small apartment, Anthony sat in the stillness trying to deal with the news about his mother. His feelings grouped into distinctly opposing forces. What his dad told him clarified so much, but if he accepted it as fact, the rage he'd nursed since the dawn of memory could no longer be fueled. If his mother was as sick as Seamus said, and he had no reason to doubt it, then it had always been there, growing unchecked in the dark places of Margaret's mind. He could not hate sickness. Not the way he hated her. It was a new ball game—and he wasn't sure of the rules.

And for the first time in his life, he felt a connection with his mother. Sympathy, a sympathy born of knowledge. Mental illness was a trip to hell—he should know.

Hatred and sympathy. Conflict. Here it comes again, he thought. Standing, he shook the tension from his shoulders. His head cleared, and he began to call on what he'd learned during therapy, during those long months in the hospital. He would telephone Dr. Jaffee first thing in the morning. And then he'd contact his own doctor and give permission to release his records. Schizophrenia? Wasn't that genetic?

CHAPTER

❧31❧

"We got to do something, Mama."

"I know, Teresa."

"She walks around like she don't hear nothin', see nothin', or want nothin'. I hear her bumpin' around that room all night long. Don't seem natural the way she just stares into space. And the twins, well, they stare at her starin', their eyes all fearful. Lately, I been noticing they sorta run from her. If she comes in the room, they leave. Can't you talk to her again?"

"I've talked till my face is blue. Talkin' don't do no good."

"She ain't interested in nothin'. Why, I found that book she's been writin' on stuffed under her bed. Pages all out of order. She dumped it in a cardboard box, and now she never looks at it. Never writes nothin'."

Carrie watched as Teresa picked up a knife and whacked

at the green peppers. All that Teresa said was true. And Carrie didn't have the foggiest notion what to do.

"You know, Mama, I think I understand what she's goin' through." The knife, suspended in air, remained there. "I know she don't act like me when I was troubled. She never hid in the church. I ain't talked about it much, Mama. I'm not good with words like Delaney. But I've learned that God don't intend us to hide. We got to face what comes, take it in, and keep on goin'."

Teresa glanced at her mother. Carrie was standing quite still, her head nodding slightly, spurring Teresa on.

"What I'm trying to say is Delaney ain't been nowhere except Atlanta and Charlotte since the twins were born. Now, I admit, that's further than we went as kids, but the world has changed, Mama. Those kids have needs, and Delaney ain't meetin' them right now. She's hidin' in her own mind, and right now, that's not a good place to be."

"How," Carrie began, "did you suddenly become so wise?"

Teresa blushed bright red. "This cuttin' board's seen better days," she fumed. "And them twins is always leavin' a trail of crumbs everywhere they go." She wiped the counter furiously.

Carrie watched, amused and satisfied. Teresa had come a long way. And since her daughter had opened the door, it was time to broach another tender subject.

"Have you talked to Joe about it?"

"Joe?" Teresa blurted, her face reddening again.

"Yes, Joe. The two of you spend a lot of time talkin' lately, and I just wondered if you'd talked about Delaney."

"We talked some." With the mention of Joe's name, Teresa picked up her pace, now quarreling with the canister set. "These are too small," she stated irritably.

So I'm right, Carrie thought.

"Teresa, why don't you talk to Delaney?"

"Me? Talk to Delaney?" She stared at Carrie, completely astonished. "But Delaney's the one who's always tellin' me what to do. She won't listen."

"You're right. She won't. And that's too bad. Delaney could learn a lot from you. It's time she started listenin'."

"I don't know what you're sayin', Mama. I never have been big on talkin'. But I'm big on doin'."

"What you got in mind, baby?"

"Now, Mama. You don't need to know everything," Teresa said, her eyes narrowing.

That's right, Carrie thought with satisfaction. I don't need to know everything.

Joe was worried. For Joe, it was a rare condition. And he didn't like it. For weeks he skidded over that feeling, hoping it would go away. But each time he saw Delaney, saw the twins, it deepened.

He cursed himself, cursed Delaney, and cursed most everything that crossed his path. For it had been Delaney and the birth of the twins that had tripped the switch to his isolation, leaving him wide open for that most fearful of all conditions—caring.

In fact, even if he never admitted it to himself, the twins had affected him almost as much as Delaney. He'd been struck with wonder that a human being weighing in around four pounds could survive. And he felt a responsibility. It didn't matter why he felt it, for Joe didn't put much stock in self-examination. Things just were or they weren't.

Shortly after the twins were born, he'd begun to do some repairs around the Rollins farm. "Hell," he told himself, "some things women weren't meant to do." He fixed the leak in the barn, mended the pasture fence, and began to tinker with the combine until he had it in mint condition. No big deal.

And he watched the twins grow like kudzu. It seemed to take all three women just to handle them. It was only fitting that he took up the slack. At least, that's what Joe told himself.

They never insisted he sit and talk or stay for dinner, like most people would. Instead, Delaney brought his meals to the field or to the barn, wherever he happened to be working. Every once in a while, she'd eat with him, mostly in silence. She'd gather up the empty dishes, put them in a basket, and leave.

Joe wasn't sure when he started talking to her. But he had, and that was a fact. He told her about being from Alabama, about how his daddy was a farmer by trade but a carpenter by heart. He told her about going to the university on a football scholarship, and how he hated it and stayed only two months. All those people. And all those books. He told her how his dropping out had caught the attention of the local draft board, so he'd joined up before they took him. But he hadn't told her about Vietnam—and she hadn't asked. He knew intuitively that talking to her would be hard, and if his intuition hadn't spoken, that peace charm she wore around her neck would have.

Delaney, in time, had told him David did not exist. She'd almost cried, apologizing for using the war to protect her children. Hell, Joe didn't care much one way or the other—then. But Teresa had hinted something about this guy surfacing somewhere. And Delaney began moping around like a cowed pup.

It was at nightfall, around the time the tree frogs started hollering, that Joe made a decision. He was, for the first

273

time in his life, getting ready to interfere in something that didn't concern him, and he couldn't for the life of him think why.

"Mommy, why don't you marry Uncle Joe?" Abigail asked. The question startled Delaney, and the shampoo bottle slipped through her fingers, spilling in the bath water. Abigail giggled, churning the water into great mounds of bubbles.

"Now I'm gonna smell like shampoo all over, Mommy!"

For a moment, Abigail played quietly, her chubby hands appearing and disappearing in the frothy water.

"So? Why don't you marry Uncle Joe?"

Delaney pushed up from her knees and wiped her hands on a towel. "You know perfectly well why I don't marry Joe," she replied.

"No I don't, Mommy. I don't know anything perfectly well. You're always saying I do, but I don't. When I grow up will I know everything perfectly well?"

Delaney looked down at her daughter. How was she supposed to field *that* question? For if she answered honestly, she'd say no. Growing up meant more questions and fewer answers.

"Well, you'll know more than you know now, Abbie. We never have all the answers."

"But if you married Joe—"

"Please, Abbie. Can we talk about something else? Besides, Joe hasn't asked me. And if Joe has his eyes on anyone, it's your Aunt Teresa."

"Aunt Teresa?" Abbie's eyes widened with delight.

"Yes, but don't you say a word. They're both very shy. It's best to ignore it."

"Oh, I won't, Mommy. You know, I don't care if he

274

marries you or Teresa. Either one would be fine, since he won't marry me."

"He won't marry you?" Delaney echoed.

"No. I asked him already. He said no. He said I was too young."

"I see," Delaney said, running her fingers through Abigail's soapy hair.

"Thanks, Mommy."

"For what?"

"For talking to me."

"For talking to you?"

"Yes. You haven't talked to me in a long time."

"I've come to speak to Delaney," Joe announced when he appeared at the kitchen door. His voice was solemn and his features were set solid. Never mind it was a strange hour, though seven Sunday morning was, and never mind his pronouncement sent Carrie and Teresa scrambling from the kitchen. Joe stood his ground, fidgeting with the hat in his hands, eyes pinned to Delaney as she poured his coffee.

He sat in a chair, stiff and determined until Delaney faced him across the table.

"I'm listening, Joe."

"What you're doin' is wrong, Delaney," he began awkwardly.

"Wrong? What am I doing?"

"Nothin', and that's what's wrong. Now, when I did nothin', thought nothin', felt nothin', well, that was different. I didn't hurt nobody but me. But you have kids. And you can hurt them bad if you don't get hold of it."

"Get hold of it?" She tried to think. What did Joe want her to get hold of?

"Yes, do somethin'. You got to come to terms with it. Get back to life, Delaney."

"Joe, I know how hard this is for you, but I really don't understand what you're talking about."

"Give me a minute. Maybe it'll come clear. First, I want to tell you about something, something I've never told anyone. It's about my time in Nam. And it's about me." He dropped his eyes, gazing at the toe of his boot. Slowly, he began to talk again, and with each word he drifted further and further into himself.

"When I joined up, I believed in what I was doin'. My country needed me, and I went. I never questioned why, never needed to know. That may sound really stupid to you, 'cause I've listened to you with the kids, and you're always askin' why—makin' them think things through— answers and all. But it ain't in my nature to question things. You just do them."

Delaney listened quietly. He hesitated, grappling for words in a manner that was almost tangible. A mocking-bird began to sing, and the silence stretched. For a moment she thought he'd finished, but he leaned forward, his elbows on his knees, and went on.

"I wish I could say I was okay with it from the start, but I wasn't. Hell, nobody was. It seems like, now, that we were a bunch of pissants, runnin' here and there, tryin' to defend our territory, and that territory kept changing. But none of it was really ours, and we all knew it. Mostly, it came down to just survivin'.

"We was out on patrol. We'd been told the VC were in the area, so we were nervous, jumpin' at every noise comin' from the jungle. We'd been out about four hours and seen nothin' when we stumbled on a village. Most of it was in flames—what was left, anyway. There was bodies all over. Well, at first, we didn't know who'd done it, us or them, and by this time it didn't seem to matter much. Still, we had to check it out, see if they was hidin' anythin', VC or weapons—you know. In that kind of heat, things start to smell in no time, and some of them villagers was burned bad. We started siftin' through it all, lookin' for tunnels, weapons, whatever we could find. We'd been there 'bout half a hour and findin' nothin' when this sound kind of floated out of nowhere. It was like a scream, a stranglin' scream, and it was a woman's voice. It was comin' from the outskirts of the village, in the trees. The sarge sent me to find out who was hurt or what was goin' on. I followed that awful sound, comin' every few minutes, until I found it." He stopped again, swallowed hard, and continued, his words coming slow and heavy. "Under a tree there was this woman, this pregnant woman. And she was in a lot of pain tryin' to deliver. Beside her was a toddler. Couldn't of been more than two. That toddler sat still as a mouse, just starin' at his mama like he'd been trained to be quiet. She rolled her head and looked at me. She looked at me with eyes so full of pain and hate that I just stood there. I couldn't take my eyes off her face. I saw her move, give somethin' to that baby, and I watched him stand up and start comin' to me. I didn't notice what he was carryin'. Behind him, the woman was screamin', I don't know what, and that baby just kept comin'. The next thing I can remember is they was yellin' my name, and I saw it was a live grenade. I froze. Just stood there while that grenade went off, and all I saw was white, blindin' white. When I come to, I was in a hospital." Joe's voice had dropped so low, Delaney strained to hear him. "And after a while, the doctors told me I'd never be a man again—you know—a real man." He stopped talking.

Delaney was never quite sure how long they remained in that silence. Long enough for her heart to crack.

"Why are you telling me this, Joe?"

"Because if it weren't for your family, them kids, I don't think I would have ever felt again. And I see you slippin' away inside yourself like I did. Bad things happen, Delaney. Sometimes, there ain't no justice. And maybe you're sittin' there thinkin' I ought to say I wouldn't go again, but I would. I did what I had to do. This is the only country I got. Ain't no guarantees that it's always gonna do the right thing. And you ain't got no guarantees, Delaney. You won't always do the right thing. Now, I don't know what happened between you and the daddy of them babies, but I do know this. You're alive and he's alive—and that's all you need to get on with it. Maybe your life ain't perfect, but it's the only one you got. And you're the only mama them twins got. Be there for them."

It was the longest speech Joe had ever made in his life. The toll was enormous. Without another word he passed through the door. It was never mentioned again. Once had been enough.

CHAPTER

❧ 32 ❧

"Why don't you listen to your agent, Anthony?"

"I'm listening, I'm listening," Anthony replied irritably. "And I don't like what I'm hearing. When I don't like what I hear, I react."

"React is a mild word. Try overreact."

Anthony scowled. "I like it in New York, Dave. I like my apartment. It suits me. I have a great drama coach here. Who the hell knows what I'll find in Hollywood? Come on, Dave. I don't even like the state of California, and you want me to move there!"

"Not move there, Anthony. We've been over and over this. You'd be insane to turn down—" Dave stopped short, his face reddening.

"Stop it, Dave," Anthony stated smoothly. "Don't measure words with me. I'm not sensitive about it. If you think I'm insane, just say it."

"How about temporarily insane?"

"I've *always* been temporarily insane."

Dave laughed. "And ladies and gentlemen, the preceding was filmed before a live studio audience."

"Which is better than a dead studio audience."

"Touché," Dave capitulated. He leaned forward and changed his tack, lowering his voice. "I still think you should take the offer."

Anthony rolled his eyes. "Okay, Dave. Run it by me one more time."

"You're doing well in the theater, Anthony. The reviews have been spectacular, particularly for a newcomer, but that's exactly what you are—a newcomer. For the most part, you're still an unknown. A few good reviews and a couple of commercials do not make a star."

"How do you know I want to be a star?"

"Give me a break, Anthony," Dave groaned. "Let me finish."

"Sorry," Anthony mumbled.

"You're always griping about artistic freedom, the ability to pick and choose the roles you want to do. That's a hard-won privilege in the business. You have to earn it, pay your dues. Then, and *only* then, will you have the clout it takes to do it."

"But I'm doing it now," Anthony argued.

"Granted, but that's because you're independently wealthy. Your old man's seen to that. You're fortunate you don't have to earn your living from the theater."

"I know, Dave. I've seen what people give up, what they go through. But this isn't a career for me."

"Well, I don't know what the hell you'd call it," Dave interrupted. "Do you do anything else?"

"Yeah. I manage my money. That's my career. This acting thing is just a sideline for me. You know it, and I know it."

"But it's a sideline you take seriously, Anthony. Remember who you're talking to. I know you. You love it. You feel guilty because you're not struggling like most other actors." Dave sighed. "Sometimes I wish you were broke. Then you'd have to take my advice. The fact is, you'll never be a heavyweight if you don't establish a reputation. Film can do that for you—it's the fastest way."

"Then why do I feel like it's a sell-out?"

"It doesn't have to be, Anthony. This is a good role, one that's right for you. I mean, this character is bad, but he has so many charming, redeeming qualities that you like him anyway."

"It sounds like typecasting to me," Anthony said stubbornly.

"Don't be shortsighted, Anthony. And don't be such a snob. Have I ever steered you wrong? If you feel so strongly about staying in theater, why did you do the damned commercials?"

Anthony hesitated, then shot Dave a quick grin. "It was fun?"

"So look at this as fun. Go out there, do this one bit, and enjoy it. Okay?" He sat back and waited for Anthony's answer.

"Okay, Carter," Anthony agreed reluctantly. "You set the program. I'll be there."

"Great! And by the way, when it's over, if you liked it, tell me. If you didn't, lie."

"I'll lie to you either way. You'll have to draw your own conclusions. And in that field, you're world-class, Carter."

Dave watched Anthony walk out of the office and reached for the phone.

"Les? He'll do it. It took some heavy selling, but he'll do it." A grin spread across his mouth as he hung up. He tapped a finger against the top of his desk as he pondered the absurdity of life. Who would have thought, so many years ago, that Anthony would become who he was about to become—the next genuine star. Right up there with Redford and Newman. Nine years ago he would have bet that Anthony wouldn't live to see thirty. Proves how wrong you can be. God, he hoped Anthony could find something to like in Hollywood, even if it was only the weather. If he didn't . . .

"Nah," he muttered aloud. "I'm not wrong. My instincts say go with it, and my instincts have never been wrong . . . yet."

Eighteen months later, Delaney watched as Anthony accepted an Oscar for best supporting actor.

CHAPTER

❧ 33 ❦

"How is she today?" Seamus asked as he entered the kitchen. Anna Lobetti looked up from the cup of tea she was sipping and shook her head.

"About the same, Mr. Callahan. But the new drug is helping. At least she's sleeping better, and she's not quite as hostile."

"Has she been hallucinating?"

Anna nodded.

"Still about Anthony?"

"I'm afraid so. She's convinced he's trying to kill her. Today it was poison in her food. She wouldn't eat unless I ate first. She's already lost too much weight."

"I know. Has she said why Anthony's trying to kill her?"

"Not really. Not in so many words. She mumbles something about deserving to die, and Anthony knows why."

Seamus sank into a chair. "I don't suppose it would help to have Anthony come by again, would it?"

"I don't think so. Last time it seemed to make her worse." Anna's eyes brimmed with sympathy. "We don't understand why some schizophrenics respond to drugs and some don't, Mr. Callahan. She doesn't know what she's saying. It's best to try to go on with what's normal."

"Normal?" Seamus laughed bitterly. Margaret roamed the house all night, and he'd been sleeping in snatches for so long, he'd forgotten what eight hours of solid rest felt like.

"Let me get you some tea, Mr. Callahan. I know you're a coffee drinker, but there are times when tea soothes the soul. And if you don't mind my saying so, your soul looks rather bruised."

Seamus looked up. Anna's gray eyes fixed him with gentleness. How long had it been since anyone cared how he felt?

"Tea would be nice, Anna."

He sat quietly while Anna filled the teakettle and lit the stove. Anna was a godsend. He'd been through four nurses before he'd found her. Two of them quit of their own accord, unable to tolerate Margaret's sudden outbursts of temper. One left when Margaret hit her, and he'd fired the last one for incompetence. The stupid woman had been sleeping when Margaret found the car keys. Then she'd insisted it was no fault of hers when the police called. Margaret had run three red lights and crashed into a parked car.

Each time he brought her home, he thought it would be good for her. But it hadn't worked, and it wasn't working this time either. It seemed endless.

"Mr. Callahan," Anna said, placing a cup in front of him.

"Please, Anna. Call me Seamus. I feel old when you call me Mr. Callahan. Anyway, you've seen me at my best and at my worst. Anyone that familiar with my personal life should call me by my first name."

Anna smiled. "Well, you might feel old, but you don't look it. For what it's worth, I don't know of a single person who bears up under these conditions, who doesn't lose it every now and then."

"You don't."

"It's easier for me. I have objectivity. I'm not emotionally involved. It's difficult to make rational decisions when you care so much."

Seamus avoided her eyes. Care? He wasn't sure if that was the proper term. Duty, yes. But care? He'd stopped caring long ago. That was one part of his personal life Anna didn't know. He had admitted it to nobody, not even Margaret's psychiatrist. Even at this moment, he did not like to think of it.

"Have you had dinner?"

He looked up, and there were those gentle eyes again, still and deep.

"I grabbed something before I came home. I've got to find a cook, Anna. Do you think we could keep Margaret out of the kitchen? That's the only way a cook will stay longer than a week."

Anna studied his face thoughtfully. "Mr. Callahan . . . I mean Seamus," she corrected. "I'm never less than honest with family members. I think nurturing false hope is devastating under these circumstances." She hesitated, sipped her tea, and went on. "But I don't see Margaret ever functioning as a normal person. There are always miracles, I won't dispute it, but it's hard to structure your life around the possibility of that happening. Maybe you should make a decision, for both yourself and Margaret, that hospitalization is the only option." She paused for breath, watching his eyes for a reaction. "I wouldn't like to see your life destroyed along with hers. There comes a time to save yourself."

Seamus felt the last ounce of energy drain from his body. Anna was right. The kind of life he'd been living was killing him. And it wasn't helping Margaret.

"I'll consider what you said, Anna. I'll want to discuss it with Anthony and Michael, and we'll see."

Do it soon, Anna urged inwardly. Before all your spirit is destroyed.

"I've got to know, Rebecca. If it's there, if that's what's been wrong with me, if that's what I can expect, I have to know."

Rebecca Tyson's gaze held steady. Anthony's eyes were charged. His body vibrated with tension. She had not seen him this anxious in years.

"Anthony," she said, her voice moderated yet solid, "why didn't you come to me sooner?"

"Denial?" The word as an answer and a question. "I didn't want to think about it. And I was probably afraid of the answer."

"But I've given you an answer. During all the years I treated you, I never saw symptoms of schizophrenia. You had a wretched childhood, Anthony. Such a childhood scars the psyche. And what happened in Vietnam was too much for you to bear. You blocked it. You escaped because you didn't have the coping skills to deal with it. And you are not alone. Post-traumatic stress syndrome, the condition that so many returning vets manifest, can be treated successfully. It was in your case, Anthony."

She halted, reading his eyes, watching the body tension begin to dissipate as his shoulders seemed to relax.

"Anthony, listen to me. Really hear me. I'm not at all surprised about your mother's condition. It's a piece of the puzzle that fits too well. And if you're looking for absolutes, I can't give them. Nobody can. But I can give you an educated opinion. I've never seen symptoms of schizophrenia in you."

He was standing now, pacing in front of her desk, long strides, crossing and recrossing like a metronome. He stopped by the window, and she could see his eyes flickering rapidly.

"I'm thinking of getting married," he announced slowly.

"Anthony! I think that's wonderful! Who is she?"

"Heather Riley."

"Heather Riley? Isn't she in music? I know I've heard that name."

"Your age is showing, Rebecca. How do you manage to treat teenagers if you don't know their music?" he teased. "She's a singer. Rock. You know, rock 'n' roll? Have you heard the term?"

"Once or twice." Rebecca sniffed, looking at him down the bridge of her upturned nose. "And my age isn't showing, my *taste* is showing. I can't help it if I like Mozart. Call me a throwback. There's a limit to what I'll do for my patients, and listening to those horrible sounds exceeds that limit."

"And you're a snob." He grinned. "A musical snob."

"If I recall correctly, and I usually do," she teased back, "you're partial to jazz. So I'm not alone in my snobbery." She watched him smile again, watched the anxiety dissolve

CURRENTS OF LOVE

even further. "She must be special, Anthony. I'm happy for
you, and I wish you my very best. Now, is there anything
else? Anything you want to add or ask before I chase you
out of here? I have a legitimate patient in the waiting room.
Someone who still needs my attention, unlike you, Mr.
Callahan."

"I'm being dismissed?"

"You are."

"And I'm not going to be schizophrenic?"

"I see no signs of it."

"But you won't guarantee it?"

"Anthony, I had a great-grandfather who was killed
when a tree branch fell on his head. Now, the odds of your
getting schizophrenia are a little higher. But if I spent my
life worrying that a tree branch would fall on my head, you
would recommend therapy for me."

"Thanks, Rebecca."

"Don't mention it. And send me an announcement or an
invitation—whatever the case."

"You bet. After all the money you've earned off me, it's
time I got something back, even if it's only a wedding
present."

She laughed as he closed the door. A smile lingered on
Dr. Rebecca Tyson's lips. Momentarily, she indulged herself, basking in the glow of a success story. Anthony Callahan. God, he had come a long way.

"Okay, Rebecca, you've had your pat on the back for
today." Her finger pressed the buzzer signaling the receptionist to admit her next patient. A manic-depressive.
Someone still in trouble.

CHAPTER

❧ 34 ❧

Like a day lily at sundown, Delaney closed in on herself. Days passed. Months passed. The children grew, and the restaurant flourished. The outward appearance of her life seemed adequate as she smiled at customers, paid the bills, looked after the twins, and took care of the minutiae of life. But the silence in which she moved deepened.

She never knew when Anthony's image would spring at her. It was happening with increasing frequency, on television, magazine covers, even in the newspapers. And when it happened, the breath would leave her lungs. Cushing, which had been her haven, was no longer safe.

It came to a head the day Carrie took the twins for a tetanus shot. She'd accidentally overheard her grumbling to Teresa.

"Too bad I can't take Delaney for a shot. Get her immunized against that television set."

"Hmmph!" Teresa had replied. "Delaney? I don't know any Delaney." There had been a pause, and then Teresa had continued. "Oh. You mean that woman who lives upstairs? She used to be Delaney, but I don't know who she is anymore."

"Why, Teresa. That's downright mean," Carrie had chided.

"You're right, Mama. It is mean. Mean but true."

That night, while everyone slept, Delaney tried to take a long, hard look at herself. But the harder she looked, the emptier the space she should have occupied became. She'd vanished. Everything she was and everything she'd wanted to be had simply disappeared.

The next day, she drove to Asheville. She checked into the Holiday Inn, bought a newspaper, and went to the movie theater. And when Anthony appeared on screen—that familiar body, that familiar face—the tears she thought she was done with broke again. And she fled the theater, returning to the motel, the bed shaking as she slammed her fists into the pillow. And when she was through, she was through.

Twenty-four hours later, she slipped into the darkness of the theater again. And she watched the screen until she was sated with his image, until it had no impact. Only then did she leave.

On the drive back to Cushing, she was overcome with a mass of dormant emotions, each fighting for attention. But mostly she was angry. She'd been a fool expecting someone else to meet her needs. A fool for believing in love. And more of a fool to expect it from Anthony. He'd been about as real as the image on the screen. He was hollow, like an empty papershell pecan. He lacked the basics, the real stuff of life.

She raged at herself. How could she have been so blind? How could she have considered a life with someone whose values, background, family were so different from her own? Why had she thought that because something was different, it was better?

She was done with scapegoats. Done with excuses. It had been her own stupidity, her choices alone that had brought her to this point. Joe was right. Life wasn't fair. It wasn't just. And tomorrow held no promise. But it was the only life she had.

The rage she had intentionally incited grew, and that was good. For her anger proved she was still there. But what was she to do with it? What was she to do with all that anger?

Hours later, in the heaviest part of the night, she rose and went to her typewriter. Momentarily, she stared at the blank piece of paper lying beside it. Then she began.

CHAPTER

❧ 35 ❧

Heather Riley—the *real* Heather Riley, not the one on the concert tours—was an anomaly, for she had none of the stereotypical hang-ups of her generation. Heather was aware of herself, aware of her strengths and limitations, and she had her feet, for the most part, solidly planted in the here and now. Her ego was the proper size, and her psyche, with the exception of a few minor dents, was sound. All this combined to make Heather Riley as close to normal as a person could be, and in the music industry, that made her different.

She had grown up in Fort Lauderdale when parts of it still had the flavor of a small town. Her mother taught piano, and her father, when he wasn't building houses, played a mean guitar. He liked both equally.

Heather's home was comfortable, loving, and most of all, accepting. She could be who she was with emotional impunity. Her mother loved her. Her father loved her. And she learned to love herself.

Her musical interest bloomed when she was two years old. She'd stand in front of the stereo, mesmerized. Her father would sing into a teaspoon as though it were a microphone, and every once in a while he'd hold it in front of Heather's mouth, and she would sing with him. Eventually, she got her own spoon.

At seventeen, she was singing in a local club, drawing exceptional crowds. Heather was the first to dye her hair bright orange, and if it was a problem for her mother, it wasn't for Heather. After all, it was only image. When she finally landed a recording contract, she dyed her hair back to its original color, except for the green streak down the middle. By the time other members of the rock scene were mimicking she'd stopped, and her hair hung down in one long braid—dark brown. She wore what she pleased— from feathers to burlap. In fact, one of her favorite costumes was a flour sack cinched at the waist with a rubber snake. And since she never washed the sacks, flour, like an aurora, pouffed from her body when she sang.

Her voice was unmistakable. It was a powerful voice, husky, sultry; but more than that, it held a singularity that identified her immediately to the listener. You might not like her, but you never forgot her.

The growth of her career was as steady as Heather herself. And in spite of all the trappings, the grueling hours, the outrageous personalities that peppered the music world, Heather never confused who she was with what she was.

And if it surprised the press and paparazzi when she started seeing Anthony Callahan, the blueblood, it didn't surprise Heather Riley. Not only was he drop-dead gorgeous, but he *looked* normal, and Heather liked that. He took show business seriously, but he knew it for what it was—a business. And Heather liked that. He'd been through a lot and come out of it all with a sense of himself, his own personal identity that wasn't locked into his image on the screen or his megabucks. And Heather liked that. In fact, there was nothing about him she didn't like, except for the fact that sometimes she felt he withheld something from her, something very personal . . . but then, Heather rationalized, nobody's perfect.

Usually Heather was conspicuous only by her absence at the ongoing round of Hollywood bashes, but Dave Carter was her agent. Besides, she liked him. So when she received the invitation that included a handwritten plea from Dave, she made an exception. She put on a simple white sundress and drove her Porsche to Dave's richly understated home in Beverly Hills. She'd put in an appearance, kiss Dave on the cheek, and leave.

But before she ran into her host, she spotted Anthony Callahan, trapped in a corner with John Tolbert, the film critic, renowned first for his vicious dismembering of everything he viewed, and second for his obesity. He was a thoroughly disgusting man. If Heather had tried, she could not have wished anyone worse on Anthony. She smiled to herself a delicious, spiteful little smile. Revenge was sweet, even if it was vicarious.

Heather moved through the crowd, drifting closer, anticipating the expression of misery on Anthony's face. She had seen Anthony only once since he'd bloodied her lip (except in his films, of course), and that had been at the Academy Award circus where he had accepted his Oscar. Heather had not applauded. She inched closer, now only a few feet away, and as she nonchalantly reached for a shrimp she observed Anthony through lowered lashes.

Squirm, she thought to herself. What goes round comes round. In a matter of seconds that spiteful little smile faded. For on close examination, she'd seen something in his eyes that checked her glee. He wasn't miserable. He was *laughing*, laughing at this self-inflated whale whose words dictated the box-office success or failure of too many movies.

And then he looked up, caught her eye, and she realized he'd seen her laughing at him laughing at the critic. From that point on, things just happened.

They were married three months later. And divorced nine months after that. Heather was hurt, but the damage was not permanent. She'd gone back to Fort Lauderdale to nurse her wounds in the comfort of her parents' love.

"You know, Mom," she said, "he's truly terrific, but he can't, or won't, give of himself. Not completely. He's like a person who started out with a limited supply, and he gave too much the first time out of the gate. Now there's not enough left—not for me, anyway. I deserve more."

Heather was right.

CHAPTER

ᕗ 36 ᕕ

When Seamus had looked in on her, she'd pretended to be sleeping. She'd learned to do that in the hospital. She would be still, holding her breath until the attendant walked away, footsteps muffled on the floor. Then and only then would she strip her bed. Pull off the blanket, the sheets, the mattress cover, and shove them in the closet, out of sight. She'd take a chair, wedge it under the door knob. And sleep would come.

She had tried to explain it. Tried to explain that when night fell the covers formed shapes, took on life, a spirit, an evil spirit, creeping over her body to her neck, trying to choke the life from her. But no matter how many times she told it, nobody believed her. Oh, they pretended to believe, but they didn't.

And to make matters worse, they were the wrong spirits! Not the ones she was expecting. And it was crucial that the spirits be right! Crucial that she made no mistakes! Why didn't anyone understand?

But she was growing weaker. And they were getting stronger. The voices were loud now, not soft like they were in the beginning. Beginning? There was no beginning. They'd been there forever, whispering in her sleep. No! No! That wasn't true either. They'd come with Anthony. That was the beginning. They'd sent Anthony. Sent him as a baby. But she'd outsmarted them for a while. She'd had nothing to do with Anthony.

But now he was big, and she was so small. She held an arm in front of her. She saw a bone covered with flesh. She felt a wave of fear. Don't look! Don't look! What had Seamus done? He'd done something to the mirror. Relief washed over her, and she glanced up. A towel was draped over it. Good! For when she looked in a mirror, she no longer saw herself. She saw something else. She could see through her skin. Her skin no longer protected her. Where her face should have been was a skull, her own skull. It was horrible!

That stupid, stupid woman Seamus had staying in this house. Not like Anna. Where was Anna? What had Seamus told her about Anna? Michigan? She'd gone to Michigan for the holiday. That was it. Margaret frowned. Which holiday? Her brain tossed up answers. Christmas? The Fourth of July? Thanksgiving? Yes, that was it. Thanksgiving! And Seamus had brought her home. And she had been here three days, long enough to make the plan, figure it all out.

And she'd been watching, watching when no one saw her. And this time, she'd listen to the voices. Do what they said, and nobody could stop her. Because it was the only way. One way. Then Anthony would understand. He'd know she'd had no choices. She had done what she'd been told to do. She'd been a good girl. Margaret was a good girl.

Slowly, she lowered herself onto the bare mattress. The cook was coming early. Early because of Thanksgiving. And Margaret would be awake. Little Margaret wide awake, waiting for the cook.

And that stupid, stupid woman would be sleeping. Asleep in the den with the television droning. Now weren't those voices, too? Voices in her sleep? Margaret laughed. Of course they were. Stupid, stupid woman and her voices droning on and on.

And cook's purse, shoved in the kitchen cabinet by the dishwasher. Sitting there, wide open, the keys on top.

And cook would make the coffee, make the coffee while the house was still and Seamus slept. And Margaret would drink a cup, and cook would drink two cups. And shortly, she'd leave, leave the room for just a moment. She'd go to the bathroom. All Margaret had to do was wait.

It was so easy. So clear. This time she was going to follow instructions. Do exactly what she was told to do. Her eyes sparkled like the crystals on the chandelier. Oh, yes, she'd do exactly what they said. Then she would be pure. Purged. Delivered. Hadn't her voices told her so? And weren't they always right?

She glanced at the clock. Four A.M. Not long now. Not long.

The article in the newspaper was brief. Margaret Callahan, wife of developer Seamus T. Callahan, died as a result of injuries sustained in an accident on the Connecticut Turnpike. Mrs. Callahan was sixty-three. No mention of her hospitalization. No mention that she'd been traveling at eighty miles an hour when she struck the abutment of an underpass. Those facts would surface only in the Los Angeles papers, where sordid details were the food of life.

Graveside services Saturday at eleven o'clock. Family only.

Did Anthony grieve? If he did, it was for that which never was. And now it never could be. For a while he experienced a certain lingering sadness accompanied by release, utter and complete. He closed his thoughts around this strange new feeling, and by degrees it clarified, forming softly in his mind like a coming together, a truce of sorts. For Margaret was released, too. Released from whatever drove her into that abutment. It was over. Finally over.

CHAPTER

⍟37⍟

1983

The flight attendant was announcing their approach to Asheville. The plane lurched into an air pocket, then leveled off. Delaney felt an aching dullness as she reached under her seat to retrieve her purse. Los Angeles to Atlanta. Atlanta to Asheville. During the trip the sky had darkened rapidly due to the time change. City lights flickered like the fireflies at the farm.

She'd had one goal when she left Anthony's office. She wanted to get away from Los Angeles as quickly as possible. Once back at the hotel, she'd called the airline and changed her flight to an earlier one. She'd thrown her clothing in the small suitcase, caught a cab, and made it to the airport with little time to spare.

She did not think until the plane was airborne. From then on, she could not stop her mind. Anthony would come. She did not know when, but he would come. She'd look up one day, and he'd be there. And the twins would be there. And there was no way on earth to prevent it from happening.

She could not whisk the twins away, although that's what she wanted to do. Their life was in Cushing. Her life was in Cushing. As much as she wanted, she could not run away . . . not again.

She had to tell them. But how? How would she ever explain the way it was? The way she was? Facts were cold, barren, always denying the power of feelings. And yet the facts were bound to the feelings. She had been unable to separate them as they had jointly propelled her life.

The plain truth was that she'd been pregnant and had chosen not to tell Anthony. She had denied her children a chance for a living father. Instead, she'd substituted a myth, a figment of her imagination. It wouldn't matter why she'd done it. It would only matter that she *had* done it.

She closed her eyes and tried to picture Abigail and Adam seated in front of her. How would they react? Abigail was so rebellious, so strong-willed. She'd always been more difficult to control than Adam. And she was hard to read, for she covered all her emotions with a full measure of bluff. She appeared fearless. Always the first one to do something dangerous. Hadn't she been the first to jump from Killer's Rock into the creek too far below? And hadn't she broken her arm? And had she been sorry? No. And lately, her moods had been even more difficult, challenging, as she crept into womanhood. If Delaney liked something, Abigail didn't. Daughter against mother, an emotional battleground. Once, in the heat of an argument, Abigail had even gone so far as to say she'd never let her life turn out like Delaney's. Nobody was going to keep her in Cushing, shoveling food to strangers day in and day out.

No way! So how would Abigail react when told she had a father, a living father, let alone one as famous as Anthony?

And Adam? What about Adam? So introspective. Abigail's counterpoint. Adam, who weighed each decision, determined the best and worst that could result before acting? Adam, incapable of deceit, unequipped for the presence of it in his mother?

What would Anthony do? She hadn't really known him fifteen years ago, and she certainly didn't know him now.

The plane shuddered as the wheels touched the runway. The engines roared in protest as it slowed. By the time it had docked at the gate, Delaney's mind was set. It didn't matter what Anthony would do. It mattered what *she* did. After tomorrow, she would have no secrets. She would tell them. And whatever was going to happen, would happen.

CHAPTER

❧ 38 ❧

Well? What is it, Mom?" Adam was repeating. He sat on the steps, his long brown legs stretched in front of him, the ubiquitous basketball propped on his lap. Delaney looked at his eyes; they were expectant, patiently waiting for her to speak, and it was like seeing him for the first time. He was almost a man. Almost six feet and still growing. Almost a man, but not quite.

"Mom, can we get on with it? I'm supposed to be at Ginny's by five o'clock. Her brothers are letting us use their bikes, finally," she tacked on. "You know how I've wanted to go dirt biking, and I'd like to get there before they change their minds. Honestly, Mom, why don't you let me have a bike of my own? Dirt biking isn't that dangerous, and—"

"Abigail, will you hush? This is not about dirt bikes. It's

about something more important. It's about your father."
There. It was out.

"My father?" Abigail echoed. "What about him?"

"What I'm going to say will be a shock. And I don't know a gentle way to do it. Believe me, I wish I did." Her voice broke as her throat contracted. She paused a second longer, then spoke again. "There's no easy way to say it. Your father is alive." Her words hit the air like four explosions.

"What are you talking about, Mom? You said he died in Vietnam."

"I know what I said. But it wasn't true. He's alive. And you'll probably meet him soon."

"Mom," Adam said slowly. "I know you're serious because I can tell by the look on your face, but I don't know what you are talking about. I mean, was he a prisoner of war, and they suddenly released him? Did the government make a mistake thinking he was dead? What happened?"

Delaney tried, but she couldn't speak.

"Come on, Mom," Adam prodded, barely containing the excitement in his voice. "Just tell us."

"Your father was not killed in Vietnam. And his name's not David Anderson."

Abigail laughed. "This is a joke, isn't it? 'Cause if it is, it isn't very funny. Is it April Fool's, and I missed it? Come on, Mom."

"No, Abigail. It's no joke. I've never been more serious in my life."

And she told them.

Abigail did not go to Ginny's. Adam missed basketball practice.

When it was over, Adam had gone to his room. He'd

fallen in bed, one arm over his eyes, his leg bent at an angle, one foot still on the floor. He'd stayed there a long time, thinking. Only the tapping on his door, two slow taps and then three quick ones, had gotten him up. When he passed down the steps and into the kitchen, he had run into neither Grandma Carrie or his mother. It took about a minute for his long legs to cross the pasture and enter the barn.

It was early evening, and the setting sun colored the interior of the barn a dusty pink. The air was ripe with newly mown grass and the musky smell of animals. Adam closed the heavy door behind him and looked around for Abbie. Softly he called her name, but no answer.

He climbed to the loft and waited. The signal, although long abandoned, had been unmistakable. They'd been using it since they were small, and it meant "I'm in trouble. Meet me in the hayloft." But nothing had been as serious as this.

The door reopened. A slash of light fell across the floor and disappeared. He heard Abbie scampering like a mouse as she crossed the floor. In seconds, the top of her head appeared, then her whole body.

For a moment, neither said anything. Adam chewed on a piece of straw, and Abbie chewed gum.

"What are you going to do, Adam?"

"Do? I don't know. Nothing, I guess. So I've got an old man, and he's famous. It's nothing to me."

"Yeah, and you've got a mom that's famous. Daria Rogers." Abigail snorted. She tossed the book she was carrying in the hay. "Seems like Mom's into secrets. Wonder what else she's lied about."

A pained look crossed Adam's face. "Come on, Abbie. Mom's not a liar, and you know it."

"Then if she's not, what would you call all that stuff

about Dad? A fairy tale? Get a grip, Adam. She lied to us. She's always lied to us." She threw a magazine on top of the book. It was an old issue of *People*. On the cover was Anthony Callahan. Underneath was written "The Man and the Myth." Abbie leaned back against a beam and closed her eyes. "Interesting reading material," she murmured.

"Not to me," Adam stated grimly. "I don't care who he is, he's nothing to me."

"Why are you mad at Anthony Callahan? What'd he do to you?"

"Nothing. And I'm not mad at him. I just don't know him, and don't care if I ever do."

"You are really weird, Adam Anderson." Suddenly, she sat straight and crossed her legs like an Indian. "Or should I say Adam Callahan?"

Adam's neck snapped in her direction. "Abbie, you're a first-class moron. It's not Callahan. It's not Anderson. It's Rollins. In case the thought hasn't crossed your mind, any way you cut it, I'm a bastard. And so are you!"

"Sired by Anthony Callahan. Out of Daria Rogers. Will the real parents of these poor children please stand up?"

"God, you're a bitch."

"So, who you going to tell?"

"Nobody. And neither are you, Abigail. This is nobody's business. I swear, you'll live to regret it if you—"

"God, Adam. You are such a nerd. You believe everything everybody says."

"And you don't?"

"No!" Abigail stormed. "Not anymore I don't."

The night music of crickets began to fill the air. For a while, neither said anything, listening to the sound rise and fall. Finally, Abbie spoke, and for the first time, a sadness shaded her words.

"I still don't understand, Adam."

"Mom said we wouldn't. She said you had to be there, know him, know who she was at the time. She said we—"

"I don't give a damn what Mom said," Abbie exploded. "I feel like a total fool, mooning over some man named David Anderson, wondering what he was like, imagining what life would have been like if he'd lived. Oh, Adam, I feel like somebody really died, and that's absurd, because he never lived. No wonder Mom's Daria Rogers. She's so good at fiction." Her voice was now bitter, angry.

Adam's eyes fell to the magazine cover. "Did you read that junk?" he asked, his gaze thoughtfully studying Anthony's image.

Abbie sighed. "Yeah. I read it. That dude is forty years old. He's ancient! And Heather Riley was married to him once. Heather Riley! Can you believe it?"

"What else?" Adam asked.

"Why don't you read it, Adam?"

"I don't want to! Why don't you just tell me what's in it?"

"A lot of stuff about how great an actor he is and how although he doesn't take it seriously, he does take it seriously, whatever that's supposed to mean. He's *rich*, Adam, I mean really rich. His old man made a ton in real estate and handed a bunch of it over to his son. Just gave it to him! If he'd married Mom, we'd have been rich and wouldn't be living in this pitiful little town with nothing to do. We'd be living in Hollywood, Adam."

Adam's eyes darkened. "Who cares? Nothing but a bunch of phonies running around wearing makeup."

"Adam?"

"What?" Adam's voice was filled with exasperation.

"Maybe we're rich. I mean, maybe Mom made a lot of

money off that book. I know it was a big seller. Have you read it?"

"No."

"I did."

"So what's new? You read everything."

"It's good, Adam. I hate to admit it, but it's good. If Anthony Callahan was like that character in Mom's book —well, I can sort of understand—"

"Well, I can't!" Adam stormed. "And I don't want to. I'm sick of his name. I'm sick of this whole thing. I'm just plain sick."

"That's right, Adam. You're sick—period."

"And you're a twit."

"Aren't you the least bit curious?"

"No."

"Well, I am. What are you going to do if he comes here?"

"I'll go to Joe's. I don't want to meet him."

Abigail stood and shook out her hair. "Well, I do," she stated emphatically. "But more than that, I want him to meet me."

"You think you're so great. You just want to meet him so he'll say 'Ohhh, look what I missed!'"

"Something like that," Abigail answered, picking straw from her jeans.

"Well, count me out. And," he added menacingly, "if you breathe a word to anyone—I mean it, Abbie, anyone —I'll kill you. Mom's right about the press being all over this place. I'd just as soon the world didn't know I'm a bastard, if you don't mind."

"Don't worry, Adam. Not a word."

She slipped down the ladder and out the door, leaving Adam to his own thoughts. And they were jumbled, a real mess. And at the bottom of it all was hurt. His mother had lied to him, he knew that, but she'd done it to protect him. But why had she lied about her writing? Why had she pretended she'd never sold anything? She's said it was to insure their privacy, but Adam, in his naïveté, couldn't imagine anyone caring about a book enough to seek out its author. All that stuff about his dad being a hero in Vietnam. He'd even had a fight with Jimmy Owens over it. He'd been nine years old, and Jimmy said he didn't believe Adam had a daddy. It was the cold cruelty of innocence, something to rub in Adam's face for hitting three home runs in Little League. If Jimmy only knew.

He'd seen the movies, mostly on television. A cowboy, a card shark, a Wall Street broker. Those were the three roles he could remember. Who the hell was Anthony Callahan? He buried his head in the straw. It stuck in the back of his neck. Who cared? It didn't matter. He was nothing to Adam Anderson . . . Rollins.

CHAPTER

❧ 39 ❦

At the sound of the rapping, Abigail shoved the magazine under the covers.

"Come in."

The door opened and Delaney stepped through. Abigail kept her eyes straight ahead and her voice level.

"Hi, Mom."

"Hi, honey. I wanted to see if you were okay."

From the corner of her eye Abigail watched her mother cross the room. Abigail said nothing. She felt Delaney's hesitation, that slight stillness, before she sat on the side of the bed. And when Delaney lifted a hand to touch her, Abigail deliberately flinched. It was only then that she looked directly at her mother. Yes, there was hurt. Good. Her mother needed to pay for what she'd done. You must accept the consequences of your own actions. Weren't those Delaney's exact words? She could eat those words now.

She returned her eyes to the foot of her bed. Delaney said nothing. Abigail felt a sense of power. It was a recent sensation, this power. Sometimes she felt it in the presence of boys, but she'd never felt it with her mother. But now it was there. With the boys it felt good—exciting and good. But with her mother, it wasn't what she expected. It made her uncomfortable, as though she'd stumbled into danger. Maybe she did strain against Delaney's control, but within those controls was a sense of security. And now, in spite of herself, she, Abigail, was threatening that security, and she couldn't stop.

"Abbie, I know you have questions. And I'm here to answer anything—"

"I don't have questions, Mom. I know everything I want to know."

Again the look of pain. The power to inflict it.

Delaney stood. She moved toward the door, looked back once, and stepped through.

"Good night, Abbie."

"Good night, Mom."

The door closed.

Abigail's rejection burned Delaney as though she'd been branded. She knew its source. Youth. The self-righteousness of innocence. Had she not been that way herself? Judged her parents? Found them wanting?

She passed by Adam's empty room. He'd gone to Joe's. Yes. He would run to Joe for comfort. And Joe would handle it. Somehow, he managed to get through to Adam. He gave Adam what he needed most—time.

It was out, and it was over. What would come now were aftershocks. When Anthony appeared, the twins would be ready for him. Or as ready as they could be.

But would she? Where was the truth? He had used sub-terfuge to get her to California. And she had used the same on her children. And she had justified it in the name of necessity. He had done the same. She had spent years blaming herself for what happened. Some weakness in her. A form of blindness. A need to understand, so real that she would make the pieces fit, force them into place, regard-less of the outcome. And Anthony alone exposed that weakness, that blindness. And she had loved him because of it—and she had hated him because of it.

And now, Abigail and Adam, hiding weaknesses and blind spots. And eventually, they would encounter some-one who shed light on these dark places—and they would love and destroy just as she and Anthony had done. It was inevitable, and even if she could, she didn't want to stop it.

As for Anthony and the twins, they'd find their own way. The twins would choose or not choose to let him into their lives. He would choose or not choose to be there. She had paved the way, told the truth, and she was prepared for Anthony to come.

But she was not prepared for Abigail to leave.

The voice on the answering machine was John Wise-man, his attorney. He listened to the message twice, then again to make sure he was hearing right. His first impulse was to reach for the phone. He had it in his hand, dialing the numbers when, abruptly, he hung up.

What was he going to say?

If only he hadn't gone sailing. The call had come yester-day afternoon, when he was on his boat, well out of con-tact. And he could tell by John Wiseman's voice that even *he* wasn't sure what was going on. Inappropriately, An-thony laughed. John Wiseman never lost his cool.

"Okay, okay, Callahan," he instructed himself. "Think. You have a daughter. Her name is Abigail. And she's probably on her way to see you." He laughed again. "Congratulations, Daddy." He didn't believe it. He didn't believe his own voice.

He snapped on the answering machine and listened for the fourth time. The message was the same, no change. Call Delaney Rollins. A daughter. Abigail. Missing for two days. Possibly on her way to Los Angeles. APB. Delaney Rollins frantic. And John had ended his message with a question. Delaney Rollins?

He wanted to shout and he wanted to cry. A daughter. Goddamnit, missing! How did it happen? And how would a fourteen-year-old girl fare alone? His heart jumped. Los Angeles wasn't the world, but he knew what could happen to kids in the city. But *his* daughter? Something might happen before he had a chance to see her. Know her.

He grabbed the phone again. So he wasn't thinking straight. Wasn't ready. It didn't matter.

There was an answer after the first ring.

"Delaney? I just got the message. I was sailing and—"

"Have you heard anything?"

Her voice sounded steady. Tense but steady. "No. I just got the message."

"They told me you were sailing."

"Delaney, why do you think she's headed here?"

"I told her about you, about us. Two days ago. That night she slipped out. She left an old issue of *People* on the bed. It's a guess, Anthony, but it's all we have."

"I assume the police—"

"Yes," she interrupted again. The conversation was in shorthand.

"Has she ever run away before?"

313

"Never."

"What about money? I mean, did she have any?"

"About twenty-eight dollars."

"That's all?"

"That's all."

There was a pause. Anthony rubbed his brow, trying to think of something, anything.

"Anthony? Are you there?"

"Yes. I'm here. I don't know what to say. No, that's not true. I'm *afraid* to say anything. It'll be wrong. What do you want me to do?"

"Wait. Stay close to the phone. If the police pick her up—"

"They may not believe her. I'll make a call . . . no, I'll have my attorney call. Get the word out to the right people. I know you want to keep this quiet, but we might not be able to, Delaney."

"I know. Can you try?"

"Yes. I'll have John handle it. Maybe we can keep the lid on for a while. She is a juvenile. We'll see. But don't be surprised if it breaks. Are you ready for that?"

"No, I'm not."

He heard the catch in her voice. He wanted to leap through the lines. Hold off the world.

"Delaney, I have connections. I'll use them. We'll find her if she comes anywhere near Los Angeles. Now, if you can answer some questions, it might help—that is, if I can think of the right ones to ask."

When he hung up, he was sweating. He stripped the sweatshirt from his body and picked the phone up again.

"John? This is Anthony. Get comfortable. This is going to take a few minutes . . ."

CHAPTER

❧ 40 ❧

"We have her in here, Mr. Callahan." The officer in charge waved an arm at a closed door halfway down a corridor badly in need of paint.

"Are you sure she's all right? I mean, nothing's happened to her, has it? Something you're not telling me?"

"She seems fine, Mr. Callahan. She could use a bath, but that's not uncommon for runaways. You know what we know. We found one joint on her." The juvenile officer shook his head in resignation.

Anthony's center core, his point of view careened. He racked his brain for a role, any role he could assume, put on like a second skin. Robert Young came to mind, and he almost laughed, caught himself, and frowned instead. "Father Knows Best" he was not. And laughter was not appropriate. Never mind that it was coming as a release, like funereal giggles. Instantly, that urge was gone. In its place stood fear—naked fear. Get real, he told himself. How much damage can a fourteen-year-old female do? God, if he only had time to think. His mind popped an image—dark hair, dark eyes—a carbon copy of Delaney. Beyond that, nothing.

"Mr. Callahan?" The officer was looking at him intently. Anthony noticed that he had tired eyes, old eyes set in a young face.

Anthony cleared his throat. "I'm sorry. I was thinking. I'm kind of rattled."

"You're not alone. Everyone here is rattled. Are you ready to see your daughter?"

"Let's go."

His Reeboks squeaked against the waxed tile floor. The door opened. A blond head turned, and he looked straight into his own eyes. There was his face, refined, delicately sculpted, and utterly feminine. The faintest of smiles, or was it a smile, crossed her mouth.

"Well. If it isn't dear old Dad."

"Delaney? I've got her."

"Thank God. Is she all right? I mean, is she hurt? Are you sure she's all right?"

"She seems okay. Right now, she's in the bathtub."

"Listen, Anthony, I'm driving to Columbia, and I'll be on the next plane to Los Angeles. I'll take a cab—"

"Whoaaa," he interrupted. "I don't think that's a good idea, Delaney."

"Why not?" Her voice prickled.

"Well, she's tired, for openers. And you're probably exhausted. Maybe I'm wrong, but I think a little rest would do wonders—probably for both of you. Anyway," he hemmed, "I'd like a day or so to get to know her."

"You think you're going to know Abigail in a couple of days?" Her voice prickled more.

"No, Delaney," he replied cautiously. "No, I don't think that at all. As a matter of fact, I don't know what I think. The important thing is she's safe. I promise I won't let her out of my sight. I'll bring her home in my plane."

"You have a plane?"

"A small one." Why did he lie? And why did he feel embarrassed?

"Is it safe?" She sounded anxious, frazzled.

"It's better than a commercial flight, Delaney. Please don't worry. I promise a safe delivery. Door to door."

"Well, she better worry. I think I'm going to kill her—or at least ground her forever."

Anthony laughed nervously. "I think she'd find a way around it."

"You figured that out already."

"It took about two minutes."

"I see you're still as perceptive as ever, Anthony."

"I'd better be. I think I'm going to need it. Look, Delaney, I'll call you tonight and in the morning. As soon as she's rested, we're on our way."

"Thanks, Anthony. I know this has been a shock to you. It's been a shock to all of us—particularly . . . well, it's been a shock." Her voice dwindled.

"Delaney, this is the very least I could do." A heavy silence hummed through the telephone. "I'll talk to you."

"Why didn't you marry my mother?"

The question came at him hard. The answer he'd carefully prepared vanished as though written in invisible ink.

"I thought a lot about that, Abigail. And, in time, I hope

I can explain it to your satisfaction. But for now, let's just say I was a total asshole and let it go."

For the first time, she really smiled at him. Her freshly scrubbed face glowed, and right then, at that precise moment, he was hooked. This was his daughter.

"Do I have to go home tomorrow? I mean, since I'm here, couldn't we go out? See somebody famous? I mean, I know you're famous and all, but I'd like to see *something*. I hate to go home and tell everyone I just stayed in this house and didn't even see Sunset Strip. I hear it's really sleazy. I like sleaze. Mom hates it, but I *love* it." She stopped and shot him an anxious look. She'd been caught acting her age. He watched as a slow blush crept across her face. It was utterly charming.

Immediately, her face sullened up, and Anthony read the message. If he thought he was making inroads, he was wrong. She would not make it easy. He had to earn it—whatever it was he wanted from her—and he had to do it the hard way.

"I was kidding," she said finally.

So much for honesty, he thought. Now, back to bravura.

"I'm tired. I think I will go to bed. Got any good tapes I could listen to on my Walkman? Got Michael Jackson? Or The Police?"

"No, Abigail, I don't. I usually listen to jazz. The only rock tapes I have are Heather Riley's."

"Well, I guess you would. Why'd she leave you?"

Anthony looked at her, trying to hold on to his equilibrium. The light shimmered in her hair and on her face. The face kept altering, and he had trouble assimilating. It threw him off guard, looking into his own eyes. Here was this woman-child, hurling complicated questions and waiting for simple answers. He was being tested in an unknown arena, and he badly wanted to pass.

"Are all teenagers this direct, or is it only you?"

She shrugged. "I don't know. Mom says being direct is important." She laughed one short laugh. "But Mom says honesty's important, too. So much for Mom."

"That's enough!" His voice came from a core of iron. It surprised him. And it scared him. How was he supposed to handle this?

"Okay, okay. You don't have to yell at me." She shoved her hands into the pockets of his terry-cloth bathrobe. Her hair, still damp, clung to her forehead. She looked lost in his large robe. She looked like what she was. A child. He shouldn't have raised his voice. After all, he had no right. An uncomfortable silence followed.

"Well?"

"Well, what?"

"Why'd Heather Riley leave you?"

This time he thought before answering. "She didn't leave me. It was a mutual decision. And it's none of your business."

He heard his own voice. He sounded fourteen. During the brief course of their conversation, she'd reduced him to her level. He tried again.

"Look, Abigail. We don't know each other. That's an odd condition for a father and daughter. I don't know how to respond to you, and you don't know how to take me. Let's go easy. I won't ask you anything too personal, and you show me the same courtesy. That's all we can offer each other right now. Common courtesy."

"Okay." She stood and floated across the room. Yes, the word was float. She was taller than he'd expected her to be. And she was lean, streamlined. He kept staring at her, still not believing she was real.

"I really think you should go to bed. We've got a long flight tomorrow, and I have a feeling you're going to need all your energy to face your mother."

"If you say go to bed, I guess I have no choice. After all, it's your house."

How long had it been since he'd felt the sting of blatant sarcasm?

"No, Abigail. It's not my house. I lease it."

"Whatever."

God! This was maddening.

"Don't you think it would be a good idea to get some sleep?" he asked. "Three days on the road must have been tiring."

"I'm going." She dragged on the words, stalling. She stood and headed for the stairs, her bare feet sinking into the deep pile of the carpet. She turned to face him at the entranceway. "Besides, the truck drivers let me sleep most of the way." She veered to another subject. "I'll watch television, since you don't have any tapes. Seems a waste. I can do that at home."

His mind considered, for the first time, his cable connection. He could see her with the remote control flipping from one channel to another, and there were things he didn't want her to see.

"No," he answered, his voice too loud.

Her eyes flickered with disgust. The look was lethal. Without a word, she left the room.

He sat in his chair, undone.

CHAPTER

❧ 41 ❧

Bᵤt, Mom, *why* do I have to meet him? I don't care who he is, he's not my father! You made that decision for me years ago! And I trust you, Mom! I trust you completely. If it had been the right thing, you would have told him, but something was wrong, because you didn't! You didn't want him in your life. Why should I want him in mine?"

Adam's eyes were black. Two black stones set in a sea of white. His broad shoulders were hunched over, one hand flattened on the table. It was a large hand, already callused, and right now it was stiff with tension.

"Adam, you're going to meet him sooner or later. I'd rather it happen here, where everything's familiar, where you feel secure." She searched his eyes. He wasn't buying anything she said. She tried again.

"Listen, baby. He's a very famous man. And people are interested in famous personalities. Someone will—and we

321

don't know where or when—tip the media to the fact that you and Abigail exist, that you are Anthony Callahan's children—and that will be news. Your sister let the cat out of the bag in Los Angeles. She swore she was Anthony Callahan's daughter. If Anthony hadn't picked her up, she'd still be swearing it to whoever would listen to her. We can't undo that. Eventually, some reporter will be on it. It's hard to have secrets when you're as well known as your father."

"He's not my father!"

Delaney felt hollow with exhaustion. Adam's words had been delivered in a half shout. She had been talking, talking, talking, trying to explain what was, even to her, inexplicable. She tried one more time.

"Adam, do you want me to agree? Okay. He's not your father. Does that make you feel better?"

"No!"

"Then what would make you feel better?"

"Nothing. Nothing can make it better, Mom. I want my old father back."

Delaney watched his hand ball into a fist. He sounded small again. Even his choice of words sounded small. She recognized the look on his face. Anger and fear.

"Adam, look at me. Really look at me. I'm afraid, too. I bear enormous responsibility for this mess. I had plans for my life, Adam. And nothing's turned out the way I planned it, except for my writing."

Her voice subsided, took on a different shade as she continued. "And I kept my success a secret because I was afraid Anthony would find me, find you. He's famous, wealthy, powerful, and I was terrified that if he knew you and Abigail existed, he'd take you from me. And you'd want to go. I was more comfortable with the father I created for you. But David Anderson was the myth, not Anthony. David existed only in your mind. Only in my mind."

She paused to swallow the strain in her voice. And when she continued, the past had faded.

"Have you considered the possibility that Anthony won't interfere in your life? Maybe he doesn't want a son any more than you want a father."

"But I did want one, Mom! I've wanted one all my life. I wanted you to marry Joe. Then I wanted you to marry anyone, so I could have a normal home, with two parents. I've grown up in a house full of females. If it hadn't been for Joe—"

"I know, Adam. But you wouldn't want me to marry solely to give you a father, would you?"

Adam dropped his head. His eyes slowly closed, then opened. "I used to. But I don't anymore."

"Good. Because I wouldn't have done it anyway. Look, Adam, we don't choose our families. They just are. Sometimes we try to run away from them. I did. But I found out, no matter how far you run, that family goes with you. It's in your heart, in your brain, even in your blood. You may not like it, but that's what you have, and now Anthony's a knowledge that you have to live with. For he's in your blood, too. Whether or not you let him in your life, or he wants to be part of your life, is another matter. That's up to you. And it's up to Anthony. Everyone faces a fire sooner or later, Adam. And sometimes that fire burns, and you're never the same afterward. How you face it is your decision. After this is over, settled down—and it will settle down—you have to live with yourself. You might as well get it over with."

Delaney had been watching Adam's face closely, looking for a crack in the impregnable will belonging to her son. It came to her slowly that he looked like a man. Suddenly, she was talking to a man, and a sense of new loss wrenched her heart.

"You're saying the same thing Joe said, only in different words, Mom." Now his head was between his hands, and she could no longer read his face.

"Do you want to tell me?"

"Awww, Mom. Joe said stuff about not knowing what goes on in anyone's life. That what we see isn't always what's really there. And not to judge too quickly. You know, Mom, sometimes I think adults have a conspiracy going. And kids have to figure it out." Adam laughed nervously. "But by the time we've figured it out, we probably will have created our own conspiracy."

"And how did you get so wise in fourteen years?"

Adam grinned. "What does Grandma Carrie say? 'The apple don't fall far from the tree'?"

Delaney smiled. It was a compliment, rare indeed from Adam. "I have a feeling it's a persimmon tree, Adam, if I'm any example. Taste the fruit before it's ripened, and it's sure to be sour."

Adam laughed again, and this time it sounded normal. His body was slack, unexpectedly that of an adolescent.

"What the hell, Mom. Bring him on. The worst that can happen is I'll hate his guts. The best that can happen is he knows how to shoot a rifle like he did in *Showdown*."

CHAPTER

❧ 42 ❧

The two-lane highway coiled around the mountains like a strip of thin black leather. Fifteen miles back, he'd seen the first sign pointing to Cushing, but it had already taken thirty minutes to cover the distance. Air, heavy with honeysuckle, rushed at his face through the open window. The mountains, stately and serene, dominated the landscape with haughty splendor. Unlike the Rockies, which ruptured the sky with flaunted youth, these mountains proclaimed supremacy by virtue of age. Thousands of years had passed since they had raged, hurling stone, heaving the earth with their fury. And now they rested, shrouded in the inexplicable blue haze, cloaked with the lushness of summer growth. Green tangled with green. Occasional spots of gold, like mustard seed, hinted at the breathtaking self-portraits they would paint in October. Goldenrod choked the roadside as kudzu climbed over hills, trees, rocks, occasionally swallowing the entire landscape with ruthless appetite.

Anthony had been here before, once, and although he found it beautiful, he'd seen other places equally lovely. But now he viewed it from a different perspective. This was Delaney's home. This was Abigail's home, and he wanted to see everything, note everything, from the creek meandering beside the highway to the hawk he'd seen circling overhead. For the mountains now held a special significance.

"Boring," Abigail had declared when he'd expressed delight at the small waterfalls spilling through the tears in the steep rock walls imprisoning the road. And she'd promptly gone to sleep.

He watched her from the corner of his eye, just as he'd watched her on the plane. Once over the excitement of being in a private jet, staring in restrained awe at the cockpit, offering a shy hand to his pilot, George Canton, she'd settled into a seat and slept most of the trip. He'd had hours to absorb everything about her, and when he thought he'd had his fill, believing her image indelibly lodged in his mind, he would look away, only to find himself doubting her existence, and he would begin again. The blue-veined eyelids. The soft curve of her chin. She was a mystery, a child born fully grown, and he was ravaged by a sharp hunger, a need to know everything, instantly, immediately, and completely.

She would chatter, then fall into long silences. She would smile, laugh, and if he blinked, the laughter would be gone, and she'd be staring into space, her lips slightly parted, provocative and enchanting. A feeling was growing in him, a possessiveness he had not felt since Delaney. He wanted something. For the first time in years, he wanted something.

Abigail stirred, her lean arms relaxed, then taut as she stretched them over her head. Her smooth brow creased with annoyance as her hand bumped the ceiling of the car. Her eyes flew open, staring blankly, finally registering where she was, who he was. Her head rolled toward the passenger window.

"There's the sign," she mumbled.

If she hadn't spoken, Anthony would have missed it. A small sign etched in weather-beaten wood. "The Rollins Farm." Two miles.

"I wish it wasn't Monday," Abigail grumbled, running splayed fingers through her hair.

"What's wrong with Monday, other than the fact today's Monday?" he said lightly, rubbing his right hand on the front of his shirt. Damn, his palms were starting to sweat.

"The restaurant's closed on Mondays. Any other day Mom would be too busy to jump my case. At least until after dinner. Now there's no reprieve."

"You get jumped often?" he asked, more to fill the silence than out of a need to know, for he'd been witness to Abigail's impetuosity. That was a given.

She flung him a quick look and grinned.

"Somebody has to do something around here, or the whole town would die from boredom."

Anthony's eyes lighted as he answered her look. Yes, she would be that way. He didn't ask, nor was he ready to know, what she did to alleviate the boredom. He knew what he'd done at her age, and the remembrance struck terror in his soul. He thought of the joint she'd had hidden in her purse. She had sworn she didn't smoke, never had. "Don't tell Mom," she'd pleaded desperately. "I bought it from a kid at a truck stop. I wanted to impress you." Jesus! What other mistaken concepts did she hold? What had been her source materials for his life? Inwardly, he cringed. Ninety-five percent of the stuff written about him wasn't true. His life, outside of working, was rather solitary. He avoided star status, evaded the media, seldom gave interviews. But no one of his stature could completely avoid being the target of sensational journalism. And although he ignored what was printed, maybe she hadn't. He was swept with a new and violent emotion. Goddamnit, he cared what she thought. He'd have his secretary bring him everything that had been written about him, and he'd read it, be ready to deny, explain. Oh, Jesus, what had been written about him?

"Turn right around the next curve," she was saying. His heart thumped like a jackhammer. He hadn't felt this nerve-filled since Nam. He tried to laugh at himself, at the mental image he'd conjured up. A full-grown man as nervous over a fourteen-year-old girl as he was facing a landing on the *Chicamauga*. During monsoon. At night.

He rounded the curve, and the wide entrance to the restaurant came up fast. He braked, too hard, and Abigail lurched forward, bracing herself on the dash.

"I think you fly better than you drive," she said archly.

He said nothing as he wound up the paved drive, absorbing the house, large, rambling, seated at the foot of the valley. It appeared freshly painted, white against deep red shutters. A wide covered porch stretched the full length and turned a corner. On it were an array of rockers, chairs, and swing. A large pasture swept to the west, and a clump of Charolais cattle completely ignored their arrival, grazing languidly in the afternoon sun. An orchard, probably apple, stretched up the hillside behind the house, and there were rectangular fields, acres and acres, tired from summer growth, languishing with exhaustion. It was a sight taken straight from a postcard. Unreal and yet too real.

Abigail now slumped in the car seat, her face miserable. He kept his a blank but felt as miserable. Jesus. What had he missed? Why did he keep saying Jesus?

He pulled the car into one of the parking slots nearest the front porch.

He hesitated as Abigail reached for the door handle, and unexpectedly she smiled at him, a smile from someone in trouble to someone in even deeper trouble. Something happened in that small exchange that Anthony recognized, felt, and internalized in the deepest part of his heart. It was the beginning of bonding, and with it came courage. He opened the door and stepped out.

When the car wound its way up the long driveway leading to the house, Carrie and Teresa had positioned themselves behind the curtain of the front bedroom window while Delaney and Adam waited in the main dining room. It pulled into the parking space closest to the front entrance. Carrie silently uttered a thankful prayer that it was Monday, for the restaurant was closed on Monday. What if he'd arrived yesterday, when the place was swarming with people? Somebody would have recognized him, sure as she lived and breathed.

"I can't see him yet," Teresa complained loudly, barely able to contain the excitement in her voice.

"Now, this ain't none of our concern," Carrie huffed.

"Then how come you're standin' here just like me, Mama? I know that look on your face. Nothin' but a dozer could budge you from this window!"

"Hush, Teresa. I just want to see Abigail's safe and

329

sound." But that wasn't true. Carrie knew it, and Teresa knew it.

"Well, there she is," Teresa hissed as Abigail popped out of the car. "You can stop lookin'."

"Not if a dozer were comin' full at me, Teresa."

Anthony emerged, and Carrie studied the top of his head, blond like Abigail's. She noted his walk, for a lot could be told about a man by his walk. This one moved smooth but proud, like he wasn't afraid to set his foot on the earth, like he knew where he was going. He stopped at the bottom of the steps and looked around, and Carrie caught the set of his chin, the sharpness in his eyes. Yes, she thought. Delaney had her hands full. And about time.

Slowly, Anthony walked to the steps, then stopped, watching as Abigail climbed them two at a time. He felt awkward, not knowing what to do with his body. He stared at the bed of giant zinnias bordering the porch, spilling over onto the stone-paved walkway. At the sound of the door opening, he lifted his eyes.

Delaney emerged. She stood in the doorway, tanned arms against the white of a T-shirt, feet clad in sandals, dark hair loose around her face, ruffling in the slight breeze coming off the mountains. Abbie, poised at the top step, her head lowered, waited. It was a scene from a film, a film that existed only in his mind, one that he could never capture. Two women caught in the act of life. And then Abbie was in Delaney's arms, and she was crying. Delaney was speaking, soothing sounds, words of love. The scene tore at his heart, ripped at his stomach, and he dropped his eyes, unable to witness that from which he was excluded.

He heard the door open again but kept his eyes averted. Delaney's voice droned for a few seconds longer, the words unrecognizable but the message clear. And a second voice responded, deep and clean. Anthony raised his eyes, and Abbie was wrapped in the arms of a boy, a boy much taller than she. She was still crying as he pulled away and said something, something that made her laugh, and she slipped into the house as the boy turned to face him. Delaney was coming down the steps, coming toward him, and the boy followed. She halted in front of Anthony, caught in his shadow, her dark eyes a barometer, searching his face, pleading for something, something she needed desperately.

She reached behind her and caught the boy's hand, pulling him to her side. The boy was looking at him, and as Anthony returned the look, more from discomfort than curiosity, he felt the impact of those eyes. Something hurtled at him. Primordial challenge. One man to another. It threw him off his guard, so that when Delaney spoke, her female voice sounded alien, as though it had accidentally blown into the male arena of territorial claims raging in the boy's eyes.

"Anthony." His name came off her lips softly, tentatively. She paused. Her eyes returned to the boy's face, bestowing that look of desperation, the same one she'd initially given to Anthony. Her vision remained fastened, but the boy's returned to Anthony, less threatening, defused by some unspoken signal received from Delaney, but still black and hard.

Anthony said nothing, knowing intuitively to wait for her to take the lead. Finally, she swung her head to face him, and she spoke again, each word floating in the summer air, standing first alone, then crashing wildly to confer the meaning.

"This is Adam. Adam, this is your father."

CHAPTER

❧ 43 ❧

Delaney had caught it, caught that message in Anthony's eyes, although she was never able to label it. Later, when she was alone in her bedroom, she tried. For wasn't she the writer? Wasn't she supposed to be tuned in to what people said, and how they said it? Wasn't she always processing the meaning behind the words, the body language, the slight movement in the eyes, around the mouth, the shuffling of feet?

And yet, she could not come up with the proper words to describe that look in Anthony's eyes. Confusion? Anger? Astonishment? And there it was, the one she hooked into, because she'd never seen it in Anthony before—helplessness.

The minute the words were out of her mouth, she knew he had not known of Adam. With lightning speed, she replayed her telephone conversation with Anthony. She'd been frantic about Abigail. The conversation had been limited to that subject, and she had not mentioned Adam. There had been no reason to mention him. The focus was on Abigail.

In her relief that Abigail was safe, she'd forgotten Adam again. But there was no way Abigail had forgotten Adam. Abigail had done it intentionally. And Delaney would have bet her life that once Abigail had slipped through the doorway after her teary reunion on the porch, she had stood listening in the hallway, not brazen enough to peek through the window, but thoroughly enjoying the demise of Anthony's control. Yes, Abigail would do that. And she'd smile as she did it.

And Delaney knew, if questioned, Abigail would claim she was innocent. "Just an oversight, Mom," she would say. "Adam's name never came up." In spite of herself, Delaney laughed. Abigail's sweet revenge. She would not let Anthony in, no matter who he was, without the rites of passage. Being Abigail's father would not come easily.

And Adam, for which she had feared more than for Abigail, had come through with flying colors. He'd been polite, proffering his hand to Anthony, meeting Anthony's stunned blue eyes like a man. Delaney smiled again. Well, maybe he'd overdone the handshake, his grip a bit crushing, but Adam was entitled to his moment, too.

Still, she was angry, but not at the twins. It was self-directed. She had jumped in to smooth it over. She'd come to Anthony's aid, hurrying everyone into the house, introducing Carrie and Teresa, taking Anthony on a tour of the dining rooms. She'd created enough activity, allowed enough time to lapse for Anthony to find his bearings.

My God! She had felt sorry for Anthony Callahan! She was suddenly and thoroughly furious with herself. She should have let him squirm, stand there, his faculties decomposing before her very eyes. But no. She had rescued him as though he were a wounded puppy. And, in all honesty, that's what he'd looked like.

Strangely, she had calmed in direct proportion to Anthony's rising level of nervousness. And she had seen to it that she was never alone with him. That would come tomorrow. There would be no rescuing in the morning—not even first aid. From now on, he was on his own.

"I heard it all, Adam. I wanted to look so bad I almost died! What did his face look like? Oh, God, it was wonderful!"

Adam grinned at Abigail, who perched at the foot of his bed like an owl.

"Keep your voice down, Abbie. I don't want Mom to hear."

"Then tell me what his face looked like, Adam," Abigail hissed. "Was he totally unglued?"

"That, Abigail, is an understatement. And you know what? It made it easier for me! He was so messed up, I kinda felt sorry for him. How did you know Mom hadn't told him about me?"

"I didn't. But he never asked, so I never mentioned it, hoping, hoping, hoping Mom wouldn't blow it. I figured she was too rattled by what I'd done and where I'd gone to talk about you. And what do you mean saying you felt sorry for him? That's just too weird, Adam!"

"I don't know," Adam replied vaguely as he poked at the pillow and turned to his side. "I guess I expected someone like him—I mean, someone who has everything he wants in the world—to be on top of things. And when he wasn't

—when he acted, well, normal—I couldn't help but feel a little sorry for him."

"Well, I don't, and you shouldn't! I'm sure he's quite capable of taking care of himself," Abbie sniffed sanctimoniously. "He sure as hell hasn't been taking care of us all these years!"

"Awww, Abbie, give him a break. He didn't know we existed."

"That doesn't matter."

Adam rolled his eyes. "Joe's right. Women are totally devoid of logic."

"We are not, you chauvinistic throwback!" She was quiet for a moment, staring at the floor. When she spoke, her voice had softened. "Do you think he'll be recognized at the inn? I mean, what if somebody pegs him? What's he gonna say?"

"No way. He checked in after dark. And in that hat and those glasses, it won't happen. Besides, famous people don't stay at places like The Cushing Inn. And they don't drive Fords. They drive Maseratis and shit."

"How do you know? You've never met anyone famous in your life!"

"I just know," Adam said, shutting his eyes.

"He's leaving tomorrow," Abbie added wistfully. "Do you think he'll want to see us again? I mean, visit us, or let us visit him?"

"Who knows?" Adam muttered gruffly. "Anyway, why should anyone want to see you? Unless he's deranged. Now me, that's a different matter—"

The pillow was on his face in a split second.

"You're a sicko, Adam!" she squealed. "A very sick person!"

* * *

Teresa knocked lightly before opening the door. Carrie recognized the look on her face. Teresa had something to say, and neither hell nor high water would stop her from saying it. Carrie waited.

"Mama, it's driving me crazy. When he talks, I keep wantin' to turn off the television set. He sounds exactly like he does on TV and in the movies! So? What do you think?"

Carrie sighed deeply, sinking further under the covers. She knew it didn't matter what she thought. She might as well speak her mind.

"I like him," Carrie said flatly. "He don't put on airs." Her mouth clamped shut. It was none of her business. At least for now.

Anthony made it into the inn virtually unnoticed. The young man at the desk shoved the registration form at him, yawning. Anthony signed his name "Sean Callahan" and gave his father's address in Connecticut.

"That's a right odd name," the desk clerk had mused. "How do you say that? 'Seen'?"

Anthony had smiled. "No. It's pronounced like Shawn. It's Irish."

"Do tell. I never was much good at spellin'. It's a mystery to me why words ain't spelled the way folks say them. Now take John. Why we don't say that 'h' in John. So, as far as I can see, ain't no reason for it to be there." He'd kept up the patter until Anthony was safely ensconced in the high-ceilinged, perfectly square room.

He did not sleep. And there was no television or radio to act as an opiate. By morning, he knew every square inch of that room. He stared at himself in the bathroom mirror. His eyes might be bleary, but his mind wasn't. He was ready for Delaney.

CHAPTER

❧ 44 ❧

The front door opened, and Delaney slipped through. He stepped out of the car and moved toward her.

"Feel like taking a walk?" she asked.

"On a bed of hot coals?"

"No, Anthony." She laughed lightly. "Although there were times when I've imagined that, and worse."

"What's in there?" he asked, his eyes dropping to the basket.

"Coffee. Biscuits. I remembered that you don't do well —I mean, you don't think clearly—until you've had morning coffee, and considering the time change, it's the middle of the night for you."

Anthony heard the slight stammer in her voice. The gesture was an admission of memory, a *personal* memory, and it embarrassed her. She avoided his eyes as she continued speaking, her words coming in a flurry.

"We could walk down by the creek. The cooks are here, so the kitchen isn't safe, and the waitresses will arrive by midmorning. Someone might recognize—"

"That's fine, Delaney. You lead, and I'll follow."

"Now, that has to be a first."

"What? Do I detect a note of skepticism?" he teased, relieved that some of the ice had broken.

"No, Anthony, you are hearing a symphony of skepticism. I think it's a by-product of age."

"A symphony of skepticism?" he repeated. "Don't tell me." His eyes circled the sky in feigned thought. "Are you a writer by any chance?"

"Okay, okay." She laughed again. "Sometimes I get carried away."

She headed toward the pasture, and he followed. He had not looked at her, really looked at her, since arriving in Cushing. And he did not do so now. The truth was, he didn't dare. It was better to keep it light, at least until he'd had his chance.

She walked swiftly, crossing the pasture and heading down a gently sloping road. Eventually, she turned onto a path that descended steeply and steadily toward the sound of water. She confined her words to a minimum, pointing out an occasional rock or leaf-hidden root that might cause him to stumble.

Occasionally, they passed through patches of tattered fog, then into speckled sunlight dappling through the tree-tops. His feet fell on emerald moss, slippery from morning dew. A wind rose. The tired leaves of summer skimmed the air, and a few, stained terra-cotta, drifted to the ground. The sound of rushing water grew, the path took a steeper turn, and the creek came into sight. Delaney halted by a large, flat rock and turned to face him.

"Here," she said. "This is my favorite spot."

He looked at her, at that face, that familiar face, so near. He quelled the urge to touch it, to verify reality. A small leaf was caught in her hair. He reached to remove it, and she flinched. His heart was felled by that small movement. He must remember not to touch her. She might bolt, and he would lose his only chance.

He settled on the rock as she opened the thermos and poured the coffee. He thanked her as she handed him the mug. The creek roared beneath him. A squirrel quarreled with a jaybird. Everything seemed exaggerated. The green of the trees. The blue of the sky. He picked up a twig and began to break it in small pieces, his eyes now on the water careening below him.

"Why didn't you tell me?"

Her eyes came to him quickly.

"Because you didn't want to hear it."

He hesitated, caught in the rightness of her words. "But later, later you could have . . ."

"By then, I didn't want to tell you."

Blood roared through his head. Her words were spoken with such finality. A silence converged, and he let it settle. He watched her watching the creek until she sensed his eyes, knew her words had found their mark, that the meaning behind them was unmistakable. Now she was ready to hear him again.

"Delaney," he began, his mind structuring the words like delicate crystal, "I want to reassure you that I'm not going to do anything you don't want me to do. You're calling all the shots. All I want is a chance to explain. I want you to listen. And afterward, if you want me to disappear, that's what I'll do. Is that okay?"

Delaney heard the hesitancy in his voice. She turned to

face him. He was staring at the creek, unable to meet her eyes.

"That's why I'm here, Anthony. To listen. I need it for myself and for the twins. There are too many unanswered questions, and they deserve to know." Her voice dropped. "Go on."

"I know you've drawn your own conclusions, Delaney, and knowing you, some of them are probably dead-on right. But some of them are wrong. I never wanted to leave you." Her eyes flickered, and he rushed on. "I know. I know. Physically, I did leave you, but you were never out of my mind. I was out of my mind." He laughed cynically. "Literally. But you weren't. Not even during the blackest times, when I barely knew my name. In fact, you were the only thing there when I got back from Vietnam."

"I hope," she said slowly, letting his words sink in, "that you intend to explain what you just said. It's a little obscure, Anthony, even for me."

"I lost it, Delaney. I was in the process of losing it during my first tour in Nam—no, even before that. But I really lost it during my second tour. The shrinks—and I use the word collectively, for there were a lot of them—told me that what happened had been coming on for a long time. It was a seed waiting to germinate, and Nam was the right climate." He shook his head slowly. "Sort of the catalyst that triggered the inevitable.

"It began with Mother. She died three years ago, Delaney. She rammed into an overpass on the turnpike." Delaney started to interrupt, but he stopped her. "Please do me one favor and let me finish. I have a lot to say in a short time."

"Okay, Anthony. I'll grant you the moment."

It was a stinging comment, breaking his train of thought.

His mind grappled for traction as he went on. "Mother was sick, Delaney. She may have committed suicide. We'll never know. By sick, I mean very disturbed. But it wasn't diagnosed until about a year and a half before she died. By then, it was so bad, Dad *had* to do something. She was paranoid. Accused me of trying to kill her. Finally, Dad sought help, put her in a hospital. A psychiatric hospital. She was diagnosed as schizophrenic. Probably always had been."

He felt her eyes on him, and he turned away, not wanting pity. No, that was not his purpose.

"The long and short of it is that I caught the fallout from her illness. I never received any nurturing, any love. So I didn't know what love was, how to recognize it. And I sure didn't know how to give it. There was always this little boy in me, crying under a rosebush, wanting someone to find him, convinced that no one ever would. And when I got older, I quit caring. I simply didn't give a damn."

Delaney felt a wash of anger as she heard his words. The feeling was pronounced as Margaret's face flashed through her memory. She studied Anthony's profile, and within that profile she saw the child, hurt, rejected. The first glimmering of understanding began to surface.

He started to talk again, his features still, immobile with the telling.

"I always thought it was my fault. That's common among children, to blame themselves. Even when I knew, intellectually, it wasn't true, I still blamed myself. I knew I had done something terrible, something unforgivable for Mother to treat me the way she did. But I could never figure out what it was.

"I was isolated as a child. It was something I did in order to survive. And I found it necessary to do the same during my first tour in Nam." His face hardened. "Nam accelerated everything. I made some good friends in the navy, Delaney, and most of them died. They simply disappeared, as though they'd never existed, never been there. I convinced myself it was true. In order to fly, do my duty, *in order to survive,* I cut everyone off. But you were a problem. A major problem. I'd never been in love before. I didn't know it would be so hard, make me feel vulnerable, and believe me, Delaney, at that time, I couldn't handle vulnerability. So you had to go, too."

"Anthony, I—"

"No. Let me finish, Delaney. That was the deal, remember?" He watched her nod, then turned away again. "When I returned to the States, all I could think about were the people I'd killed, burned to death, blown up—men, women, children—and facing you was like facing an accusation. Oh, I know we never talked about it. But I knew how you felt. Not talking about it didn't make it go away. And the climate in this country was hostile. I was so damned confused, and confusion makes truth elusive. I'm still not sure what was true about Nam, for it seems like a bad dream. A bad dream that I wanted desperately to talk about, to try to defuse, but nobody wanted to listen. We were all too concerned with taking sides to listen.

"Anyway, I felt useless at home. I was equipped to do one thing, and one thing only. Drop those bombs. And I did that well, Delaney. It became an obsession, and anything that got in the way of that obsession had to be destroyed. That meant you. I had to forget you in order to be *me,* or at least who I was at the time. So I went back to Nam."

He stood, shook the tenseness from his shoulders, and rubbed his neck. He glanced at Delaney, looking for some sign that she understood, but her face was unreadable. Then she spoke, and her words granted him momentum, what he needed to continue.

"Go on, Anthony. I want to hear."

He sat back down, closed his eyes, then opened them, seeing something she didn't see, someplace she'd never been. He began again, trying to describe it, needing to make her see it with him.

"After I returned to duty, got back to what I thought I understood, my world really fell apart." He halted again, and for the first time, he asked her a question.

"Do you remember me talking about Terry?" She nodded, and he looked back at the creek, his voice low and tight. "I always wanted you to meet him. You would have liked each other, Delaney. He was with me on my first sortie. We were hit. There was a fire, and we had to eject over enemy territory. It was night, dark, and I lost Terry, couldn't find him anywhere. I stumbled around in that jungle for hours, and I was terrified. You know, as pilots, we're conditioned to stay emotionally detached. Right up my alley, huh? But being on that ground, in that jungle, alone, blew the hell out of that detachment. I made contact with SAR, and—"

"SAR?" she repeated.

"Search and Rescue. But they couldn't pick me up until morning. I kept trying to raise Terry on the radio, but he never answered. I thought maybe he was hurt, unconscious, and I kept looking." Now Anthony's voice fell so low that it was barely audible above the roar of the creek. "I found him, at dawn. I'd stumbled out of the jungle, or woods, or whatever the hell I was in, and found myself at the edge of a rice paddy. I could see his chute clearly. I hid, Delaney. I hid in a clump of trees, trying to decide what to do, trying to decide if I should make a run for him, fear eating at my gut while I damned myself for being a coward. It was getting lighter every second, and before I could decide, some villagers appeared, so I stayed hidden."

Sweat had broken out on his forehead. He wiped it with the back of his arm, drew a long breath, and continued.

"The next part is what put me over the line. I didn't remember it for months. On my report, I kept insisting the villagers were playing ball, some kind of ballgame. But the chopper that came in for me spotted Terry's chute, knew that he had been somewhere around. I don't know all that I said, but it was enough to land me in a VA hospital.

"I'd be days acting normal, talking, laughing, and then suddenly I'd lose it, and I'd think I was back in that jungle watching those villagers play ball.

"They tried a series of drugs on me, none of which did any good. I was doing the thorazine shuffle most of the time, drifting around in my own private world. Luckily, Dad surmised what was happening, and he had me transferred to a private hospital. Otherwise, I might still be there.

"I've been lucky, Delaney. I finally touched base with an excellent shrink. I spent months in analysis, all about my childhood, ad nauseam, but when we'd reach the part about Nam, nothing. I was sticking to my story about the ballgame.

"Finally, she hypnotized me, and the truth came out." Anthony dropped his head. The muscles in his neck corded, and his breathing became shallow. "What I was calling a ballgame might have been an execution. The hard part is, I'll never know. Terry was there, all right. And the villagers had found him. But the ball"—his voice cracked —"the ball was Terry's head."

He heard the small sound erupt from Delaney's throat. She started to rise, to come to him, but he held out his palm, stopping her.

"No, don't. Not pity, Delaney. I don't want pity. There were others who had it worse. Why some of us made it and some of us didn't, I'll never understand. Maybe I don't even have to. But I was one who did."

He halted again, throat dry from his long monologue. This time he did not look at her. He did not want to see what was in her eyes. He did not want to see judgment.

"I'll never know if Terry was alive or dead when it happened. I've told myself that he had to be dead, or at least unconscious, or he would have answered my radio call. I can live with that better than I can the alternative.

"It took a long time, Delaney, to heal. I had to quit blaming myself, quit feeling like a coward. I couldn't have done it without Dr. Tyson. In fact, I don't think I'd be alive if it weren't for her."

For the first time, a faint smile appeared on his lips. "She's responsible for my career. Sometimes she used Gestalt therapy on me. And she told me I was so good at it I ought to be an actor. She said it could be an extension of my therapy. It would give me something to do, put me in touch with people, yet keep them at a distance until I was ready to let someone into my life. And I found it comfortable, easy to play a role, be someone else, anyone other than myself."

He turned to face her, and she felt the full impact of his eyes. It was the blue of the sky all focused on her.

"I tried to find you when I was well enough. But you'd

disappeared. There was no listing for a Rollins in Valhalla. And Mary Sue was nowhere to be found. I thought I'd lost you forever."

She could not stop the question. It tumbled from her mouth, unwanted and damning. "What about Heather?"

"Heather?" he repeated. "Heather had the good sense to leave me and look for someone who would give her what I couldn't. I didn't love her, Delaney, and she knew it. It was short and relatively painless. An attempt at normalcy."

She sat silently. Imagination, the asset she possessed in abundance, had failed her completely where Anthony was concerned. All of her assumptions had been wrong.

"I don't know what you're thinking, Delaney. But if I could only make you understand. I had no plans to interfere in your life, but when I saw you in Los Angeles, all of that changed. Maybe I'm a selfish bastard, but there's no use kidding myself, or you. I would have done anything to see you, find you. But I had no idea what was waiting for me at the end of that search. Adam, maybe. But Abigail?"

He felt his resolve tottering as his eyes sought her face. Panic, real and overwhelming, spilled into his voice.

"Please, Delaney. Tell me what's been going on with you."

She raised her eyes and started to speak, but he lifted his hand, stopping her, and she waited.

"I don't mean about what you've been doing. Abigail filled me in on that. I mean what you felt. I need to hear what it's been like for you, Delaney."

Her eyes turned to the creek. She reached for a blade of grass and broke it off, then turned it over and over in her fingers.

"What I felt?" Her eyes scanned the distance as though

she were gathering in her thoughts, collecting them from unseen places, condensing them to a manageable entity.

"At first," she began tentatively, "I was heartbroken. I was a mass of raw feelings. Anguish, regret, longing, fear. Then, eventually, I realized that it was all fantasy, you were all fantasy, and I could not lose what I'd never had in the first place. I was in love with someone as mythical as the husband I'd invented. And that made it easier to pretend he actually existed, and you were dead.

"When the twins were born, they consumed most of my life. And, with time, I thought I was over it." She stopped. She glanced at him quickly, then looked away. For a moment, she seemed lost in some memory, a memory of pain. His heart wrenched in his chest while he watched her.

"And then, I saw you on television, and all that loss came hurtling at me like a backwash. It was years before I knew I wouldn't die from hurting. Years of loss, grieving, pain, until I finally accepted it. Then, and only then, did I start to live again."

"And now I've crashed back into your life."

"It seems that way, Anthony. It seems that's the only way you enter my life—crashing." Her lips parted as a faint and poignant smile appeared, then faded. She turned to face him, her eyes clear and intense.

"What is it you want from me, Anthony? Is it the children?"

"No, Delaney. I would never want them to be parted from you." He watched as relief flooded her face.

"Then what is it?" she asked again.

He looked at the leaf still lodged in her hair. His thoughts fused together as the words formed in his mind.

"I want," he began, "another chance. I want to find out

347

who you are now. And I want you to know me. Will you give me that chance, Delaney?" ·

And there it was. The question she never thought she'd hear and therefore couldn't answer.

"I don't know, Anthony."

It wasn't yes, he thought, but it wasn't no either. It was enough for him. Gently, he reached for the leaf.